THE WORLD'S CLASSICS

THE WAVES

GILLIAN BEER is Professor of English at the University of Cambridge and a Fellow of Girton College. Among her books are *Darwin's Plots* (Routledge, 1983), *George Eliot* (Harvester, 1986), and *Arguing with the Past* (Routledge, 1989) which includes several of her essays on Virginia Woolf.

THE WORLD'S CLASSICS

VIRGINIA WOOLF

The Waves

Edited with an Introduction by
GILLIAN BEER

OXFORD UNIVERSITY PRESS

Oxford University Press, Walton Street, Oxford OX2 6DP

Oxford New York
Athens Auckland Bangkok Bombay
Calcutta Cape Town Dar es Salaam Delhi
Florence Hong Kong Istanbul Karachi
Kuala Lumpur Madras Madrid Melbourne
Mexico City Nairobi Paris Singapore
Taipei Tokyo Toronto

and associated companies in
Berlin Ibadan

Oxford is a trade mark of Oxford University Press

Published in the United States by
Oxford University Press Inc., New York

First published as a World's Classics paperback 1992

British Library Cataloguing in Publication Data
Data available
ISBN 0-19 281820-1

5 7 9 10 8 6

Printed in Great Britain by
BPC Paperbacks Ltd.
Aylesbury, Bucks

CONTENTS

CONTENTS

BIOGRAPHICAL PREFACE

VIRGINIA WOOLF was born Adeline Virginia Stephen on 25 January 1882 at 22 Hyde Park Gate, Kensington. Her father, Leslie Stephen, himself a widower, had married in 1878 Julia Jackson, widow of Herbert Duckworth. Between them they already had four children; a fifth, Vanessa, was born in 1879, a sixth, Thoby, in 1880. There followed Virginia and, in 1883, Adrian.

Both of the parents had strong family associations with literature. Leslie Stephen was the son of Sir James Stephen, a noted historian, and brother of Sir James Fitzjames Stephen, a distinguished lawyer and writer on law. His first wife was a daughter of Thackeray, his second had been an admired associate of the Pre-Raphaelites, and also, like her first husband, had aristocratic connections. Stephen himself is best remembered as the founding editor of the *Dictionary of National Biography*, and as an alpinist, but he was also a remarkable journalist, biographer, and historian of ideas; his *History of English Thought in the Eighteenth Century* (1876) is still of great value. No doubt our strongest idea of him derives from the character of Mr Ramsay in *To the Lighthouse*; for a less impressionistic portrait, which conveys a strong sense of his centrality in the intellectual life of the time, one can consult Noël Annan's *Leslie Stephen* (revised edition, 1984).

Virginia had the free run of her father's library, a better substitute for the public school and university education she was denied than most women of the time could aspire to; her brothers, of course, were sent to Clifton and Westminster. Her mother died in 1895, and in that year she had her first breakdown, possibly related in some way to the sexual molestation of which her half-brother George Duckworth is accused. By 1897 she was able to read again, and did so voraciously: 'Gracious, child, how you gobble,' remarked her father, who, with a liberality and good sense at odds with the age in which they lived, allowed her to choose her reading freely. In other respects her relationship with her father was difficult; his deafness and melancholy, his excessive emotionalism, not helped by successive bereavements, all increased her nervousness.

Stephen fell ill in 1902 and died in 1904. Virginia suffered another breakdown, during which she heard the birds singing in Greek, a language in which she had acquired some competence. On her recovery she moved, with her brothers and sister, to a house in Gordon Square, Bloomsbury; there, and subsequently at several other nearby addresses, what eventually became famous as the Bloomsbury Group took shape.

Virginia had long considered herself a writer. It was in 1905 that she began to write for publication in the *Times Literary Supplement*. In her circle (more loosely drawn than is sometimes supposed) were many whose names are now half-forgotten, but some were or became famous: J. M. Keynes and E. M. Forster and Roger Fry; also Clive Bell, who married Vanessa, Lytton Strachey, who once proposed marriage to her, and Leonard Woolf. Despite much ill health in these years, she travelled a good deal, and had an interesting social life in London. She did a little adult-education teaching, worked for female suffrage, and shared the excitement of Roger Fry's Post-Impressionist Exhibition in 1910. In 1912, after another bout of illness, she married Leonard Woolf.

She was thirty, and had not yet published a book, though *The Voyage Out* was in preparation. It was accepted for publication by her half-brother Gerald Duckworth in 1913 (it appeared in 1915). She was often ill with depression and anorexia, and in 1913 attempted suicide. But after a bout of violent madness her health seemed to settle down, and in 1917 a printing press was installed at Hogarth House, Richmond, where she and her husband were living. The Hogarth Press, later an illustrious institution, but at first meant in part as therapy for Virginia, was now inaugurated. She began *Night and Day*, and finished it in 1918. It was published by Duckworth in 1919, the year in which the Woolfs bought Monk's House, Rodmell, for £700. There, in 1920, she began *Jacob's Room*, finished, and published by the Woolfs' own Hogarth Press, in 1922. In the following year she began *Mrs Dalloway* (finished in 1924, published 1925), when she was already working on *To the Lighthouse* (finished and published, after intervals of illness, in 1927). *Orlando*, a fantastic 'biography' of a man–woman, and a tribute to Virginia's close friendship with Vita Sackville-West, was written quite rapidly over the winter of 1927–8, and published, with considerable success, in October. *The Waves* was written and rewritten in 1930 and 1931 (published in October of that year). She had already started on *Flush*, the story of Elizabeth Barrett Browning's pet dog—another success with the public— and in 1932 began work on what became *The Years*.

This brief account of her work during the first twenty years of her marriage is of course incomplete; she had also written and published many shorter works, as well as both series of *The Common Reader*, and *A Room of One's Own*. There have been accounts of the marriage very hostile to Leonard Woolf, but he can hardly be accused of cramping her talent or hindering the development of her career.

Preface

The Years proved an agonizingly difficult book to finish, and was completely rewritten at least twice. Her friend Roger Fry having died in 1934, she planned to write a biography, but illnesses in 1936 delayed the project; towards the end of that year she began instead the polemical *Three Guineas*, published in 1938. *The Years* had meanwhile appeared in 1937, by which time she was again at work on the Fry biography, and already sketching in her head the book that was to be *Between the Acts*. *Roger Fry* was published in the terrifying summer of 1940. By the autumn of that year many of the familiar Bloomsbury houses had been destroyed or badly damaged by bombs. Back at Monk's House, she worked on *Between the Acts*, and finished it in February 1941. Thereafter her mental condition deteriorated alarmingly, and on 28 March, unable to face another bout of insanity, she drowned herself in the River Ouse.

Her career as a writer of fiction covers the years 1912–41, thirty years distracted by intermittent serious illness as well as by the demands, which she regarded as very important, of family and friends, and by the need or desire to write literary criticism and social comment. Her industry was extraordinary—nine highly-wrought novels, two or three of them among the great masterpieces of the form in this century, along with all the other writings, including the copious journals and letters that have been edited and published in recent years. Firmly set though her life was in the 'Bloomsbury' context—the agnostic ethic transformed from that of her forebears, the influence of G. E. Moore and the Cambridge Apostles, the individual brilliance of J. M. Keynes, Strachey, Forster, and the others—we have come more and more to value the distinctiveness of her talent, so that she seems more and more to stand free of any context that might be thought to limit her. None of that company—except, perhaps, T. S. Eliot, who was on the fringe of it—did more to establish the possibilities of literary innovation, or to demonstrate that such innovation must be brought about by minds familiar with the innovations of the past. This is true originality. It was Eliot who said of *Jacob's Room* that in that book she had freed herself from any compromise between the traditional novel and her original gift; it was the freedom he himself sought in *The Waste Land*, published in the same year, a freedom that was dependent upon one's knowing with intimacy that with which compromise must be avoided, so that the knowledge became part of the originality. In fact she had 'gobbled' her father's books to a higher purpose than he could have understood.

Frank Kermode

INTRODUCTION

As she at last reached the final page of *The Waves*, on 7 February 1931, Woolf wrote in her diary: 'I have netted that fin in the waste of waters which appeared to me over the marshes out of my window at Rodmell when I was coming to an end of To the Lighthouse.' The arc through time of that glimpsed fin is remarkable. *The Waves* was conceived, brooded on, and written during a highly political phase in Woolf's career, when she was speaking at public and private meetings on issues of gender and of class. This was the period, too, when her love-affair with Vita Sackville-West was at its most intense. Yet the work is often described as if it were the product of a secluded, disembodied sensibility. It might more aptly be described as seeking out the rhythms of the body.

To the Lighthouse was published in May 1927. Over the winter of 1927/8 Woolf wrote *Orlando: A Biography*. That work triumphs over death and over patriarchal succession, but not grandly: rather, in a speedy, lightfooted mode of satire, pastiche, and disrespect. The hero–heroine loosens the bonds of gender, evades history and the knowingness of the biographer's art, and collaborates mockingly with the class system. *The Waves* was meditated alongside the composition of *Orlando*, and of *A Room of One's Own* where Woolf more directly challenges the current ordering of society, particularly its disabling of women. *A Room of One's Own* issued out of papers she read to young women at Cambridge and it was finished in March 1929. At that same time Woolf began writing the first draft of *The Waves*. Towards the conclusion of the second draft, early in 1931, Woolf was seized by intense excitement over the project that was to issue in some of her most polemical writing, *The Pargiters* and *Three Guineas*.

> I have this moment, while having my bath, conceived an entire new book—a sequel to a Room of Ones Own—about the sexual life of women: to be called Professions for Women perhaps— Lord how exciting! This sprang out of my paper to be read on Wednesday to Pippa's society. Now for The Waves. Thank God—but I'm very much excited. (*Diary*, 20 January 1931)

Her excitement is focused towards the new project, yet, as often happens in writing, it is as though at this late stage of composition she can at last understand the project of the book on which she is at present engaged. *The Waves*, also, has to do with the sexual life, with the six persons of one woman.

In the paper she refers to above, 'Professions for Women', she figures the imagination as a woman, fishing:

> lying sunk in dreams on the verge of a deep lake with a rod held out over the water. She was letting her imagination sweep unchecked round every rock and cranny of the world that lies submerged in the depths of our unconscious being.[1]

The unchecked, suffusive power of the imagination explores like fish and fisher at once. The spatial image is that of descent into the depths, just as she called *The Waves* a submarine book, every atom saturated. The passage continues with an insight into how *The Waves* overcomes what she saw as a central problem for women writing: expressing the body and the passions.

> Her imagination had rushed away. It had sought the pools, the depths, the dark places, where the largest fish slumber. And then

---

[1] 'Professions for Women', in *The Death of the Moth* (London: Hogarth Press, 1942), 152.

there was a smash. There was an explosion. There was foam and confusion. The imagination had dashed itself against something hard. The girl was roused from her dream. She was indeed in a state of the most acute and difficult distress. To speak without figure she had thought of something, something about the body, about the passions which it was unfitting for her as a woman to say. Men, her reason told her, would be shocked. The consciousness of what men will say of a woman who speaks the truth about her passions had roused her from her artist's state of unconsciousness.[2]

By going down in *The Waves* into 'the world that lies submerged in our unconscious being' and by sustaining the evenness of a dream state, 'her artist's state of unconsciousness', Woolf seeks to escape the narrow bounds of social realism which, she perceives, is functioning as a form of censorship. She has found a language and a rhythm that will be less 'impeded by the extreme conventionality of the other sex'. But it is not a language that excludes 'the other sex': the six speakers of the book, three male, three female, often stand separate from each other but are as often allied across gender. They share sensory experience, though they are later sorted socially.

Far from being a pallid retreat from political issues the project of *The Waves* is innovative and substantial. Its method is not that of confrontation. Instead the work brings into question the established hierarchies of what matters, what constitutes an event, how to write life— including knives and tables, and the presence of many people in a single street on a particular day. Woolf's writing in *Mrs Dalloway* had already suggested that the most fundamental form of connection between human beings is

[2] Ibid.

being alive in the same place at the same time, rather than the chosen friendships and love-affairs that fiction ordinarily privileges. *The Waves* sustains that perception but mixes it with an intense scrutiny of particular people. By the end of the book—and more and more in rereading—what has seemed at first oblique, hard to construe, proves to have provided intimate access to the individualities of Jinny, Susan, Rhoda, Bernard, Neville, Louis: though not to Percival. *The Waves* issues out of a vigorous phase of production and feeling and the language of the work is packed with sensory experience, highly sexualized, 'quivering within the wave's intenser day'.[3]

Woolf's hints and touches in her diary from 1925 on towards the work that became *The Waves* make it clear that this was to be experimental work, work that would fundamentally challenge the bounds of fiction. It would bring into question what gets left out when life is described. It would test the established demarcations between individual and communal experience. It would extend the reach of language and suffer its debilities. It would follow a rhythm, not a plot. It would also inhabit the body: 'Muscles, nerves, intestines, blood-vessels, all that makes the coil and spring of our being, the unconscious hum of the engine, as well as the dart and flicker of the tongue' (pp. 217–18).

This insistence on substantiality goes alongside a sense of how objects warp, bend, deliquesce and how the senses

---

[3] My allusion to Shelley's 'Ode to the West Wind' is not casual. Woolf quotes Shelley directly at a number of moments in *The Waves*, particularly his elegiac poems, and his cosmic images of seas, suns, stars, waves, mingled with flowers and passionate outcry are crucial in the imaginative economy of the book's vocabulary. See below, pp. xxix ff. and Explanatory Notes.

seize a world always irretrievably altered, endlessly contingent: at sunrise '*Everything became softly amorphous, as if the china of the plate flowed and the steel of the knife were liquid. Meanwhile the concussion of the waves breaking fell with muffled thuds, like logs falling, on the shore.*' (p. 21)

The observation is exact. Waves are fluid, logs solid, yet the report of the waves' fall measures their weight. The ear registers a likeness lost on the eye. The eye's assurance wavers with the changes of light yet the mind remains determined to maintain distinctions: plates and knives are solid even while they are seen as amorphous. That double recognition permeates *The Waves*: of crusts, determined distances, carapaces, identities; of decay, shadows, accumulations, visceral softness, assembled cries.

Each of the books Woolf wrote around that time strained across genre, attempted to break through—or disturb— the limits of the essay, the novel, the biography, to touch realities denied by accepted forms. In all her work there was an astute awareness that apparently literary questions—of genre, language, plot—are questions that touch the pith of how society constitutes and contains itself.

In 'Women and Fiction' in 1929 Woolf connected the material conditions of women's lives with the forms of their expression, and saw that the two would change together: she hoped that in future women, like men, 'will deal with social evils and remedies. Their men and women will not be observed wholly in relation to each other emotionally, but as they cohere and clash in groups and classes and races.' Another, even more important, change will be that 'the greater impersonality of women's lives will encourage the poetic spirit, and it is in poetry that women's fiction is still weakest. It will lead them to be less absorbed in facts and no longer content to record . . . their own observation. They will look beyond the personal and political relationships to the wider questions which the poet tries to solve of our destiny and the meaning of life.'[4] This may seem a paradoxical proposal, offering something like de-politicization as a political project for women. But her essay 'The Narrow Bridge of Art' (1927) attempts to analyse the relations between poetry and prose and takes things in a different direction. As she wrote ruefully to Vita Sackville-West on 19 July 1926: 'my God Vita, if you happen to know do wire whats the essential difference between prose and poetry—It cracks my poor brain to consider.'[5]

What she seeks for fiction is the possibility of detachment and feeling at once, an assaying of those experiences ordinarily reserved for poetry, avoiding the hubbub of demands, retaining humour. Instead of mirroring directly, this new form should be able to 'stand further back from life.'[6] But where the observer should be placed exercised her as she wrote:

I have thought of this device: to put

The Lonely Mind

separately in The Moths, as if it were a person. (*Diary*, 4 September 1929)

In the first draft an enigmatic figure, obscurely male or female, scrutinizes the scene from behind a veil. But this did not satisfy her. Again she writes in the diary, on 25 September 1929: 'Yesterday morning I made another start

[4] *Collected Essays*, 4 vols. (London: Hogarth Press, 1966–7), ii. 147.
[5] *The Letters of Virginia Woolf*, ed. Nigel Nicolson and Joanne Trautmann, 6 vols. (London: Hogarth Press, 1975–84), iii. 281.
[6] *Collected Essays*, ii. 224–5.

on The Moths, but that won't be its title. & several problems cry out at once to be solved. Who thinks it? And am I outside the thinker? One wants some device which is not a trick.' In the final work that device is the lady writing, the gardeners sweeping, at Elvedon, glimpsed once only in the children's elated and secret invasion of that foreign territory, yet perpetually present—and referred to—throughout the book (for example, on pp. 12, 224). The image is of absorbed, indeflectable activity. The lady is thinking and inscribing, not outwardly observing. The children watch, the lady writes, the gardeners sweep: the work turns its eyes upon itself, but entirely through the eyes of the actors. There is no outside place for the observer. The reader, too, must immerse in this submarine, eyeless (I-less) medium.

One of the first references in the diary to what will eventually form the enquiry of *The Waves* proposes a new kind of biography (or autobiography):

I am now & then haunted by some semimystic very profound life of a woman, which shall all be told on one occasion; & time shall be utterly obliterated; future shall somehow blossom out of the past. One incident—say the fall of a flower—might contain it. My theory being that the actual event practically does not exist— nor time either. But I don't want to force this. (*Diary*, 23 November 1926)

She has described this impulse at the end of October as 'a dramatisation of my mood at Rodmell ... an endeavour at something mystic, spiritual; the thing that exists when we aren't there' (*Diary*, 30 October 1926).

That first mood survives in the accomplished work, but it is lightened by her indefatigable sense of absurdity. Things will not stay still. The scale of experience constantly shifts. What looks large to one looks trivial to another. And in the same instant experience may be extended and doggedly contained. The pettiness of life may produce much of its meaning: trains and pillar-boxes, hide-and-seek and school lessons, jaunts and meals in humdrum cafés, walks through the streets of London, solitary suppers, belching and flowers.

Food is particularly vital to *The Waves*, functioning as ceremonial, aesthetic form, and rank appetite. Two dinner parties order the narrative: that before Percival leaves for India and that at Hampton Court when all the other characters meet again in middle age. The last scene, Bernard's consummating soliloquy, also takes place in a restaurant. Bernard, driven by the curiosity of language, the need to make phrases, is also the most primitive of the characters in his relation to food and drink. Language and appetite are fundamentally at one. In his young adulthood, newly engaged to be married, he reflects: 'Having dropped off satisfied like a child from the breast, I am at liberty now to sink down, deep, into what passes, this omnipresent, general life.' (p. 92) Sexual fulfilment takes the individual back deep into the common life of first consciousness at the breast. At the end of the work Bernard thinks with pleasure of the appetites which live alongside the 'shadows of people one might have been; unborn selves'.

There is the old brute, too, the savage, the hairy man who dabbles his fingers in ropes of entrails; and gobbles and belches, whose speech is guttural, visceral—well, he is here. He squats in me. Tonight he has been feasted on quails, salad, and sweetbread. He now holds a glass of fine old brandy in his paw. He brindles, purrs and shoots warm thrills all down my spine as I sip. It is true, he washes his hands before dinner, but they are still hairy.

He buttons on trousers and waistcoats, but they contain the same organs. . . . That man, the hairy, the ape-like, has contributed his part to my life. He has given a greener glow to green things . . . (pp. 241–2)

Alongside this often ebullient emphasis on primary desires goes the evocation of temperature, touch (and the evasion of touch): 'Let me then feel pressing against me some human hand.'[7] Jinny's body,

my companion . . . is always sending its signals . . . All my senses stand erect. Now I feel the roughness of the fibre of the curtain through which I push; now I feel the cold iron railing and its blistered paint beneath my palm. (p. 146)

While she was writing *Mrs Dalloway* Woolf copied a passage from Book VII of Wordsworth's *The Prelude* and added a comment:

> The matter that detains us now may seem,
> To many, neither dignified enough
> Nor arduous, yet will not be scorned by them,
> Who, looking inward, have observed the ties
> That bind the perishable hours of life
> Each to the other, & the curious props
> By which the world of memory and thought
> Exists & is sustained.
>
> Good quotation for one of my books.[8]

The quotation is quite as pertinent for *The Waves* as for *Mrs Dalloway*, and indeed Woolf copied exactly the same passage into her diary on 22 August 1929. The 'curious

---

[7] *Virginia Woolf, The Waves: The Two Holograph Drafts*, transcribed and edited by J. W. Graham (London: Hogarth Press, 1976), 7.

[8] Brenda R. Silver, *Virginia Woolf's Reading Notebooks* (Princeton: Princeton University Press, 1983), 30.

props' that memory selects, often apparently captiously, form the recurrent medium of experience for the reader of *The Waves*. Memory melds events and fantasies. Rhoda's bowl of petals and desert sands, Neville's knife blade and his spotless bookshelves, Louis's father 'a banker in Brisbane' and his humiliated memory of being given a Union Jack from the Christmas tree because no one had thought to prepare a present for him: recurrent phrases, intense knots of time, produce a rhythm that both partakes of everyday life and guides the reader through the welter of impressions. The new literary form that Woolf hoped for in 'The Narrow Bridge of Art' was to have 'something of the exaltation of poetry, but much of the ordinariness of prose. It will be dramatic, and yet not a play. It will be read, not acted.'[9]

This mingling of the humdrum with the high style, and particularly that dangerous word 'mystical' that Woolf associates with the work, may account for the relative neglect of *The Waves* in recent criticism. Although it has traditionally been treated as Woolf's 'masterpiece', it gets short shrift in a number of important recent studies. The comments of critics range from the cautious to the downright hostile, and several people skirt the problem that the book evidently presents to current thinking by leaving it out altogether, though often with a brief obeisance to its absence.

The demurrals and exclusions practised by these studies are in themselves revealing. Jane Marcus in her essay 'The Niece of a Nun: Virginia Woolf, Caroline Stephen, and the Cloistered Imagination' is forthright about the problem and imaginative in her response to it:

[9] *Collected Essays*, ii. 224.

As a feminist critic I had avoided the subject of Woolf's mysticism, and of *The Waves*, feeling that acknowledging her as a visionary was a trap that would allow her to be dismissed as another female crank, irrational and eccentric. I was drawn to her most anti-capitalist, anti-imperialist novels, to Woolf the socialist and feminist, logical, witty, and devastating in argument.[10]

Marcus suggests that it may be possible 'to see the structure of *The Waves* as a Quaker meeting': that is, an occasion which gives particular value to communal silence and to individual utterance bearing profoundly shared concerns. This, she suggests, links the book to the particular exploration of silence and being silenced focused by Adrienne Rich and Tillie Olsen as part of women's experience. But Marcus has not, so far as I know, written at length about the book.

Perry Meisel makes briefly the telling point that 'Ironically, *To The Lighthouse* is a far more abstract account of the way the self is situated in the common life than *The Waves*, Woolf's apparently more oblique achievement. Here she is exceedingly concrete.'[11] In contrast, Alex Zwerdling asserts: 'The relentlessly elevated discourse of the book denied entry to the prosaic, the comic, the particular.'[12] This seems a surprising judgement in the light of the characters' preoccupation with the humdrum detail and the winning incongruities of daily life, 'the way some old woman sits, arms akimbo, in an omnibus with a

[10] Jane Marcus (ed.), *Virginia Woolf: A Feminist Slant* (Lincoln: Nebraska University Press, 1984), 27.

[11] Perry Meisel, *The Absent Father: Virginia Woolf and Walter Pater* (New Haven: Yale University Press, 1980), 200.

[12] Alex Zwerdling, *Virginia Woolf and the Real World* (Berkeley: University of California Press), 12.

basket'. (p. 148) Louis relishes, with self-aware satire, his part in the business of the Empire:

This is life; Mr Prentice at four; Mr Eyres at four-thirty. I like to hear the soft rush of the lift and the thud with which it stops on my landing and the heavy male tread of responsible feet down the corridors. So by dint of our united exertions we sent ships to the remotest parts of the globe; replete with lavatories and gymnasiums. The weight of the world is on our shoulders. This is life. (p. 140)

Susan describes her cooking with sensuous particularity, registering wet and dry, weight and temperature—and the live bodily forms of yeasty bread: 'I go then to the cupboard, and take the damp bags of rich sultanas: I lift the heavy flour on to the clean scrubbed kitchen table. I knead; I stretch; I pull, plunging my hands in the warm inwards of the dough.' (p. 80) Zwerdling's outstanding study of Woolf's 'real world' takes *The Waves* as his adverse point of departure rather than exploring it fully.

Zwerdling cites to support his view of the work's insubstantial bias Woolf's own comment that 'there's no quite solid table on which to put it'. Woolf was here very probably responding also to contemporary scientific and philosophical writing. The distinguished physicist and writer Arthur Eddington observed in *The Nature of the Physical World* (1928):

we have seen that substance is one of the greatest of our illusions ... Perhaps, indeed, reality is a child which cannot survive without its nurse illusion. .... In the world of physics we watch a shadowgraph performance of the drama of familiar life. The shadow of my elbow rests on the shadow table as the shadow ink flows over the shadow paper. It is all symbolic, and as a symbol the physicist leaves it.[13]

---

[13] Eddington, op. cit. (Cambridge: Cambridge University Press), xvi.

Doubting substance and solidity does not make work insubstantial. The overlaps and contradictions between substance and shadow that are so passionately explored in *The Waves* are (as I argue in a forthcoming book) part of the mainstream of enquiry in Woolf's time, not a limitation on her responsiveness to life.

The very unfamiliarity of Woolf's presentation of 'reality' in the work is tonic. It is not an issue that can be settled out of some secure position of observation. The then popular and highly regarded novelist Hugh Walpole complained that: 'Much of it beat me because I couldn't feel it to be real.'[14] Woolf counter-attacked with a shaft against Walpole's new novel, *Judith Paris*:

Well, I'm very much interested about unreality and the Waves— we must discuss it I mean why do you think The Waves unreal, and why was that the very word I was using of Judith Paris— ... 'These people aren't *real* to me'— ... . But unreality does take the colour out of a book of course; at the same time, I don't see that it's a final judgment on either of us. You're real to some—I to others. Who's to decide what reality is?[15]

Many of the objections to *The Waves* as an image of reality resolve into questions of tense. The interludes, which describe the progress of the sun through a single day and across the world, are put in past tense. The episodes are chiefly in the present, and not always even the progressive present. 'I go to the bookcase' ... 'I come back from the office'; 'I detect; I perceive': such statements suggest habitual and repeated acts and avoid placing the event in a single moment of time. The pure present tense also implic-

---

[14] Quoted in Quentin Bell, *Virginia Woolf: A Biography*, 2 vols. (London: Hogarth Press, 1972), ii. 162.
[15] 8 Nov. 1931; *Letters*, iv. 402.

itly suggests self-observation and a kind of instantaneous act of memory, the activity of the watching mind.[16] Only Bernard's concluding soliloquy is in the past tense, supposedly addressed to a listener casually encountered (someone first met long ago on board ship on a journey outside the narrative). That listener is also the reader who at last resolves and orders the group's lives through time, sharing them anew, recognizing stark individualities as well as the overlap of identities.

The Waves, as Makiko Minow Pinkney well observes in one of the few extended recent discussions, maintains for most of its length 'a precarious dialectic between identity and its loss, the symbolic and its unrepresentable Other—an unsettling and unsettlable alternation prefigured in the sexual metamorphoses of *Orlando*'.[17] Elizabeth Abel, however, in her otherwise excellent study of the psychoanalytic context of Woolf's working community, surprisingly decides to 'omit *The Waves* (1931) whose experiment in dissolving identity sets it outside my concerns'. The omission is the more surprising since she continues, suggestively: 'the very disembodiment that characterizes the text, however, suggests a heightened ambivalence toward the body's origin. *The Waves* marks the terminus of Woolf's progression through the 1920s toward an ambivalent engagement with maternal origins.'[18]

Her comments focus the need now for a fuller study of

[16] For a fuller discussion of tense and point of view, see J. W. Graham, 'Point of View in *The Waves: Some Services of the Style*', in Thomas Lewis (ed.), *Virginia Woolf: A Collection of Criticism* (New York: McGraw-Hill, 1975).

[17] Makiko Minow Pinkney, *Virginia Woolf and the Problem of the Subject* (Brighton: Harvester Press, 1988), 155.

[18] Elizabeth Abel, *Virginia Woolf and the Fictions of Psychoanalysis* (Chicago: Chicago University Press, 1989), Notes, p. 132.

the movement from the early drafts to the final version of the work. The first version of *The Waves* includes, very near the opening, the image of the maternal sea:

Many mothers, & before them many mothers, & again many mothers, have groaned, & fallen ~~back, while the child crowed~~. Like one wave, ~~& then~~ succeeding each other. Wave after wave, endlessly sinking & falling as far as the eye can stretch. And all these waves have been the prostrate forms of mothers, in their ~~flowing~~ nightgowns, with the tumbled sheets about them holding up, with a groan, as they sink back into the sea, ~~infin innumerable children.~~[19]

Labour, self-loss, origins prolonged beyond memory: the anonymity of childbirth and succession in this passage lends further resonance to Woolf's often-cited remark that women 'think back through their mothers'. In the finished novel the inchoate is replaced by the specific. Susan becomes the living presence who is typified by maternal conflict and maternal pleasure and who, late in the book, seeks to be free of that identification.

The most antagonistic recent comments on *The Waves* are those of Mark Hussey who sees *The Waves* as 'useful as a store-house of typical ideas, but not much more than this. It is a kind of warehouse in which are found the materials from which novels such as *To The Lighthouse* or *Between the Acts* may be created.'[20] Hussey's principal objection, apart from this suggestion of discrete parcels awaiting delivery, is to the novel's resistance to the reader. Woolf herself was anxious about the reader's skills in this new form. She wrote to Ethel Smyth on 28 August 1930:

[19] *The Waves*, ed. Graham.

[20] Mark Hussey, *The Singing of the Real World: The Philosophy of Virginia Woolf's Fiction* (Columbus, Ohio: Ohio State University Press, 1986), 82.

What question in particular was it about the Waves that delicacy
forbade? . . . I think then that my difficulty is that I am writing
to a rhythm and not to a plot. Does this convey anything? And
thus though the rhythmical is more natural to me than the
narrative, it is completely opposed to the tradition of fiction and
I am casting about all the time for some rope to throw to the
reader. This is rough and ready; but not wilfully inaccurate.[21]

If the rope the reader needs is information, it is there.
(Readers may prefer to read the novel before considering
the list of events I offer later in this paragraph, so be
warned!) We are given a considerable number of statements
about what are usually considered key events and emotions. What makes those statements strange, indeed difficult to read, is that they are presented dead-pan, as part of
a sentence, in the midst of a paragraph, without comment
or emphasis. Susan loves Louis, Percival loves Susan,
Neville loves Percival. Percival leaves for India, Susan is
married to a farmer. Bernard is engaged. His son is born
just as he hears the news of Percival's death. Jinny has
many lovers. Neville seeks the one, and after Percival's
death finds him in a succession. Louis is successful in
business, Neville distinguished. Louis writes poems, perhaps of lasting value. Louis and Rhoda are lovers. She
leaves him. Bernard goes to Rome for ten days. At some
time, Rhoda has killed herself. Rhoda was fatherless (the
children's parentage is laconically summarized by Louis on
p. 14).

In sexual orientation the six characters are fanned across
a spectrum that includes Neville's heartfelt and unwaver-
ing homo-eroticism, Susan's passionately maternal preoccupation, Jinny's promiscuous and cheerful narcissism,

---

[21] *Letters*, iv. 204.

Bernard's heterosexual marriage and fatherhood, Louis and Rhoda's twinned isolations, celibacies. This, then, is the 'semimystic, very profound life of a woman', the rhythm through which at that time Woolf found it possible to speak of 'the body, the passions'.[22]

The turning-point of the book is Percival's death and here Woolf pays death the tribute of narrative pattern. Woolf removed from the final version the particular irony that his horse stumbled over a molehill, which is much dwelt upon in the earlier drafts. Percival remains opaque, a figure whose consciousness the reader never enters. Percival is cricket captain, and later rows, rides, and hunts. He appears to be entirely unreflective and like his namesake Parsifal is both pure and ignorant. He is the man at ease in the world of Empire and action, beloved, absurd, mocked and adored by the other characters in their youth. Like Parsifal he is the perfect knight who is also maladroit, unable to ask the right question at the right time. He is also *past*, a focus for memory and community, but no saviour. In the complicated cross-allusions to T. S. Eliot's work in *The Waves* his name may have significance too. In Arthurian legend Parsifal found the Holy Grail at Chapel Perilous. In *The Waste Land* the chapel is empty: 'There is the empty chapel, only the wind's home.' Woolf may also have had Wagner's drama moving in her mind. She had already visited the Bayreuth festival in 1909 and remarks in her diary on 20 September 1927, as she is thinking her way into *The Waves*, that the young Quentin Bell 'wont let us play him Wagner: prefers Bach'. Be that as it may, Percival is an obscured, even blanked out figure whose passage to

---

[22] See quotations above, pp. xxvi, xxvii.

India as part of the apparatus of Empire results in his pointless death.

The treatment of his death is remarkably different from that of Rhoda. We never know when that has occurred. Rhoda is absent for the length of two episodes but is present again at Hampton Court, the last episode before Bernard's summation. It is only from Bernard's last speech that we know that she has killed herself. From the outset she has been at odds with time; as a child, left behind to do her sums, the figures on the blackboard 'fill with time'. When she joins up the o, the zero, her reverie becomes nightmare: 'The world is entire, and I am outside of it, crying, "Oh save me, from being blown for ever outside the loop of time!"' (p. 15)

Rhoda is particularly closely associated with the language of Shelley, whose work forms so strong a strand in the elegiac allusions to other poets that I gloss in the notes. This submerged level of intertextuality in the book has not, I think, previously been brought to light. It bears on Woolf's feelings for her dead brother Thoby, friend of her youth, whose presence she longed to mark by writing his name on the first page, but did not.[23] Instead she drew upon the elegiac poems of Catullus and Shelley, Arnold and Milton, Ben Jonson, Shakespeare, and an anonymous medieval writer fleetingly to mark her tribute. Many of the fugitive literary allusions in *The Waves* are to scenes of death or mourning. They vary from the initial image of an arm rising through water that glancingly conjures Tennyson's 'The Passing of Arthur': 'an arm/Clothed in white

---

[23] Thoby Stephen died of typhoid contracted when they and other members of the family were on holiday together in Greece. When he died he was 26 and Virginia 24.

samite, mystic, wonderful', to the reference to Arnold whose elegy for his friend Clough, 'Thyrsis', is organized around his search for a remembered tree, in *The Waves* the 'immitigable tree' (p. 18).[24]

Some of these allusions are indirect and wavering, but many others are quite precise and placed in quotation marks. Some have a proleptic function, suggesting Percival's journey to India before it has occurred or been mentioned. Shelley's poem 'The Indian Serenade' becomes part of Rhoda's physical experience long before Percival's journey is announced. Catullus is frequently invoked: his 'Odi et amo', I hate and I love, becomes Susan's recurring phrase. Her passionate and unquestioning immediacy is sustained by

> Odi et amo: quare id faciam, fortasse requiris.
> nescio, sed fieri sentio et excrucior.

I hate and I love. Why I do so, perhaps you ask. I know not, but I feel it, and am in torment.[25]

That poem might also, for a reader saturated as Neville and Louis are said to be in Catullus's language, summon up other nearby poems for his works:

> Friends, who profess your ardour to explore
> The ends of the earth with me, on India's shore
> The long wave breaking calls for evermore
> Clamorously.[26]

[24] *The Poems of Tennyson*, ed. Christopher Ricks (London: Longman, 1969), 1750. Lines 312–13 ; *The Poems of Matthew Arnold*, ed. Kenneth Allott (London: Longmans, 1965), 506.

[25] *Catullus*, ed. F. W. Cornish, Loeb Classical Library (Boston, Mass.: Harvard University Press, 1962), 162–3.

[26] E. A. Havelock, *The Lyric Genius of Catullus* (Oxford: Basil Blackwell, 1939), 67.

Shelley is directly and pointedly quoted on a number of occasions in the text. His presence is crucial beyond the elegiac, although of course Shelley did die young and tragically. In her rewriting of 'life' Woolf responded to the energy of his writing, and its constant shifting of scale and distances. Indeed, the opening image of the sun rising may include a response to his final, unfinished, and deeply equivocal poem 'The Triumph of Life' with its vigorous first lines when 'the Sun their father rose':

> Swift as a spirit hastening to his task
> Of glory and of good, the Sun sprang forth
> Rejoicing in his splendour.[27]

Woolf's sun is no Apollonian figure but a woman, no father but a girl.

In September 1927, Woolf records in her diary, she was working on a review of Walter Peck's biography of Shelley. His poetry provides a language at once sensorily intense and intellectually distanced that in particular reinforces Rhoda's abstruse relation to life. Rhoda's reading of his poem 'The Question' as a child provides the yearning phrase that becomes Rhoda's leitmotiv, just as 'Odi et amo' is Susan's. The poem describes a dream where 'Bare Winter suddenly was changed to Spring' and the dreamer gathers 'wild roses, and ivy serpentine'. The poem ends:

> then, elate and gay,
> I hastened to the spot whence I had come,
> That I might there present it!—Oh! to whom?[28]

---

[27] *The Complete Poetical Works of Percy Bysshe Shelley*, ed. Thomas Hutchinson (Oxford: Oxford University Press, 1934), 507.
[28] Shelley, ed. cit. 614.

As the child Rhoda falls asleep just after this passage, phrases from another Shelley poem merge into the physical symptoms of the sleep-state:

> I die! I faint! I fail!
> Let thy love in kisses rain
> On my lips and eyelids pale.[29]

Rhoda's language as a child and adolescent is everywhere erotically charged. In adulthood she is in flight from intimacy, though she and Louis are for a time lovers. When Bernard goes to visit them (though they prove to be absent) the line 'Away! the moor is dark beneath the moon' comes into his mind as he mounts their stairs. Shelley's melancholy poem of loss and ghostly presences ends with a stanza equivocally connected here with the narrative of Percival's death and the lovers' absence:

> Thou in the grave shalt rest—yet till the phantoms flee
> Which that house and heath and garden made dear to thee
>   erewhile,
> Thy remembrance, and repentance, and deep musings are not
>   free
> From the music of two voices and the light of one sweet
>   smile.[30]

However that harmonious last line may mock the outcome, Rhoda and Louis, alone among the characters, address each other on one occasion by name and converse. They are said to be 'conspirators': they share private knowledge and they con-spire, that is, breathe together.

The language associated with Louis is perhaps the most allusively charged of all, since it shares so many of the qualities of T. S. Eliot's verse (as passages such as those on

[29] Shelley, ed. cit. 579.   [30] Ibid. 521.

pages 168 and 211 demonstrate). Circumstantially, also, Louis bears some resemblances to Eliot: in his non-English ('colonial') background, in his banking career, classical learning, and fascination with the poetics of history and 'vile and famished' humdrum life. Tiresias-like, he remembers the ancient Nile 'and the women carrying pitchers on their heads' synchronically with chimney cowls, loose slates, slinking cats, and attic windows (p. 168). Though Bernard is the story-maker of *The Waves*, Louis is the poet and the one whose work the other characters expect will last. T. S. Eliot was born in St Louis.

Louis, the Australian whose father's bank failed in Brisbane, has political ambitions. (Woolf seams his pretensions in this direction with allusions to British politicians and lawmakers who were preoccupied with the Indian imperial enterprise, Chatham, Pitt, Burke, and Peel.) Alone among the characters Louis understands the 'third term' between literature and politics—the industrial revolution—and can avenge through business the 'beatings and other tortures' (p. 139) inflicted on him in his youth by the British upper classes.

Rhoda's childhood fantasies and images, like those of each of the other characters, revive persistently throughout her later life: the bowl of petals, the pillar, the pool, the zero. Music and geometric forms must supplement language if these experiences are to be registered, Woolf's characters discover. Life's ordered sequences are 'a convenience, a lie', Bernard thinks 'always deep below' is 'a rushing stream of broken dreams, nursery rhymes, street cries, half-finished sentences and sights—elm trees, willow trees, gardeners sweeping, women writing' (p. 213). Within the book the 'Ah' of the singer (p. 133), the 'little language' that lovers use, pain itself (p. 246), the string quartet's instruments placing a square upon an oblong (pp. 134, 170): such are Woolf's means of reaching beyond the exigencies of prose and its tendency to drive Roman roads across unnoticed territory (p. 216). Jinny, alone of the characters, lives perfectly at home in each present moment, waving her scarf, alive in her body, the alternative story-teller who understands the sign-language of clothes and physical presence:

I see what is before me. . . . This scarf, these wine-coloured spots. This glass. This mustard pot. This flower. I like what one touches, what one tastes. I like rain when it has turned to snow and become palpable, I do not temper my beauty with meanness lest it should scorch me. I gulp it down entire. It is made of flesh; it is made of stuff. (pp. 183–4)

In the image of the waves, which succeeded to her first thoughts of moths or farmyard noises, Woolf found a form that perfectly expressed at once the different measures of chronological and of psychic time. She knew the writing of the Victorian physical chemist John Tyndall and may have had passages such as this already in her imagination:

The particles in front reach in succession the crest of the wave, and as soon as the crest is passed, they begin to fall. They then reach the furrow or sinus of the wave, and can sink no further. Immediately afterwards they become the front of the succeeding wave, rise again until they reach the crest, and then sink as before. Thus, while the waves pass onward horizontally, the individual particles are simply lifted up and down vertically. Observe a sea-fowl, or, if you are a swimmer, abandon yourself to the action of the waves; you are not carried forward, but simply rocked up and down.[31]

[31] John Tyndall, *Six Lectures on Light* (London, 1873), 53.

So, the wave-form flows onwards but the substance is not transferred. Psychic life remains fluid yet strangely unchanging. Individuals do not move much: they reach the crest and then fall back. That same image of a wave-like movement is repeated through the sequence of the interludes, where the sun rises, comes to full height, and at last sets. As Diane Gillespie suggests, the descriptions of the sun can probably best be read like the impressionist painter Claude Monet's series-paintings, in which different lights transform objects such as haystacks, cathedrals, trees—and light itself becomes the topic. Woolf's verbal equivalents for the changes wrought by light are here supplemented by 'the movement of light rays and waves as well as the sounds of the sea and the chirping of birds'.[32]

Certainly, the reader of *The Waves* needs to swim, to trust to the buoyancy of the eye and the suppleness of the understanding. It is no good panicking when sequence seems lost or persons are hard to pick out. The rhythms of the work will sustain us comfortably as long as we do not flounder about trying to catch hold of events. The events are there, sure enough, but they are not sundered from the flow. This is to say that the form of the waves is acted out in the actual reading experience, and the reader must trust the medium. The rhythmic patterns of the book, this 'play-poem', provide the clues for performance.

For, despite the uncertain status of the character's soliloquies as thought or utterance, the auditory is an important component in the work's effect. Indeed, it was the area where Woolf most recognized her own limits, here, of

---

[32] Diane Filby Gillespie, *The Sisters' Arts: The Writing and Painting of Virginia Woolf and Vanessa Bell* (Syracuse: Syracuse University Press, 1988), 303.

class. Because of her uncertainty about the sounds of other kinds of voice and her fear of condescending, Woolf made her one major concession as she worked to the contemporary social order. She recognized that she had internalized some voices and not others. She drew back from her first intention to include working-class speech. She decided to concentrate her final version on middle-class people, a loss in a book that was to be, according to the title-page of the first draft ,'the life of anybody':

Albert, who would look, if you only saw his head in a crowd, ~~much~~ like ~~other pe~~ Roger; but ~~had~~ then there was a patch on his trousers & his boots were shabby—He was apprenticed to a . . . linen draper—No single person could follow lives so opposite; could speak two languages so different; The light came gradually into the room.[33]

[33] *The Waves*, ed. Graham, 68.

NOTE ON THE TEXT

THE text of this edition is that of the third and last impression (October 1933) of the 1931 first edition published by the Hogarth Press on 8 October 1931. This impression is incorrectly described on the verso of the title as a New Edition. The volume was a new edition only in the same sense that it formed part of the Uniform Edition of her novels, but it did give Virginia Woolf the opportunity to correct misprints from the first impression (for example, p. 24, 'when Percy fires at the rocks' is corrected to 'when Percy fired at the rooks'; p. 76, 'an alien' to 'am alien'). Four thousand, one hundred and thirty copies were printed. J. W. Graham's edition of *The Waves: The Two Holograph Drafts* (London: Hogarth Press, 1976) provides a complete transcription and editorial comments on the manuscripts. Virginia Woolf clearly continued to revise up to and including the proof stage, as a number of variants between the first English and first American edition (Harcourt, Brace and Co., 22 October 1931) makes clear. I have followed the English edition; the correction of misprints between the first and third issue suggests that Woolf was content to allow the English readings to stand where they differed slightly from the American edition.

This edition makes minor adjustments to hyphenation, word division ('tomorrow', 'tonight', 'someone', etc.), 'ize' for 'ise', the dropping of the full point after 'Mr' and 'Mrs', and the use of single rather than double quotes, in order to be consistent, and to follow current standard usage.

SELECT BIBLIOGRAPHY

BIBLIOGRAPHY

KIRKPATRICK, B. J., *A Bibliography of Virginia Woolf* (2nd edn.; Oxford: University Press, 1980).

BIOGRAPHY

BELL, QUENTIN, *Virginia Woolf: A Biography* (2 vols.; London: Hogarth Press, 1972).

POOLE, ROGER, *The Unknown Virginia Woolf* (Cambridge: University Press, 1978).

ROSE, PHYLLIS, *Woman of Letters: A Life of Virginia Woolf* (New York: Oxford University Press, 1978).

WOOLF, LEONARD, *An Autobiography* (2 vols.; Oxford: University Press, 1980).

EDITIONS

The Diary of Virginia Woolf, ed. Anne Olivier Bell and Andrew McNeillie (5 vols.; London: Hogarth Press, 1977–84).

The Letters of Virginia Woolf, ed. Nigel Nicolson and Joanne Trautmann (6 vols.; London: Hogarth Press, 1975–84).

GENERAL CRITICISM

BENNETT, JOAN, *Virginia Woolf: Her Art as a Novelist* (Cambridge: University Press, 1945, 1964).

BOWLBY, RACHEL, *Virginia Woolf: Feminist Destinations* (Oxford: Blackwell, 1988).

BREWSTER, DOROTHY, *Virginia Woolf* (London: Allen and Unwin, 1963).

DI BATTISTA, MARIA, *Virginia Woolf's Major Novels* (New Haven, Conn., and London: Yale University Press, 1980).

FLEISHMAN, AVROM, *Virginia Woolf: A Critical Reading* (Baltimore, Johns Hopkins University Press, 1977).

Select Bibliography

FREEDMAN, RALPH, *Virginia Woolf: Revaluation and Continuity* (Berkeley: University of California Press, 1980).

GUIGET, JEAN, *Virginia Woolf and her Works*, trans. Jean Stewart (London: Hogarth Press, 1965).

LEASKA, MITCHELL A., *The Novels of Virginia Woolf* (New York: John Jay Press, 1977).

LEE, HERMIONE, *The Novels of Virginia Woolf* (London: Methuen, 1977).

MAJUMDAR, ROBIN, and MCLAURIN, ALLEN (eds.), *Virginia Woolf: The Critical Heritage* (London: Routledge and Kegan Paul, 1975).

MARCUS, JANE (ed.), *New Feminist Essays on Virginia Woolf* (London: Macmillan, 1981).

MARDER, HERBERT, *Feminism and Art: A Study of Virginia Woolf* (New Haven, Conn., and London: Yale University Press, 1968).

MCLAURIN, ALLEN, *Virginia Woolf: The Echoes Enslaved* (Cambridge: University Press, 1973).

MINOW PINKNEY, MAKIKO, *Virginia Woolf and the Problem of the Subject* (Brighton: Harvester, 1987).

MOODY, A. D., *Virginia Woolf* (Edinburgh: Oliver and Boyd, 1963).

THAKUR, N. C., *The Symbolism of Virginia Woolf* (London: Oxford University Press, 1965).

WARNER, ERIC (ed.), *Virginia Woolf: A Centenary Perspective* (London: Macmillan, 1984).

ZWERDLING, ALEX, *Virginia Woolf and the Real World* (Berkeley: University of California Press, 1986).

ON *THE WAVES*

GRAHAM, J. W., 'Point of View in *The Waves*: Some Services of the Style', in *Virginia Woolf: A Collection of Criticism*, ed. Thomas S. W. Lewis (New York: McGraw-Hill, 1975), 94–112.

Select Bibliography

GRAHAM, J. W., (ed.), *The Waves: The Two Holograph Drafts* (London: Hogarth Press, 1976).

McCLUSKEY, KATHLEEN, OSJ, *Reverberations: Sound and Structure in the Novels of Virginia Woolf* (Ann Arbor, Michigan: UMI Research Press, 1988).

MEISEL, PERRY, *The Absent Father: Virginia Woolf and Walter Pater* (New Haven: Yale University Press, 1980).

MINOW PINKNEY, MAKIKO, *Virginia Woolf and the Problem of the Subject* (Brighton: Harvester, 1987).

STEWART, GARRETT, 'Catching the Stylistic D/rift: Sound Effects in *The Waves*', *English Literary History*, 54 (Summer 1987), 21–61.

A CHRONOLOGY OF
VIRGINIA WOOLF

1882   (25 Jan.) Born Adeline Virginia Stephen.

1895   (5 May) Death of mother, Julia Stephen. VW's first breakdown.

1896   Travels in France with sister Vanessa.

1897   (19 July) Death of half-sister Stella. VW learning Greek.

1899   VW's brother Thoby goes to Trinity College, Cambridge, where he forms friendships with Lytton Strachey, Leonard Woolf, Clive Bell, and others of the future Bloomsbury Group. (The other brother Adrian followed him to Trinity in 1902.)

1904   Death of father, Sir Leslie Stephen. In spring VW travels in Italy with Vanessa and friend Violet Dickinson. (May) VW has another serious collapse. Moves to Gordon Square.

1905   Travels in Spain and Portugal. Writes reviews and teaches at Morley College.

1906   Travels in Greece. (20 Nov.) Death of Thoby Stephen.

1907   Marriage of Vanessa to Clive Bell. VW moves with Adrian to Fitzroy Square. Works on a novel, *Melymbrosia* (working title for *The Voyage Out*)

1908   Visits Italy with the Bells.

1909   (17 Feb.) Lytton Strachey proposes marriage.

        First meets Lady Ottoline Morrell. Visits Florence and later Bayreuth.

1910   Roger Fry's first Post-Impressionist Exhibition.

1911   Travels to Turkey, where Vanessa is ill. Moves to Brunswick Square, sharing house with Adrian, Keynes, Duncan Grant, and Leonard Woolf.

1912 (10 Aug.) Marriage to Leonard Woolf; travels in Provence, Spain, and Italy. Moves to Clifford's Inn.

1913 Unwell most of summer. (9 Sept.) Suicide attempt.

1914 Moves to Richmond.

1915 Purchase of Hogarth House, Richmond. *The Voyage Out* published. Bout of violent madness.

1917 Hogarth Press commences publication with *The Mark on the Wall*. Begins work on *Night and Day*.

1918 Writes reviews and *Night and Day*; also sets type for the Press. (15 Nov.) First meets T. S. Eliot.

1919 Purchase of Monk's House, Rodmell. *Night and Day* published.

1920 Works on journalism and *Jacob's Room*.

1921 Ill for summer months. Finishes *Jacob's Room*.

1922 (14 Dec.) First meets V. Sackville-West. *Jacob's Room* published.

1923 Visits Spain. Works on first version of *Mrs Dalloway*.

1924 Purchase of lease on house in Tavistock Square. Gives lecture that became 'Mr Bennett and Mrs Brown'. Finishes *Mrs Dalloway*.

1925 *The Common Reader* published. *Mrs Dalloway* published. Ill during summer.

1926 Writes *To the Lighthouse*.

1927 *To the Lighthouse* published. Travels to Sicily. Begins *Orlando*.

1928 *Orlando* published.

1929 Travels to Berlin. *A Room of One's Own* published.

1930 Writes and rewrites *The Waves*.

1931 Tours in France. *The Waves* published. Writes *Flush*.

Chronology

1932   Death of Lytton Strachey. *The Common Reader*, 2nd series, published. Begins *The Years*.

1933   *Flush* published.

1934   Works on *The Years*. Death of Roger Fry.

1935   Rewrites *The Years*. Reads for Fry biography.

1936   (May–Oct.) Ill. Finishes *The Years*. Begins *Three Guineas*.

1937   *The Years* published. Begins *Roger Fry*. Death in Spanish Civil War of Julian Bell, son of Vanessa.

1938   *Three Guineas* published. Works on *Roger Fry*, and thinks about *Between the Acts*.

1939   Woolfs move to Mecklenburgh Square, but live mostly at Monk's House. Works on *Between the Acts*.

1940   *Roger Fry* published. Mecklenburgh Square house damaged; house in Tavistock Square destroyed. (23 Nov.) Finishes *Between the Acts*.

1941   (26 Feb.) Revises *Between the Acts*. Becomes ill. (28 Mar.) Drowns herself in River Ouse. *Between the Acts* published.

Chronology

The Waves

THE WAVES

*The sun** had not yet risen. The sea was indistinguishable
from the sky, except that the sea was slightly creased as if a
cloth had wrinkles in it. Gradually as the sky whitened a
dark line lay on the horizon dividing the sea from the sky
and the grey cloth became barred with thick strokes
moving, one after another, beneath the surface, following
each other, pursuing each other, perpetually.

As they neared the shore each bar rose, heaped itself,
broke and swept a thin veil of white water across the sand.
The wave paused, and then drew out again, sighing like a
sleeper whose breath comes and goes unconsciously. Gradually the dark bar on the horizon became clear as if the
sediment in an old wine-bottle had sunk and left the glass
green. Behind it, too, the sky cleared as if the white
sediment there had sunk, or as if the arm of a woman
couched beneath the horizon had raised a lamp and flat
bars of white, green and yellow spread across the sky like
the blades of a fan. Then she raised her lamp higher and
the air seemed to become fibrous and to tear away from the
green surface flickering and flaming in red and yellow fibres
like the smoky fire that roars from a bonfire. Gradually the
fibres of the burning bonfire were fused into one haze, one
incandescence which lifted the weight of the woollen grey
sky on top of it and turned it to a million atoms of soft blue.
The surface of the sea slowly became transparent and lay
rippling and sparkling until the dark stripes were almost
rubbed out. Slowly the arm that held the lamp raised it

*higher and then higher until a broad flame became visible;
an arc of fire burnt on the rim of the horizon, and all round
it the sea blazed gold.*

*The light struck upon the trees in the garden, making one
leaf transparent and then another. One bird chirped high
up; there was a pause; another chirped lower down. The
sun sharpened the walls of the house, and rested like the tip
of a fan upon a white blind and made a blue finger-print of
shadow under the leaf by the bedroom window. The blind
stirred slightly, but all within was dim and unsubstantial.
The birds sang their blank melody outside.*

'I SEE a ring,' said Bernard, 'hanging above me. It quivers and hangs in a loop of light.'

'I see a slab of pale yellow,' said Susan, 'spreading away until it meets a purple stripe.'

'I hear a sound,' said Rhoda, 'cheep, chirp; cheep chirp; going up and down.'

'I see a globe,' said Neville, 'hanging down in a drop against the enormous flanks of some hill.'

'I see a crimson tassel,' said Jinny, 'twisted with gold threads.'

'I hear something stamping,' said Louis. 'A great beast's foot is chained. It stamps, and stamps, and stamps.'

'Look at the spider's web on the corner of the balcony,' said Bernard. 'It has beads of water on it, drops of white light.'

'The leaves are gathered round the window like pointed ears,' said Susan.

'A shadow falls on the path,' said Louis, 'like an elbow bent.'

'Islands of light are swimming on the grass,' said Rhoda. 'They have fallen through the trees.'

'The birds' eyes are bright in the tunnels between the leaves,' said Neville.

'The stalks are covered with harsh, short hairs,' said Jinny, 'and drops of water have stuck to them.'

'A caterpillar is curled in a green ring,' said Susan, 'notched with blunt feet.'

'The grey-shelled snail draws across the path and flattens the blades behind him,' said Rhoda.

'And burning lights from the window-panes flash in and out on the grasses,' said Louis.

'Stones are cold to my feet,' said Neville. 'I feel each one, round or pointed, separately.'

'The back of my hand burns,' said Jinny, 'but the palm is clammy and damp with dew.'

'Now the cock crows like a spurt of hard, red water in the white tide,' said Bernard.

'Birds are singing up and down and in and out all round us,' said Susan.

'The beast stamps; the elephant with its foot chained; the great brute on the beach stamps,' said Louis.

'Look at the house,' said Jinny, 'with all its windows white with blinds.'

'Cold water begins to run from the scullery tap,' said Rhoda, 'over the mackerel in the bowl.'

'The walls are cracked with gold cracks,' said Bernard, 'and there are blue, finger-shaped shadows of leaves beneath the windows.'

'Now Mrs Constable pulls up her thick black stockings,' said Susan.

'When the smoke rises, sleep curls off the roof like a mist,' said Louis.

'The birds sang in chorus first,' said Rhoda. 'Now the scullery door is unbarred. Off they fly. Off they fly like a fling of seed. But one sings by the bedroom window alone.'

'Bubbles form on the floor of the saucepan,' said Jinny. 'Then they rise, quicker and quicker, in a silver chain to the top.'

'Now Billy scrapes the fish-scales with a jagged knife on to a wooden board,' said Neville.

'The dining-room window is dark blue now,' said Bernard, 'and the air ripples above the chimneys.'

'A swallow is perched on the lightning-conductor,' said Susan. 'And Biddy has smacked down the bucket on the kitchen flags.'

'That is the first stroke of the church bell,' said Louis. 'Then the others follow; one, two; one, two; one, two.'

'Look at the table-cloth, flying white along the table,' said Rhoda. 'Now there are rounds of white china, and silver streaks beside each plate.'

'Suddenly a bee booms in my ear,' said Neville. 'It is here; it is past.'

'I burn, I shiver,' said Jinny, 'out of this sun, into this shadow.'

'Now they have all gone,' said Louis. 'I am alone. They have gone into the house for breakfast, and I am left standing by the wall among the flowers. It is very early, before lessons. Flower after flower is specked on the depths of green. The petals are harlequins. Stalks rise from the black hollows beneath. The flowers swim like fish made of light upon the dark, green waters. I hold a stalk in my hand. I am the stalk.* My roots go down to the depths of the world, through earth dry with brick, and damp earth, through veins of lead and silver. I am all fibre. All tremors shake me, and the weight of the earth is pressed to my ribs. Up here my eyes are green leaves, unseeing. I am a boy in grey flannels with a belt fastened by a brass snake up here. Down there my eyes are the lidless eyes of a stone figure in a desert by the Nile. I see women passing with red pitchers to the river; I see camels swaying and men in turbans. I hear tramplings, tremblings, stirrings round me.

'Up here Bernard, Neville, Jinny and Susan (but not

Rhoda) skim the flower-beds with their nets. They skim the butterflies from the nodding tops of the flowers. They brush the surface of the world. Their nets are full of fluttering wings. "Louis! Louis! Louis!" they shout. But they cannot see me. I am on the other side of the hedge. There are only little eye-holes among the leaves. Oh Lord, let them pass. Lord, let them lay their butterflies on a pocket-handkerchief on the gravel. Let them count out their tortoise-shells, their red admirals and cabbage whites. But let me be unseen. I am green as a yew tree in the shade of the hedge. My hair is made of leaves. I am rooted to the middle of the earth. My body is a stalk. I press the stalk. A drop oozes from the hole at the mouth and slowly, thickly, grows larger and larger. Now something pink passes the eye-hole. Now an eye-beam is slid through the chink. Its beam strikes me. I am a boy in a grey flannel suit. She has found me. I am struck on the nape of the neck. She has kissed me. All is shattered.'

'I was running,' said Jinny, 'after breakfast. I saw leaves moving in a hole in the hedge. I thought "That is a bird on its nest." I parted them and looked; but there was no bird on a nest. The leaves went on moving. I was frightened. I ran past Susan, past Rhoda, and Neville and Bernard in the tool-house talking. I cried as I ran, faster and faster. What moved the leaves? What moves my heart, my legs? And I dashed in here, seeing you green as a bush, like a branch, very still, Louis, with your eyes fixed. "Is he dead?" I thought, and kissed you, with my heart jumping under my pink frock like the leaves, which go on moving, though there is nothing to move them. Now I smell geraniums; I smell earth mould. I dance. I ripple. I am thrown over you like a net of light. I lie quivering flung over you.'

'Through the chink in the hedge,' said Susan, 'I saw her

kiss him. I raised my head from my flower-pot and looked through a chink in the hedge. I saw her kiss him. I saw them, Jinny and Louis, kissing. Now I will wrap my agony inside my pocket-handkerchief. It shall be screwed tight into a ball. I will go to the beech wood alone, before lessons. I will not sit at a table, doing sums. I will not sit next Jinny and next Louis. I will take my anguish and lay it upon the roots under the beech trees. I will examine it and take it between my fingers. They will not find me. I shall eat nuts and peer for eggs through the brambles and my hair will be matted and I shall sleep under hedges and drink water from ditches and die there.'

'Susan has passed us,' said Bernard. 'She has passed the tool-house door with her handkerchief screwed into a ball. She was not crying, but her eyes, which are so beautiful, were narrow as cats' eyes before they spring. I shall follow her, Neville. I shall go gently behind her, to be at hand, with my curiosity, to comfort her when she bursts out in a rage and thinks, "I am alone".

'Now she walks across the field with a swing, nonchalantly, to deceive us. Then she comes to the dip; she thinks she is unseen; she begins to run with her fists clenched in front of her. Her nails meet in the ball of her pocket-handkerchief. She is making for the beech woods out of the light. She spreads her arms as she comes to them and takes to the shade like a swimmer. But she is blind after the light and trips and flings herself down on the roots under the trees, where the light seems to pant in and out, in and out. The branches heave up and down. There is agitation and trouble here. There is gloom. The light is fitful. There is anguish here. The roots make a skeleton on the ground, with dead leaves heaped in the angles. Susan has spread her anguish out. Her pocket-handkerchief is laid on the roots of the beech trees and she sobs, sitting crumpled where she has fallen.'

'I saw her kiss him,' said Susan. 'I looked between the leaves and saw her. She danced in flecked with diamonds light as dust. And I am squat, Bernard, I am short. I have eyes that look close to the ground and see insects in the grass. The yellow warmth in my side turned to stone when I saw Jinny kiss Louis. I shall eat grass and die in a ditch in the brown water where dead leaves have rotted.'

'I saw you go,' said Bernard. 'As you passed the door of the tool-house I heard you cry "I am unhappy". I put down my knife. I was making boats out of firewood with Neville. And my hair is untidy, because when Mrs Constable told me to brush it there was a fly in a web, and I asked, "Shall I free the fly? Shall I let the fly be eaten?" So I am late always. My hair is unbrushed and these chips of wood stick in it. When I heard you cry I followed you, and saw you put down your handkerchief, screwed up, with its rage, with its hate, knotted in it. But soon that will cease. Our bodies are close now. You hear me breathe. You see the beetle too carrying off a leaf on its back. It runs this way, then that way, so that even your desire while you watch the beetle, to possess one single thing (it is Louis now) must waver, like the light in and out of the beech leaves; and then words, moving darkly, in the depths of your mind will break up this knot of hardness, screwed in your pocket-handkerchief.'

'I love,' said Susan, 'and I hate.* I desire one thing only. My eyes are hard. Jinny's eyes break into a thousand lights. Rhoda's are like those pale flowers to which moths come in the evening. Yours grow full and brim and never break. But I am already set on my pursuit. I see insects in the grass. Though my mother still knits white socks for me and hems pinafores and I am a child, I love and I hate.'

'But when we sit together, close,' said Bernard, 'we melt into each other with phrases. We are edged with mist. We make an unsubstantial territory.'

'I see the beetle,' said Susan. 'It is black, I see; it is green, I see; I am tied down with single words. But you wander off; you slip away; you rise up higher, with words and words in phrases.'

'Now,' said Bernard, 'let us explore. There is the white house lying among the trees. It lies down there ever so far beneath us. We shall sink like swimmers just touching the ground with the tips of their toes. We shall sink through the green air of the leaves, Susan. We sink as we run. The waves close over us, the beech leaves meet above our heads. There is the stable clock with its gilt hands shining. Those are the flats and heights of the roofs of the great house. There is the stable-boy clattering in the yard in rubber boots. That is Elvedon.

'Now we have fallen through the tree-tops to the earth. The air no longer rolls its long, unhappy, purple waves over us. We touch earth; we tread ground. That is the close-clipped hedge of the ladies' garden. There they walk at noon, with scissors, clipping roses. Now we are in the ringed wood with the wall round it. This is Elvedon. I have seen signposts at the cross-roads with one arm pointing "To Elvedon". No one has been there. The ferns smell very strong, and there are red funguses growing beneath them. Now we wake the sleeping daws who have never seen a human form; now we tread on rotten oak apples, red with age and slippery. There is a ring of wall round this wood; nobody comes here. Listen! That is the flop of a giant toad in the undergrowth; that is the patter of some primeval fir-cone falling to rot among the ferns.

'Put your foot on this brick. Look over the wall. That is Elvedon. The lady sits between the two long windows, writing. The gardeners sweep the lawn with giant brooms. We are the first to come here. We are the discoverers of an unknown land. Do not stir; if the gardeners saw us they would shoot us. We should be nailed like stoats to the stable door. Look! Do not move. Grasp the ferns tight on the top of the wall.'

'I see the lady writing. I see the gardeners sweeping,' said Susan. 'If we died here, nobody would bury us.'

'Run!' said Bernard. 'Run! The gardener with the black beard has seen us! We shall be shot! We shall be shot like jays and pinned to the wall! We are in a hostile country. We must escape to the beech wood. We must hide under the trees. I turned a twig as we came. There is a secret path. Bend as low as you can. Follow without looking back. They will think we are foxes. Run!

'Now we are safe. Now we can stand upright again. Now we can stretch our arms in this high canopy, in this vast wood. I hear nothing. That is only the murmur of the waves in the air. That is a wood-pigeon breaking cover in the tops of the beech trees. The pigeon beats the air; the pigeon beats the air with wooden wings.'

'Now you trail away,' said Susan, 'making phrases. Now you mount like an air-ball's string, higher and higher through the layers of the leaves, out of reach. Now you lag. Now you tug at my skirts, looking back, making phrases. You have escaped me. Here is the garden. Here is the hedge. Here is Rhoda on the path rocking petals to and fro in her brown basin.'

'All my ships are white,' said Rhoda. 'I do not want red

petals of hollyhocks or geranium. I want white petals that
float when I tip the basin up. I have a fleet now swimming
from shore to shore. I will drop a twig in as a raft for a
drowning sailor. I will drop a stone in and see bubbles rise
from the depths of the sea. Neville has gone and Susan has
gone; Jinny is in the kitchen garden picking currants with
Louis perhaps. I have a short time alone, while Miss
Hudson spreads our copy-books on the schoolroom table.
I have a short space of freedom. I have picked all the fallen
petals and made them swim. I have put raindrops in some.
I will plant a lighthouse here, a head of Sweet Alice. And I
will now rock the brown basin from side to side so that
my ships may ride the waves. Some will founder. Some
will dash themselves against the cliffs. One sails alone.*
That is my ship. It sails into icy caverns where the sea-bear
barks and stalactites swing green chains. The waves rise;
their crests curl; look at the lights on the mastheads. They
have scattered, they have foundered, all except my ship,
which mounts the wave and sweeps before the gale and
reaches the islands where the parrots chatter and the
creepers . . .'

'Where is Bernard?' said Neville. 'He has my knife. We
were in the tool-shed making boats, and Susan came past
the door. And Bernard dropped his boat and went after
her taking my knife, the sharp one that cuts the keel. He is
like a dangling wire, a broken bell-pull, always twangling.
He is like the seaweed hung outside the window, damp
now, now dry. He leaves me in the lurch; he follows
Susan; and if Susan cries he will take my knife and tell her
stories. The big blade is an emperor; the broken blade a
Negro. I hate dangling things; I hate dampish things. I hate
wandering and mixing things together. Now the bell rings
and we shall be late. Now we must drop our toys. Now

we must go in together. The copy-books are laid out side by side on the green baize table.'

'I will not conjugate the verb,' said Louis, 'until Bernard has said it. My father is a banker in Brisbane and I speak with an Australian accent. I will wait and copy Bernard. He is English. They are all English. Susan's father is a clergyman. Rhoda has no father. Bernard and Neville are the sons of gentlemen. Jinny lives with her grandmother in London. Now they suck their pens. Now they twist their copy-books, and, looking sideways at Miss Hudson, count the purple buttons on her bodice. Bernard has a chip in his hair. Susan has a red look in her eyes. Both are flushed. But I am pale; I am neat, and my knickerbockers are drawn together by a belt with a brass snake. I know the lesson by heart. I know more than they will ever know. I know my cases and my genders; I could know everything in the world if I wished. But I do not wish to come to the top and say my lesson. My roots are threaded, like fibres in a flower-pot, round and round about the world. I do not wish to come to the top and live in the light of this great clock, yellow-faced, which ticks and ticks. Jinny and Susan, Bernard and Neville bind themselves into a thong with which to lash me. They laugh at my neatness, at my Australian accent. I will now try to imitate Bernard softly lisping Latin.'

'Those are white words,' said Susan, 'like stones one picks up by the seashore.'

'They flick their tails right and left as I speak them,' said Bernard. 'They wag their tails; they flick their tails; they move through the air in flocks, now this way, now that way, moving all together, now dividing, now coming together.'

'Those are yellow words, those are fiery words,' said

Jinny. 'I should like a fiery dress, a yellow dress, a fulvous dress to wear in the evening.'

'Each tense,' said Neville, 'means differently. There is an order in this world; there are distinctions, there are differences in this world, upon whose verge I step. For this is only a beginning.'

'Now Miss Hudson,' said Rhoda, 'has shut the book. Now the terror is beginning. Now taking her lump of chalk she draws figures, six, seven, eight, and then a cross and then a line on the blackboard. What is the answer? The others look; they look with understanding. Louis writes; Susan writes; Neville writes; Jinny writes; even Bernard has now begun to write. But I cannot write. I see only figures. The others are handing in their answers, one by one. Now it is my turn. But I have no answer. The others are allowed to go. They slam the door. Miss Hudson goes. I am left alone to find an answer. The figures mean nothing now. Meaning has gone. The clock ticks. The two hands are convoys marching through a desert. The black bars on the clock face are green oases. The long hand has marched ahead to find water. The other, painfully stumbles among hot stones in the desert. It will die in the desert. The kitchen door slams. Wild dogs bark far away. Look, the loop of the figure is beginning to fill with time; it holds the world in it. I begin to draw a figure and the world is looped in it, and I myself am outside the loop; which I now join— so—and seal up, and make entire. The world is entire, and I am outside of it, crying, "Oh save me, from being blown for ever outside the loop of time!"'

'There Rhoda sits staring at the blackboard,' said Louis, 'in the schoolroom, while we ramble off, picking here a bit of thyme, pinching here a leaf of southernwood while Bernard tells a story. Her shoulder-blades meet across her back like the wings of a small butterfly. And as she stares at the chalk figures, her mind lodges in those white circles, it steps through those white loops into emptiness, alone. They have no meaning for her. She has no answer for them. She has no body as the others have. And I, who speak with an Australian accent, whose father is a banker in Brisbane, do not fear her as I fear the others.'

'Let us now crawl,' said Bernard, 'under the canopy of the currant leaves, and tell stories. Let us inhabit the underworld. Let us take possession of our secret territory, which is lit by pendant currants like candelabra, shining red on one side, black on the other. Here, Jinny, if we curl up close, we can sit under the canopy of the currant leaves and watch the censers swing. This is our universe. The others pass down the carriage-drive. The skirts of Miss Hudson and Miss Curry sweep by like candle extinguishers. Those are Susan's white socks. Those are Louis' neat sand-shoes firmly printing the gravel. Here come warm gusts of decomposing leaves, of rotting vegetation. We are in a swamp now; in a malarial jungle. There is an elephant white with maggots, killed by an arrow shot dead in its eye. The bright eyes of hopping birds—eagles, vultures—are apparent. They take us for fallen trees. They pick at a worm—that is a hooded cobra—and leave it with a festering brown scar to be mauled by lions. This is our world, lit with crescents and stars of light; and great petals half transparent block the openings like purple windows. Everything is strange. Things are huge and very small. The stalks of flowers are thick as oak trees. Leaves are high as the domes of vast cathedrals. We are giants, lying here, who can make forests quiver.'

'This is here,' said Jinny, 'this is now. But soon we shall go. Soon Miss Curry will blow her whistle. We shall walk.

We shall part. You will go to school. You will have masters wearing crosses with white ties. I shall have a mistress in a school on the East Coast who sits under a portrait of Queen Alexandra.* That is where I am going, and Susan and Rhoda. This is only here; this is only now. Now we lie under the currant bushes and every time the breeze stirs we are mottled all over. My hand is like a snake's skin. My knees are pink floating islands. Your face is like an apple tree netted under.'

'The heat is going,' said Bernard, 'from the Jungle. The leaves flap black wings over us. Miss Curry has blown her whistle on the terrace. We must creep out from the awning of the currant leaves and stand upright. There are twigs in your hair, Jinny. There is a green caterpillar on your neck. We must form, two by two. Miss Curry is taking us for a brisk walk, while Miss Hudson sits at her desk settling her accounts.'

'It is dull,' said Jinny, 'walking along the high road with no windows to look at, with no bleared eyes of blue glass let into the pavement.'

'We must form into pairs,' said Susan, 'and walk in order, not shuffling our feet, not lagging, with Louis going first to lead us, because Louis is alert and not a wool-gatherer.'

'Since I am supposed,' said Neville, 'to be too delicate to go with them, since I get so easily tired and then am sick, I will use this hour of solitude, this reprieve from conversation, to coast round the purlieus of the house and recover, if I can, by standing on the same stair half-way up the landing, what I felt when I heard about the dead man through the swing-door last night when cook was shoving in and out the dampers. He was found with his throat cut. The apple-tree leaves became fixed in the sky; the moon

[17]

glared; I was unable to lift my foot up the stair. He was found in the gutter. His blood gurgled down the gutter. His jowl was white as a dead codfish. I shall call this stricture, this rigidity, "death among the apple trees" for ever. There were the floating, pale-grey clouds; and the immitigable tree; the implacable tree* with its greaved silver bark. The ripple of my life was unavailing. I was unable to pass by. There was an obstacle. "I cannot surmount this unintelligible obstacle", I said. And the others passed on. But we are doomed, all of us, by the apple trees, by the immitigable tree which we cannot pass.

'Now the stricture and rigidity are over; and I will continue to make my survey of the purlieus of the house in the late afternoon, in the sunset, when the sun makes oleaginous spots on the linoleum, and a crack of light kneels on the wall, making the chair legs look broken.'

'I saw Florrie in the kitchen garden,' said Susan, 'as we came back from our walk, with the washing blown out round her, the pyjamas, the drawers, the night-gowns blown tight. And Ernest kissed her. He was in his green baize apron, cleaning silver; and his mouth was sucked like a purse in wrinkles and he seized her with the pyjamas blown out hard between them. He was blind as a bull, and she swooned in anguish, only little veins streaking her white cheeks red. Now though they pass plates of bread and butter and cups of milk at tea-time I see a crack in the earth and hot steam hisses up; and the urn roars as Ernest roared, and I am blown out hard like the pyjamas, even while my teeth meet in the soft bread and butter, and I lap the sweet milk. I am not afraid of heat, nor of the frozen winter. Rhoda dreams, sucking a crust soaked in milk; Louis regards the wall opposite with snail-green eyes; Bernard moulds his bread into pellets and calls them "people". Neville with his clean and decisive ways has finished. He has rolled his napkin and slipped it through the silver ring. Jinny spins her fingers on the table-cloth, as if they were dancing in the sunshine, pirouetting. But I am not afraid of the heat or of the frozen winter.'

'Now,' said Louis, 'we all rise; we all stand up. Miss Curry spreads wide the black book on the harmonium. It is difficult not to weep as we sing, as we pray that God may keep us safe while we sleep, calling ourselves little children.* When we are sad and trembling with apprehension it is sweet to sing together, leaning slightly, I towards Susan, Susan towards Bernard, clasping hands, afraid of much, I of my accent, Rhoda of figures; yet resolute to conquer.'

'We troop upstairs like ponies,' said Bernard, 'stamping, clattering one behind another to take our turns in the bathroom. We buffet, we tussle, we spring up and down on the hard, white beds. My turn has come. I come now.

'Mrs Constable, girt in a bath-towel, takes her lemon-coloured sponge and soaks it in water; it turns chocolate-brown; it drips; and, holding it high above me, shivering beneath her, she squeezes it. Water pours down the runnel of my spine. Bright arrows of sensation shoot on either side. I am covered with warm flesh. My dry crannies are wetted; my cold body is warmed; it is sluiced and gleaming. Water descends and sheets me like an eel. Now hot towels envelop me, and their roughness, as I rub my back, makes my blood purr. Rich and heavy sensations form on the roof of my mind; down showers the day—the woods; and Elvedon; Susan and the pigeon. Pouring down the walls of my mind, running together, the day falls copious, resplendent. Now I tie my pyjamas loosely round me, and lie under this thin sheet afloat in the shallow light which is like a film of water drawn over my eyes by a wave. I hear through it far off, far away, faint and far, the chorus beginning; wheels; dogs; men shouting; church bells; the chorus beginning.'

'As I fold up my frock and my chemise,' said Rhoda, 'so I put off my hopeless desire to be Susan, to be Jinny. But I will stretch my toes so that they touch the rail at the end of the bed; I will assure myself, touching the rail, of something hard. Now I cannot sink; cannot altogether fall through the thin sheet now. Now I spread my body on this frail mattress and hang suspended. I am above the earth now. I am no longer upright, to be knocked against and damaged. All is soft, and bending. Walls and cupboards whiten and bend their yellow squares on top of which a pale glass gleams. Out of me now my mind can pour. I can think of my Armadas* sailing on the high waves. I am relieved of hard contacts and collisions. I sail on alone under white cliffs. Oh, but I sink, I fall! That is the corner of the cupboard; that is the nursery looking-glass. But they stretch, they elongate. I sink down on the black plumes of sleep; its thick wings are pressed to my eyes. Travelling through darkness I see the stretched flower-beds, and Mrs Constable runs from behind the corner of the pampas-grass to say my aunt has come to fetch me in a carriage. I mount; I escape; I rise on spring-heeled boots over the tree-tops. But I am now fallen into the carriage at the hall door, where she sits nodding yellow plumes with eyes hard like glazed marbles. Oh, to awake from dreaming! Look, there is the chest of drawers. Let me pull myself out of these waters. But they heap themselves on me; they sweep me between their great shoulders; I am turned; I am tumbled; I am stretched, among these long lights, these long waves, these endless paths, with people pursuing, pursuing.'

The sun rose higher. Blue waves, green waves swept a quick fan over the beach, circling the spike of sea-holly and leaving shallow pools of light here and there on the sand. A faint black rim was left behind them. The rocks which had been misty and soft hardened and were marked with red clefts.

Sharp stripes of shadow lay on the grass, and the dew dancing on the tips of the flowers and leaves made the garden like a mosaic of single sparks not yet formed into one whole. The birds, whose breasts were specked canary and rose, now sang a strain or two together, wildly, like skaters rollicking arm-in-arm, and were suddenly silent, breaking asunder.

The sun laid broader blades upon the house. The light touched something green in the window corner and made it a lump of emerald, a cave of pure green like stoneless fruit. It sharpened the edges of chairs and tables and stitched white table-cloths with fine gold wires. As the light increased a bud here and there split asunder and shook out flowers, green veined and quivering, as if the effort of opening had set them rocking, and pealing a faint carillon as they beat their frail clappers against their white walls. Everything became softly amorphous, as if the china of the plate flowed and the steel of the knife were liquid. Meanwhile the concussion of the waves breaking fell with muffled thuds, like logs falling, on the shore.

'Now,' said Bernard, 'the time has come. The day has come. The cab is at the door. My huge box bends George's bandy-legs even wider. The horrible ceremony is over, the tips, and the good-byes in the hall. Now there is this gulping ceremony with my mother, this hand-shaking ceremony with my father; now I must go on waving, I must go on waving, till we turn the corner. Now that ceremony is over. Heaven be praised, all ceremonies are over. I am alone; I am going to school for the first time.

'Everybody seems to be doing things for this moment only; and never again. Never again. The urgency of it all is fearful. Everybody knows I am going to school, going to school for the first time. "That boy is going to school for the first time", says the housemaid, cleaning the steps. I must not cry. I must behold them indifferently. Now the awful portals of the station gape; "the moon-faced clock regards me".* I must make phrases and phrases and so interpose something hard between myself and the stare of housemaids, the stare of clocks, staring faces, indifferent faces, or I shall cry. There is Louis, there is Neville, in long coats, carrying handbags, by the booking-office. They are composed. But they look different.'

'Here is Bernard,' said Louis. 'He is composed; he is easy. He swings his bag as he walks. I will follow Bernard, because he is not afraid. We are drawn through the booking-office on to the platform as a stream draws twigs and straws round the piers of a bridge. There is the very

[22]

powerful, bottle-green engine without a neck, all back and thighs, breathing steam. The guard blows his whistle; the flag is dipped; without an effort, of its own momentum, like an avalanche started by a gentle push, we start forward. Bernard spreads a rug and plays knuckle-bones. Neville reads. London crumbles. London heaves and surges. There is a bristling of chimneys and towers. There a white church; there a mast among the spires. There a canal. Now there are open spaces with asphalt paths upon which it is strange that people should now be walking. There is a hill striped with red houses. A man crosses a bridge with a dog at his heels. Now the red boy begins firing at a pheasant. The blue boy shoves him aside. "My uncle is the best shot in England. My cousin is Master of Foxhounds." Boasting begins. And I cannot boast, for my father is a banker in Brisbane, and I speak with an Australian accent.'

'After all this hubbub,' said Neville, 'all this scuffling and hubbub, we have arrived. This is indeed a moment— this is indeed a solemn moment. I come, like a lord to his halls appointed. That is our founder; our illustrious founder, standing in the courtyard with one foot raised. I salute our founder. A noble Roman air hangs over these austere quadrangles. Already the lights are lit in the form rooms. Those are laboratories perhaps; and that a library, where I shall explore the exactitude of the Latin language, and step firmly upon the well-laid sentences, and pronounce the explicit, the sonorous hexameters of Virgil, of Lucretius; and chant with a passion that is never obscure or formless the loves of Catullus,* reading from a big book, a quarto with margins. I shall lie, too, in the fields among the tickling grasses. I shall lie with my friends under the towering elm trees.

'Behold, the Headmaster. Alas, that he should excite my ridicule. He is too sleek, he is altogether too shiny and black, like some statue in a public garden. And on the left side of his waistcoat, his taut, his drum-like waistcoat, hangs a crucifix.'

'Old Crane,' said Bernard, 'now rises to address us. Old Crane, the Headmaster, has a nose like a mountain at sunset, and a blue cleft in his chin, like a wooded ravine, which some tripper has fired; like a wooded ravine seen from the train window. He sways slightly, mouthing out his tremendous and sonorous words. I love tremendous and sonorous words. But his words are too hearty to be true. Yet he is by this time convinced of their truth. And when he leaves the room, lurching rather heavily from side to side, and hurls his way through the swing-doors, all the masters, lurching rather heavily from side to side, hurl themselves also through the swing-doors. This is our first night at school, apart from our sisters.'

'This is my first night at school,' said Susan, 'away from my father, away from my home. My eyes swell; my eyes prick with tears. I hate the smell of pine and linoleum. I hate the wind-bitten shrubs and the sanitary tiles. I hate the cheerful jokes and the glazed look of everyone. I left my squirrel and my doves for the boy to look after. The kitchen door slams, and shot patters among the leaves when Percy fires at the rooks. All here is false; all is meretricious. Rhoda and Jinny sit far off in brown serge, and look at Miss Lambert who sits under a picture of Queen Alexandra reading from a book before her. There is also a blue scroll of needlework embroidered by some old girl. If I do not purse my lips, if I do not screw my handkerchief, I shall cry.'

'The purple light,' said Rhoda, 'in Miss Lambert's ring passes to and fro across the black stain on the white page of the Prayer Book. It is a vinous, it is an amorous light. Now that our boxes are unpacked in the dormitories, we sit herded together under maps of the entire world. There are desks with wells for the ink. We shall write our exercises in ink here. But here I am nobody. I have no face. This great company, all dressed in brown serge, has robbed me of my identity. We are all callous, unfriended. I will seek out a face, a composed, a monumental face, and will endow it with omniscience, and wear it under my dress like a talisman and then (I promise this) I will find some dingle in a wood where I can display my assortment of curious treasures. I promise myself this. So I will not cry.'

'That dark woman,' said Jinny, 'with high cheek-bones, has a shiny dress, like a shell, veined, for wearing in the evening. That is nice for summer, but for winter I should like a thin dress shot with red threads that would gleam in the firelight. Then when the lamps were lit, I should put on my red dress and it would be thin as a veil, and would wind about my body, and billow out as I came into the room, pirouetting. It would make a flower shape as I sank down, in the middle of the room, on a gilt chair. But Miss Lambert wears an opaque dress, that falls in a cascade from her snow-white ruffle as she sits under a picture of Queen Alexandra pressing one white finger firmly on the page. And we pray.'

'Now we march, two by two,' said Louis, 'orderly, processional, into chapel. I like the dimness that falls as we enter the sacred building. I like the orderly progress. We file in; we seat ourselves. We put off our distinctions as we enter. I like it now, when, lurching slightly, but only from his momentum, Dr Crane mounts the pulpit and reads the lesson from a Bible spread on the back of the brass eagle. I rejoice; my heart expands in his bulk, in his authority. He lays the whirling dust clouds in my tremulous, my ignominiously agitated mind—how we danced round the Christmas tree and handing parcels they forgot me, and the fat woman said, "This little boy has no present", and gave me a shiny Union Jack from the top of the tree, and I cried with fury—to be remembered with pity. Now all is laid by his authority, his crucifix, and I feel come over me the sense of the earth under me, and my roots going down and down till they wrap themselves round some hardness at the centre. I recover my continuity, as he reads. I become a figure in the procession, a spoke in the huge wheel that turning, at last erects me, here and now. I have been in the dark; I have been hidden; but when the wheel turns (as he reads) I rise into this dim light where I just perceive, but scarcely, kneeling boys, pillars and memorial brasses. There is no crudity here, no sudden kisses.'

'The brute menaces my liberty,' said Neville, 'when he prays. Unwarmed by imagination, his words fall cold on my head like paving-stones, while the gilt cross heaves on his waistcoat. The words of authority are corrupted by those who speak them. I gibe and mock at this sad religion, at these tremulous, grief-stricken figures advancing, cadaverous and wounded, down a white road shadowed by fig trees where boys sprawl in the dust—naked boys; and goatskins distended with wine hang at the tavern door. I was in Rome travelling with my father at Easter; and the trembling figure of Christ's mother was borne niddle-noddling along the streets; there went by also the stricken figure of Christ in a glass case.

'Now I will lean sideways as if to scratch my thigh. So I shall see Percival. There he sits, upright among the smaller fry. He breathes through his straight nose rather heavily. His blue and oddly inexpressive eyes are fixed with pagan indifference upon the pillar opposite. He would make an admirable churchwarden. He should have a birch and beat little boys for misdemeanours. He is allied with the Latin phrases on the memorial brasses. He sees nothing; he hears nothing. He is remote from us all in a pagan universe. But look—he flicks his hand to the back of his neck. For such gestures one falls hopelessly in love for a lifetime. Dalton, Jones, Edgar and Bateman flick their hands to the back of their necks likewise. But they do not succeed.'

'At last,' said Bernard, 'the growl ceases. The sermon ends. He has minced the dance of the white butterflies at the door to powder. His rough and hairy voice is like an unshaven chin. Now he lurches back to his seat like a drunken sailor. It is an action that all the other masters will try to imitate; but, being flimsy, being floppy, wearing grey trousers, they will only succeed in making themselves ridiculous. I do not despise them. Their antics seem pitiable in my eyes. I note the fact for future reference with many others in my notebook. When I am grown up I shall carry a notebook—a fat book with many pages, methodically lettered. I shall enter my phrases. Under B shall come "Butterfly powder". If, in my novel, I describe the sun on the window-sill, I shall look under B and find butterfly powder. That will be useful. The tree "shades the window with green fingers". That will be useful. But alas! I am so soon distracted—by a hair like twisted candy, by Celia's Prayer Book, ivory covered. Louis can contemplate nature, unwinking, by the hour. Soon I fail, unless talked to. "The lake of my mind, unbroken by oars, heaves placidly and soon sinks into an oily somnolence." That will be useful.'

'Now we move out of this cool temple, into the yellow playing-fields,' said Louis. 'And, as it is a half-holiday (the Duke's birthday)* we will settle among the long grasses, while they play cricket. Could I be "they" I would choose it; I would buckle on my pads and stride across the playing-field at the head of the batsmen. Look now, how everybody follows Percival. He is heavy. He walks clumsily down the field, through the long grass, to where the great elm trees stand. His magnificence is that of some mediaeval commander. A wake of light seems to lie on the grass behind him. Look at us trooping after him, his faithful servants, to be shot like sheep, for he will certainly attempt some forlorn enterprise and die in battle. My heart turns rough; it abrades my side like a file with two edges: one, that I adore his magnificence; the other I despise his slovenly accents—I who am so much his superior—and am jealous.'

'And now,' said Neville, 'let Bernard begin. Let him burble on, telling us stories, while we lie recumbent. Let him describe what we have all seen so that it becomes a sequence. Bernard says there is always a story. I am a story. Louis is a story. There is the story of the boot-boy, the story of the man with one eye, the story of the woman who sells winkles. Let him burble on with his story while I lie back and regard the stiff-legged figures of the padded batsmen through the trembling grasses. It seems as if the whole world were flowing and curving—on the earth the trees, in the sky the clouds. I look up, through the trees, into the sky. The match seems to be played up there. Faintly among the soft, white clouds I hear the cry "Run", I hear the cry "How's that?" The clouds lose tufts of whiteness as the breeze dishevels them. If that blue could stay for ever; if that hole could remain for ever; if this moment could stay for ever——

'But Bernard goes on talking. Up they bubble—images. "Like a camel", . . . "a vulture". The camel is a vulture; the vulture a camel; for Bernard is a dangling wire, loose, but seductive. Yes, for when he talks, when he makes his foolish comparisons, a lightness comes over one. One floats, too, as if one were that bubble; one is freed; I have escaped, one feels. Even the chubby little boys (Dalton, Larpent and Baker) feel the same abandonment. They like this better than the cricket. They catch the phrases as they bubble. They let the feathery grasses tickle their noses. And then we all feel Percival lying heavy among us. His curious guffaw seems to sanction our laughter. But now he has rolled himself over in the long grass. He is, I think, chewing a stalk between his teeth. He feels bored; I too feel bored. Bernard at once perceives that we are bored. I detect a certain effort, an extravagance in his phrase, as if he said "Look!" but Percival says "No". For he is always the first to detect insincerity; and is brutal in the extreme. The sentence tails off feebly. Yes, the appalling moment has come when Bernard's power fails him and there is no longer any sequence and he sags and twiddles a bit of string and falls silent, gaping as if about to burst into tears. Among the tortures and devastations of life is this then— our friends are not able to finish their stories.'

'Now let me try,' said Louis, 'before we rise, before we go to tea, to fix the moment in one effort of supreme endeavour. This shall endure. We are parting; some to tea; some to the nets; I to show my essay to Mr Barker. This will endure. From discord, from hatred (I despise dabblers in imagery—I resent the power of Percival intensely) my

shattered mind is pieced together by some sudden perception. I take the trees, the clouds, to be witnesses of my
complete integration. I, Louis, I, who shall walk the earth
these seventy years, am born entire, out of hatred, out of
discord. Here on this ring of grass we have sat together,
bound by the tremendous power of some inner compulsion. The trees wave, the clouds pass. The time approaches
when these soliloquies shall be shared. We shall not always
give out a sound like a beaten gong as one sensation strikes
and then another. Children, our lives have been gongs
striking; clamour and boasting; cries of despair; blows on
the nape of the neck in gardens.

'Now grass and trees, the travelling air blowing empty
spaces in the blue which they then recover, shaking the
leaves which then replace themselves, and our ring here,
sitting, with our arms binding our knees, hint at some
other order, and better, which makes a reason everlastingly.
This I see for a second, and shall try tonight to fix in
words, to forge in a ring of steel, though Percival destroys
it, as he blunders off, crushing the grasses, with the small
fry trotting subservient after him. Yet it is Percival I need;
for it is Percival who inspires poetry.'

'For how many months,' said Susan, 'for how many years,
have I run up these stairs, in the dismal days of winter, in
the chilly days of spring? Now it is midsummer. We go
upstairs to change into white frocks to play tennis—Jinny
and I with Rhoda following after. I count each step as I
mount, counting each step something done with. So each
night I tear off the old day from the calendar, and screw it
tight into a ball. I do this vindictively, while Betty and

Clara are on their knees. I do not pray. I revenge myself upon the day. I wreak my spite upon its image. You are dead now, I say, school day, hated day. They have made all the days of June—this is the twenty-fifth—shiny and orderly, with gongs, with lessons, with orders to wash, to change, to work, to eat. We listen to missionaries from China. We drive off in brakes along the asphalt pavement, to attend concerts in halls. We are shown galleries and pictures.

'At home the hay waves over the meadows. My father leans upon the stile, smoking. In the house one door bangs and then another, as the summer air puffs along the empty passages. Some old picture perhaps swings on the wall. A petal drops from the rose in the jar. The farm wagons strew the hedges with tufts of hay. All this I see, I always see, as I pass the looking-glass on the landing, with Jinny in front and Rhoda lagging behind. Jinny dances. Jinny always dances in the hall on the ugly, the encaustic tiles; she turns cartwheels in the playground; she picks some flower forbiddenly, and sticks it behind her ear so that Miss Perry's dark eyes smoulder with admiration, for Jinny, not me. Miss Perry loves Jinny; and I could have loved her, but now love no one, except my father, my doves and the squirrel whom I left in the cage at home for the boy to look after.'

'I hate the small looking-glass on the stairs,' said Jinny. 'It shows our heads only; it cuts off our heads. And my lips are too wide, and my eyes are too close together; I show my gums too much when I laugh. Susan's head, with its fell look, with its grass-green eyes which poets will love, Bernard said, because they fall upon close white stitching, put mine out; even Rhoda's face, mooning, vacant, is completed, like those white petals she used to swim in her bowl. So I skip up the stairs past them, to the next landing, where the long glass hangs and I see myself entire. I see my body and head in one now; for even in this serge frock they are one, my body and my head. Look, when I move my head I ripple all down my narrow body; even my thin legs ripple like a stalk in the wind. I flicker between the set face of Susan and Rhoda's vagueness; I leap like one of those flames that run between the cracks of the earth; I move, I dance; I never cease to move and to dance. I move like the leaf that moved in the hedge as a child and frightened me. I dance over these streaked, these impersonal, distempered walls with their yellow skirting as firelight dances over teapots. I catch fire even from women's cold eyes. When I read, a purple rim runs round the black edge of the textbook. Yet I cannot follow any word through its changes. I cannot follow any thought from present to past. I do not stand lost, like Susan, with tears in my eyes remembering home; or lie, like Rhoda, crumpled among the ferns, staining my pink cotton green, while I dream of plants that flower under the sea, and rocks through which the fish swim slowly. I do not dream.

'Now let us be quick. Now let me be the first to pull off these coarse clothes. Here are my clean white stockings. Here are my new shoes. I bind my hair with a white ribbon, so that when I leap across the court the ribbon will stream out in a flash, yet curl round my neck, perfectly in its place. Not a hair shall be untidy.'

'That is my face,' said Rhoda, 'in the looking-glass behind Susan's shoulder—that face is my face. But I will duck behind her to hide it, for I am not here. I have no face. Other people have faces; Susan and Jinny have faces; they are here. Their world is the real world. The things they lift are heavy. They say Yes, they say No; whereas I shift and change and am seen through in a second. If they meet a housemaid she looks at them without laughing. But she laughs at me. They know what to say if spoken to. They laugh really; they get angry really; while I have to look first and do what other people do when they have done it.

'See now with what extraordinary certainty Jinny pulls on her stockings, simply to play tennis. That I admire. But I like Susan's way better, for she is more resolute, and less ambitious of distinction than Jinny. Both despise me for copying what they do; but Susan sometimes teaches me, for instance, how to tie a bow, while Jinny has her own knowledge but keeps it to herself. They have friends to sit by. They have things to say privately in corners. But I attach myself only to names and faces; and hoard them like amulets against disaster. I choose out across the hall some unknown face and can hardly drink my tea when she whose name I do not know sits opposite. I choke. I am rocked from side to side by the violence of my emotion. I imagine these nameless, these immaculate people, watching me from behind bushes. I leap high to excite their admiration. At night, in bed, I excite their complete wonder. I often die pierced with arrows to win their tears. If they should say, or I should see from a label on their boxes, that they were in Scarborough last holidays, the whole town runs gold, the whole pavement is illuminated. Therefore I hate looking-glasses which show me my real face. Alone, I often fall down into nothingness. I must push my foot stealthily lest I should fall off the edge of the world into nothingness. I have to bang my head against some hard door to call myself back to the body.'

'We are late,' said Susan. 'We must wait our turn to play. We will pitch here in the long grass and pretend to watch

Jinny and Clara, Betty and Mavis. But we will not watch them. I hate watching other people play games. I will make images of all the things I hate most and bury them in the ground. This shiny pebble is Madame Carlo, and I will bury her deep because of her fawning and ingratiating manners, because of the sixpence she gave me for keeping my knuckles flat when I played my scales. I buried her sixpence. I would bury the whole school: the gymnasium; the classroom; the dining-room that always smells of meat; and the chapel. I would bury the red-brown tiles and the oily portraits of old men—benefactors, founders of schools. There are some trees I like; the cherry tree with lumps of clear gum on the bark; and one view from the attic towards some far hills. Save for these, I would bury it all as I bury these ugly stones that are always scattered about this briny coast, with its piers and its trippers. At home, the waves are mile long. On winter nights we hear them booming. Last Christmas a man was drowned sitting alone in his cart.'

'When Miss Lambert passes,' said Rhoda, 'talking to the clergyman, the others laugh and imitate her hunch behind her back; yet everything changes and becomes luminous. Jinny leaps higher too when Miss Lambert passes. Suppose she saw that daisy, it would change. Wherever she goes, things are changed under her eyes; and yet when she has gone is not the thing the same again? Miss Lambert is taking the clergyman through the wicket-gate to her private garden; and when she comes to the pond, she sees a frog on a leaf, and that will change. All is solemn, all is pale where she stands, like a statue in a grove. She lets her tasselled silken cloak slip down, and only her purple ring still glows, her vinous, her amethystine ring. There is this mystery about people when they leave us. When they leave

us I can companion them to the pond and make them
stately. When Miss Lambert passes, she makes the daisy
change; and everything runs like streaks of fire when she
carves the beef. Month by month things are losing their
hardness; even my body now lets the light through; my
spine is soft like wax near the flame of the candle. I dream;
I dream.'

'I have won the game,' said Jinny. 'Now it is your turn. I
must throw myself on the ground and pant. I am out of
breath with running, with triumph. Everything in my body
seems thinned out with running and triumph. My blood
must be bright red, whipped up, slapping against my ribs.
My soles tingle, as if wire rings opened and shut in my feet.
I see every blade of grass very clear. But the pulse drums so
in my forehead, behind my eyes, that everything dances—
the net, the grass; your faces leap like butterflies; the trees
seem to jump up and down. There is nothing staid, nothing
settled, in this universe. All is rippling, all is dancing; all is
quickness and triumph. Only, when I have lain alone on the
hard ground, watching you play your game, I begin to feel
the wish to be singled out; to be summoned, to be called
away by one person who comes to find me, who is attracted
towards me, who cannot keep himself from me, but comes
to where I sit on my gilt chair, with my frock billowing
round me like a flower. And withdrawing into an alcove,
sitting alone on a balcony we talk together.

'Now the tide sinks. Now the trees come to earth; the
brisk waves that slap my ribs rock more gently, and my
heart rides at anchor, like a sailing-boat whose sails slide
slowly down on to the white deck. The game is over. We
must go to tea now.'

'The boasting boys,' said Louis, 'have gone now in a vast team to play cricket. They have driven off in their great brake,* singing in chorus. All their heads turn simultaneously at the corner by the laurel bushes. Now they are boasting. Larpent's brother played football for Oxford; Smith's father made a century at Lords. Archie and Hugh; Parker and Dalton; Larpent and Smith; then again Archie and Hugh; Parker and Dalton; Larpent and Smith—the names repeat themselves; the names are the same always. They are the volunteers; they are the cricketers; they are the officers of the Natural History Society. They are always forming into fours and marching in troops with badges on their caps; they salute simultaneously passing the figure of their general. How majestic is their order, how beautiful is their obedience! If I could follow, if I could be with them, I would sacrifice all I know. But they also leave butterflies trembling with their wings pinched off; they throw dirty pocket-handkerchiefs clotted with blood screwed up into corners. They make little boys sob in dark passages. They have big red ears that stand out under their caps. Yet that is what we wish to be, Neville and I. I watch them go with envy. Peeping from behind a curtain, I note the simultaneity of their movements with delight. If my legs were reinforced by theirs, how they would run! If I had been with them and won matches and rowed in great races, and galloped all day, how I should thunder out songs at midnight! In what a torrent the words would rush from my throat!'

'Percival has gone now,' said Neville. 'He is thinking of nothing but the match. He never waved his hand as the brake turned the corner by the laurel bush. He despises me for being too weak to play (yet he is always kind to my weakness). He despises me for not caring if they win or lose except that he cares. He takes my devotion; he accepts my tremulous, no doubt abject offering, mixed with contempt as it is for his mind. For he cannot read. Yet when I read Shakespeare or Catullus, lying in the long grass, he understands more than Louis. Not the words—but what are words? Do I not know already how to rhyme, how to imitate Pope, Dryden, even Shakespeare?* But I cannot stand all day in the sun with my eyes on the ball; I cannot feel the flight of the ball through my body and think only of the ball. I shall be a clinger to the outsides of words all my life. Yet I could not live with him and suffer his stupidity. He will coarsen and snore. He will marry and there will be scenes of tenderness at breakfast. But now he is young. Not a thread, not a sheet of paper lies between him and the sun, between him and the rain, between him and the moon as he lies naked, tumbled, hot, on his bed. Now as they drive along the high road in their brake his face is mottled red and yellow. He will throw off his coat and stand with his legs apart, with his hands ready, watching the wicket. And he will pray, "Lord let us win"; he will think of one thing only, that they should win.

'How could I go with them in a brake to play cricket? Only Bernard could go with them, but Bernard is too late to go with them. He is always too late. He is prevented by his incorrigible moodiness from going with them. He stops, when he washes his hands, to say, "There is a fly in that web. Shall I rescue that fly; shall I let the spider eat it?" He is shaded with innumerable perplexities, or he would go with them to play cricket, and would lie in the grass, watching the sky, and would start when the ball was hit. But they would forgive him; for he would tell them a story.'

'They have bowled off,' said Bernard, 'and I am too late

to go with them. The horrid little boys, who are also so beautiful, whom you and Louis, Neville, envy so deeply, have bowled off with their heads all turned the same way. But I am unaware of these profound distinctions. My fingers slip over the keyboard without knowing which is black and which white. Archie makes easily a hundred; I by a fluke make sometimes fifteen. But what is the difference between us? Wait though, Neville; let me talk. The bubbles are rising like the silver bubbles from the floor of a saucepan; image on top of image. I cannot sit down to my book, like Louis, with ferocious tenacity. I must open the little trap-door and let out these linked phrases in which I run together whatever happens, so that instead of incoherence there is perceived a wandering thread, lightly joining one thing to another. I will tell you the story of the doctor.

'When Dr Crane lurches through the swing-doors after prayers he is convinced, it seems, of his immense superiority; and indeed, Neville, we cannot deny that his departure leaves us not only with a sense of relief, but also with a sense of something removed, like a tooth. Now let us follow him as he heaves through the swing-door to his own apartments. Let us imagine him in his private room over the stables undressing. He unfastens his sock suspenders (let us be trivial, let us be intimate). Then with a characteristic gesture (it is difficult to avoid these ready-made phrases, and they are, in his case, somehow appropriate) he takes the silver, he takes the coppers from his trouser pockets and places them there, and there, on his dressing-table. With both arms stretched on the arms of his chair he reflects (this is his private moment; it is here we must try to catch him): shall he cross the pink bridge into his bedroom or shall he not cross it? The two rooms are united by a bridge of rosy light from the lamp at the bedside where Mrs Crane lies with her hair on the pillow reading a French memoir. As she reads, she sweeps her hand with an abandoned and despairing gesture over her forehead, and sighs, "Is this all?" comparing herself with some French duchess. Now, says the doctor, in two years I shall retire. I shall clip yew hedges in a west country garden. An admiral I might have been; or a judge; not a schoolmaster. What forces, he asks, staring at the gas-fire with his shoulders hunched up more hugely than we know them (he is in his shirt-sleeves remember), have brought me to this? What vast forces? he thinks, getting into the stride of his majestic phrases as he looks over his shoulder at the window. It is a stormy night; the branches of the chestnut trees are ploughing up and down. Stars flash between them. What vast forces of good and evil have brought me here? he asks, and sees with sorrow that his chair has worn a little hole in the pile of the purple carpet. So there he sits, swinging his braces. But stories that follow people into their private rooms are difficult. I cannot go on with this story. I twiddle a piece of string; I turn over four or five coins in my trouser pocket.'

'Bernard's stories amuse me,' said Neville, 'at the start. But when they tail off absurdly and he gapes, twiddling a bit of string, I feel my own solitude. He sees everyone with blurred edges. Hence I cannot talk to him of Percival. I cannot expose my absurd and violent passion to his sympathetic understanding. It too would make a "story". I need someone whose mind falls like a chopper on a block; to whom the pitch of absurdity is sublime, and a shoestring adorable. To whom can I expose the urgency of my own passion? Louis is too cold, too universal. There is nobody—here among these grey arches, and moaning pigeons, and cheerful games and tradition and emulation, all so skilfully organized to prevent feeling alone. Yet I am struck still as I walk by sudden premonitions of what is to come. Yesterday, passing the open door leading into the private garden, I saw Fenwick with his mallet raised. The steam from the tea-urn rose in the middle of the lawn. There were banks of blue flowers. Then suddenly descended upon me the obscure, the mystic sense of adoration, of completeness that triumphed over chaos. Nobody saw my poised and intent figure as I stood at the open door. Nobody guessed the need I had to offer my being to one god; and perish, and disappear. His mallet descended; the vision broke.

'Should I seek out some tree? Should I desert these form rooms and libraries, and the broad yellow page in which I read Catullus, for woods and fields? Should I walk under beech trees, or saunter along the river bank, where the trees meet united like lovers in the water? But nature is too vegetable, too vapid. She has only sublimities and vastitudes and water and leaves. I begin to wish for firelight, privacy, and the limbs of one person.'

'I begin to wish,' said Louis, 'for night to come. As I stand here with my hand on the grained oak panel of Mr Wickham's door I think myself the friend of Richelieu,* or the Duke of St Simon holding out a snuff-box to the King himself. It is my privilege. My witticisms "run like wildfire through the court". Duchesses tear emeralds from their earrings out of admiration—but these rockets rise best in darkness, in my cubicle at night. I am now a boy only with a colonial accent holding my knuckles against Mr Wickham's grained oak door. The day has been full of ignominies and triumphs concealed from fear of laughter. I am the best scholar in the school. But when darkness comes I put off this unenviable body—my large nose, my thin lips, my colonial accent—and inhabit space. I am then Virgil's companion, and Plato's.* I am then the last scion of one of the great houses of France. But I am also one who will force himself to desert these windy and moonlit territories, these midnight wanderings, and confront grained oak doors. I will achieve in my life—Heaven grant that it be not long—some gigantic amalgamation between the two discrepancies so hideously apparent to me. Out of my suffering I will do it. I will knock. I will enter.'

'I have torn off the whole of May and June,' said Susan, 'and twenty days of July. I have torn them off and screwed them up so that they no longer exist, save as a weight in my side. They have been crippled days, like moths with shrivelled wings unable to fly. There are only eight days left. In eight days' time I shall get out of the train and stand on the platform at six twenty-five. Then my freedom will unfurl, and all these restrictions that wrinkle and shrivel—hours and order and discipline, and being here and there exactly at the right moment—will crack asunder. Out the day will spring, as I open the carriage-door and see my father in his old hat and gaiters. I shall tremble. I shall burst into tears. Then next morning I shall get up at dawn. I shall let myself out by the kitchen door. I shall walk on the moor. The great horses of the phantom riders will thunder behind me and stop suddenly. I shall see the swallow skim the grass. I shall throw myself on a bank by the river and watch the fish slip in and out among the reeds. The palms of my hands will be printed with pine-needles. I shall there unfold and take out whatever it is I have made here; something hard. For something has grown in me here, through the winters and summers, on staircases, in bedrooms. I do not want, as Jinny wants, to be admired. I do not want people, when I come in, to look up with admiration. I want to give, to be given, and solitude in which to unfold my possessions.

'Then I shall come back through the trembling lanes under the arches of the nut leaves. I shall pass an old woman wheeling a perambulator full of sticks; and the shepherd. But we shall not speak. I shall come back through the kitchen garden, and see the curved leaves of the cabbages pebbled with dew, and the house in the garden, blind with curtained windows. I shall go upstairs to my room, and turn over my own things, locked carefully in the wardrobe: my shells; my eggs; my curious grasses. I shall feed my doves and my squirrel. I shall go to the kennel and comb my spaniel. So gradually I shall turn over the hard thing that has grown here in my side. But here bells ring; feet shuffle perpetually.'

'I hate darkness and sleep and night,' said Jinny, 'and lie longing for the day to come. I long that the week should be all one day without divisions. When I wake early—and the birds wake me—I lie and watch the brass handles on the cupboard grow clear; then the basin; then the towel-horse. As each thing in the bedroom grows clear, my heart beats quicker. I feel my body harden, and become pink, yellow, brown. My hands pass over my legs and body. I feel its slopes, its thinness. I love to hear the gong roar through the house and the stir begin—here a thud, there a patter. Doors slam; water rushes. Here is another day, here is another day, I cry, as my feet touch the floor. It may be a bruised day, an imperfect day. I am often scolded. I am often in disgrace for idleness, for laughing; but even as

Miss Matthews grumbles at my feather-headed carelessness, I catch sight of something moving—a speck of sun
perhaps on a picture, or the donkey drawing the mowing-
machine across the lawn; or a sail that passes between the
laurel leaves, so that I am never cast down. I cannot be
prevented from pirouetting behind Miss Matthews into
prayers.

'Now, too, the time is coming when we shall leave
school and wear long skirts. I shall wear necklaces and a
white dress without sleeves at night. There will be parties
in brilliant rooms; and one man will single me out and will
tell me what he has told no other person. He will like me
better than Susan or Rhoda. He will find in me some
quality, some peculiar thing. But I shall not let myself be
attached to one person only. I do not want to be fixed, to
be pinioned. I tremble, I quiver, like the leaf in the hedge,
as I sit dangling my feet, on the edge of the bed, with a
new day to break open. I have fifty years, I have sixty
years to spend. I have not yet broken into my hoard. This
is the beginning.'

'There are hours and hours,' said Rhoda, 'before I can
put out the light and lie suspended on my bed above the
world, before I can let the day drop down, before I can let
my tree grow, quivering in green pavilions above my head.
Here I cannot let it grow. Somebody knocks through it.
They ask questions, they interrupt, they throw it down.

'Now I will go to the bathroom and take off my shoes
and wash; but as I wash, as I bend my head down over the
basin, I will let the Russian Empress's veil flow about my
shoulders. The diamonds of the Imperial crown blaze on
my forehead. I hear the roar of the hostile mob as I step
out on to the balcony. Now I dry my hands, vigorously,
so that Miss, whose name I forget, cannot suspect that I

am waving my fist at an infuriated mob. "I am your Empress, people." My attitude is one of defiance. I am fearless. I conquer.

'But this is a thin dream. This is a papery tree. Miss Lambert blows it down. Even the sight of her vanishing down the corridor blows it to atoms. It is not solid; it gives me no satisfaction—this Empress dream. It leaves me, now that it has fallen, here in the passage rather shivering. Things seem paler. I will go now into the library and take out some book, and read and look; and read again and look. Here is a poem about a hedge. I will wander down it and pick flowers, green cowbind and the moonlight-coloured May, wild roses and ivy serpentine.* I will clasp them in my hands and lay them on the desk's shiny surface. I will sit by the river's trembling edge and look at the water-lilies, broad and bright, which lit the oak that overhung the hedge with moonlight beams of their own watery light. I will pick flowers; I will bind flowers in one garland and clasp them and present them—Oh! to whom? There is some check in the flow of my being; a deep stream presses on some obstacle; it jerks; it tugs; some knot in the centre resists. Oh, this is pain, this is anguish! I faint, I fail.* Now my body thaws; I am unsealed, I am incandescent. Now the stream pours in a deep tide fertilizing, opening the shut, forcing the tight-folded, flooding free. To whom shall I give all that now flows through me, from my warm, my porous body? I will gather my flowers and present them—Oh! to whom?

'Sailors loiter on the parade, and amorous couples; the omnibuses rattle along the sea front to the town. I will give; I will enrich; I will return to the world this beauty. I will bind my flowers in one garland and advancing with my hand outstretched will present them—Oh! to whom?'

dancer; but I hear always the sullen thud of the waves; and the chained beast stamps on the beach. It stamps and stamps.'

'Now we have received,' said Louis, 'for this is the last day of the last term—Neville's and Bernard's and my last day—whatever our masters have had to give us. The introduction has been made; the world presented. They stay, we depart. The great Doctor, whom of all men I most revere, swaying a little from side to side among the tables, the bound volumes, has dealt out Horace, Tennyson, the complete works of Keats and Matthew Arnold,* suitably inscribed. I respect the hand which gave them. He speaks with complete conviction. To him his words are true, though not to us. Speaking in the gruff voice of deep emotion, fiercely, tenderly, he has told us that we are about to go. He has bid us "quit ourselves like men".* (On his lips quotations from the Bible, from *The Times*, seem equally magnificent.) Some will do this; others that. Some will not meet again. Neville, Bernard and I shall not meet here again. Life will divide us. But we have formed certain ties. Our boyish, our irresponsible years are over. But we have forged certain links. Above all, we have inherited traditions. These stone flags have been worn for six hundred years. On these walls are inscribed the names of men of war, of statesmen, of some unhappy poets (mine shall be among them). Blessings be on all traditions, on all safeguards and circumscriptions! I am most grateful to you men in black gowns, and you, dead, for your leading, for your guardianship; yet after all, the problem remains. The differences are not yet solved. Flowers toss their heads outside the window. I see wild birds, and impulses wilder than the wildest birds strike from my wild heart. My eyes are wild; my lips tight pressed. The bird flies; the flower dances; but I hear always the sullen thud of the waves; and the chained beast stamps on the beach. It stamps and stamps.'

'This is the final ceremony,' said Bernard. 'This is the last of all our ceremonies. We are overcome by strange feelings. The guard holding his flag is about to blow his whistle; the train breathing steam in another moment is about to start. One wants to say something, to feel something, absolutely appropriate to the occasion. One's mind is primed; one's lips are pursed. And then a bee drifts in and hums round the flowers in the bouquet which Lady Hampton, the wife of the General, keeps smelling to show her appreciation of the compliment. If the bee were to sting her nose? We are all deeply moved; yet irreverent; yet penitent; yet anxious to get it over; yet reluctant to part. The bee distracts us; its casual flight seems to deride our intensity. Humming vaguely, skimming widely, it is settled now on the carnation. Many of us will not meet again. We shall not enjoy certain pleasures again, when we are free to go to bed, or to sit up, when I need no longer smuggle in bits of candle-ends and immoral literature. The bee now hums round the head of the great Doctor. Larpent, John, Archie, Percival, Baker and Smith—I have liked them enormously. I have known one mad boy only. I have hated one mean boy only. I enjoy in retrospect my terribly awkward breakfasts at the Headmaster's table with toast and marmalade. He alone does not notice the bee. If it were to settle on his nose he would flick it off with one magnificent gesture. Now he has made his joke; now his voice has almost broken but not quite. Now we are dismissed—Louis, Neville and I for ever. We take our highly polished books, scholastically inscribed in a little crabbed hand. We rise, we disperse; the pressure is removed. The bee has become an insignificant, a disregarded insect, flown through the open window into obscurity. Tomorrow we go.'

'We are about to part,' said Neville. 'Here are the boxes; here are the cabs. There is Percival in his billycock hat. He will forget me. He will leave my letters lying about among guns and dogs unanswered. I shall send him poems and he will perhaps reply with a picture post card. But it is for that that I love him. I shall propose meeting—under a clock, by some Cross; and shall wait, and he will not come. It is for that that I love him. Oblivious, almost entirely ignorant, he will pass from my life. And I shall pass, incredible as it seems, into other lives; this is only an escapade perhaps, a prelude only. I feel already, though I cannot endure the Doctor's pompous mummery and faked emotions, that things we have only dimly perceived draw near. I shall be free to enter the garden where Fenwick raises his mallet. Those who have despised me shall acknowledge my sovereignty. But by some inscrutable law of my being sovereignty and the possession of power will not be enough; I shall always push through curtains to privacy, and want some whispered words alone. Therefore I go, dubious, but elate; apprehensive of intolerable pain; yet I think bound in my adventuring to conquer after huge suffering, bound, surely, to discover my desire in the end. There, for the last time, I see the statue of our pious founder with the doves about his head. They will wheel for ever about his head, whitening it, while the organ moans in the chapel. So I take my seat; and, when I have found my place in the corner of our reserved compartment, I will shade my eyes with a book to hide one tear; I will shade my eyes to observe; to peep at one face. It is the first day of the summer holidays.'

'It is the first day of the summer holidays,' said Susan. 'But the day is still rolled up. I will not examine it until I step out on to the platform in the evening. I will not let myself even smell it until I smell the cold green air off the fields. But already these are not school fields; these are not school hedges; the men in these fields are doing real things; they fill carts with real hay; and those are real cows, not school cows. But the carbolic smell of corridors and the chalky smell of schoolrooms is still in my nostrils. The glazed, shiny look of matchboard is still in my eyes. I must wait for fields and hedges, and woods and fields, and steep railway cuttings, sprinkled with gorse bushes, and trucks in sidings, and tunnels and suburban gardens with women hanging out washing, and then fields again and children swinging on gates, to cover it over, to bury it deep, this school that I have hated.

'I will not send my children to school nor spend a night all my life in London. Here in this vast station everything echoes and booms hollowly. The light is like the yellow light under an awning. Jinny lives here. Jinny takes her dog for walks on these pavements. People here shoot through the streets silently. They look at nothing but shop-windows. Their heads bob up and down all at about the same height. The streets are laced together with telegraph wires. The houses are all glass, all festoons and glitter; now all front doors and lace curtains, all pillars and white steps. But now I pass on, out of London again; the fields begin again; and the houses, and women hanging washing, and trees and fields. London is now veiled, now vanished, now crumbled, now fallen. The carbolic and the pitch-pine begin to lose their savour. I smell corn and turnips. I undo a paper packet tied with a piece of white cotton. The egg-shells slide into the cleft between my knees. Now we stop at station after station, rolling out milk cans. Now women kiss each other and help with baskets. Now I will let myself lean out of the window. The air rushes down my nose and throat—the cold air, the salt air with the smell of turnip fields in it. And there is my father, with his back turned, talking to a farmer. I tremble. I cry. There is my father in gaiters. There is my father.'

'I sit snug in my own corner going north,' said Jinny, 'in this roaring express which is yet so smooth that it flattens hedges, lengthens hills. We flash past signal-boxes; we make the earth rock slightly from side to side. The distance closes for ever in a point; and we for ever open the distance wide again. The telegraph poles bob up incessantly; one is felled, another rises. Now we roar and swing into a tunnel. The gentleman pulls up the window. I see reflections on the shining glass which lines the tunnel. I see him lower his paper. He smiles at my reflection in the tunnel. My body instantly of its own accord puts forth a frill under his gaze. My body lives a life of its own. Now the black window glass is green again. We are out of the tunnel. He reads his paper. But we have exchanged the approval of our bodies. There is then a great society of bodies, and mine is introduced; mine has come into the room where the gilt chairs are. Look—all the windows of the villas and their white-tented curtains dance; and the men sitting in the hedges in the cornfields with knotted blue handkerchiefs are aware too, as I am aware, of heat and rapture. One waves as we pass him. There are bowers and arbours in these villa gardens and young men in shirt-sleeves on ladders trimming roses. A man on a horse canters over the field. His horse plunges as we pass. And the rider turns to look at us. We roar again through blackness. And I lie back; I give myself up to rapture; I think that at the end of the tunnel I enter a lamp-lit room with chairs, into one of which I sink, much admired, my dress billowing round me. But behold, looking up, I meet the eyes of a sour woman, who suspects me of rapture. My body shuts in her face, impertinently, like a parasol. I open my body, I shut my body at my will. Life is beginning. I now break into my hoard of life.'

'It is the first day of the summer holidays,' said Rhoda. 'And now, as the train passes by these red rocks, by this blue sea, the term, done with, forms itself into one shape behind me. I see its colour. June was white. I see the fields white with daisies, and white with dresses; and tennis courts marked with white. Then there was wind and violent thunder. There was a star riding through clouds one night, and I said to the star, "Consume me". That was at midsummer, after the garden party and my humiliation at the garden party. Wind and storm coloured July. Also, in the middle, cadaverous, awful, lay the grey puddle in the courtyard, when, holding an envelope in my hand, I carried a message. I came to the puddle.* I could not cross it. Identity failed me. We are nothing, I said, and fell. I was blown like a feather, I was wafted down tunnels. Then very gingerly, I pushed my foot across. I laid my hand against a brick wall. I returned very painfully, drawing myself back into my body over the grey, cadaverous space of the puddle. This is life then to which I am committed.

'So I detach the summer term. With intermittent shocks, sudden as the springs of a tiger, life emerges heaving its dark crest from the sea. It is to this we are attached; it is to this we are bound, as bodies to wild horses. And yet we

have invented devices for filling up the crevices and dis-
guising these fissures. Here is the ticket collector. Here are
two men; three women; there is a cat in a basket; myself
with my elbow on the window-sill—this is here and now.
We draw on, we make off, through whispering fields of
golden corn. Women in the fields are surprised to be left
behind there, hoeing. The train now stamps heavily,
breathes stertorously, as it climbs up and up. At last we are
on the top of the moor. Only a few wild sheep live here; a
few shaggy ponies; yet we are provided with every comfort; with tables to hold our newspapers, with rings to
hold our tumblers. We come carrying these appliances with
us over the top of the moor. Now we are on the summit.
Silence will close behind us. If I look back over that bald
head, I can see silence already closing and the shadows of
clouds chasing each other over the empty moor; silence
closes over our transient passage. This I say is the present
moment; this is the first day of the summer holidays. This
is part of the emerging monster to whom we are attached.'

'Now we are off,' said Louis. 'Now I hang suspended
without attachments. We are nowhere. We are passing
through England in a train. England slips by the window,
always changing from hill to wood, from rivers and
willows to towns again. And I have no firm ground to
which I go. Bernard and Neville, Percival, Archie, Larpent
and Baker go to Oxford or Cambridge, to Edinburgh,
Rome, Paris, Berlin, or to some American University. I go
vaguely, to make money vaguely. Therefore a poignant
shadow, a keen accent, falls on these golden bristles, on
these poppy-red fields, this flowing corn that never over-

flows its boundaries; but runs rippling to the edge. This is the first day of a new life, another spoke of the rising wheel. But my body passes vagrant as a bird's shadow. I should be transient as the shadow on the meadow, soon fading, soon darkening and dying there where it meets the wood, were it not that I coerce my brain to form in my forehead; I force myself to state, if only in one line of unwritten poetry, this moment; to mark this inch in the long, long history that began in Egypt, in the time of the Pharaohs, when women carried red pitchers to the Nile. I seem already to have lived many thousand years. But if I now shut my eyes, if I fail to realize the meeting-place of past and present, that I sit in a third-class railway carriage full of boys going home for the holidays, human history is defrauded of a moment's vision. Its eye, that would see through me, shuts—if I sleep now, through slovenliness, or cowardice, burying myself in the past, in the dark; or acquiesce, as Bernard acquiesces, telling stories; or boast, as Percival, Archie, John, Walter, Lathom, Larpent, Roper, Smith boast—the names are the same always, the names of the boasting boys. They are all boasting, all talking, except Neville, who slips a look occasionally over the edge of a French novel, and so will always slip into cushioned firelit rooms, with many books and one friend, while I tilt on an office chair behind a counter. Then I shall grow bitter and mock at them. I shall envy them their continuance down the safe traditional ways under the shade of old yew trees while I consort with cockneys and clerks, and tap the pavements of the city.

'But now disembodied, passing over fields without lodgement—(there is a river; a man fishes; there is a spire, there is the village street with its bow-windowed inn)—all is dreamlike and dim to me. These hard thoughts, this envy, this bitterness, make no lodgement in me. I am the ghost of Louis, an ephemeral passer-by, in whose mind dreams have power, and garden sounds when in the early morning petals float on fathomless depths and the birds sing. I dash and sprinkle myself with the bright waters of childhood. Its thin veil quivers. But the chained beast stamps and stamps on the shore.'

'Louis and Neville,' said Bernard, 'both sit silent. Both are absorbed. Both feel the presence of other people as a separating wall. But if I find myself in company with other people, words at once make smoke rings—see how phrases at once begin to wreathe off my lips. It seems that a match is set to a fire; something burns. An elderly and apparently prosperous man, a traveller, now gets in. And I at once wish to approach him; I instinctively dislike the sense of his presence, cold, unassimilated, among us. I do not believe in separation. We are not single. Also I wish to add to my collection of valuable observations upon the true nature of human life. My book will certainly run to many volumes, embracing every known variety of man and woman. I fill my mind with whatever happens to be the contents of a room or a railway carriage as one fills a fountain-pen in an inkpot. I have a steady unquenchable thirst. Now I feel by imperceptible signs, which I cannot yet interpret but will later, that his defiance is about to thaw. His solitude shows signs of cracking. He has passed a remark about a country house. A smoke ring issues from my lips (about crops) and circles him, bringing him into contact. The human voice has a disarming quality—(we are not single, we are one). As we exchange these few but amiable remarks about country houses, I furbish him up and make him concrete. He is indulgent as a husband but not faithful; a small builder who employs a few men. In local society he is important; is already a councillor, and perhaps in time will be mayor. He wears a large ornament, like a double tooth torn up by the roots, made of coral, hanging at his watch-chain. Walter J. Trumble is the sort of name that would fit him. He has been in America, on a business trip with his wife, and a double room in a smallish hotel cost him a whole month's wages. His front tooth is stopped with gold.

'The fact is that I have little aptitude for reflection. I require the concrete in everything. It is so only that I lay hands upon the world. A good phrase, however, seems to me to have an independent existence. Yet I think it is likely that the best are made in solitude. They require some final refrigeration which I cannot give them, dabbling always in warm soluble words. My method, nevertheless, has certain advantages over theirs. Neville is repelled by the grossness of Trumble. Louis, glancing, tripping with the high step of a disdainful crane, picks up words as if in sugar-tongs. It is true that his eyes—wild, laughing, yet desperate—express something that we have not gauged. There is about both Neville and Louis a precision, an exactitude, that I admire and shall never possess. Now I begin to be aware that action is demanded. We approach a junction; at a junction I have to change. I have to board a train for Edinburgh. I cannot precisely lay fingers on this fact—it lodges loosely among my thoughts like a button, like a small coin. Here is the jolly old boy who collects tickets. I had one—I had one certainly. But it does not matter. Either I shall find it, or I shall not find it. I examine my note-case. I look in all my pockets. These are the things that for ever interrupt the process upon which I am eternally engaged of finding some perfect phrase that fits this very moment exactly.'

'Bernard has gone,' said Neville, 'without a ticket. He

has escaped us, making a phrase, waving his hand. He talked as easily to the horse-breeder or to the plumber as to us. The plumber accepted him with devotion. "If he had a son like that," he was thinking, "he would manage to send him to Oxford." But what did Bernard feel for the plumber? Did he not only wish to continue the sequence of the story which he never stops telling himself? He began it when he rolled his bread into pellets as a child. One pellet was a man, one was a woman. We are all pellets. We are all phrases in Bernard's story, things he writes down in his notebook under A or under B. He tells our story with extraordinary understanding, except of what we most feel. For he does not need us. He is never at our mercy. There he is, waving his arms on the platform. The train has gone without him. He has missed his connection. He has lost his ticket. But that does not matter. He will talk to the barmaid about the nature of human destiny. We are off; he has forgotten us already; we pass out of his view; we go on, filled with lingering sensations, half bitter, half sweet, for he is somehow to be pitied, breasting the world with half-finished phrases, having lost his ticket: he is also to be loved.

'Now I pretend again to read. I raise my book, till it almost covers my eyes. But I cannot read in the presence of horse-dealers and plumbers. I have no power of ingratiating myself. I do not admire that man; he does not admire me. Let me at least be honest. Let me denounce this piffling, trifling, self-satisfied world; these horse-hair seats; these coloured photographs of piers and parades. I could shriek aloud at the smug self-satisfaction, at the mediocrity of this world, which breeds horse-dealers with coral ornaments hanging from their watch-chains. There is that in me which will consume them entirely. My laughter shall make them twist in their seats; shall drive them howling before me. No; they are immortal. They triumph. They will make it impossible for me always to read Catullus in a third-class railway carriage. They will drive me in October to take refuge in one of the universities, where I shall become a don;* and go with schoolmasters to Greece; and lecture on the ruins of the Parthenon. It would be better to breed horses and live in one of those red villas than to run in and out of the skulls of Sophocles and Euripides like a maggot, with a high-minded wife, one of those University women. That, however, will be my fate. I shall suffer. I am already at eighteen capable of such contempt that horse-breeders hate me. That is my triumph; I do not compromise. I am not timid; I have no accent. I do not finick about fearing what people think of "my father a banker at Brisbane" like Louis.

'Now we draw near the centre of the civilized world. There are the familiar gasometers. There are the public gardens intersected by asphalt paths. There are the lovers lying shamelessly mouth to mouth on the burnt grass. Percival is now almost in Scotland; his train draws through the red moors; he sees the long line of the Border hills and the Roman wall. He reads a detective novel, yet understands everything.

'The train slows and lengthens, as we approach London, the centre, and my heart draws out too, in fear, in exultation. I am about to meet—what? What extraordinary adventure waits me, among these mail vans, these porters, these swarms of people calling taxis? I feel insignificant, lost, but exultant. With a soft shock we stop. I will let the others get out before me. I will sit still one moment before I emerge into that chaos, that tumult. I will not anticipate what is to come. The huge uproar is in my ears. It sounds

and resounds, under this glass roof like the surge of a sea.
We are cast down on the platform with our handbags. We
are whirled asunder. My sense of self almost perishes; my
contempt. I become drawn in, tossed down, thrown sky-
high. I step out on to the platform, grasping tightly all that
I possess—one bag.'

The sun rose. Bars of yellow and green fell on the shore, gilding the ribs of the eaten-out boat and making the sea-holly and its mailed leaves gleam blue as steel. Light almost pierced the thin swift waves as they raced fan-shaped over the beach. The girl who had shaken her head and made all the jewels, the topaz, the aquamarine, the water-coloured jewels with sparks of fire in them, dance, now bared her brows and with wide-opened eyes drove a straight pathway over the waves. Their quivering mackerel sparkling was darkened; they massed themselves; their green hollows deepened and darkened and might be traversed by shoals of wandering fish. As they splashed and drew back they left a black rim of twigs and cork on the shore and straws and sticks of wood, as if some light shallop had foundered and burst its sides and the sailor had swum to land and bounded up the cliff and left his frail cargo to be washed ashore.

In the garden the birds that had sung erratically and spasmodically in the dawn on that tree, on that bush, now sang together in chorus, shrill and sharp; now together, as if conscious of companionship, now alone as if to the pale blue sky. They swerved, all in one flight, when the black cat moved among the bushes, when the cook threw cinders on the ash heap and startled them. Fear was in their song, and apprehension of pain, and joy to be snatched quickly now at this instant. Also they sang emulously in the clear morning air, swerving high over the elm tree, singing together as they chased each other, escaping, pursuing, *pecking each other as they turned high in the air. And then tiring of pursuit and flight, lovelily* they came descending, delicately declining, dropped down and sat silent on the tree, on the wall, with their bright eyes glancing, and their heads turned this way, that way; aware, awake; intensely conscious of one thing, one object in particular.*

Perhaps it was a snail shell, rising in the grass like a grey cathedral, a swelling building burnt with dark rings and shadowed green by the grass. Or perhaps they saw the splendour of the flowers making a light of flowing purple over the beds, through which dark tunnels of purple shade were driven between the stalks. Or they fixed their gaze on the small bright apple leaves, dancing yet withheld, stiffly sparkling among the pink-tipped blossoms. Or they saw the rain drop on the hedge, pendent but not falling, with a whole house bent in it, and towering elms; or, gazing straight at the sun, their eyes became gold beads.

Now glancing this side, that side, they looked deeper, beneath the flowers, down the dark avenues into the unlit world where the leaf rots and the flower has fallen. Then one of them, beautifully darting, accurately alighting, spiked the soft, monstrous body of the defenceless worm, pecked again and yet again, and left it to fester. Down there among the roots where the flowers decayed, gusts of dead smells were wafted; drops formed on the bloated sides of swollen things. The skin of rotten fruit broke, and matter oozed too thick to run. Yellow excretions were exuded by slugs, and now and again an amorphous body with a head at either end swayed slowly from side to side. The gold-eyed birds darting in between the leaves observed that purulence, that wetness, quizzically. Now and then they plunged the tips of their beaks savagely into the sticky mixture.

Now, too, the rising sun came in at the window, touching the red-edged curtain, and began to bring out circles and lines. Now in the growing light its whiteness settled in the plate; the blade condensed its gleam. Chairs and cupboards loomed behind so that though each was separate they seemed inextricably involved. The looking-glass whitened its pool upon the wall. The real flower on the window-sill was attended by a phantom flower. Yet the phantom was part of the flower, for when a bud broke free the paler flower in the glass opened a bud too.

The wind rose. The waves drummed on the shore, like turbaned warriors, like turbaned men with poisoned assegais who, whirling their arms on high, advance upon the feeding flocks, the white sheep.

'THE complexity of things becomes more close,' said Bernard, 'here at college, where the stir and pressure of life are so extreme, where the excitement of mere living becomes daily more urgent. Every hour something new is unburied in the great bran-pie. What am I? I ask. This? No, I am that. Especially now, when I have left a room, and people talking, and the stone flags ring out with my solitary footsteps, and I behold the moon rising, sublimely, indifferently, over the ancient chapel—then it becomes clear that I am not one and simple, but complex and many. Bernard, in public, bubbles; in private, is secretive. That is what they do not understand, for they are now undoubtedly discussing me, saying I escape them, am evasive. They do not understand that I have to effect different transitions; have to cover the entrances and exits of several different men who alternately act their parts as Bernard. I am abnormally aware of circumstances. I can never read a book in a railway carriage without asking, Is he a builder? Is she unhappy? I was aware today acutely that poor Simes, with his pimple, was feeling, how bitterly, that his chance of making a good impression upon Billy Jackson was remote. Feeling this painfully, I invited him to dinner with ardour. This he will attribute to an admiration which is not mine. That is true. But "joined to the sensibility of a woman" (I am here quoting my own biographer) "Bernard possessed the logical sobriety of a man". Now people who make a single impression, and that, in the main, a good one (for there seems to be a virtue in simplicity), are those who keep their equilibrium in mid-stream. (I instantly see fish with their noses one way, the stream rushing past another.) Canon, Lycett, Peters, Hawkins, Larpent, Neville—all fish in mid-stream. But *you* understand, *you*, my self, who always comes at a call (that would be a harrowing experience to call and for no one to come; that would make the midnight hollow, and explains the expression of old men in clubs—they have given up calling for a self who does not come*), you understand that I am only superficially represented by what I was saying tonight. Underneath, and, at the moment when I am most disparate, I am also integrated. I sympathize effusively; I also sit, like a toad in a hole, receiving with perfect coldness whatever comes. Very few of you who are now discussing me have the double capacity to feel, to reason. Lycett, you see, believes in running after hares; Hawkins has spent a most industrious afternoon in the library. Peters has his young lady at the circulating library. You are all engaged, involved, drawn in, and absolutely energized to the top of your bent—all save Neville, whose mind is far too complex to be roused by any single activity. I also am too complex. In my case something remains floating, unattached.

'Now, as a proof of my susceptibility to atmosphere, here, as I come into my room, and turn on the light, and see the sheet of paper, the table, my gown lying negligently over the back of the chair, I feel that I am that dashing yet reflective man, that bold and deleterious figure, who, lightly throwing off his cloak, seizes his pen and at once flings off the following letter to the girl with whom he is passionately in love.

'Yes, all is propitious. I am now in the mood. I can write the letter straight off which I have begun ever so many

times. I have just come in; I have flung down my hat and
my stick; I am writing the first thing that comes into my
head without troubling to put the paper straight. It is going
to be a brilliant sketch which, she must think, was written
without a pause, without an erasure. Look how unformed
the letters are—there is a careless blot. All must be
sacrificed to speed and carelessness. I will write a quick,
running, small hand, exaggerating the down stroke of the
"y" and crossing the "t" thus—with a dash. The date shall
be only Tuesday, the 17th, and then a question mark. But
also I must give her the impression that though he—for
this is not myself—is writing in such an off-hand, such a
slap-dash way, there is some subtle suggestion of intimacy
and respect. I must allude to talks we have had together—
bring back some remembered scene. But I must seem to
her (this is very important) to be passing from thing to
thing with the greatest ease in the world. I shall pass from
the service for the man who was drowned (I have a phrase
for that) to Mrs Moffat and her sayings (I have a note of
them), and so to some reflections apparently casual but full
of profundity (profound criticism is often written casually)
about some book I have been reading, some out-of-the-
way book. I want her to say as she brushes her hair or puts
out the candle, "Where did I read that? Oh, in Bernard's
letter." It is the speed, the hot, molten effect, the laval flow
of sentence into sentence that I need. Who am I thinking
of? Byron of course. I am, in some ways, like Byron.*
Perhaps a sip of Byron will help to put me in the vein. Let
me read a page. No; this is dull; this is scrappy. This is
rather too formal. Now I am getting the hang of it. Now I
am getting his beat into my brain (the rhythm is the main
thing in writing). Now, without pausing I will begin, on
the very lilt of the stroke——.

'Yet it falls flat. It peters out. I cannot get up steam enough to carry me over the transition. My true self breaks off from my assumed. And if I begin to re-write it, she will feel "Bernard is posing as a literary man; Bernard is thinking of his biographer" (which is true). No, I will write the letter tomorrow directly after breakfast.

'Now let me fill my mind with imaginary pictures. Let me suppose that I am asked to stay at Restover, King's Laughton, Station Langley three miles. I arrive in the dusk. In the courtyard of this shabby but distinguished house there are two or three dogs, slinking, long-legged. There are faded rugs in the hall; a military gentleman smokes a pipe as he paces the terrace. The note is of distinguished poverty and military connections. A hunter's hoof on the writing-table—a favourite horse. "Do you ride?" "Yes, sir, I love riding." "My daughter expects us in the drawing-room." My heart pounds against my ribs. She is standing at a low table; she has been hunting; she munches sandwiches like a tomboy. I make a fairly good impression on the Colonel. I am not too clever, he thinks; I am not too raw. Also I play billiards. Then the nice maid who has been with the family thirty years comes in. The pattern on the plates is of Oriental long-tailed birds. Her mother's portrait in muslin hangs over the fireplace. I can sketch the surroundings up to a point with extraordinary ease. But can I make it work? Can I hear her voice—the precise tone with which, when we are alone, she says "Bernard"? And then what next?

'The truth is that I need the stimulus of other people. Alone, over my dead fire, I tend to see the thin places in my own stories. The real novelist, the perfectly simple human being, could go on, indefinitely, imagining. He would not integrate, as I do. He would not have this devastating sense of grey ashes in a burnt-out grate. Some blind flaps in my eyes. Everything becomes impervious. I cease to invent.

'Let me recollect. It has been on the whole a good day. The drop that forms on the roof of the soul in the evening is round, many-coloured. There was the morning, fine; there was the afternoon, walking. I like views of spires across grey fields. I like glimpses between people's shoulders. Things kept popping into my head. I was imaginative, subtle. After dinner, I was dramatic. I put into concrete form many things that we had dimly observed about our common friends. I made my transitions easily. But now let me ask myself the final question, as I sit over this grey fire, with its naked promontories of black coal, which of these people am I? It depends so much upon the room. When I say to myself, "Bernard", who comes? A faithful, sardonic man, disillusioned, but not embittered. A man of no particular age or calling. Myself, merely. It is he who now takes the poker and rattles the cinders so that they fall in showers through the grate. "Lord", he says to himself, watching them fall, "what a pother!" and then he adds, lugubriously, but with some sense of consolation, "Mrs Moffat will come and sweep it all up——" I fancy I shall often repeat to myself that phrase, as I rattle and bang through life, hitting first this side of the carriage, then the other, "Oh, yes, Mrs Moffat will come and sweep it all up". And so to bed.'

'In a world which contains the present moment,' said Neville, 'why discriminate? Nothing should be named lest by so doing we change it. Let it exist, this bank, this beauty, and I, for one instant, steeped in pleasure. The sun is hot. I see the river. I see trees specked and burnt in the autumn sunlight. Boats float past, through the red, through the green. Far away a bell tolls, but not for death. There are bells that ring for life. A leaf falls, from joy. Oh, I am in love with life! Look how the willow shoots its fine sprays into the air! Look how through them a boat passes, filled with indolent, with unconscious, with powerful young men. They are listening to the gramophone; they are eating fruit out of paper bags. They are tossing the skins of bananas, which then sink eel-like, into the river. All they do is beautiful. There are cruets behind them and ornaments; their rooms are full of oars and oleographs but they have turned all to beauty. That boat passes under the bridge. Another comes. Then another. That is Percival, lounging on the cushions, monolithic, in giant repose. No, it is only one of his satellites, imitating his monolithic, his giant repose. He alone is unconscious of their tricks, and when he catches them at it he buffets them good-humouredly with a blow of his paw. They, too, have passed under the bridge through "the fountains of the pendant trees", through its fine strokes of yellow and plum colour. The breeze stirs; the curtain quivers; I see behind the leaves the grave, yet eternally joyous buildings, which seem porous, not gravid; light, though set so immemorially on the ancient turf. Now begins to rise in me the familiar rhythm; words that have lain dormant now lift, now toss their crests, and fall and rise, and fall and rise again. I am a poet, yes. Surely I am a great poet. Boats and youth passing and distant trees, "the falling fountains of the pendant trees". I see it all. I feel it all. I am inspired. My eyes fill with tears. Yet even as I feel this, I lash my frenzy higher and higher. It foams. It becomes artificial, insincere. Words and words and words, how they gallop—how they lash their long manes and tails, but for some fault in me I cannot give myself to their backs; I cannot fly with them, scattering women and string bags. There is some flaw in me—some fatal hesitancy, which, if I pass it over, turns to foam and falsity. Yet it is incredible that I should not be a great poet. What did I write last night if it was not good poetry? Am I too fast, too facile? I do not know. I do not know myself sometimes, or how to measure and name and count out the grains that make me what I am.

'Something now leaves me; something goes from me to meet that figure who is coming, and assures me that I know him before I see who it is. How curiously one is changed by the addition, even at a distance, of a friend. How useful an office one's friends perform when they recall us. Yet how painful to be recalled, to be mitigated, to have one's self adulterated, mixed up, become part of another. As he approaches I become not myself but Neville mixed with somebody—with whom?—with Bernard? Yes, it is Bernard, and it is to Bernard that I shall put the question, Who am I?'

'How strange,' said Bernard, 'the willow looks seen together. I was Byron, and the tree was Byron's tree, lachrymose, down-showering, lamenting. Now that we look at the tree together, it has a combined look, each branch distinct, and I will tell you what I feel, under the compulsion of your clarity.

'I feel your disapproval, I feel your force. I become, with you, an untidy, an impulsive human being whose bandanna handkerchief is for ever stained with the grease of crumpets. Yes, I hold Gray's *Elegy** in one hand; with the other I scoop out the bottom crumpet, that has absorbed all the butter and sticks to the bottom of the plate. This offends you; I feel your distress acutely. Inspired by it and anxious to regain your good opinion, I proceed to tell you how I have just pulled Percival out of bed; I describe his slippers, his table, his guttered candle; his surly and complaining accents as I pull the blankets off his feet; he burrowing like some vast cocoon meanwhile. I describe all this in such a way that, centred as you are upon some private sorrow (for a hooded shape presides over our encounter), you give way, you laugh and delight in me. My charm and flow of language, unexpected and spontaneous as it is, delights me too. I am astonished, as I draw the veil off things with words, how much, how infinitely more than I can say, I have observed. More and more bubbles into my mind as I talk, images and images. This, I say to myself, is what I need; why, I ask, can I not finish the letter that I am writing? For my room is always scattered with unfinished letters. I begin to suspect, when I am with you, that I am among the most gifted of men. I am filled with the delight of youth, with potency, with the sense of what is to come. Blundering, but fervid, I see myself buzzing round flowers, humming down scarlet cups, making blue funnels resound with my prodigious booming. How richly I shall enjoy my youth (you make me feel). And London. And freedom. But stop. You are not listening. You are making some protest, as you slide, with an inexpressibly familiar gesture, your hand along your knee. By such signs we diagnose our friends' diseases. "Do not, in your affluence and plenty," you seem to say, "pass me by." "Stop," you say. "Ask me what I suffer."

'Let me then create you. (You have done as much for me.) You lie on this hot bank, in this lovely, this fading, this still bright October day, watching boat after boat float through the combed-out twigs of the willow tree. And you wish to be a poet; and you wish to be a lover. But the splendid clarity of your intelligence, and the remorseless honesty of your intellect (these Latin words I owe you;

these qualities of yours make me shift a little uneasily and see the faded patches, the thin strands in my own equipment) bring you to a halt. You indulge in no mystifications. You do not fog yourself with rosy clouds, or yellow.

'Am I right? Have I read the little gesture of your left hand correctly? If so, give me your poems; hand over the sheets you wrote last night in such a fervour of inspiration that you now feel a little sheepish. For you distrust inspiration, yours or mine. Let us go back together, over the bridge, under the elm trees, to my room, where, with walls round us and red serge curtains drawn, we can shut out these distracting voices, scents and savours of lime trees, and other lives; these pert shop-girls, disdainfully tripping, these shuffling, heavy-laden old women; these furtive glimpses of some vague and vanishing figure—it might be Jinny, it might be Susan, or was that Rhoda disappearing down the avenue? Again, from some slight twitch I guess your feeling; I have escaped you; I have gone buzzing like a swarm of bees, endlessly vagrant, with none of your power of fixing remorselessly upon a single object. But I will return.'

'When there are buildings like these,' said Neville, 'I cannot endure that there should be shop-girls. Their titter, their gossip, offends me; breaks into my stillness, and nudges me, in moments of purest exultation, to remember our degradation.

'But now we have regained our territory after that brief brush with the bicycles and the lime scent and the vanishing figures in the distracted street. Here we are masters of tranquillity and order; inheritors of proud tradition. The lights are beginning to make yellow slits across the square. Mists from the river are filling these ancient spaces. They cling, gently, to the hoary stone. The leaves now are thick in country lanes, sheep cough in the damp fields; but here in your room we are dry. We talk privately. The fire leaps and sinks, making some knob bright.

'You have been reading Byron. You have been marking the passages that seem to approve of your own character. I find marks against all those sentences which seem to express a sardonic yet passionate nature; a moth-like impetuosity dashing itself against hard glass. You thought, as you drew your pencil there, "I too throw off my cloak like that. I too snap my fingers in the face of destiny." Yet Byron never made tea as you do, who fill the pot so that when you put the lid on the tea spills over. There is a brown pool on the table—it is running among your books and papers. Now you mop it up, clumsily, with your pocket-handkerchief. You then stuff your handkerchief back into your pocket—that is not Byron; that is you; that is so essentially you that if I think of you in twenty years' time, when we are both famous, gouty and intolerable, it will be by that scene: and if you are dead, I shall weep. Once you were Tolstoy's young man; now you are Byron's young man; perhaps you will be Meredith's young man;* then you will visit Paris in the Easter vacation and come back wearing a black tie, some detestable Frenchman whom nobody has ever heard of. Then I shall drop you.

'I am one person—myself. I do not impersonate Catullus, whom I adore. I am the most slavish of students, with here a dictionary, there a notebook in which I enter curious uses of the past participle. But one cannot go on for ever cutting these ancient inscriptions clearer with a knife. Shall I always draw the red serge curtain close and see my book, laid like a block of marble, pale under the lamp? That would be a glorious life, to addict oneself to perfection; to follow the curve of the sentence wherever it might lead, into deserts, under drifts of sand, regardless of lures, of seductions; to be poor always and unkempt; to be ridiculous in Piccadilly.

'But I am too nervous to end my sentence properly. I speak quickly, as I pace up and down, to conceal my agitation. I hate your greasy handkerchiefs—you will stain your copy of *Don Juan*. You are not listening to me. You are making phrases about Byron. And while you gesticulate, with your cloak, your cane, I am trying to expose a secret told to nobody yet; I am asking you (as I stand with my back to you) to take my life in your hands and tell me whether I am doomed always to cause repulsion in those I love?

'I stand with my back to you fidgeting. No, my hands are now perfectly still. Precisely, opening a space in the bookcase, I insert *Don Juan*; there. I would rather be loved, I would rather be famous than follow perfection through the sand. But am I doomed to cause disgust? Am I a poet? Take it. The desire which is loaded behind my lips, cold as lead, fell as a bullet, the thing I aim at shop-girls, women, the pretence, the vulgarity of life (because I love it) shoots at you as I throw—catch it—my poem.'

'He has shot like an arrow from the room,' said Bernard. 'He has left me his poem. O friendship, I too will press flowers between the pages of Shakespeare's sonnets! O friendship, how piercing are your darts—there, there, again there. He looked at me, turning to face me; he gave me his poem. All mists curl off the roof of my being. That confidence I shall keep to my dying day. Like a long wave, like a roll of heavy waters, he went over me, his devastating presence—dragging me open, laying bare the pebbles on the shore of my soul. It was humiliating; I was turned to small stones. All semblances were rolled up. "You are not

Byron; you are your self." To be contracted by another person into a single being—how strange.

'How strange to feel the line that is spun from us lengthening its fine filament across the misty spaces of the intervening world. He is gone; I stand here, holding his poem. Between us is this line. But now, how comfortable, how reassuring to feel that alien presence removed, that scrutiny darkened and hooded over! How grateful to draw the blinds, and admit no other presence; to feel returning from the dark corners in which they took refuge, those shabby inmates, those familiars, whom, with his superior force, he drove into hiding. The mocking, the observant spirits who, even in the crisis and stab of the moment, watched on my behalf now come flocking home again. With their addition, I am Bernard; I am Byron; I am this, that and the other. They darken the air and enrich me, as of old, with their antics, their comments, and cloud the fine simplicity of my moment of emotion. For I am more selves than Neville thinks. We are not simple as our friends would have us to meet their needs. Yet love is simple.

'Now they have returned, my inmates, my familiars. Now the stab, the rent in my defences that Neville made with his astonishing fine rapier, is repaired. I am almost whole now; and see how jubilant I am, bringing into play all that Neville ignores in me. I feel, as I look from the window, parting the curtains, "That would give him no pleasure; but it rejoices me". (We use our friends to measure our own stature.) My scope embraces what Neville never reaches. They are shouting hunting-songs over the way. They are celebrating some run with the beagles. The little boys in caps who always turned at the same moment when the brake went round the corner are clapping each other on the shoulder and boasting. But

Neville, delicately avoiding interference, stealthily, like a conspirator, hastens back to his room. I see him sunk in his low chair gazing at the fire which has assumed for the moment an architectural solidity. If life, he thinks, could wear that permanence, if life could have that order—for above all he desires order, and detests my Byronic untidiness; and so draws his curtain; and bolts his door. His eyes (for he is in love; the sinister figure of love presided at our encounter) fill with longing; fill with tears. He snatches the poker and with one blow destroys that momentary appearance of solidity in the burning coals. All changes. And youth and love. The boat has floated through the arch of the willows and is now under the bridge. Percival, Tony, Archie, or another, will go to India. We shall not meet again. Then he stretches his hand for his copy-book—a neat volume bound in mottled paper—and writes feverishly long lines of poetry, in the manner of whomever he admires most at the moment.

'But I want to linger; to lean from the window; to listen. There again comes that rollicking chorus. They are now smashing china—that also is the convention. The chorus, like a torrent jumping rocks, brutally assaulting old trees, pours with splendid abandonment headlong over precipices. On they roll; on they gallop; after hounds, after footballs; they pump up and down attached to oars like sacks of flour. All divisions are merged—they act like one man. The gusty October wind blows the uproar in bursts of sound and silence across the court. Now again they are smashing the china—that is the convention. An old, unsteady woman carrying a bag trots home under the fire-red windows. She is half afraid that they will fall on her and tumble her into the gutter. Yet she pauses as if to warm her knobbed, her rheumaticky hands at the bonfire which flares away with streams of sparks and bits of blown paper. The old woman pauses against the lit window. A contrast. That I see and Neville does not see; that I feel and Neville does not feel. Hence he will reach perfection and I shall fail and shall leave nothing behind me but imperfect phrases littered with sand.

'I think of Louis now. What malevolent yet searching light would Louis throw upon this dwindling autumn evening, upon this china-smashing and trolling of hunting-songs, upon Neville, Byron and our life here? His thin lips are somewhat pursed; his cheeks are pale; he pores in an office over some obscure commercial document. "My father, a banker at Brisbane"—being ashamed of him he always talks of him—failed. So he sits in an office, Louis, the best scholar in the school. But I seeking contrasts often feel his eye on us, his laughing eye, his wild eye, adding us up like insignificant items in some grand total which he is for ever pursuing in his office. And one day, taking a fine pen and dipping it in red ink, the addition will be complete; our total will be known; but it will not be enough.

'Bang! They have thrown a chair now against the wall. We are damned then. My case is dubious too. Am I not indulging in unwarranted emotions? Yes, as I lean out of the window and drop my cigarette so that it twirls lightly to the ground, I feel Louis watching even my cigarette. And Louis says, "That means something. But what?"'

'People go on passing,' said Louis. 'They pass the window of this eating-shop incessantly. Motor-cars, vans, motor-omnibuses; and again motor-omnibuses, vans, motor-cars—they pass the window. In the background I perceive shops and houses; also the grey spires of a city church. In the foreground are glass shelves set with plates of buns and ham sandwiches. All is somewhat obscured by steam from a tea-urn. A meaty, vapourish smell of beef and mutton, sausages and mash, hangs down like a damp net in the middle of the eating-house. I prop my book against a bottle of Worcester sauce* and try to look like the rest.

'Yet I cannot. (They go on passing, they go on passing in disorderly procession.) I cannot read my book, or order my beef, with conviction. I repeat, "I am an average Englishman; I am an average clerk", yet I look at the little men at the next table to be sure that I do what they do. Supple-faced, with rippling skins, that are always twitching with the multiplicity of their sensations, prehensile like monkeys, greased to this particular moment, they are discussing with all the right gestures the sale of a piano. It blocks up the hall; so he would take a tenner. People go on passing; they go on passing against the spires of the church and the plates of ham sandwiches. The streamers of my consciousness waver out and are perpetually torn and distressed by their disorder. I cannot therefore concentrate on my dinner. "I would take a tenner. The case is handsome; but it blocks up the hall." They dive and plunge like guillemots whose feathers are slippery with oil. All excesses beyond that norm are vanity. That is the mean; that is the average. Meanwhile the hats bob up and down; the door perpetually shuts and opens. I am conscious of flux, of disorder; of annihilation and despair. If this is all, this is worthless. Yet I feel, too, the rhythm of the eating-house. It is like a waltz tune, eddying in and out, round and round. The waitresses, balancing trays, swing in and out, round and round, dealing plates of greens, of apricot and custard, dealing them at the right time, to the right customers. The average men, including her rhythm in their rhythm ("I would take a tenner; for it blocks up the hall") take their greens, take their apricots and custard. Where then is the break in this continuity? What the fissure through which one sees disaster? The circle is unbroken; the harmony complete. Here is the central rhythm; here the common mainspring. I watch it expand, contract; and then expand again. Yet I am not included. If I speak, imitating their accent, they prick their ears, waiting for me to speak again, in order that they may place me—if I come from Canada or Australia, I, who desire above all things to be taken to the arms with love, am alien, external. I, who would wish to feel close over me the protective waves of the ordinary, catch with the tail of my eye some far horizon; am aware of hats bobbing up and down in perpetual disorder. To me is addressed the plaint of the wandering and distracted spirit (a woman with bad teeth falters at the counter), "Bring us back to the fold, we who pass so disjectedly, bobbing up and down, past windows with plates of ham sandwiches in the foreground." Yes; I will reduce you to order.

'I will read in the book that is propped against the bottle of Worcester sauce. It contains some forged rings, some perfect statements, a few words, but poetry. You, all of you, ignore it. What the dead poet said, you have forgotten. And I cannot translate it to you so that its binding power ropes you in, and makes it clear to you that you are aimless; and the rhythm is cheap and worthless; and so remove that degradation which, if you are unaware of your aimlessness, pervades you, making you senile, even while you are young. To translate that poem so that it is easily read is to be my endeavour. I, the companion of Plato, of Virgil, will knock at the grained oak door. I oppose to what is passing this ramrod of beaten steel. I will not submit to this aimless passing of billycock hats and Hom-

burg hats and all the plumed and variegated head-dresses
of women. (Susan, whom I respect, would wear a plain
straw hat on a summer's day.) And the grinding and the
steam that runs in unequal drops down the window-pane;
and the stopping and the starting with a jerk of motor-
omnibuses; and the hesitations at counters; and the words
that trail drearily without human meaning; I will reduce
you to order.

'My roots go down through veins of lead and silver,
through damp, marshy places that exhale odours, to a knot
made of oak roots bound together in the centre. Sealed and
blind, with earth stopping my ears, I have yet heard
rumours of wars; and the nightingale; have felt the hurrying of many troops of men flocking hither and thither in
quest of civilization like flocks of birds migrating seeking
the summer; I have seen women carrying red pitchers to
the banks of the Nile. I woke in a garden, with a blow on
the nape of my neck, a hot kiss, Jinny's; remembering all
this as one remembers confused cries and toppling pillars
and shafts of red and black in some nocturnal conflagration. I am for ever sleeping and waking. Now I sleep; now
I wake. I see the gleaming tea-urn; the glass cases full of
pale-yellow sandwiches; the men in round coats perched
on stools at the counter; and also behind them, eternity.*
It is a stigma burnt on my quivering flesh by a cowled man
with a red-hot iron. I see this eating-shop against the
packed and fluttering birds' wings, many feathered, folded,
of the past. Hence my pursed lips, my sickly pallor; my
distasteful and uninviting aspect as I turn my face with
hatred and bitterness upon Bernard and Neville, who
saunter under yew trees; who inherit armchairs; and draw
their curtains close, so that lamplight falls on their books.

'Susan, I respect; because she sits stitching. She sews

under a quiet lamp in a house where the corn sighs close to the window and gives me safety. For I am the weakest, the youngest of them all. I am a child looking at his feet and the little runnels that the stream has made in the gravel. That is a snail, I say; that is a leaf. I delight in the snails; I delight in the leaf. I am always the youngest, the most innocent, the most trustful. You are all protected. I am naked. When the waitress with the plaited wreaths of hair swings past, she deals you your apricots and custard unhesitatingly, like a sister. You are her brothers. But when I get up, brushing the crumbs from my waistcoat, I slip too large a tip, a shilling, under the edge of my plate, so that she may not find it till I am gone, and her scorn, as she picks it up with laughter, may not strike on me till I am past the swing-doors.'

'Now the wind lifts the blind,' said Susan, 'jars, bowls, matting and the shabby armchair with the hole in it are now become distinct. The usual faded ribbons sprinkle the wallpaper. The bird chorus is over, only one bird now sings close to the bedroom window. I will pull on my stockings and go quietly past the bedroom doors, and down through the kitchen, out through the garden past the greenhouse into the field. It is still early morning. The mist is on the marshes. The day is stark and stiff as a linen shroud. But it will soften; it will warm. At this hour, this still early hour, I think I am the field, I am the barn, I am the trees; mine are the flocks of birds, and this young hare who leaps, at the last moment when I step almost on him. Mine is the heron that stretches its vast wings lazily; and the cow that creaks as it pushes one foot before another munching; and the wild, swooping swallow; and the faint red in the sky, and the green when the red fades; the silence and the bell; the call of the man fetching cart-horses from the fields—all are mine.

'I cannot be divided, or kept apart. I was sent to school; I was sent to Switzerland to finish my education. I hate linoleum; I hate fir trees and mountains. Let me now fling myself on this flat ground under a pale sky where the clouds pace slowly. The cart grows gradually larger as it comes along the road. The sheep gather in the middle of the field. The birds gather in the middle of the road—they need not fly yet. The wood smoke rises. The starkness of the dawn is going out of it. Now the day stirs. Colour returns. The day waves yellow with all its crops. The earth hangs heavy beneath me.

'But who am I, who lean on this gate and watch my setter nose in a circle? I think sometimes (I am not twenty yet) I am not a woman, but the light that falls on this gate, on this ground. I am the seasons, I think sometimes, January, May, November; the mud, the mist, the dawn. I cannot be tossed about, or float gently, or mix with other people. Yet now, leaning here till the gate prints my arm, I feel the weight that has formed itself in my side. Something has formed, at school, in Switzerland, some hard thing. Not sighs and laughter, not circling and ingenious phrases; not Rhoda's strange communications when she looks past us, over our shoulders; nor Jinny's pirouetting, all of a piece, limbs and body. What I give is fell. I cannot float gently, mixing with other people. I like best the stare of shepherds met in the road; the stare of gipsy women beside a cart in a ditch suckling their children as I shall suckle my children. For soon in the hot midday when the bees hum round the hollyhocks my lover will come. He will stand

[79]

under the cedar tree. To his one word I shall answer my one word. What has formed in me I shall give him. I shall have children; I shall have maids in aprons; men with pitchforks; a kitchen where they bring the ailing lambs to warm in baskets, where the hams hang and the onions glisten. I shall be like my mother, silent in a blue apron locking up the cupboards.

'Now I am hungry. I will call my setter. I think of crusts and bread and butter and white plates in a sunny room. I will go back across the fields. I will walk along this grass path with strong, even strides, now swerving to avoid the puddle, now leaping lightly to a clump. Beads of wet form on my rough skirt; my shoes become supple and dark. The stiffness has gone from the day; it is shaded with grey, green and umber. The birds no longer settle on the high road.

'I return, like a cat or fox returning, whose fur is grey with rime, whose pads are hardened by the coarse earth. I push through the cabbages, making their leaves squeak and their drops spill. I sit waiting for my father's footsteps as he shuffles down the passage pinching some herb between his fingers. I pour out cup after cup while the unopened flowers hold themselves erect on the table among the pots of jam, the loaves and the butter. We are silent.

'I go then to the cupboard, and take the damp bags of rich sultanas; I lift the heavy flour on to the clean scrubbed kitchen table. I knead; I stretch; I pull, plunging my hands in the warm inwards of the dough. I let the cold water stream fanwise through my fingers. The fire roars; the flies buzz in a circle. All my currants and rices, the silver bags and the blue bags, are locked again in the cupboard. The meat is stood in the oven; the bread rises in a soft dome under the clean towel. I walk in the afternoon down to the river. All the world is breeding. The flies are going from grass to grass. The flowers are thick with pollen. The swans ride the stream in order. The clouds, warm now, sun-spotted, sweep over the hills, leaving gold in the water, and gold on the necks of the swans. Pushing one foot before the other, the cows munch their way across the field. I feel through the grass for the white-domed mushroom; and break its stalk and pick the purple orchid that grows beside it and lay the orchid by the mushroom with the earth at its root, and so home to make the kettle boil for my father among the just reddened roses on the tea-table.

'But evening comes and the lamps are lit. And when evening comes and the lamps are lit they make a yellow fire in the ivy. I sit with my sewing by the table. I think of Jinny; of Rhoda; and hear the rattle of wheels on the pavement as the farm horses plod home; I hear traffic roaring in the evening wind. I look at the quivering leaves in the dark garden and think "They dance in London. Jinny kisses Louis."'

'How strange,' said Jinny, 'that people should sleep, that people should put out the lights and go upstairs. They have taken off their dresses, they have put on white night-gowns. There are no lights in any of these houses. There is a line of chimney-pots against the sky; and a street lamp or two burning, as lamps burn when nobody needs them. The only people in the streets are poor people hurrying. There is no one coming or going in this street; the day is over. A few policemen stand at the corners. Yet night is beginning. I feel myself shining in the dark. Silk is on my knee. My silk legs rub smoothly together. The stones of a necklace lie cold on my throat. My feet feel the pinch of shoes. I sit bolt upright so that my hair may not touch the back of the seat. I am arrayed, I am prepared. This is the momentary pause; the dark moment. The fiddlers have lifted their bows.

'Now the car slides to a stop. A strip of pavement is lighted. The door is opening and shutting. People are arriving; they do not speak; they hasten in. There is the swishing sound of cloaks falling in the hall. This is the prelude, this is the beginning. I glance, I peep, I powder. All is exact, prepared. My hair is swept in one curve. My lips are precisely red. I am ready now to join men and women on the stairs, my peers. I pass them, exposed to their gaze, as they are to mine. Like lightning we look but do not soften or show signs of recognition. Our bodies communicate. This is my calling. This is my world. All is decided and ready; the servants, standing here, and again here, take my name, my fresh, my unknown name, and toss it before me. I enter.

'Here are gilt chairs in the empty, the expectant rooms, and flowers, stiller, statelier, than flowers that grow, spread green, spread white, against the walls. And on one small table is one bound book. This is what I have dreamt; this is what I have foretold. I am native here. I tread naturally on thick carpets. I slide easily on smooth-polished floors, I now begin to unfurl, in this scent, in this radiance, as a fern when its curled leaves unfurl. I stop. I take stock of this world. I look among the groups of unknown people. Among the lustrous green, pink, pearl-grey women stand upright the bodies of men. They are black and white; they are grooved beneath their clothes with deep rills. I feel again the reflection in the window of the tunnel; it moves. The black-and-white figures of unknown men look at me as I lean forward; as I turn aside to look at a picture, they turn too. Their hands go fluttering to their ties. They touch their waistcoats, their pocket-handkerchiefs. They are very young. They are anxious to make a good impression. I feel a thousand capacities spring up in me. I am arch, gay, languid, melancholy by turns. I am rooted, but I flow. All gold, flowing that way, I say to this one, "Come". Rippling black, I say to that one, "No". One breaks off from his station under the glass cabinet. He approaches. He makes towards me. This is the most exciting moment I have ever known. I flutter. I ripple. I stream like a plant in the river, flowing this way, flowing that way, but rooted, so that he may come to me. "Come," I say, "come." Pale, with dark hair, the one who is coming is melancholy, romantic. And I am arch and fluent and capricious; for he is melancholy, he is romantic. He is here; he stands at my side.

'Now with a little jerk, like a limpet broken from a rock, I am broken off: I fall with him; I am carried off. We yield to this slow flood. We go in and out of this hesitating music. Rocks break the current of the dance; it jars, it shivers. In and out, we are swept now into this large figure; it holds us together; we cannot step outside its sinuous, its hesitating, its abrupt, its perfectly encircling walls. Our bodies, his hard, mine flowing, are pressed together within its body; it holds us together; and then lengthening out, in smooth, in sinuous folds, rolls us between it, on and on. Suddenly the music breaks. My blood runs on but my body stands still. The room reels past my eyes. It stops.

'Come, then, let us wander whirling to the gilt chairs. The body is stronger than I thought. I am dizzier than I supposed. I do not care for anything in the world. I do not care for anybody save this man whose name I do not know. Are we not acceptable, moon? Are we not lovely sitting together here, I in my satin; he in black and white? My peers may look at me now. I look straight back at you, men and women. I am one of you. This is my world. Now

I take this thin-stemmed glass and sip. Wine has a drastic, an astringent taste. I cannot help wincing as I drink. Scent and flowers, radiance and heat, are distilled here to a fiery, to a yellow liquid. Just behind my shoulder-blades some dry thing, wide-eyed, gently closes, gradually lulls itself to sleep. This is rapture; this is relief. The bar at the back of my throat lowers itself. Words crowd and cluster and push forth one on top of another. It does not matter which. They jostle and mount on each other's shoulders. The single and the solitary mate, tumble and become many. It does not matter what I say. Crowding, like a fluttering bird, one sentence crosses the empty space between us. It settles on his lips. I fill my glass again. I drink. The veil drops between us. I am admitted to the warmth and privacy of another soul. We are together, high up, on some Alpine pass. He stands melancholy on the crest of the road. I stoop. I pick a blue flower and fix it, standing on tiptoe to reach him, in his coat. There! That is my moment of ecstasy. Now it is over.

'Now slackness and indifference invade us. Other people brush past. We have lost consciousness of our bodies uniting under the table. I also like fair-haired men with blue eyes. The door opens. The door goes on opening. Now I think, next time it opens the whole of my life will be changed. Who comes? But it is only a servant, bringing glasses. That is an old man—I should be a child with him. That is a great lady—with her I should dissemble. There are girls of my own age, for whom I feel the drawn swords of an honourable antagonism. For these are my peers. I am a native of this world. Here is my risk, here is my adventure. The door opens. O come, I say to this one, rippling gold from head to heels. "Come", and he comes towards me.'

'I shall edge behind them,' said Rhoda, 'as if I saw someone I know. But I know no one. I shall twitch the curtain and look at the moon. Draughts of oblivion shall quench my agitation. The door opens; the tiger leaps. The door opens; terror rushes in; terror upon terror, pursuing me. Let me visit furtively the treasures I have laid apart. Pools lie on the other side of the world reflecting marble columns. The swallow dips her wing in dark pools. But here the door opens and people come; they come towards me. Throwing faint smiles to mask their cruelty, their indifference, they seize me. The swallow dips her wings; the moon rides through the blue seas alone. I must take his hand; I must answer. But what answer shall I give? I am thrust back to stand burning in this clumsy, this ill-fitting body, to receive the shafts of his indifference and his scorn, I who long for marble columns and pools on the other side of the world where the swallow dips her wings.

'Night has wheeled a little further over the chimney-pots. I see out of the window over his shoulder some unembarrassed cat, not drowned in light, not trapped in silk, free to pause, to stretch, and to move again. I hate all details of the individual life. But I am fixed here to listen. An immense pressure is on me. I cannot move without dislodging the weight of centuries. A million arrows pierce me. Scorn and ridicule pierce me. I, who could beat my breast against the storm and let the hail choke me joyfully, am pinned down here; am exposed. The tiger leaps. Tongues with their whips are upon me. Mobile, incessant, they flicker over me. I must prevaricate and fence them off with lies. What amulet is there against this disaster? What face can I summon to lay cool upon this heat? I think of names on boxes; of mothers from whose wide knees skirts descend; of glades where the many-backed steep hills come down. Hide me, I cry, protect me, for I am the youngest, the most naked of you all. Jinny rides like a gull on the wave, dealing her looks adroitly here and there, saying this, saying that, with truth. But I lie; I prevaricate.

'Alone, I rock my basins; I am mistress of my fleet of ships. But here, twisting the tassels of this brocaded curtain in my hostess's window, I am broken into separate pieces; I am no longer one. What then is the knowledge that Jinny has as she dances; the assurance that Susan has as, stooping quietly beneath the lamplight, she draws the white cotton through the eye of her needle? They say, Yes; they say, No; they bring their fists down with a bang on the table. But I doubt; I tremble; I see the wild thorn tree shake its shadow in the desert.

'Now I will walk, as if I had an end in view, across the room, to the balcony under the awning. I see the sky, softly feathered with its sudden effulgence of moon. I also see the railings of the square, and two people without faces, leaning like statues against the sky. There is, then, a world immune from change. When I have passed through this drawing-room flickering with tongues that cut me like knives, making me stammer, making me lie, I find faces rid of features, robed in beauty. The lovers crouch under the plane tree. The policeman stands sentinel at the corner. A man passes. There is, then, a world immune from change. But I am not composed enough, standing on tiptoe on the verge of fire, still scorched by the hot breath, afraid of the door opening and the leap of the tiger, to make even one sentence. What I say is perpetually contradicted. Each time the door opens I am interrupted. I am not yet twenty-one. I am to be broken. I am to be derided all my life. I am to be cast up and down among these men and women, with their twitching faces, with their lying tongues, like a cork

on a rough sea. Like a ribbon of weed I am flung far every
time the door opens. I am the foam that sweeps and fills
the uttermost rims of the rocks with whiteness; I am also a
girl, here in this room.'

THE WAVES

The sun, risen, no longer couched on a green mattress darting a fitful glance through watery jewels, bared its face and looked straight over the waves. They fell with a regular thud. They fell with the concussion of horses' hooves on the turf. Their spray rose like the tossing of lances and assegais over the riders' heads. They swept the beach with steel blue and diamond-tipped water. They drew in and out with the energy, the muscularity, of an engine which sweeps its force out and in again. The sun fell on cornfields and woods. Rivers became blue and many-plaited, lawns that sloped down to the water's edge became green as birds' feathers softly ruffling their plumes. The hills, curved and controlled, seemed bound back by thongs, as a limb is laced by muscles; and the woods which bristled proudly on their flanks were like the curt, clipped mane on the neck of a horse.

In the garden where the trees stood thick over flower-beds, ponds, and greenhouses the birds sang in the hot sunshine, each alone. One sang under the bedroom window; another on the topmost twig of the lilac bush; another on the edge of the wall. Each sang stridently, with passion, with vehemence, as if to let the song burst out of it, no matter if it shattered the song of another bird with harsh discord. Their round eyes bulged with brightness; their claws gripped the twig or rail. They sang, exposed without shelter, to the air and the sun, beautiful in their new plumage, shell-veined or brightly mailed, here barred with soft blues, here splashed with gold, or striped with one *bright feather. They sang as if the song were urged out of them by the pressure of the morning. They sang as if the edge of being were sharpened and must cut, must split the softness of the blue-green light, the dampness of the wet earth; the fumes and steams of the greasy kitchen vapour; the hot breath of mutton and beef; the richness of pastry and fruit; the damp shreds and peelings thrown from the kitchen bucket, from which a slow steam oozed on the rubbish heap. On all the sodden, the damp-spotted, the curled with wetness, they descended, dry-beaked, ruthless, abrupt. They swooped suddenly from the lilac bough or the fence. They spied a snail and tapped the shell against a stone. They tapped furiously, methodically, until the shell broke and something slimy oozed from the crack. They swept and soared sharply in flights high into the air, twittering short, sharp notes, and perched in the upper branches of some tree, and looked down upon leaves and spires beneath, and the country white with blossom, flowing with grass, and the sea which beat like a drum that raises a regiment of plumed and turbaned soldiers. Now and again their songs ran together in swift scales like the interlacings of a mountain stream whose waters, meeting, foam and then mix, and hasten quicker and quicker down the same channel, brushing the same broad leaves. But there is a rock; they sever.*

The sun fell in sharp wedges inside the room. Whatever the light touched became dowered with a fanatical existence. A plate was like a white lake. A knife looked like a dagger of ice. Suddenly tumblers revealed themselves upheld by streaks of light. Tables and chairs rose to the surface as if they had been sunk under water and rose, filmed with red, orange, purple like the bloom on the skin of ripe fruit. The veins on the glaze of the china, the grain of the wood, the fibres of the matting became more and more finely engraved. Everything was without shadow. A jar was so green that the eye seemed sucked up through a funnel by its intensity and stuck to it like a limpet. Then shapes took on mass and edge. Here was the boss of a chair; here the bulk of a cupboard. And as the light increased, flocks of shadow were driven before it and conglomerated and hung in many-pleated folds in the background.

'How fair, how strange,' said Bernard, 'glittering, many-pointed and many-domed London lies* before me under mist. Guarded by gasometers, by factory chimneys, she lies sleeping as we approach. She folds the ant-heap to her breast. All cries, all clamour, are softly enveloped in silence. Not Rome herself looks more majestic. But we are aimed at her. Already her maternal somnolence is uneasy. Ridges fledged with houses rise from the mist. Factories, cathedrals, glass domes, institutions and theatres erect themselves. The early train from the north is hurled at her like a missile. We draw a curtain as we pass. Blank expectant faces stare at us as we rattle and flash through stations. Men clutch their newspapers a little tighter, as our wind sweeps them, envisaging death. But we roar on. We are about to explode in the flanks of the city like a shell in the side of some ponderous, maternal, majestic animal. She hums and murmurs; she awaits us.

'Meanwhile as I stand looking from the train window, I feel strangely, persuasively, that because of my great happiness (being engaged to be married) I am become part of this speed, this missile hurled at the city. I am numbed to tolerance and acquiescence. My dear sir, I could say, why do you fidget, taking down your suitcase and pressing into it the cap that you have worn all night? Nothing we can do will avail. Over us all broods a splendid unanimity. We are enlarged and solemnized and brushed into uniformity as with the grey wing of some enormous goose (it is a fine

but colourless morning) because we have only one desire—
to arrive at the station. I do not want the train to stop with
a thud. I do not want the connection which has bound us
together sitting opposite each other all night long to be
broken. I do not want to feel that hate and rivalry have
resumed their sway; and different desires. Our community
in the rushing train, sitting together with only one wish, to
arrive at Euston, was very welcome. But behold! It is over.
We have attained our desire. We have drawn up at the
platform. Hurry and confusion and the wish to be first
through the gate into the lift assert themselves. But I do
not wish to be first through the gate, to assume the burden
of individual life. I, who have been since Monday, when
she accepted me, charged in every nerve with a sense of
identity, who could not see a tooth-brush in a glass without
saying, "*My* tooth-brush", now wish to unclasp my hands
and let fall my possessions, and merely stand here in the
street, taking no part, watching the omnibuses, without
desire; without envy; with what would be boundless
curiosity about human destiny if there were any longer an
edge to my mind. But it has none. I have arrived; am
accepted. I ask nothing.

'Having dropped off satisfied like a child from the breast,
I am at liberty now to sink down, deep, into what passes,
this omnipresent, general life. (How much, let me note,
depends upon trousers; the intelligent head is entirely
handicapped by shabby trousers.) One observes curious
hesitations at the door of the lift. This way, that way, the
other? Then individuality asserts itself. They are off. They
are all impelled by some necessity. Some miserable affair
of keeping an appointment, of buying a hat, severs these
beautiful human beings once so united. For myself, I have
no aim. I have no ambition. I will let myself be carried on

by the general impulse. The surface of my mind slips along like a pale-grey stream reflecting what passes. I cannot remember my past, my nose, or the colour of my eyes, or what my general opinion of myself is. Only in moments of emergency, at a crossing, at a kerb, the wish to preserve my body springs out and seizes me and stops me, here, before this omnibus. We insist, it seems, on living. Then again, indifference descends. The roar of the traffic, the passage of undifferentiated faces, this way and that way, drugs me into dreams; rubs the features from faces. People might walk through me. And, what is this moment of time, this particular day in which I have found myself caught? The growl of traffic might be any uproar—forest trees or the roar of wild beasts. Time has whizzed back an inch or two on its reel; our short progress has been cancelled. I think also that our bodies are in truth naked. We are only lightly covered with buttoned cloth; and beneath these pavements are shells, bones and silence.

'It is, however, true that my dreaming, my tentative advance like one carried beneath the surface of a stream, is interrupted, torn, pricked and plucked at by sensations, spontaneous and irrelevant, of curiosity, greed, desire, irresponsible as in sleep. (I covet that bag—etc.) No, but I wish to go under; to visit the profound depths; once in a while to exercise my prerogative not always to act, but to explore; to hear vague, ancestral sounds of boughs creaking, of mammoths; to indulge impossible desires to embrace the whole world with the arms of understanding—impossible to those who act. Am I not, as I walk, trembling with strange oscillations and vibrations of sympathy, which, unmoored as I am from a private being, bid me embrace these engrossed flocks; these starers and trippers; these errand-boys and furtive and fugitive girls who, ignoring their doom, look in at shop-windows? But I am aware of our ephemeral passage.

'It is, however, true that I cannot deny a sense that life for me is now mysteriously prolonged. Is it that I may have children, may cast a fling of seed wider, beyond this generation, this doom-encircled population, shuffling each other in endless competition along the street? My daughters shall come here, in other summers; my sons shall turn new fields. Hence we are not raindrops, soon dried by the wind; we make gardens blow and forests roar; we come up differently, for ever and ever. This, then, serves to explain my confidence, my central stability, otherwise so monstrously absurd as I breast the stream of this crowded thoroughfare, making always a passage for myself between people's bodies, taking advantage of safe moments to cross. It is not vanity; for I am emptied of ambition; I do not remember my special gifts, or idiosyncrasy, or the marks I bear on my person; eyes, nose or mouth. I am not, at this moment, myself.

'Yet behold, it returns. One cannot extinguish that persistent smell. It steals in through some crack in the structure—one's identity. I am not part of the street—no, I observe the street. One splits off, therefore. For instance, up that back street a girl stands waiting; for whom? A romantic story. On the wall of that shop is fixed a small crane, and for what reason, I ask, was that crane fixed there? and invent a purple lady swelling, circumambient, hauled from a barouche landau by a perspiring husband sometime in the sixties. A grotesque story. That is, I am a natural coiner of words, a blower of bubbles through one thing and another. And, striking off these observations spontaneously, I elaborate myself; differentiate myself and, listening to the voice that says as I stroll past, "Look! Take note of that!" I conceive myself called upon to provide, some winter's night, a meaning for all my observations—a line that runs from one to another, a summing up that completes. But soliloquies in back streets soon pall. I need an audience. That is my downfall. That always ruffles the edge of the final statement and prevents it from forming. I cannot seat myself in some sordid eating-house and order the same glass day after day and imbue myself entirely in one fluid—this life. I make my phrase and run off with it to some furnished room where it will be lit by dozens of candles. I need eyes on me to draw out these frills and furbelows. To be myself (I note) I need the illumination of other people's eyes, and therefore cannot be entirely sure what is my self. The authentics, like Louis, like Rhoda, exist most completely in solitude. They resent illumination, reduplication. They toss their pictures once painted face downward on the field. On Louis's words the ice is packed thick. His words issue pressed, condensed, enduring.

'I wish, then, after this somnolence to sparkle, many-faceted under the light of my friends' faces. I have been traversing the sunless territory of non-identity. A strange land. I have heard in my moment of appeasement, in my moment of obliterating satisfaction, the sigh, as it goes in, comes out, of the tide that draws beyond this circle of bright light, this drumming of insensate fury. I have had one moment of enormous peace. This perhaps is happiness. Now I am drawn back by pricking sensations; by curiosity, greed (I am hungry) and the irresistible desire to be myself. I think of people to whom I could say things: Louis, Neville, Susan, Jinny and Rhoda. With them I am many-sided. They retrieve me from darkness. We shall meet tonight, thank Heaven. Thank Heaven, I need not be alone. We shall dine together. We shall say good-bye to

Percival, who goes to India.* The hour is still distant, but I feel already those harbingers, those outriders, figures of one's friends in absence. I see Louis, stone-carved, sculpturesque; Neville, scissor-cutting, exact; Susan with eyes like lumps of crystal; Jinny dancing like a flame, febrile, hot, over dry earth; and Rhoda the nymph of the fountain always wet.* These are fantastic pictures—these are figments, these visions of friends in absence, grotesque, dropsical, vanishing at the first touch of the toe of a real boot. Yet they drum me alive. They brush off these vapours. I begin to be impatient of solitude—to feel its draperies hang sweltering, unwholesome about me. Oh, to toss them off and be active! Anybody will do. I am not fastidious. The crossing-sweeper will do; the postman; the waiter in this French restaurant; better still the genial proprietor, whose geniality seems reserved for oneself. He mixes the salad with his own hands for some privileged guest. Which is the privileged guest, I ask, and why? And what is he saying to the lady in ear-rings; is she a friend or a customer? I feel at once, as I sit down at a table, the delicious jostle of confusion, of uncertainty, of possibility, of speculation. Images breed instantly. I am embarrassed by my own fertility. I could describe every chair, table, luncher here copiously, freely. My mind hums hither and thither with its veil of words for everything. To speak, about wine even to the waiter, is to bring about an explosion. Up goes the rocket. Its golden grain falls, fertilizing, upon the rich soil of my imagination. The entirely unexpected nature of this explosion—that is the joy of intercourse. I, mixed with an unknown Italian waiter—what am I? There is no stability in this world. Who is to say what meaning there is in anything? Who is to foretell the flight of a word? It is a balloon that sails over tree-tops. To speak of knowledge is futile. All is experiment and adventure. We are for ever mixing ourselves with unknown quantities. What is to come? I know not. But as I put down my glass I remember: I am engaged to be married. I am to dine with my friends tonight. I am Bernard, myself.'

'It is now five minutes to eight,' said Neville. 'I have come early. I have taken my place at the table ten minutes before the time in order to taste every moment of anticipation; to see the door open and to say, "Is it Percival? No; it is not Percival." There is a morbid pleasure in saying: "No, it is not Percival". I have seen the door open and shut twenty times already; each time the suspense sharpens. This is the place to which he is coming. This is the table at which he will sit. Here, incredible as it seems, will be his actual body. This table, these chairs, this metal vase with its three red flowers are about to undergo an extraordinary transformation. Already the room, with its swing-doors, its tables heaped with fruit, with cold joints, wears the wavering, unreal appearance of a place where one waits expecting something to happen. Things quiver as if not yet in being. The blankness of the white table-cloth glares. The hostility, the indifference of other people dining here is oppressive. We look at each other; see that we do not know each other, stare, and go off. Such looks are lashes. I feel the whole cruelty and indifference of the world in them. If he should not come I could not bear it. I should go. Yet somebody must be seeing him now. He must be in some cab; he must be passing some shop. And every moment he seems to pump into this room this prickly light, this intensity of being, so that things have lost their normal uses—this knife-blade is only a flash of light, not a thing to cut with. The normal is abolished.

'The door opens, but he does not come. That is Louis hesitating there. That is his strange mixture of assurance and timidity. He looks at himself in the looking-glass as he comes in; he touches his hair; he is dissatisfied with his appearance. He says, "I am a Duke—the last of an ancient race". He is acrid, suspicious, domineering, difficult (I am comparing him with Percival). At the same time he is formidable, for there is laughter in his eyes. He has seen me. Here he is.'

'There is Susan,' said Louis. 'She does not see us. She has not dressed, because she despises the futility of London. She stands for a moment at the swing-door, looking about her like a creature dazed by the light of a lamp. Now she moves. She has the stealthy yet assured movements (even among tables and chairs) of a wild beast. She seems to find her way by instinct in and out among these little tables, touching no one, disregarding waiters, yet comes straight to our table in the corner. When she sees us (Neville, and myself) her face assumes a certainty which is alarming, as if she had what she wanted. To be loved by Susan would be to be impaled by a bird's sharp beak, to be nailed to a barnyard door. Yet there are moments when I could wish to be speared by a beak, to be nailed to a barnyard door, positively, once and for all.

'Rhoda comes now, from nowhere, having slipped in while we were not looking. She must have made a tortuous course, taking cover now behind a waiter, now behind some ornamental pillar, so as to put off as long as possible the shock of recognition, so as to be secure for one more moment to rock her petals in her basin. We wake her. We torture her. She dreads us, she despises us, yet comes cringing to our sides because for all our cruelty there is always some name, some face, which sheds a radiance, which lights up her pavements and makes it possible for her to replenish her dreams.'

'The door opens, the door goes on opening,' said Neville, 'yet he does not come.'

'There is Jinny,' said Susan. 'She stands in the door. Everything seems stayed. The waiter stops. The diners at the table by the door look. She seems to centre everything; round her tables, lines of doors, windows, ceilings, ray themselves, like rays round the star in the middle of a smashed window-pane. She brings things to a point, to order. Now she sees us, and moves, and all the rays ripple and flow and waver over us, bringing in new tides of sensation. We change. Louis puts his hand to his tie. Neville, who sits waiting with agonized intensity, nervously straightens the forks in front of him. Rhoda sees her with surprise, as if on some far horizon a fire blazed. And I, though I pile my mind with damp grass, with wet fields, with the sound of rain on the roof and the gusts of wind that batter at the house in winter and so protect my soul against her, feel her derision steal round me, feel her laughter curl its tongues of fire round me and light up unsparingly my shabby dress, my square-tipped finger-nails, which I at once hide under the table-cloth.'

'He has not come,' said Neville. 'The door opens and he does not come. That is Bernard. As he pulls off his coat he shows, of course, the blue shirt under his arm-pits. And then, unlike the rest of us, he comes in without pushing open a door, without knowing that he comes into a room full of strangers. He does not look in the glass. His hair is untidy, but he does not know it. He has no perception that we differ, or that this table is his goal. He hesitates on his way here. Who is that? he asks himself, for he half knows a woman in an opera cloak. He half knows everybody; he knows nobody (I compare him with Percival). But now, perceiving us, he waves a benevolent salute; he bears down with such benignity, with such love of mankind (crossed with humour at the futility of "loving mankind"), that, if it were not for Percival, who turns all this to vapour, one would feel, as the others already feel: Now is our festival; now we are together. But without Percival there is no solidity. We are silhouettes, hollow phantoms moving mistily without a background.'

'The swing-door goes on opening,' said Rhoda. 'Strangers keep on coming, people we shall never see again, people who brush us disagreeably with their familiarity, their indifference, and the sense of a world continuing without us. We cannot sink down, we cannot forget our faces. Even I who have no face, who make no difference when I come in (Susan and Jinny change bodies and faces), flutter unattached, without anchorage anywhere, unconsolidated, incapable of composing any blankness or continuity or wall against which these bodies move. It is because of Neville and his misery. The sharp breath of his misery scatters my being. Nothing can settle; nothing can subside. Every time the door opens he looks fixedly at the table—he dare not raise his eyes—then looks for one second and says, "He has not come". But here he is.'

'Now,' said Neville, 'my tree flowers. My heart rises. All oppression is relieved. All impediment is removed. The reign of chaos is over. He has imposed order. Knives cut again.'

'Here is Percival,' said Jinny. 'He has not dressed.'

'Here is Percival,' said Bernard, 'smoothing his hair, not from vanity (he does not look in the glass), but to propitiate the god of decency. He is conventional; he is a hero. The little boys trooped after him across the playing-fields. They blew their noses as he blew his nose, but unsuccessfully, for he is Percival. Now, when he is about to leave us, to go to India, all these trifles come together. He is a hero. Oh yes, that is not to be denied, and when he takes his seat by Susan, whom he loves, the occasion is crowned. We who yelped like jackals biting at each other's heels now assume the sober and confident air of soldiers in the presence of their captain. We who have been separated by our youth (the oldest is not yet twenty-five), who have sung like eager birds each his own song and tapped with the remorseless and savage egotism of the young our own snail-shell till it cracked (I am engaged), or perched solitary outside some bedroom window and sang of love, of fame and other single experiences so dear to the callow bird with a yellow tuft on its beak, now come nearer; and shuffling closer on our perch in this restaurant where everybody's interests are at variance, and the incessant passage of traffic chafes us with distractions, and the door opening perpetually its glass cage solicits us with myriad temptations and offers insults and wounds to our confidence—sitting together here we love each other and believe in our own endurance.'

'Now let us issue from the darkness of solitude,' said Louis.

'Now let us say, brutally and directly, what is in our minds,' said Neville. 'Our isolation, our preparation, is over. The furtive days of secrecy and hiding, the revelations on staircases, moments of terror and ecstasy.'

'Old Mrs Constable lifted her sponge and warmth poured over us,' said Bernard. 'We became clothed in this changing, this feeling garment of flesh.'

'The boot-boy made love to the scullery-maid in the kitchen garden,' said Susan, 'among the blown-out washing.'

'The breath of the wind was like a tiger panting,' said Rhoda.

'The man lay livid with his throat cut in the gutter,' said Neville. 'And going upstairs I could not raise my foot against the immitigable apple tree with its silver leaves held stiff.'

'The leaf danced in the hedge without anyone to blow it,' said Jinny.

'In the sun-baked corner,' said Louis, 'the petals swam on depths of green.'

'At Elvedon the gardeners swept and swept with their great brooms, and the woman sat at a table writing,' said Bernard.

'From these close-furled balls of string we draw now every filament,' said Louis, 'remembering, when we meet.'

'And then,' said Bernard, 'the cab came to the door, and, pressing our new bowler hats tightly over our eyes to hide our unmanly tears, we drove through streets in which even the housemaids looked at us, and our names painted in white letters on our boxes proclaimed to all the world that we were going to school with the regulation number of socks and drawers, on which our mothers for some nights previously had stitched our initials, in our boxes. A second severance from the body of our mother.'

'And Miss Lambert, Miss Cutting and Miss Bard,' said Jinny, 'monumental ladies, white-ruffed, stone-coloured, enigmatic, with amethyst rings moving like virginal tapers, dim glow-worms over the pages of French, geography and arithmetic, presided; and there were maps, green-baize boards, and rows of shoes on a shelf.'

'Bells rang punctually,' said Susan, 'maids scuffled and giggled. There was a drawing in of chairs and a drawing out of chairs on the linoleum. But from one attic there was a blue view, a distant view of a field unstained by the corruption of this regimented, unreal existence.'

'Down from our heads veils fell,' said Rhoda. 'We clasped the flowers with their green leaves rustling in garlands.'

'We changed, we became unrecognizable,' said Louis. 'Exposed to all these different lights, what we had in us (for we are all so different) came intermittently, in violent patches, spaced by blank voids, to the surface as if some acid had dropped unequally on the plate. I was this, Neville that, Rhoda different again, and Bernard too.'

'Then canoes slipped through palely tinted yellow branches,' said Neville, 'and Bernard, advancing in his casual way against breadths of green, against houses of very ancient foundation, tumbled in a heap on the ground beside me. In an access of emotion—winds are not more raving, nor lightning more sudden—I took my poem, I flung my poem, I slammed the door behind me.'

'I, however,' said Louis, 'losing sight of you, sat in my office and tore the date from the calendar, and announced to the world of ship-brokers, corn-chandlers and actuaries that Friday the tenth, or Tuesday the eighteenth, had dawned on the city of London.'

'Then,' said Jinny, 'Rhoda and I, exposed in bright dresses, with a few precious stones nestling on a cold ring round our throats, bowed, shook hands and took a sandwich from a plate with a smile.'

'The tiger leapt, and the swallow dipped her wings in dark pools on the other side of the world,' said Rhoda.

'But here and now we are together,' said Bernard. 'We have come together, at a particular time, to this particular spot. We are drawn into this communion by some deep, some common emotion. Shall we call it, conveniently, "love"? Shall we say "love of Percival" because Percival is going to India?

'No, that is too small, too particular a name. We cannot attach the width and spread of our feelings to so small a mark. We have come together (from the North, from the South, from Susan's farm, from Louis's house of business) to make one thing, not enduring—for what endures?—but seen by many eyes simultaneously. There is a red carnation in that vase. A single flower as we sat here waiting, but now a seven-sided flower,* many-petalled, red, puce, purple-shaded, stiff with silver-tinted leaves—a whole flower to which every eye brings its own contribution.'

'After the capricious fires, the abysmal dullness of youth,' said Neville, 'the light falls upon real objects now. Here are knives and forks. The world is displayed, and we too, so that we can talk.'

'We differ, it may be too profoundly,' said Louis, 'for explanation. But let us attempt it. I smoothed my hair when I came in, hoping to look like the rest of you. But I cannot, for I am not single and entire as you are. I have lived a thousand lives already. Every day I unbury—I dig up. I find relics of myself in the sand that women made thousands of years ago, when I heard songs by the Nile and the chained beast stamping. What you see beside you, this man, this Louis, is only the cinders and refuse of something once splendid. I was an Arab prince; behold my free gestures. I was a great poet in the time of Elizabeth. I was a Duke at the court of Louis the Fourteenth. I am very vain, very confident; I have an immeasurable desire that women should sigh in sympathy. I have eaten no lunch today in order that Susan may think me cadaverous and that Jinny may extend to me the exquisite balm of her sympathy. But while I admire Susan and Percival, I hate the others, because it is for them that I do these antics, smoothing my hair, concealing my accent. I am the little ape who chatters over a nut, and you are the dowdy women with shiny bags of stale buns; I am also the caged tiger, and you are the keepers with red-hot bars. That is, I am fiercer and stronger than you are, yet the apparition that appears above ground after ages of non-entity will be spent in terror lest you should laugh at me, in veerings with the wind against the soot storms, in efforts to make a steel ring of clear poetry that shall connect the gulls and the women with bad teeth, the church spire and the bobbing billycock hats as I see them when I take my luncheon and prop my poet—is it Lucretius?—against a cruet and the gravy-splashed bill of fare.'

'But you will never hate me,' said Jinny. 'You will never see me, even across a room full of gilt chairs and ambassadors, without coming to me across the room to seek my sympathy. When I came in just now everything stood still in a pattern. Waiters stopped, diners raised their forks and held them. I had the air of being prepared for what would happen. When I sat down you put your hands to your ties, you hid them under the table. But I hide nothing. I am prepared. Every time the door opens I cry "More!" But my imagination is the bodies. I can imagine nothing beyond the circle cast by my body. My body goes before me, like a lantern down a dark lane, bringing one thing after another out of darkness into a ring of light. I dazzle you; I make you believe that this is all.'

'But when you stand in the door,' said Neville, 'you inflict stillness, demanding admiration, and that is a great impediment to the freedom of intercourse. You stand in the door making us notice you. But none of you saw me approach. I came early; I came quickly and directly, *here*, to sit by the person whom I love. My life has a rapidity that yours lack. I am like a hound on the scent. I hunt from dawn to dusk. Nothing, not the pursuit of perfection through the sand, nor fame, nor money, has meaning for me. I shall have riches; I shall have fame. But I shall never have what I want, for I lack bodily grace and the courage that comes with it. The swiftness of my mind is too strong for my body. I fail before I reach the end and fall in a heap, damp, perhaps disgusting. I excite pity in the crises of life, not love. Therefore I suffer horribly. But I do not suffer, as Louis does, to make myself a spectacle. I have too fine a sense of fact to allow myself these juggleries, these pretences. I see everything—except one thing—with complete clarity. That is my saving. That is what gives my suffering an unceasing excitement. That is what makes me dictate, even when I am silent. And since I am, in one respect, deluded, since the person is always changing, though not the desire, and I do not know in the morning by whom I shall sit at night, I am never stagnant; I rise from my worst disasters, I turn, I change. Pebbles bounce off the mail of my muscular, my extended body. In this pursuit I shall grow old.'

'If I could believe,' said Rhoda, 'that I should grow old in pursuit and change, I should be rid of my fear: nothing persists. One moment does not lead to another. The door opens and the tiger leaps. You did not see me come. I circled round the chairs to avoid the horror of the spring. I am afraid of you all. I am afraid of the shock of sensation that leaps upon me, because I cannot deal with it as you do—I cannot make one moment merge in the next. To me they are all violent, all separate; and if I fall under the shock of the leap of the moment you will be on me, tearing me to pieces. I have no end in view. I do not know how to run minute to minute and hour to hour, solving them by some natural force until they make the whole and indivisible mass that you call life. Because you have an end in view—one person, is it, to sit beside, an idea is it, your beauty is it? I do not know—your days and hours pass like the boughs of forest trees and the smooth green of forest rides to a hound running on the scent. But there is no single scent, no single body for me to follow. And I have no face. I am like the foam that races over the beach or the moonlight that falls arrowlike here on a tin can, here on a spike of the mailed sea-holly, or a bone or a half-eaten boat. I am whirled down caverns, and flap like paper against endless corridors, and must press my hand against the wall to draw myself back.

'But since I wish above all things to have lodgement, I pretend, as I go upstairs lagging behind Jinny and Susan, to have an end in view. I pull on my stockings as I see them pull on theirs. I wait for you to speak and then speak like you. I am drawn here across London to a particular spot, to a particular place, not to see you or you or you, but to light my fire at the general blaze of you who live wholly, indivisibly and without caring.'

'When I came into the room tonight,' said Susan, 'I stopped, I peered about like an animal with its eyes near to the ground. The smell of carpets and furniture and scent disgusts me. I like to walk through the wet fields alone, or to stop at a gate and watch my setter nose in a circle, and to ask: Where is the hare? I like to be with people who twist herbs, and spit into the fire, and shuffle down long passages in slippers like my father. The only sayings I understand are cries of love, hate, rage and pain. This talking is undressing an old woman whose dress had seemed to be part of her, but now, as we talk, she turns pinkish underneath, and has wrinkled thighs and sagging breasts. When you are silent you are again beautiful. I shall never have anything but natural happiness. It will almost content me. I shall go to bed tired. I shall lie like a field bearing crops in rotation; in the summer heat will dance over me; in the winter I shall be cracked with the cold. But heat and cold will follow each other naturally without my willing or unwilling. My children will carry me on; their teething, their crying, their going to school and coming back will be like the waves of the sea under me. No day will be without its movement. I shall be lifted higher than any of you on the backs of the seasons. I shall possess more than Jinny, more than Rhoda, by the time I die. But on the other hand, where you are various and dimple a million times to the ideas and laughter of others, I shall be sullen, storm-tinted and all one purple. I shall be debased and hide-bound by the bestial and beautiful passion of maternity. I shall push the fortunes of my children unscrupulously. I shall hate those who see their faults. I shall lie basely to help them. I shall let them wall me away from you, from you and from you. Also, I am torn with jealousy. I hate Jinny because she shows me that my hands are red, my nails bitten. I love with such ferocity that it kills me when the object of my love shows by a phrase that he can escape. He escapes, and I am left clutching at a string that slips in and out among the leaves on the tree-tops. I do not understand phrases.'

'Had I been born,' said Bernard, 'not knowing that one word follows another I might have been, who knows, perhaps anything. As it is, finding sequences everywhere, I cannot bear the pressure of solitude. When I cannot see words curling like rings of smoke round me I am in darkness—I am nothing. When I am alone I fall into lethargy, and say to myself dismally as I poke the cinders through the bars of the grate, Mrs Moffat will come. She will come and sweep it all up. When Louis is alone he sees with astonishing intensity, and will write some words that may outlast us all. Rhoda loves to be alone. She fears us because we shatter the sense of being which is so extreme in solitude—see how she grasps her fork—her weapon against us. But I only come into existence when the plumber, or the horse-dealer, or whoever it may be, says something which sets me alight. Then how lovely the smoke of my phrase is, rising and falling, flaunting and falling, upon red lobsters and yellow fruit, wreathing them into one beauty. But observe how meretricious the phrase is—made up of what evasions and old lies. Thus my character is in part made of the stimulus which other people provide, and is not mine, as yours are. There is some fatal streak, some wandering and irregular vein of silver, weakening it. Hence the fact that used to enrage Neville at school, that I left him. I went with the boasting boys with little caps and badges, driving off in big brakes— there are some here tonight, dining together, correctly dressed, before they go off in perfect concord to the music hall; I loved them. For they bring me into existence as certainly as you do. Hence, too, when I am leaving you and the train is going, you feel that it is not the train that is going, but I, Bernard, who does not care, who does not feel, who has no ticket, and has lost perhaps his purse. Susan, staring at the string that slips in and out among the leaves of the beech trees, cries: "He is gone! He has escaped me!" For there is nothing to lay hold of. I am made and remade continually. Different people draw different words from me.

'Thus there is not one person but fifty people whom I

want to sit beside tonight. But I am the only one of you who is at home here without taking liberties. I am not gross; I am not a snob. If I lie open to the pressure of society I often succeed with the dexterity of my tongue in putting something difficult into the currency. See my little toys, twisted out of nothing in a second, how they entertain. I am no hoarder—I shall leave only a cupboard of old clothes when I die—and I am almost indifferent to the minor vanities of life which cause Louis so much torture. But I have sacrificed much. Veined as I am with iron, with silver and streaks of common mud, I cannot contract into the firm fist which those clench who do not depend upon stimulus. I am incapable of the denials, the heroisms of Louis and Rhoda. I shall never succeed, even in talk, in making a perfect phrase. But I shall have contributed more to the passing moment than any of you; I shall go into more rooms, more different rooms, than any of you. But because there is something that comes from outside and not from within I shall be forgotten; when my voice is silent you will not remember me, save as the echo of a voice that once wreathed the fruit into phrases.'

'Look,' said Rhoda; 'listen. Look how the light becomes richer, second by second, and bloom and ripeness lie everywhere; and our eyes, as they range round this room with all its tables, seem to push through curtains of colour, red, orange, umber and queer ambiguous tints, which yield like veils and close behind them, and one thing melts into another.'

'Yes,' said Jinny, 'our senses have widened. Membranes, webs of nerve that lay white and limp, have filled and spread themselves and float round us like filaments, making the air tangible and catching in them far-away sounds unheard before.'

'The roar of London,' said Louis, 'is round us. Motor-cars, vans, omnibuses pass and repass continuously. All are merged in one turning wheel of single sound. All separate sounds—wheels, bells, the cries of drunkards, of merry-makers—are churned into one sound, steel blue, circular. Then a siren hoots. At that shores slip away, chimneys flatten themselves, the ship makes for the open sea.'

'Percival is going,' said Neville. 'We sit here, surrounded, lit up, many-coloured; all things—hands, curtains, knives and forks, other people dining—run into each other. We are walled in here. But India lies outside.'

'I see India,' said Bernard. 'I see the low, long shore; I see the tortuous lanes of stamped mud that lead in and out among ramshackle pagodas; I see the gilt and crenellated buildings which have an air of fragility and decay as if they were temporarily run up buildings in some Oriental exhibi-tion. I see a pair of bullocks who drag a low cart along the sun-baked road. The cart sways incompetently from side to side. Now one wheel sticks in the rut, and at once innumerable natives in loin-cloths swarm round it, chatter-ing excitely. But they do nothing. Time seems endless, ambition vain. Over all broods a sense of the uselessness of human exertion. There are strange sour smells. An old man in a ditch continues to chew betel and to contemplate his navel. But now, behold, Percival advances; Percival rides a flea-bitten mare, and wears a sun helmet. By applying the standards of the West, by using the violent language that is natural to him, the bullock-cart is righted in less than five minutes. The Oriental problem is solved.* He rides on; the multitude cluster round him, regarding him as if he were—what indeed he is—a God.'

'Unknown, with or without a secret, it does not matter,' said Rhoda, 'he is like a stone fallen into a pond round which minnows swarm. Like minnows, we who had been shooting this way, that way, all shot round him when he came. Like minnows, conscious of the presence of a great stone, we undulate and eddy contentedly. Comfort steals over us. Gold runs in our blood. One, two; one, two; the heart beats in serenity, in confidence, in some trance of well-being, in some rapture of benignity; and look—the outermost parts of the earth—pale shadows on the utmost horizon, India for instance, rise into our purview. The world that had been shrivelled, rounds itself; remote provinces are fetched up out of darkness; we see muddy roads, twisted jungle, swarms of men, and the vulture that feeds on some bloated carcass as within our scope, part of our proud and splendid province, since Percival, riding alone on a flea-bitten mare, advances down a solitary path, has his camp pitched among desolate trees, and sits alone, looking at the enormous mountains.'

'It is Percival,' said Louis, 'sitting silent as he sat among the tickling grasses when the breeze parted the clouds and they formed again, who makes us aware that these attempts to say, "I am this, I am that", which we make, coming together, like separated parts of one body and soul, are false. Something has been left out from fear. Something has been altered, from vanity. We have tried to accentuate differences. From the desire to be separate we have laid stress upon our faults, and what is particular to us. But there is a chain whirling round, round, in a steel-blue circle beneath.'

'It is hate, it is love,' said Susan. 'That is the furious coal-black stream that makes us dizzy if we look down into it. We stand on a ledge here, but if we look down we turn giddy.'

'It is love,' said Jinny, 'it is hate, such as Susan feels for me because I kissed Louis once in the garden; because equipped as I am, I make her think when I come in, "My hands are red", and hide them. But our hatred is almost indistinguishable from our love.'

'Yet these roaring waters,' said Neville, 'upon which we build our crazy platforms are more stable than the wild, the weak and inconsequent cries that we utter when, trying to speak, we rise; when we reason and jerk out these false sayings, "I am this; I am that!" Speech is false.

'But I eat. I gradually lose all knowledge of particulars as I eat. I am becoming weighed down with food. These delicious mouthfuls of roast duck, fitly piled with vegetables, following each other in exquisite rotation of warmth, weight, sweet and bitter, past my palate, down my gullet, into my stomach, have stabilized my body. I feel quiet, gravity, control. All is solid now. Instinctively my palate now requires and anticipates sweetness and lightness, something sugared and evanescent; and cool wine, fitting glove-like over those finer nerves that seem to tremble from the roof of my mouth and make it spread (as I drink) into a domed cavern, green with vine leaves, musk-scented, purple with grapes. Now I can look steadily into the mill-race that foams beneath. By what particular name are we to call it? Let Rhoda speak, whose face I see reflected mistily in the looking-glass opposite; Rhoda whom I interrupted when she rocked her petals in a brown basin, asking for the pocket-knife that Bernard had stolen. Love is not a whirlpool to her. She is not giddy when she looks down. She looks far away over our heads, beyond India.'

'Yes, between your shoulders, over your heads, to a landscape,' said Rhoda, 'to a hollow where the many-backed steep hills come down like birds' wings folded. There, on the short, firm turf, are bushes, dark leaved, and against their darkness I see a shape, white, but not of stone, moving, perhaps alive. But it is not you, it is not you, it is not you; not Percival, Susan, Jinny, Neville or Louis. When the white arm rests upon the knee it is a triangle; now it is upright—a column; now a fountain, falling. It makes no sign, it does not beckon, it does not see us. Behind it roars the sea. It is beyond our reach. Yet there I venture. There I go to replenish my emptiness, to stretch my nights and fill them fuller and fuller with dreams. And for a second even now, even here, I reach my object and say, "Wander no more. All else is trial and make-believe. Here is the end." But these pilgrimages, these moments of departure, start always in your presence, from this table, these lights, from Percival and Susan, here and now. Always I see the grove over your heads, between your shoulders, or from a window when I have crossed the room at a party and stand looking down into the street.'

'But his slippers?' said Neville. 'And his voice downstairs in the hall? And catching sight of him when he does not see one? One waits and he does not come. It gets later and later. He has forgotten. He is with someone else. He is faithless, his love meant nothing. Oh, then the agony— then the intolerable despair! And then the door opens. He is here.'

'Rippling gold, I say to him, "Come",' said Jinny. 'And he comes; he crosses the room to where I sit, with my dress like a veil billowing round me on the gilt chair. Our hands touch, our bodies burst into fire. The chair, the cup, the table—nothing remains unlit. All quivers, all kindles, all burns clear.'

('Look, Rhoda,' said Louis, 'they have become nocturnal, rapt. Their eyes are like moths' wings moving so quickly that they do not seem to move at all.'

'Horns and trumpets,' said Rhoda, 'ring out. Leaves unfold; the stags blare in the thicket. There is a dancing and a drumming, like the dancing and the drumming of naked men with assagais.'

'Like the dance of savages,' said Louis, 'round the camp-fire. They are savage; they are ruthless. They dance in a circle, flapping bladders. The flames leap over their painted faces, over the leopard skins and the bleeding limbs which they have torn from the living body.'

'The flames of the festival rise high,' said Rhoda. 'The great procession passes, flinging green boughs and flowering branches. Their horns spill blue smoke; their skins are dappled red and yellow in the torchlight. They throw violets. They deck the beloved with garlands and with laurel leaves, there on the ring of turf where the steep-backed hills come down. The procession passes.* And while it passes, Louis, we are aware of downfalling, we forebode decay. The shadow slants. We who are conspira-tors, withdrawn together to lean over some cold urn, note how the purple flame flows downwards.'

'Death is woven in with the violets,' said Louis. 'Death and again death.')

'How proudly we sit here,' said Jinny, 'we who are not yet twenty-five! Outside the trees flower; outside the women linger; outside the cabs swerve and sweep. Emerged from the tentative ways, the obscurities and dazzle of youth, we look straight in front of us, ready for what may come (the door opens, the door keeps on opening). All is real; all is firm without shadow or illusion. Beauty rides our brows. There is mine, there is Susan's. Our flesh is firm and cool. Our differences are clear-cut as the shadows of rocks in full sunlight. Beside us lie crisp rolls, yellow-glazed and hard; the table-cloth is white; and our hands lie half curled, ready to contract. Days and days are to come; winter days, summer days; we have scarcely broken into our hoard. Now the fruit is swollen beneath the leaf. The room is golden, and I say to him, "Come".'

'He has red ears,' said Louis, 'and the smell of meat hangs down in a damp net while the city clerks take snacks at the lunch bar.'

'With infinite time before us,' said Neville, 'we ask what shall we do? Shall we loiter down Bond Street, looking here and there, and buying perhaps a fountain-pen because it is green, or asking how much is the ring with the blue stone? Or shall we sit indoors and watch the coals turn crimson? Shall we stretch our hands for books and read here a passage and there a passage? Shall we shout with laughter for no reason? Shall we push through flowering meadows and make daisy chains? Shall we find out when the next train starts for the Hebrides and engage a reserved compartment? All is to come.'

'For you,' said Bernard, 'but yesterday I walked bang into a pillar-box. Yesterday I became engaged.'

'How strange,' said Susan, 'the little heaps of sugar look by the side of our plates. Also the mottled peelings of pears, and the plush rims to the looking-glasses. I had not seen them before. Everything is now set; everything is fixed. Bernard is engaged. Something irrevocable has happened. A circle has been cast on the waters; a chain is imposed. We shall never flow freely again.'

'For one moment only,' said Louis. 'Before the chain breaks, before disorder returns, see us fixed, see us displayed, see us held in a vice.

'But now the circle breaks. Now the current flows. Now we rush faster than before. Now passions that lay in wait down there in the dark weeds which grow at the bottom rise and pound us with their waves. Pain and jealousy, envy and desire, and something deeper than they are, stronger than love and more subterranean. The voice of action speaks. Listen, Rhoda (for we are conspirators, with our hands on the cold urn), to the casual, quick, exciting voice of action, of hounds running on the scent. They speak now without troubling to finish their sentences. They talk a little language such as lovers use. An imperious brute possesses them. The nerves thrill in their thighs. Their hearts pound and churn in their sides. Susan screws her pocket-handkerchief. Jinny's eyes dance with fire.'

'They are immune,' said Rhoda, 'from picking fingers and searching eyes. How easily they turn and glance; what poses they take of energy and pride! What life shines in Jinny's eyes; how fell, how entire Susan's glance is, searching for insects at the roots! Their hair shines lustrous. Their eyes burn like the eyes of animals brushing through leaves on the scent of the prey. The circle is destroyed. We are thrown asunder.'

'But soon, too soon,' said Bernard, 'this egotistic exultation fails. Too soon the moment of ravenous identity is over, and the appetite for happiness, and happiness, and still more happiness is glutted. The stone is sunk; the moment is over. Round me there spreads a wide margin of indifference. Now open in my eyes a thousand eyes of curiosity. Anyone now is at liberty to murder Bernard, who is engaged to be married, so long as they leave untouched this margin of unknown territory, this forest of the unknown world. Why, I ask (whispering discreetly), do women dine alone together there? Who are they? And what has brought them on this particular evening to this particular spot? The youth in the corner, judging from the nervous way in which he puts his hand from time to time to the back of his head, is from the country. He is suppliant, and so anxious to respond suitably to the kindness of his father's friend, his host, that he can scarcely enjoy now what he will enjoy very much at about half-past eleven tomorrow morning. I have also seen that lady powder her nose three times in the midst of an absorbing conversation—about love perhaps, about the unhappiness of their dearest friend perhaps. "Ah, but the state of my nose!" she thinks, and out comes her powder-puff, obliterating in its passage all the most fervent feelings of the human heart. There remains, however, the insoluble problem of the solitary man with the eyeglass; of the elderly lady drinking champagne alone. Who and what are these unknown people? I ask. I could make a dozen stories of what he said, of what she said—I can see a dozen pictures. But what are stories? Toys I twist, bubbles I blow, one ring passing through another. And sometimes I begin to doubt if there are stories. What is my story? What is Rhoda's? What is Neville's? There are facts, as, for example: "The handsome young man in the grey suit, whose reserve contrasted so strangely with the loquacity of the others, now brushed the crumbs from his waistcoat and, with a characteristic gesture at once commanding and benign, made a sign to the waiter, who came instantly and returned a moment later with the bill discreetly folded upon a plate". That is the truth; that is the fact, but beyond it all is darkness and conjecture.'

'Now once more,' said Louis, 'as we are about to part, having paid our bill, the circle in our blood, broken so often, so sharply, for we are so different, closes in a ring. Something is made. Yes, as we rise and fidget, a little nervously, we pray, holding in our hands this common feeling, "Do not move, do not let the swing-door cut to pieces the thing that we have made, that globes itself here, among these lights, these peelings, this litter of bread-crumbs and people passing. Do not move, do not go. Hold it for ever."'

'Let us hold it for one moment,' said Jinny; 'love, hatred, by whatever name we call it, this globe whose walls are made of Percival, of youth and beauty, and something so deep sunk within us that we shall perhaps never make this moment out of one man again.'

'Forests and far countries on the other side of the world,' said Rhoda, 'are in it; seas and jungles; the howlings of jackals and moonlight falling upon some high peak where the eagle soars.'

'Happiness is in it,' said Neville, 'and the quiet of ordinary things. A table, a chair, a book with a paper-knife stuck between the pages. And the petal falling from the rose, and the light flickering as we sit silent, or, perhaps, bethinking us of some trifle, suddenly speak.'

'Week-days are in it,' said Susan, 'Monday, Tuesday, Wednesday; the horses going up to the fields, and the horses returning; the rooks rising and falling, and catching the elm-trees in their net, whether it is April, whether it is November.'

'What is to come is in it,' said Bernard. 'That is the last drop and the brightest that we let fall like some supernal quicksilver into the swelling and splendid moment created by us from Percival. What is to come? I ask, brushing the crumbs from my waistcoat, what is outside? We have proved, sitting eating, sitting talking, that we can add to the treasury of moments. We are not slaves bound to suffer incessantly unrecorded petty blows on our bent backs. We are not sheep either, following a master. We are creators. We too have made something that will join the innumerable

THE WAVES

congregations of past time. We too, as we put on our hats
and push open the door, stride not into chaos, but into a
world that our own force can subjugate and make part of
the illumined and everlasting road.

'Look, Percival, while they fetch the taxi, at the prospect
which you are so soon to lose. The street is hard and
burnished with the churning of innumerable wheels. The
yellow canopy of our tremendous energy hangs like a
burning cloth above our heads. Theatres, music halls and
lamps in private houses make that light.'

'Peaked clouds,' said Rhoda, 'voyage over a sky dark
like polished whalebone.'

'Now the agony begins; now the horror has seized me
with its fangs,' said Neville. 'Now the cab comes; now
Percival goes. What can we do to keep him? How bridge
the distance between us? How fan the fire so that it blazes
for ever? How signal to all time to come that we, who
stand in the street, in the lamplight, loved Percival? Now
Percival is gone.'

The sun had risen to its full height. It was no longer half seen and guessed at, from hints and gleams, as if a girl couched on her green-sea mattress tired her brows with water-globed jewels that sent lances of opal-tinted light falling and flashing in the uncertain air like the flanks of a dolphin leaping, or the flash of a falling blade. Now the sun burnt uncompromising, undeniable. It struck upon the hard sand, and the rocks became furnaces of red heat; it searched each pool and caught the minnow hiding in the cranny, and showed the rusty cartwheel, the white bone, or the boot without laces stuck, black as iron, in the sand. It gave to everything its exact measure of colour; to the sandhills their innumerable glitter, to the wild grasses their glancing green; or it fell upon the arid waste of the desert, here wind-scourged into furrows, here swept into desolate cairns, here sprinkled with stunted dark-green jungle trees. It lit up the smooth gilt mosque, the frail pink-and-white card houses of the southern village, and the long-breasted, white-haired women who knelt in the river bed beating wrinkled cloths upon stones. Steamers thudding slowly over the sea were caught in the level stare of the sun, and it beat through the yellow awnings upon passengers who dozed or paced the deck, shading their eyes to look for the land, while day after day, compressed in its oily throbbing sides, the ship bore them on monotonously over the waters.

The sun beat on the crowded pinnacles of southern hills and glared into deep, stony river beds where the water was

*shrunk beneath the high slung bridge so that washerwomen
kneeling on hot stones could scarcely wet their linen; and
lean mules went picking their way among the chattering
grey stones with panniers slung across their narrow shoulders. At midday the heat of the sun made the hills grey as
if shaved and singed in an explosion, while, further north,
in cloudier and rainier countries hills smoothed into slabs as
with the back of a spade had a light in them as if a warder,
deep within, went from chamber to chamber carrying a
green lamp. Through atoms of grey-blue air the sun struck
at English fields and lit up marshes and pools, a white gull
on a stake, the slow sail of shadows over blunt-headed
woods and young corn and flowing hayfields. It beat on the
orchard wall, and every pit and grain of the brick was
silver pointed, purple, fiery as if soft to touch, as if touched
it must melt into hot-baked grains of dust. The currants
hung against the wall in ripples and cascades of polished
red; plums swelled out their leaves, and all the blades of
the grass were run together in one fluent green blaze. The
trees' shadow was sunk to a dark pool at the root. Light
descending in floods dissolved the separate foliation into one
green mound.*

*The birds sang passionate songs addressed to one ear only
and then stopped. Bubbling and chuckling they carried little
bits of straw and twig to the dark knots in the higher
branches of the trees. Gilt and purpled they perched in the
garden where cones of laburnum and purple shook down
gold and lilac, for now at midday the garden was all
blossom and profusion and even the tunnels under the
plants were green and purple and tawny as the sun beat
through the red petal, or the broad yellow petal, or was
barred by some thickly furred green stalk.*

The sun struck straight upon the house, making the white

*walls glare between the dark windows. Their panes, woven
thickly with green branches, held circles of impenetrable
darkness. Sharp-edged wedges of light lay upon the
window-sill and showed inside the room plates with blue
rings, cups with curved handles, the bulge of a great bowl,
the criss-cross pattern in the rug, and the formidable corners
and lines of cabinets and bookcases. Behind their conglom-
eration hung a zone of shadow in which might be a further
shape to be disencumbered of shadow or still denser depths
of darkness.*

*The waves broke and spread their waters swiftly over the
shore. One after another they massed themselves and fell;
the spray tossed itself back with the energy of their fall. The
waves were steeped deep-blue save for a pattern of dia-
mond-pointed light on their backs which rippled as the
backs of great horses ripple with muscles as they move. The
waves fell; withdrew and fell again, like the thud of a great
beast stamping.*

THE WAVES

'HE is dead,' said Neville. 'He fell. His horse tripped. He was thrown. The sails of the world have swung round and caught me on the head. All is over. The lights of the world have gone out. There stands the tree which I cannot pass.

'Oh, to crumple this telegram in my fingers—to let the light of the world flood back—to say this has not happened! But why turn one's head hither and thither? This is the truth. This is the fact. His horse stumbled; he was thrown. The flashing trees and white rails went up in a shower. There was a surge; a drumming in his ears. Then the blow; the world crashed; he breathed heavily. He died where he fell.*

'Barns and summer days in the country, rooms where we sat—all now lie in the unreal world which is gone. My past is cut from me. They came running. They carried him to some pavilion, men in riding-boots, men in sun helmets; among unknown men he died. Loneliness and silence often surrounded him. He often left me. And then, returning, "See where he comes!" I said.

'Women shuffle past the window as if there were no gulf cut in the street; no tree with stiff leaves which we cannot pass. We deserve then to be tripped by molehills. We are infinitely abject, shuffling past with our eyes shut. But why should I submit? Why try to lift my foot and mount the stair? This is where I stand; here, holding the telegram. The past, summer days and rooms where we sat, stream away like burnt paper with red eyes in it. Why meet and resume? Why talk and eat and make up other combinations with other people? From this moment I am solitary. No one will know me now. I have three letters, "I am about to play quoits with a colonel, so no more", thus he ends our friendship, shouldering his way through the crowd with a wave of his hand. This farce is worth no more formal celebration. Yet if someone had but said: "Wait"; had pulled the strap three holes tighter—he would have done justice for fifty years, and sat in Court and ridden alone at the head of troops and denounced some monstrous tyranny, and come back to us.

'Now I say there is a grinning, there is a subterfuge. There is something sneering behind our backs. That boy almost lost his footing as he leapt on the bus. Percival fell; was killed; is buried; and I watch people passing; holding tight to the rails of omnibuses; determined to save their lives.

'I will not lift my foot to climb the stair. I will stand for one moment beneath the immitigable tree, alone with the man whose throat is cut, while downstairs the cook shoves in and out the dampers. I will not climb the stair. We are doomed, all of us. Women shuffle past with shopping-bags. People keep on passing. Yet you shall not destroy me. For this moment, this one moment, we are together. I press you to me. Come, pain, feed on me. Bury your fangs in my flesh. Tear me asunder. I sob, I sob.'

'Such is the incomprehensible combination,' said Bernard, 'such is the complexity of things, that as I descend the staircase I do not know which is sorrow, which joy. My son is born; Percival is dead. I am upheld by pillars, shored up on either side by stark emotions; but which is sorrow, which is joy? I ask, and do not know, only that I need silence, and to be alone and to go out, and to save one hour to consider what has happened to my world, what death has done to my world.

'This then is the world that Percival sees no longer. Let me look. The butcher delivers meat next door; two old men stumble along the pavement; sparrows alight. The machine then works; I note the rhythm, the throb, but as a thing in which I have no part, since he sees it no longer. (He lies pale and bandaged in some room.) Now then is my chance to find out what is of great importance, and I must be careful, and tell no lies. About him my feeling was: he sat there in the centre. Now I go to that spot no longer. The place is empty.

'Oh yes, I can assure you, men in felt hats and women carrying baskets—you have lost something that would have been very valuable to you. You have lost a leader whom you would have followed; and one of you has lost happiness and children. He is dead who would have given you that. He lies on a camp-bed, bandaged, in some hot Indian hospital while coolies squatted on the floor agitate those fans—I forget how they call them. But this is important; "You are well out of it", I said, while the doves descended over the roofs and my son was born, as if it were a fact. I remember, as a boy, his curious air of detachment. And I go on to say (my eyes fill with tears and then are dry), "But this is better than one had dared to hope". I say, addressing what is abstract, facing me eyeless at the end of the avenue, in the sky, "Is this the utmost you can do?" Then we have triumphed. You have done your utmost, I say, addressing that blank and brutal face (for he was twenty-five and should have lived to be eighty) without avail. I am not going to lie down and weep away a life of care. (An entry to be made in my pocket-book; contempt for those who inflict meaningless death.) Further, this is important; that I should be able to place him in trifling and ridiculous situations, so that he may not feel himself absurd, perched on a great horse. I must be able to say, "Percival, a ridiculous name". At the same time let me tell you, men and women, hurrying to the tube station, you would have had to respect him. You would have had to form up and follow behind him. How strange to oar one's way through crowds seeing life through hollow eyes, burning eyes.

'Yet already signals begin, beckonings, attempts to lure me back. Curiosity is knocked out for only a short time. One cannot live outside the machine for more perhaps than half an hour. Bodies, I note, already begin to look ordinary; but what is behind them differs—the perspective. Behind that newspaper placard is the hospital; the long room with black men pulling ropes; and then they bury him. Yet since it says a famous actress has been divorced, I ask instantly, Which? Yet I cannot take out my penny; I cannot buy a paper; I cannot suffer interruption yet.

'I ask, if I shall never see you again and fix my eyes on that solidity, what form will our communication take? You have gone across the court, further and further, drawing finer and finer the thread between us. But you exist somewhere. Something of you remains. A judge. That is, if I discover a new vein in myself I shall submit it to you privately. I shall ask, What is your verdict? You shall remain the arbiter. But for how long? Things will become too difficult to explain: there will be new things; already my son. I am now at the zenith of an experience. It will decline. Already I no longer cry with conviction, "What luck!" Exaltation, the flight of doves descending, is over. Chaos, detail return. I am no longer amazed by names written over shop-windows. I do not feel Why hurry?

Why catch trains? The sequence returns; one thing leads to another—the usual order.

'Yes, but I still resent the usual order. I will not let myself be made yet to accept the sequence of things. I will walk; I will not change the rhythm of my mind by stopping, by looking; I will walk. I will go up these steps into the gallery and submit myself to the influence of minds like mine outside the sequence. There is little time left to answer the question; my powers flag; I become torpid. Here are pictures. Here are cold madonnas among their pillars. Let them lay to rest the incessant activity of the mind's eye, the bandaged head, the men with ropes, so that I may find something unvisual beneath. Here are gardens; and Venus among her flowers; here are saints and blue madonnas. Mercifully these pictures make no reference;* they do not nudge; they do not point. Thus they expand my consciousness of him and bring him back to me differently. I remember his beauty. "Look, where he comes", I said.

'Lines and colours almost persuade me that I too can be heroic, I, who make phrases so easily, am so soon seduced, love what comes next, and cannot clench my fist, but vacillate weakly making phrases according to my circumstances. Now, through my own infirmity I recover what he was to me: my opposite. Being naturally truthful, he did not see the point of these exaggerations, and was borne on by a natural sense of the fitting, was indeed a great master of the art of living so that he seems to have lived long, and to have spread calm round him, indifference one might almost say, certainly to his own advancement, save that he had also great compassion. A child playing—a summer evening—doors will open and shut, will keep opening and shutting, through which I see sights that make me weep. For they cannot be imparted. Hence our loneliness; hence our desolation. I turn to that spot in my mind and find it empty. My own infirmities oppress me. There is no longer him to oppose them.

'Behold, then, the blue madonna streaked with tears. This is my funeral service. We have no ceremonies, only private dirges and no conclusions, only violent sensations, each separate. Nothing that has been said meets our case. We sit in the Italian room at the National Gallery picking up fragments. I doubt that Titian* ever felt this rat gnaw. Painters live lives of methodical absorption, adding stroke to stroke. They are not like poets—scapegoats; they are not chained to the rock. Hence the silence, the sublimity. Yet that crimson must have burnt in Titian's gizzard. No doubt he rose with the great arms holding the cornucopia, and fell, in that descent. But the silence weighs on me— the perpetual solicitation of the eye. The pressure is intermittent and muffled. I distinguish too little and too vaguely. The bell is pressed and I do not ring or give out irrelevant clamours all jangled. I am titillated inordinately by some splendour; the ruffled crimson against the green lining; the march of pillars; the orange light behind the black, pricked ears of the olive trees. Arrows of sensation strike from my spine, but without order.

'Yet something is added to my interpretation. Something lies deeply buried. For one moment I thought to grasp it. But bury it, bury it; let it breed, hidden in the depths of my mind some day to fructify. After a long lifetime, loosely, in a moment of revelation, I may lay hands on it, but now the idea breaks in my hand. Ideas break a thousand times for once that they globe themselves entire. They break; they fall over me. "Line and colours they survive, therefore . . ."

'I am yawning. I am glutted with sensations. I am exhausted with the strain and the long, long time—twenty-five minutes, half an hour—that I have held myself alone outside the machine. I grow numb; I grow stiff. How shall I break up this numbness which discredits my sympathetic heart? There are others suffering—multitudes of people suffering. Neville suffers. He loved Percival. But I can no longer endure extremities; I want someone with whom to laugh, with whom to yawn, with whom to remember how he scratched his head; someone he was at ease with and liked (not Susan, whom he loved, but Jinny rather). In her room also I could do penance. I could ask, Did he tell you how I refused him when he asked me to go to Hampton Court that day?* Those are the thoughts that will wake me leaping in anguish in the middle of the night—the crimes for which one would do penance in all the markets of the world bareheaded; that one did not go to Hampton Court that day.

'But now I want life round me, and books and little ornaments, and the usual sounds of tradesmen calling on which to pillow my head after this exhaustion, and shut my eyes after this revelation. I will go straight, then, down the stairs, and hail the first taxi and drive to Jinny.'

'There is the puddle,' said Rhoda, 'and I cannot cross it. I hear the rush of the great grindstone within an inch of my head. Its wind roars in my face. All palpable forms of life have failed me. Unless I can stretch and touch something hard, I shall be blown down the eternal corridors for ever. What, then, can I touch? What brick, what stone? and so draw myself across the enormous gulf into my body safely?

'Now the shadow has fallen and the purple light slants downwards. The figure that was robed in beauty is now clothed in ruin. The figure that stood in the grove where the steep-backed hills come down falls in ruin, as I told them when they said they loved his voice on the stair, and his old shoes and moments of being together.

'Now I will walk down Oxford Street envisaging a world rent by lightning; I will look at oaks cracked asunder and red where the flowering branch has fallen. I will go to Oxford Street* and buy stockings for a party. I will do the usual things under the lightning flash. On the bare ground I will pick violets* and bind them together and offer them to Percival, something given him by me. Look now at what Percival has given me. Look at the street now that Percival is dead. The houses are lightly founded to be puffed over by a breath of air. Reckless and random the cars race and roar and hunt us to death like bloodhounds. I am alone in a hostile world. The human face is hideous. This is to my liking. I want publicity and violence and to be dashed like a stone on the rocks. I like factory chimneys and cranes and lorries. I like the passing of face and face and face, deformed, indifferent. I am sick of prettiness; I am sick of privacy. I ride rough waters and shall sink with no one to save me.

'Percival, by his death, has made me this present, has revealed this terror, has left me to undergo this humiliation—faces and faces, served out like soup-plates by scullions; coarse, greedy, casual; looking in at shop-windows with pendent parcels; ogling, brushing, destroying everything, leaving even our love impure, touched now by their dirty fingers.

'Here is the shop where they sell stockings. And I could believe that beauty is once more set flowing. Its whisper comes down these aisles, through these laces, breathing among baskets of coloured ribbons. There are then warm hollows grooved in the heart of the uproar; alcoves of silence where we can shelter under the wing of beauty from truth which I desire. Pain is suspended as a girl silently slides open a drawer. And then, she speaks; her voice wakes me. I shoot to the bottom among the weeds and see envy, jealousy, hatred and spite scuttle like crabs over the sand as she speaks. These are our companions. I will pay my bill and take my parcel.

'This is Oxford Street. Here are hate, jealousy, hurry, and indifference frothed into the wild semblance of life. These are our companions. Consider the friends with whom we sit and eat. I think of Louis, reading the sporting column of an evening newspaper, afraid of ridicule; a snob. He says, looking at the people passing, he will shepherd us if we will follow. If we submit he will reduce us to order. Thus he will smooth out the death of Percival to his satisfaction, looking fixedly over the cruet, past the houses at the sky. Bernard, meanwhile, flops red-eyed into some armchair. He will have out his notebook; under D, he will enter "Phrases to be used on the deaths of friends". Jinny, pirouetting across the room, will perch on the arm of his chair and ask, "Did he love me?" "More than he loved Susan?" Susan, engaged to her farmer in the country, will stand for a second with the telegram before her, holding a plate; and then, with a kick of her heel, slam to the oven door. Neville, after staring at the window through his tears, will see through his tears, and ask, "Who passes the window?"—"What lovely boy?" This is my tribute to Percival; withered violets, blackened violets.

'Where shall I go then?* To some museum, where they keep rings under glass cases, where there are cabinets, and the dresses that queens have worn? Or shall I go to Hampton Court and look at the red walls and courtyards and the seemliness of herded yew trees making black pyramids symmetrically on the grass among flowers? There shall I recover beauty, and impose order upon my raked, my dishevelled soul? But what can one make in loneliness? Alone I should stand on the empty grass and say, Rooks fly; somebody passes with a bag; there is a gardener with a wheelbarrow. I should stand in a queue and smell sweat, and scent as horrible as sweat; and be hung with other people like a joint of meat among other joints of meat.

'Here is a hall where one pays money and goes in, where one hears music among somnolent people who have come here after lunch on a hot afternoon. We have eaten beef and pudding enough to live for a week without tasting food. Therefore we cluster like maggots on the back of something that will carry us on. Decorous, portly—we have white hair waved under our hats; slim shoes; little bags; clean-shaven cheeks; here and there a military moustache; not a speck of dust has been allowed to settle anywhere on our broadcloth. Swaying and opening programmes, with a few words of greeting to friends, we settle down, like walruses stranded on rocks, like heavy bodies incapable of waddling to the sea, hoping for a wave to lift us, but we are too heavy, and too much dry shingle lies between us and the sea. We lie gorged with food, torpid in the heat. Then, swollen but contained in slippery satin, the sea-green woman comes to our rescue. She sucks in her lips, assumes an air of intensity, inflates herself and hurls herself precisely at the right moment as if she saw an apple and her voice was the arrow into the note, "Ah!"

'An axe has split a tree to the core; the core is warm; sound quivers within the bark. "Ah!" cried a woman to her lover, leaning from her window in Venice. "Ah, ah!" she cried, and again she cries "Ah!" She has provided us with a cry. But only a cry. And what is a cry?* Then the beetle-shaped men come with their violins; wait; count; nod; down come their bows. And there is ripple and laughter like the dance of olive trees and their myriad-tongued grey leaves when a seafarer, biting a twig between his lips where the many-backed steep hills come down, leaps on shore.

'"Like" and "like" and "like"—but what is the thing that lies beneath the semblance of the thing? Now that lightning has gashed the tree and the flowering branch has fallen and Percival, by his death, has made me this gift, let me see the thing. There is a square; there is an oblong. The players take the square and place it upon the oblong. They place it very accurately; they make a perfect dwelling-place. Very little is left outside. The structure is now visible; what is inchoate is here stated; we are not so various or so mean; we have made oblongs and stood them upon squares. This is our triumph; this is our consolation.

'The sweetness of this content overflowing runs down the walls of my mind, and liberates understanding. Wander no more, I say; this is the end. The oblong has been set upon the square; the spiral is on top. We have been hauled over the shingle, down to the sea. The players come again. But they are mopping their faces. They are no longer so spruce or so debonair. I will go. I will set aside this afternoon. I will make a pilgrimage. I will go to Greenwich.* I will fling myself fearlessly into trams, into omnibuses. As we lurch down Regent Street, and I am flung upon this woman, upon this man, I am not injured, I am not outraged by the collision. A square stands upon an oblong. Here are mean streets where chaffering goes on in street markets, and every sort of iron rod, bolt and screw is laid out, and people swarm off the pavement, pinching raw meat with thick fingers. The structure is visible. We have made a dwelling-place.

'These, then, are the flowers that grow among the rough grasses of the field which the cows trample, wind-bitten, almost deformed, without fruit or blossom. These are what I bring, torn up by the roots from the pavement of Oxford Street, my penny bunch, my penny bunch of violets. Now from the window of the tram I see masts among chimneys; there is the river; there are ships that sail to India. I will walk by the river. I will pace this embankment, where an old man reads a newspaper in a glass shelter. I will pace this terrace and watch the ships bowling down the tide. A woman walks on deck, with a dog barking round her. Her skirts are blown; her hair is blown; they are going out to sea; they are leaving us; they are vanishing this summer evening. Now I will relinquish; now I will let loose. Now I will at last free the checked, the jerked-back desire to be spent, to be consumed. We will gallop together over desert hills where the swallow dips her wings in dark pools and the pillars stand entire. Into the wave that dashes upon the shore, into the wave that flings its white foam to the uttermost corners of the earth, I throw my violets, my offering to Percival.'

The sun no longer stood in the middle of the sky. Its light slanted, falling obliquely. Here it caught on the edge of a cloud and burnt it into a slice of light, a blazing island on which no foot could rest. Then another cloud was caught in the light and another and another, so that the waves beneath were arrow-struck with fiery feathered darts that shot erratically across the quivering blue.

The topmost leaves of the tree were crisped in the sun. They rustled stiffly in the random breeze. The birds sat still save that they flicked their heads sharply from side to side. Now they paused in their song as if glutted with sound, as if the fullness of midday had gorged them. The dragon-fly poised motionless over a reed, then shot its blue stitch further through the air. The far hum in the distance seemed made of the broken tremor of fine wings dancing up and down on the horizon. The river water held the reeds now fixed as if glass had hardened round them; and then the glass wavered and the reeds swept low. Pondering, sunken headed, the cattle stood in the fields and cumbrously moved one foot and then another. In the bucket near the house the tap stopped dripping, as if the bucket were full, and then the tap dripped one, two, three separate drops in succession.

The windows showed erratically spots of burning fire, the elbow of one branch, and then some tranquil space of pure clarity. The blind hung red at the window's edge and within the room daggers of light fell upon chairs and tables making cracks across their lacquer and polish. The green pot bulged enormously, with its white window elongated in its side. Light driving darkness before it spilt itself profusely upon the corners and bosses; and yet heaped up darkness in mounds of unmoulded shape.

The waves massed themselves, curved their backs and crashed. Up spurted stones and shingle. They swept round the rocks, and the spray, leaping high, spattered the walls of a cave that had been dry before, and left pools inland, where some fish stranded lashed its tail as the wave drew back.

'I HAVE signed my name,' said Louis, 'already twenty times. I, and again I, and again I. Clear, firm, unequivocal, there it stands, my name. Clear-cut and unequivocal am I too. Yet a vast inheritance of experience is packed in me. I have lived thousands of years. I am like a worm that has eaten its way through the wood of a very old oak beam. But now I am compact; now I am gathered together this fine morning.

'The sun shines from a clear sky. But twelve o'clock brings neither rain nor sunshine. It is the hour when Miss Johnson brings me my letters in a wire tray. Upon these white sheets I indent my name. The whisper of leaves, water running down gutters, green depths flecked with dahlias or zinnias; I, now a duke, now Plato, companion of Socrates; the tramp of dark men and yellow men migrating east, west, north and south; the eternal procession, women going with attaché cases down the Strand as they went once with pitchers to the Nile; all the furled and close-packed leaves of my many-folded life are now summed in my name; incised cleanly and barely on the sheet. Now a full-grown man; now upright standing in sun or rain. I must drop heavy as a hatchet and cut the oak with my sheer weight, for if I deviate, glancing this way, or that way, I shall fall like snow and be wasted.

'I am half in love with the typewriter and the telephone. With letters and cables and brief but courteous commands on the telephone to Paris, Berlin, New York, I have fused my many lives into one; I have helped by my assiduity and decision to score those lines on the map there by which the different parts of the world are laced together. I love punctually at ten to come into my room; I love the purple glow of the dark mahogany; I love the table and its sharp edge; and the smooth-running drawers. I love the telephone with its lip stretched to my whisper, and the date on the wall; and the engagement book. Mr Prentice at four; Mr Eyres sharp at four-thirty.

'I like to be asked to come to Mr Burchard's private room and report on our commitments to China. I hope to inherit an armchair and a Turkey carpet. My shoulder is to the wheel; I roll the dark before me, spreading commerce where there was chaos in the far parts of the world. If I press on, from chaos making order, I shall find myself where Chatham stood, and Pitt, Burke and Sir Robert Peel.* Thus I expunge certain stains, and erase old defilements; the woman who gave me a flag from the top of the Christmas tree; my accent; beatings and other tortures; the boasting boys; my father, a banker at Brisbane.

'I have read my poet in an eating-house, and, stirring my coffee, listened to the clerks making bets at the little tables, watched the women hesitating at the counter. I said that nothing should be irrelevant, like a piece of brown paper dropped casually on the floor. I said their journeys should have an end in view; they should earn their two pound ten a week at the command of an august master; some hand, some robe, should fold us about in the evening. When I have healed these fractures and comprehended these monstrosities so that they need neither excuse nor apology, which both waste our strength, I shall give back to the street and the eating-shop what they lost when they fell on these hard times and broke on these stony beaches. I shall assemble a few words and forge round us a hammered ring of beaten steel.

'But now I have not a moment to spare. There is no respite here, no shadow made of quivering leaves, or alcove to which one can retreat from the sun, to sit, with a lover, in the cool of the evening. The weight of the world is on our shoulders; its vision is through our eyes; if we blink or look aside, or turn back to finger what Plato said or remember Napoleon and his conquests, we inflict on the world the injury of some obliquity. This is life; Mr Prentice at four; Mr Eyres at four-thirty. I like to hear the soft rush of the lift and the thud with which it stops on my landing and the heavy male tread of responsible feet down the corridors. So by dint of our united exertions we send ships to the remotest parts of the globe; replete with lavatories and gymnasiums. The weight of the world is on our shoulders. This is life. If I press on, I shall inherit a chair and a rug; a place in Surrey with glass houses, and some rare conifer, melon or flowering tree which other merchants will envy.

'Yet I still keep my attic room. There I open the usual little book; there I watch the rain glisten on the tiles till they shine like a policeman's waterproof; there I see the broken windows in poor people's houses; the lean cats; some slattern squinting in a cracked looking-glass as she arranges her face for the street corner; there Rhoda sometimes comes. For we are lovers.

'Percival has died (he died in Egypt;* he died in Greece; all deaths are one death). Susan has children; Neville mounts rapidly to the conspicuous heights. Life passes. The clouds change perpetually over our houses. I do this, do that, and again do this and then that. Meeting and parting, we assemble different forms, make different patterns. But if I do not nail these impressions to the board and out of the many men in me make one; exist here and now and not in streaks and patches, like scattered snow wreaths on far mountains; and ask Miss Johnson as I pass through the office about the movies and take my cup of tea and accept also my favourite biscuit, then I shall fall like snow and be wasted.

'Yet when six o'clock comes and I touch my hat to the commissionaire, being always too effusive in ceremony since I desire so much to be accepted; and struggle, leaning against the wind, buttoned up, with my jaws blue and my eyes running water, I wish that a little typist would cuddle on my knees; I think that my favourite dish is liver and bacon; and so am apt to wander to the river, to the narrow streets where there are frequent public-houses, and the shadows of ships passing at the end of the street, and women fighting. But I say to myself, recovering my sanity, Mr Prentice at four; Mr Eyres at four-thirty. The hatchet must fall on the block; the oak must be cleft to the centre. The weight of the world is on my shoulders. Here is the pen and the paper; on the letters in the wire basket I sign my name, I, I, and again I.'

'Summer comes, and winter,' said Susan. 'The seasons pass. The pear fills itself and drops from the tree. The dead leaf rests on its edge. But steam has obscured the window. I sit by the fire watching the kettle boil. I see the pear tree through the streaked steam on the window-pane.

'Sleep, sleep, I croon, whether it is summer or winter, May or November. Sleep I sing—I, who am unmelodious and hear no music save rustic music when a dog barks, a bell tinkles, or wheels crunch upon the gravel. I sing my song by the fire like an old shell murmuring on the beach. Sleep, sleep, I say, warning off with my voice all who rattle milk-cans, fire at rooks, shoot rabbits, or in any way bring the shock of destruction near this wicker cradle, laden with soft limbs, curled under a pink coverlet.

'I have lost my indifference, my blank eyes, my pear-shaped eyes that saw to the root. I am no longer January, May or any other season, but am all spun to a fine thread round the cradle, wrapping in a cocoon made of my own blood the delicate limbs of my baby. Sleep, I say, and feel within me uprush some wilder, darker violence, so that I would fell down with one blow any intruder, any snatcher, who should break into this room and wake the sleeper.

'I pad about the house all day long in apron and slippers, like my mother who died of cancer. Whether it is summer, whether it is winter, I no longer know by the moor grass, and the heath flower; only by the steam on the window-pane, or the frost on the window-pane. When the lark peels high his ring of sound and it falls through the air like an apple paring, I stoop; I feed my baby. I, who used to walk through beech woods noting the jay's feather turning blue as it falls, past the shepherd and the tramp, who stared at the woman squatted beside a tilted cart in a ditch, go from room to room with a duster. Sleep, I say, desiring sleep to fall like a blanket of down and cover these weak limbs; demanding that life shall sheathe its claws and gird its lightning and pass by, making of my own body a hollow, a warm shelter for my child to sleep in. Sleep, I say, sleep. Or I go to the window, I look at the rook's high nest; and the pear tree. "His eyes will see when mine are shut", I think. "I shall go mixed with them beyond my body and shall see India. He will come home, bringing trophies to be laid at my feet. He will increase my possessions."

'But I never rise at dawn and see the purple drops in the

cabbage leaves; the red drops in the roses. I do not watch
the setter nose in a circle, or lie at night watching the leaves
hide the stars and the stars move and the leaves hang still.
The butcher calls; the milk has to be stood under a shade
lest it should sour.

'Sleep, I say, sleep, as the kettle boils and its breath
comes thicker and thicker issuing in one jet from the spout.
So life fills my veins. So life pours through my limbs. So I
am driven forward, till I could cry, as I move from dawn
to dusk opening and shutting, "No more. I am glutted
with natural happiness." Yet more will come, more children; more cradles, more baskets in the kitchen and hams
ripening; and onions glistening; and more beds of lettuce
and potatoes. I am blown like a leaf by the gale; now
brushing the wet grass, now whirled up. I am glutted with
natural happiness; and wish sometimes that the fullness
would pass from me and the weight of the sleeping house
rise, when we sit reading, and I stay the thread at the eye
of my needle. The lamp kindles a fire in the dark pane. A
fire burns in the heart of the ivy. I see a lit-up street in the
evergreens. I hear traffic in the brush of the wind down the
lane, and broken voices, and laughter, and Jinny who cries
as the door opens, "Come, Come!"

'But no sound breaks the silence of our house, where the
fields sigh close to the door. The wind washes through the
elm trees; a moth hits the lamp; a cow lows; a crack of
sound starts in the rafter, and I push my thread through
the needle and murmur, "Sleep".'

'Now is the moment,' said Jinny. 'Now we have met,
and have come together. Now let us talk, let us tell stories.
Who is he? Who is she? I am infinitely curious and do not
know what is to come. If you, whom I meet for the first
time, were to say to me, "The coach starts at four from

Piccadilly", I would not stay to fling a few necessaries in a bandbox, but would come at once.

'Let us sit here under the cut flowers, on the sofa by the picture. Let us decorate our Christmas tree with facts and again with facts. People are so soon gone; let us catch them. That man there, by the cabinet; he lives, you say, surrounded by china pots. Break one and you shatter a thousand pounds. And he loved a girl in Rome and she left him. Hence the pots, old junk found in lodging-houses or dug from the desert sands. And since beauty must be broken daily to remain beautiful, and he is static, his life stagnates in a china sea. It is strange though; for once, as a young man, he sat on damp ground and drank rum with soldiers.

'One must be quick and add facts deftly, like toys to a tree, fixing them with a twist of the fingers. He stoops, how he stoops, even over an azalea. He stoops over the old woman even, because she wears diamonds in her ears, and, bundling about her estate in a pony carriage, directs who is to be helped, what tree felled, and who turned out tomorrow. (I have lived my life, I must tell you, all these years, and I am now past thirty, perilously, like a mountain goat, leaping from crag to crag; I do not settle long anywhere; I do not attach myself to one person in particular; but you will find that if I raise my arm, some figure at once breaks off and will come.) And that man is a judge; and that man is a millionaire, and that man, with the eyeglass, shot his governess through the heart with an arrow when he was ten years old. Afterwards he rode through deserts with despatches, took part in revolutions and now collects materials for a history of his mother's family, long settled in Norfolk. That little man with a blue chin has a right hand that is withered. But why? We do not know. That woman, you whisper discreetly, with the pearl pagodas hanging from her ears, was the pure flame who lit the life of one of our statesmen; now since his death she sees ghosts, tells fortunes, and has adopted a coffee-coloured youth whom she calls the Messiah. That man with the drooping moustache, like a cavalry officer, lived a life of the utmost debauchery (it is all in some memoir) until one day he met a stranger in a train who converted him between Edinburgh and Carlisle by reading the Bible.

'Thus, in a few seconds, deftly, adroitly, we decipher the hieroglyphs written on other people's faces. Here, in this room, are the abraded and battered shells cast on the shore. The door goes on opening. The room fills and fills with knowledge, anguish, many kinds of ambition, much indifference, some despair. Between us, you say, we could build cathedrals, dictate policies, condemn men to death, and administer the affairs of several public offices. The common fund of experience is very deep. We have between us scores of children of both sexes, whom we are educating, going to see at school with the measles, and bringing up to inherit our houses. In one way or another we make this day, this Friday, some by going to the Law Courts; others to the city; others to the nursery; others by marching and forming fours. A million hands stitch, raise hods with bricks. The activity is endless. And tomorrow it begins again; tomorrow we make Saturday. Some take train for France; others ship for India. Some will never come into this room again. One may die tonight. Another will beget a child. From us every sort of building, policy, venture, picture, poem, child, factory, will spring. Life comes; life goes; we make life. So you say.

'But we who live in the body see with the body's

imagination things in outline. I see rocks in bright sunshine. I cannot take these facts into some cave and, shading
my eyes, grade their yellows, blues, umbers into one
substance. I cannot remain seated for long. I must jump up
and go. The coach may start from Piccadilly. I drop all
these facts—diamonds, withered hands, china pots and the
rest of it—as a monkey drops nuts from its naked paws. I
cannot tell you if life is this or that. I am going to push out
into the heterogeneous crowd. I am going to be buffeted;
to be flung up, and flung down, among men, like a ship on
the sea.

'For now my body, my companion, which is always
sending its signals, the rough black "No", the golden
"Come", in rapid running arrows of sensation, beckons.
Someone moves. Did I raise my arm? Did I look? Did my
yellow scarf with the strawberry spots float and signal? He
has broken from the wall. He follows. I am pursued
through the forest. All is rapt, all is nocturnal, and the
parrots go screaming through the branches. All my senses
stand erect. Now I feel the roughness of the fibre of the
curtain through which I push; now I feel the cold iron
railing and its blistered paint beneath my palm. Now the
cool tide of darkness breaks its waters over me. We are out
of doors. Night opens; night traversed by wandering
moths; night hiding lovers roaming to adventure. I smell
roses; I smell violets; I see red and blue just hidden. Now
gravel is under my shoes; now grass. Up reel the tall backs
of houses guilty with lights. All London is uneasy with
flashing lights. Now let us sing our love song—Come,
come, come. Now my gold signal is like a dragon-fly flying
taut. Jug, jug, jug,* I sing like the nightingale whose
melody is crowded in the too narrow passage of her throat.
Now I hear crash and rending of boughs and the crack of

antlers as if the beasts of the forest were all hunting, all rearing high and plunging down among the thorns. One has pierced me. One is driven deep within me.

'And velvet flowers and leaves whose coolness has been stood in water wash me round, and sheathe me, embalming me.'

'Why, look,' said Neville, 'at the clock ticking on the mantelpiece? Time passes, yes. And we grow old. But to sit with you, alone with you, here in London, in this firelit room, you there, I here, is all. The world ransacked to its uttermost ends, and all its heights stripped and gathered of their flowers, holds no more. Look at the firelight running up and down the gold thread in the curtain. The fruit it circles droops heavy. It falls on the toe of your boot, it gives your face a red rim—I think it is the firelight and not your face; I think those are books against the wall, and that a curtain, and that perhaps an armchair. But when you come everything changes. The cups and saucers changed when you came in this morning. There can be no doubt, I thought, pushing aside the newspaper, that our mean lives, unsightly as they are, put on splendour and have meaning only under the eyes of love.

'I rose. I had done my breakfast. There was the whole day before us, and as it was fine, tender, non-committal, we walked through the Park to the Embankment, along the Strand to St Paul's, then to the shop where I bought an umbrella, always talking, and now and then stopping to look. But can this last? I said to myself, by a lion in Trafalgar Square,* by the lion seen once and for ever;—so I revisit my past life, scene by scene; there is an elm tree, and there lies Percival. For ever and ever, I swore. Then darted in the usual doubt. I clutched your hand. You left me. The descent into the Tube was like death. We were cut up, we were dissevered by all those faces and the hollow wind that seemed to roar down there over desert boulders. I sat staring in my own room. By five I knew that you were faithless. I snatched the telephone and the buzz, buzz, buzz of its stupid voice in your empty room battered my heart down, when the door opened and there you stood. That was the most perfect of our meetings. But these meetings, these partings, finally destroy us.

'Now this room seems to me central, something scooped out of the eternal night. Outside lines twist and intersect, but round us, wrapping us about. Here we are centred. Here we can be silent, or speak without raising our voices: Did you notice that and then that? we say. He said that, meaning. . . . She hesitated, and I believe suspected. Anyhow, I heard voices, a sob on the stair late at night. It is the end of their relationship. Thus we spin round us infinitely fine filaments and construct a system. Plato and Shakespeare are included, also quite obscure people, people of no importance whatsoever. I hate men who wear crucifixes on the left side of their waistcoats. I hate ceremonies and lamentations and the sad figure of Christ trembling beside another trembling and sad figure. Also the pomp and the indifference and the emphasis, always on the wrong place, of people holding forth under chandeliers in full evening dress, wearing stars and decorations. Some spray in a hedge, though, or a sunset over a flat winter field, or again the way some old woman sits, arms akimbo, in an omnibus with a basket—those we point at for the other to look at. It is so vast an alleviation to be able to point for another to look at. And then not to talk. To follow the dark paths of the mind and enter the past, to visit books, to brush aside their branches and break off some fruit. And you take it and marvel, as I take the careless movements of your body and marvel at its ease, its power—how you fling open windows and are dexterous with your hands. For alas! my mind is a little impeded, it soon tires; I fall damp, perhaps disgusting, at the goal.

'Alas! I could not ride about India in a sun helmet and return to a bungalow. I cannot tumble, as you do, like half-naked boys on the deck of a ship, squirting each other with hose-pipes. I want this fire, I want this chair. I want someone to sit beside after the day's pursuit and all its anguish, after its listenings, and its waitings, and its suspicions. After quarrelling and reconciliation I need privacy—to be alone with you, to set this hubbub in order. For I am as neat as a cat in my habits. We must oppose the waste and deformity of the world, its crowds eddying round and round disgorged and trampling. One must slip paper-knives, even, exactly through the pages of novels, and tie up packets of letters neatly with green silk, and brush up the cinders with a hearth broom. Everything must be done to rebuke the horror of deformity. Let us read writers of Roman severity and virtue; let us seek perfection through the sand. Yes, but I love to slip the virtue and severity of the noble Romans under the grey light of your eyes, and dancing grasses and summer breezes and the laughter and shouts of boys at play—of naked cabin-boys squirting each other with hose-pipes on the decks of ships. Hence I am not a disinterested seeker, like Louis, after perfection through the sand. Colours always stain the page; clouds pass over it. And the poem, I think, is only your voice speaking. Alcibiades, Ajax, Hector and Percival* are also you. They loved riding, they risked their lives wantonly, they were not great readers either. But you are not Ajax or Percival. They did not wrinkle their noses and scratch their foreheads with your precise gesture. You are you. That is

THE WAVES

what consoles me for the lack of many things—I am ugly,
I am weak—and the depravity of the world, and the flight
of youth and Percival's death, and bitterness and rancour
and envies innumerable.

'But if one day you do not come after breakfast, if one
day I see you in some looking-glass perhaps looking after
another, if the telephone buzzes and buzzes in your empty
room, I shall then, after unspeakable anguish, I shall then—
for there is no end to the folly of the human heart—seek
another, find another, you. Meanwhile, let us abolish the
ticking of time's clock with one blow. Come closer.'

The sun had now sunk lower in the sky. The islands of cloud had gained in density and drew themselves across the sun so that the rocks went suddenly black, and the trembling sea-holly lost its blue and turned silver, and shadows were blown like grey cloths over the sea. The waves no longer visited the further pools or reached the dotted black line which lay irregularly upon the beach. The sand was pearl white, smoothed and shining.

Birds swooped and circled high up in the air. Some raced in the furrows of the wind and turned and sliced through them as if they were one body cut into a thousand shreds. Birds fell like a net descending on the tree-tops. Here one bird taking its way alone made wing for the marsh and sat solitary on a white stake, opening its wings and shutting them.

Some petals had fallen in the garden. They lay shell-shaped on the earth. The dead leaf no longer stood upon its edge, but had been blown, now running, now pausing, against some stalk. Through all the flowers the same wave of light passed in a sudden flaunt and flash as if a fin cut the green glass of a lake. Now and again some level and masterly blast blew the multitudinous leaves up and down and then, as the wind flagged, each blade regained its identity. The flowers, burning their bright discs in the sun, flung aside the sunlight as the wind tossed them, and then some heads too heavy to rise again drooped slightly.

The afternoon sun warmed the fields, poured blue into

the shadows and reddened the corn. A deep varnish was laid like a lacquer over the fields. A cart, a horse, a flock of rooks—whatever moved in it was rolled round in gold. If a cow moved a leg it stirred ripples of red gold, and its horns seemed lined with light. Sprays of flaxen-haired corn lay on the hedges, brushed from the shaggy carts that came up from the meadows short legged and primeval looking. The round-headed clouds never dwindled as they bowled along, but kept every atom of their rotundity. Now, as they passed, they caught a whole village in the fling of their net and, passing, let it fly free again. Far away on the horizon, among the million grains of blue-grey dust, burnt one pane, or stood the single line of one steeple or one tree.

The red curtains and the white blinds blew in and out, flapping against the edge of the window, and the light which entered by flaps and breadths unequally had in it some brown tinge, and some abandonment as it blew through the blowing curtains in gusts. Here it browned a cabinet, there reddened a chair, here it made the window waver in the side of the green jar.

All for a moment wavered and bent in uncertainty and ambiguity, as if a great moth* sailing through the room had shadowed the immense solidity of chairs and tables with floating wings.

'AND time,' said Bernard, 'lets fall its drop. The drop that has formed on the roof of the soul falls. On the roof of my mind time, forming, lets fall its drop. Last week, as I stood shaving, the drop fell. I, standing with my razor in my hand, became suddenly aware of the merely habitual nature of my action (this is the drop forming) and congratulated my hands, ironically, for keeping at it. Shave, shave, shave, I said. Go on shaving. The drop fell. All through the day's work, at intervals, my mind went to an empty place, saying, "What is lost? What is over?" And "Over and done with," I muttered, "over and done with", solacing myself with words. People noticed the vacuity of my face and the aimlessness of my conversation. The last words of my sentence tailed away. And as I buttoned on my coat to go home I said more dramatically, "I have lost my youth".

'It is curious how, at every crisis, some phrase which does not fit insists upon coming to the rescue—the penalty of living in an old civilization with a notebook. This drop falling has nothing to do with losing my youth. This drop falling is time tapering to a point. Time, which is a sunny pasture covered with a dancing light, time, which is widespread as a field at midday, becomes pendent. Time tapers to a point. As a drop falls from a glass heavy with some sediment, time falls. These are the true cycles, these are the true events. Then as if all the luminosity of the atmosphere were withdrawn I see to the bare bottom. I see what habit covers. I lie sluggish in bed for days. I dine out and gape like a codfish. I do not trouble to finish my sentences, and my actions, usually so uncertain, acquire a mechanical precision. On this occasion, passing an office, I went in and bought, with all the composure of a mechanical figure, a ticket for Rome.*

'Now I sit on a stone seat in these gardens surveying the eternal city, and the little man who was shaving in London five days ago looks already like a heap of old clothes. London has also crumbled. London consists of fallen factories and a few gasometers. At the same time I am not involved in this pageantry. I see the violet-sashed priests and the picturesque nursemaids; I notice externals only. I sit here like a convalescent, like a very simple man who knows only words of one syllable. "The sun is hot". I say. "The wind is cold." I feel myself carried round like an insect on top of the earth and could swear that, sitting here, I feel its hardness, its turning movement. I have no desire to go the opposite way from the earth. Could I prolong this sense another six inches I have a foreboding that I should touch some queer territory. But I have a very limited proboscis. I never wish to prolong these states of detachment; I dislike them; I also despise them. I do not wish to be a man who sits for fifty years on the same spot thinking of his navel. I wish to be harnessed to a cart, a vegetable-cart that rattles over the cobbles.

'The truth is that I am not one of those who find their satisfaction in one person, or in infinity. The private room bores me, also the sky. My being only glitters when all its facets are exposed to many people. Let them fail and I am full of holes, dwindling like burnt paper. Oh, Mrs Moffat, Mrs Moffat, I say, come and sweep it all up. Things have dropped from me. I have outlived certain desires; I have lost friends, some by death—Percival—others through sheer inability to cross the street. I am not so gifted as at one time seemed likely. Certain things lie beyond my scope. I shall never understand the harder problems of philosophy. Rome is the limit of my travelling. As I drop asleep at night it strikes me sometimes with a pang that I shall never see savages in Tahiti spearing fish by the light of a blazing cresset, or a lion spring in the jungle, or a naked man eating raw flesh. Nor shall I learn Russian or read the Vedas. I shall never again walk bang into the pillar-box. (But still a few stars fall through my night, beautifully, from the violence of that concussion.) But as I think, truth has come nearer. For many years I crooned complacently, "My children . . . my wife . . . my house . . . my dog". As I let myself in with the latch-key I would go through that familiar ritual and wrap myself in those warm coverings. Now that lovely veil has fallen. I do not want possessions now. (Note: an Italian washerwoman stands on the same rung of physical refinement as the daughter of an English duke.)

'But let me consider. The drop falls; another stage has been reached. Stage upon stage. And why should there be an end of stages? and where do they lead? To what conclusion? For they come wearing robes of solemnity. In these dilemmas the devout consult those violet-sashed and sensual-looking gentry who are trooping past me. But for ourselves, we resent teachers. Let a man get up and say, "Behold, this is the truth", and instantly I perceive a sandy cat filching a piece of fish in the background. Look, you have forgotten the cat, I say. So Neville, at school, in the dim chapel, raged at the sight of the doctor's crucifix. I, who am always distracted, whether by a cat or by a bee buzzing round the bouquet that Lady Hampden keeps so diligently pressed to her nose, at once make up a story and so obliterate the angles of the crucifix. I have made up thousands of stories; I have filled innumerable notebooks with phrases to be used when I have found the true story, the one story to which all these phrases refer. But I have never yet found that story. And I begin to ask, Are there stories?

'Look now from this terrace at the swarming population beneath. Look at the general activity and clamour. That man is in difficulties with his mule. Half a dozen good-natured loafers offer their services. Others pass by without looking. They have as many interests as there are threads in a skein. Look at the sweep of the sky, bowled over by round white clouds. Imagine the leagues of level land and the aqueducts and the broken Roman pavement and the tombstones in the Campagna, and beyond the Campagna, the sea, then again more land, then the sea. I could break off any detail in all that prospect—say the mule-cart—and describe it with the greatest ease. But why describe a man in trouble with his mule? Again, I could invent stories about that girl coming up the steps. "She met him under the dark archway. . . . 'It is over,' he said, turning from the cage where the china parrot hangs." Or simply, "That was all". But why impose my arbitrary design? Why stress this and shape that and twist up little figures like the toys men sell in trays in the street? Why select this, out of all that— one detail?

'Here am I shedding one of my life-skins, and all they will say is, "Bernard is spending ten days in Rome". Here am I marching up and down this terrace alone, unoriented. But observe how dots and dashes are beginning, as I walk, to run themselves into continuous lines, how things are losing the bald, the separate identity that they had as I walked up those steps. The great red pot is now a reddish

streak in a wave of yellowish green. The world is beginning
to move past me like the banks of a hedge when the train
starts, like the waves of the sea when a steamer moves. I
am moving too, am becoming involved in the general
sequence when one thing follows another and it seems
inevitable that the tree should come, then the telegraph-
pole, then the break in the hedge. And as I move, surrounded, included and taking part, the usual phrases begin
to bubble up, and I wish to free these bubbles from the
trap-door in my head, and direct my steps therefore
towards that man, the back of whose head is half familiar
to me. We were together at school. We shall undoubtedly
meet. We shall certainly lunch together. We shall talk. But
wait, one moment wait.

'These moments of escape are not to be despised. They
come too seldom. Tahiti becomes possible. Leaning over
this parapet I see far out a waste of water. A fin turns.*
This bare visual impression is unattached to any line of
reason, it springs up as one might see the fin of a porpoise
on the horizon. Visual impressions often communicate
thus briefly statements that we shall in time to come
uncover and coax into words. I note under F., therefore,
"Fin in a waste of waters". I, who am perpetually making
notes in the margin of my mind for some final statement,
make this mark, waiting for some winter's evening.

'Now I shall go and lunch somewhere, I shall hold my
glass up, I shall look through the wine, I shall observe with
more than my usual detachment, and when a pretty woman
enters the restaurant and comes down the room between
the tables I shall say to myself, "Look where she comes
against a waste of waters". A meaningless observation, but
to me, solemn, slate-coloured, with a fatal sound of ruining
worlds and waters falling to destruction.

'So, Bernard (I recall you, you the usual partner in my enterprises), let us begin this new chapter, and observe the formation of this new, this unknown, strange, altogether unidentified and terrifying experience—the new drop—which is about to shape itself. Larpent is that man's name.'

'In this hot afternoon,' said Susan, 'here in this garden, here in this field where I walk with my son, I have reached the summit of my desires. The hinge of the gate is rusty; he heaves it open. The violent passions of childhood, my tears in the garden when Jinny kissed Louis, my rage in the schoolroom, which smelt of pine, my loneliness in foreign places, when the mules came clattering in on their pointed hoofs and the Italian women chattered at the fountain, shawled, with carnations twisted in their hair, are rewarded by security, possession, familiarity. I have had peaceful, productive years. I possess all I see. I have grown trees from the seed. I have made ponds in which goldfish hide under the broad-leaved lilies. I have netted over strawberry beds and lettuce beds, and stitched the pears and the plums into white bags to keep them safe from the wasps. I have seen my sons and daughters, once netted over like fruit in their cots, break the meshes and walk with me, taller than I am, casting shadows on the grass.

'I am fenced in, planted here like one of my own trees. I say, "My son", I say, "My daughter", and even the ironmonger looking up from his counter strewn with nails, paint and wire-fencing respects the shabby car at the door with its butterfly nets, pads and bee-hives. We hang mistletoe over the clock at Christmas, weigh our black-berries and mushrooms, count out jam-pots, and stand year by year to be measured against the shutter in the drawing-room window. I also make wreaths of white flowers, twisting silver-leaved plants among them for the dead, attaching my card with sorrow for the dead shepherd, with sympathy for the wife of the dead carter; and sit by the beds of dying women, who murmur their last terrors, who clutch my hand; frequenting rooms intolerable except to one born as I was and early acquainted with the farmyard and the dung-heap and the hens straying in and out, and the mother with two rooms and growing children. I have seen the windows run with heat, I have smelt the sink.

'I ask now, standing with my scissors among my flowers, Where can the shadow enter? What shock can loosen my laboriously gathered, relentlessly pressed down life? Yet sometimes I am sick of natural happiness, and fruit growing, and children scattering the house with oars, guns, skulls, books won for prizes and other trophies. I am sick of the body, I am sick of my own craft, industry and cunning, of the unscrupulous ways of the mother who protects, who collects under her jealous eyes at one long table her own children, always her own.

'It is when spring comes, cold, showery, with sudden yellow flowers—then as I look at the meat under the blue shade and press the heavy silver bags of tea, of sultanas, I remember how the sun rose, and the swallows skimmed the grass, and phrases that Bernard made when we were children, and the leaves shook over us, many-folded, very light, breaking the blue of the sky, scattering wandering lights upon the skeleton roots of the beech trees where I sat, sobbing. The pigeon rose. I jumped up and ran after the words that trailed like the dangling string from an air ball, up and up, from branch to branch escaping. Then like a cracked bowl the fixity of my morning broke, and putting down the bag of flour I thought, Life stands round me like a glass round the imprisoned reed.

'I hold scissors and snip off the hollyhocks, who went to Elvedon and trod on rotten oak-apples, and saw the lady writing and the gardeners with their great brooms. We ran back panting lest we should be shot and nailed like stoats to the wall. Now I measure, I preserve. At night I sit in the armchair and stretch my arm for my sewing; and hear my husband snore; and look up when the light from a passing car dazzles the windows and feel the waves of my life tossed, broken, round me who am rooted; and hear cries, and see others' lives eddying like straws round the piers of a bridge while I push my needle in and out and draw my thread through the calico.

'I think sometimes of Percival who loved me. He rode and fell in India. I think sometimes of Rhoda. Uneasy cries wake me at dead of night. But for the most part I walk content with my sons. I cut the dead petals from hollyhocks. Rather squat, grey before my time, but with clear eyes, pear-shaped eyes, I pace my fields.'

'Here I stand,' said Jinny, 'in the Tube station where everything that is desirable meets—Piccadilly South Side, Piccadilly North Side, Regent Street and the Haymarket.* I stand for a moment under the pavement in the heart of London. Innumerable wheels rush and feet press just over my head. The great avenues of civilization meet here and strike this way and that. I am in the heart of life. But look—there is my body in that looking-glass. How solitary, how shrunk, how aged! I am no longer young. I am no longer part of the procession. Millions descend those stairs in a terrible descent. Great wheels churn inexorably urging them downwards. Millions have died. Percival died. I still move. I still live. But who will come if I signal?

'Little animal that I am, sucking my flanks in and out

with fear, I stand here, palpitating, trembling. But I will not be afraid. I will bring the whip down on my flanks. I am not a whimpering little animal making for the shadow. It was only for a moment, catching sight of myself before I had time to prepare myself as I always prepare myself for the sight of myself, that I quailed. It is true; I am not young—I shall soon raise my arm in vain and my scarf will fall to my side without having signalled. I shall not hear the sudden sigh in the night and feel through the dark someone coming. There will be no reflections in window-panes in dark tunnels. I shall look into faces, and I shall see them seek some other face. I admit, for one moment the soundless flight of upright bodies down the moving stairs like the pinioned and terrible descent of some army of the dead downwards and the churning of the great engines remorselessly forwarding us, all of us, onwards, made me cower and run for shelter.

'But now I swear, making deliberately in front of the glass those slight preparations that equip me, I will not be afraid. Think of the superb omnibuses, red and yellow, stopping and starting, punctually in order. Think of the powerful and beautiful cars that now slow to a foot's pace and now shoot forward; think of men, think of women, equipped, prepared, driving onward. This is the triumphant procession; this is the army of victory with banners and brass eagles and heads crowned with laurel-leaves won in battle. They are better than savages in loin-cloths, and women whose hair is dank, whose long breasts sag, with children tugging at their long breasts. These broad thoroughfares—Piccadilly South, Piccadilly North, Regent Street and the Haymarket—are sanded paths of victory driven through the jungle. I too, with my little patent-leather shoes, my handkerchief that is but a film of gauze,

my reddened lips and my finely pencilled eyebrows, march
to victory with the band.

'Look how they show off clothes here even under
ground in a perpetual radiance. They will not let the earth
even lie wormy and sodden. There are gauzes and silks
illumined in glass cases and underclothes trimmed with a
million close stitches of fine embroidery. Crimson, green,
violet, they are dyed all colours. Think how they organize,
roll out, smooth, dip in dyes, and drive tunnels blasting
the rock. Lifts rise and fall; trains stop, trains start as
regularly as the waves of the sea. This is what has my
adhesion. I am a native of this world, I follow its banners.
How could I run for shelter when they are so magnificently
adventurous, daring, curious, too, and strong enough in
the midst of effort to pause and scrawl with a free hand a
joke upon the wall? Therefore I will powder my face and
redden my lips. I will make the angle of my eyebrows
sharper than usual. I will rise to the surface, standing erect
with the others in Piccadilly Circus. I will sign with a sharp
gesture to a cab whose driver will signify by some
indescribable alacrity his understanding of my signals. For
I still excite eagerness. I still feel the bowing of men in the
street like the silent stoop of the corn when the light wind
blows, ruffling it red.

'I will drive to my own house. I will fill the vases with
lavish, with luxurious, with extravagant flowers nodding in
great bunches. I will place one chair there, another here. I
will put ready cigarettes, glasses and some gaily covered
new unread book in case Bernard comes, or Neville or
Louis. But perhaps it will not be Bernard, Neville or Louis,
but somebody new, somebody unknown, somebody I
passed on a staircase and, just turning as we passed, I
murmured, "Come". He will come this afternoon; some-

body I do not know, somebody new. Let the silent army of the dead descend. I march forward.'

'I no longer need a room now,' said Neville, 'or walls and firelight. I am no longer young. I pass Jinny's house without envy, and smile at the young man who arranges his tie a little nervously on the doorstep. Let the dapper young man ring the bell; let him find her. I shall find her if I want her; if not, I pass on. The old corrosion has lost its bite—envy, intrigue and bitterness have been washed out. We have lost our glory too. When we were young we sat anywhere, on bare benches in draughty halls with the doors always banging. We tumbled about half naked like boys on the deck of a ship squirting each other with hose-pipes. Now I could swear that I like people pouring profusely out of the Tube when the day's work is done, unanimous, indiscriminate, uncounted. I have picked my own fruit. I look dispassionately.

'After all, we are not responsible. We are not judges. We are not called upon to torture our fellows with thumb-screws and irons; we are not called upon to mount pulpits and lecture them on pale Sunday afternoons. It is better to look at a rose, or to read Shakespeare as I read him here in Shaftesbury Avenue. Here's the fool, here's the villain, here in a car comes Cleopatra,* burning on her barge. Here are figures of the damned too, noseless men by the police-court wall, standing with their feet in fire, howling. This is poetry if we do not write it. They act their parts infallibly, and almost before they open their lips I know what they are going to say, and wait the divine moment when they speak the word that must have been written. If it were only for the sake of the play, I could walk Shaftesbury Avenue for ever.

'Then coming from the street, entering some room,

there are people talking, or hardly troubling to talk. He says, she says, somebody else says things have been said so often that one word is now enough to lift a whole weight. Argument, laughter, old grievances—they fall through the air, thickening it. I take a book and read half a page of anything. They have not mended the spout of the teapot yet. The child dances, dressed in her mother's clothes.

'But then Rhoda, or it may be Louis, some fasting and anguished spirit, passes through and out again. They want a plot, do they? They want a reason? It is not enough for them, this ordinary scene. It is not enough to wait for the thing to be said as if it were written; to see the sentence lay its dab of clay precisely on the right place, making character; to perceive, suddenly, some group in outline against the sky. Yet if they want violence, I have seen death and murder and suicide all in one room. One comes in, one goes out. There are sobs on the staircase. I have heard threads broken and knots tied and the quiet stitching of white cambric going on and on on the knees of a woman. Why ask, like Louis, for a reason, or fly like Rhoda to some far grove and part the leaves of the laurels and look for statues? They say that one must beat one's wings against the storm in the belief that beyond this welter the sun shines; the sun falls sheer into pools that are fledged with willows. (Here it is November; the poor hold out matchboxes in wind-bitten fingers.) They say truth is to be found there entire, and virtue, that shuffles along here, down blind alleys, is to be had there perfect. Rhoda flies with her neck outstretched and blind fanatic eyes, past us. Louis, now so opulent, goes to his attic window among the blistered roofs and gazes where she has vanished, but must sit down in his office among the typewriters and the telephone and work it all out for our instruction, for our regeneration, and the reform of an unborn world.

'But now in this room, which I enter without knocking, things are said as if they had been written. I go to the bookcase. If I choose, I read half a page of anything. I need not speak. But I listen. I am marvellously on the alert. Certainly, one cannot read this poem without effort. The page is often corrupt and mud-stained, and torn and stuck together with faded leaves, with scraps of verbena or geranium. To read this poem one must have myriad eyes, like one of those lamps that turn on slabs of racing water at midnight in the Atlantic, when perhaps only a spray of seaweed pricks the surface, or suddenly the waves gape and up shoulders a monster. One must put aside antipathies and jealousies and not interrupt. One must have patience and infinite care and let the light sound, whether of spiders' delicate feet on a leaf or the chuckle of water in some irrelevant drain-pipe, unfold too. Nothing is to be rejected in fear or horror. The poet who has written this page (what I read with people talking) has withdrawn. There are no commas or semi-colons. The lines do not run in convenient lengths. Much is sheer nonsense. One must be sceptical, but throw caution to the winds and when the door opens accept absolutely.* Also sometimes weep; also cut away ruthlessly with a slice of the blade soot, bark, hard accretions of all sorts. And so (while they talk) let down one's net deeper and deeper and gently draw in and bring to the surface what he said and she said and make poetry.

'Now I have listened to them talking. They have gone now. I am alone. I could be content to watch the fire burn for ever, like a dome, like a furnace; now some spike of wood takes the look of a scaffold, or pit, or happy valley; now it is a serpent curled crimson with white scales. The fruit on the curtain swells beneath the parrot's beak. Cheep, cheep, creaks the fire, like the cheep of insects in the middle of a forest. Cheep, cheep, it clicks while out there the branches thrash the air, and now, like a volley of shot, a tree falls. These are the sounds of a London night. Then I hear the one sound I wait for. Up and up it comes, approaches, hesitates, stops at my door. I cry, "Come in. Sit by me. Sit on the edge of the chair." Swept away by the old hallucination, I cry, "Come closer, closer".'

'I come back from the office,' said Louis. 'I hang my coat here, place my stick there—I like to fancy that Richelieu walked with such a cane. Thus I divest myself of my authority. I have been sitting at the right hand of a director at a varnished table. The maps of our successful undertakings confront us on the wall. We have laced the world together with our ships. The globe is strung with our lines. I am immensely respectable. All the young ladies in the office acknowledge my entrance. I can dine where I like now, and without vanity may suppose that I shall soon acquire a house in Surrey, two cars, a conservatory and some rare species of melon. But I still return, I still come back to my attic, hang up my hat and resume in solitude that curious attempt which I have made since I brought down my fist on my master's grained oak door. I open a little book. I read one poem. One poem is enough.

O western wind . . .*

O western wind, you are at enmity with my mahogany table and spats, and also, alas, with the vulgarity of my mistress, the little actress, who has never been able to speak English correctly—

O western wind, when wilt thou blow . . .

'Rhoda, with her intense abstraction, with her unseeing eyes the colour of snail's flesh, does not destroy you, western wind, whether she comes at midnight when the stars blaze or at the most prosaic hour of midday. She stands at the window and looks at the chimney-pots and the broken windows in the houses of poor people—

O western wind, when wilt thou blow . . .

'My task, my burden, has always been greater than other people's. A pyramid has been set on my shoulders. I have tried to do a colossal labour. I have driven a violent, an unruly, a vicious team. With my Australian accent I have sat in eating-shops and tried to make the clerks accept me, yet never forgotten my solemn and severe convictions and the discrepancies and incoherences that must be resolved. As a boy I dreamt of the Nile, was reluctant to awake, yet brought down my fist on the grained oak door. It would have been happier to have been born without a destiny, like Susan, like Percival, whom I most admire.

O western wind, when wilt thou blow,
That the small rain down can rain?

'Life has been a terrible affair for me. I am like some vast sucker, some glutinous, some adhesive, some insatiable mouth. I have tried to draw from the living flesh the stone lodged at the centre. I have known little natural happiness, though I chose my mistress in order that, with her cockney accent, she might make me feel at my ease. But she only tumbled the floor with dirty under-linen, and the char-woman and the shop-boys called after me a dozen times a day, mocking my prim and supercilious gait.

O western wind, when wilt thou blow,
That the small rain down can rain?

'What has my destiny been, the sharp-pointed pyramid that has pressed on my ribs all these years? That I remember the Nile and the women carrying pitchers on their heads; that I feel myself woven in and out of the long summers and winters that have made the corn flow and have frozen the streams. I am not a single and passing being. My life is not a moment's bright spark like that on the surface of a diamond. I go beneath ground tortuously, as if a warder carried a lamp from cell to cell. My destiny has been that I remember and must weave together, must plait into one cable the many threads, the thin, the thick, the broken, the enduring of our long history, of our tumultuous and varied day. There is always more to be understood; a discord to be listened for; a falsity to be reprimanded. Broken and soot-stained are these roofs with their chimney cowls, their loose slates, their slinking cats and attic windows. I pick my way over broken glass, among blistered tiles, and see only vile and famished faces.

'Let us suppose that I make reason of it all—one poem on a page, and then die. I can assure you it will not be unwillingly. Percival died. Rhoda left me. But I shall live to be gaunt and sere, to tap my way, much respected, with my gold-headed cane along the pavements of the city. Perhaps I shall never die, shall never attain even that continuity and permanence—

O western wind, when wilt thou blow,
That the small rain down can rain?

'Percival was flowering with green leaves and was laid in the earth with all his branches still sighing in the summer wind. Rhoda, with whom I shared silence when the others spoke, she who hung back and turned aside when the herd assembled and galloped with orderly, sleek backs over the

rich pastures, has gone now like the desert heat. When the
sun blisters the roofs of the city I think of her; when the
dry leaves patter to the ground; when the old men come
with pointed sticks and pierce little bits of paper as we
pierced her—

> O western wind, when wilt thou blow,
> That the small rain down can rain?
> Christ, that my love were in my arms,
> And I in my bed again!

I return now to my book; I return now to my attempt.'

'Oh, life, how I have dreaded you,' said Rhoda, 'oh,
human beings, how I have hated you! How you have
nudged, how you have interrupted, how hideous you have
looked in Oxford Street, how squalid sitting opposite each
other staring in the Tube! Now as I climb this mountain,*
from the top of which I shall see Africa, my mind is printed
with brown-paper parcels and your faces. I have been
stained by you and corrupted. You smelt so unpleasant
too, lining up outside doors to buy tickets. All were
dressed in indeterminate shades of grey and brown, never
even a blue feather pinned to a hat. None had the courage
to be one thing rather than another. What dissolution of
the soul you demanded in order to get through one day,
what lies, bowings, scrapings, fluency and servility! How
you chained me to one spot, one hour, one chair, and sat
yourselves down opposite! How you snatched from me
the white spaces that lie between hour and hour and rolled
them into dirty pellets and tossed them into the waste-
paper basket with your greasy paws. Yet those were my
life.

'But I yielded. Sneers and yawns were covered with my
hand. I did not go out into the street and break a bottle in

the gutter as a sign of rage. Trembling with ardour, I
pretended that I was not surprised. What you did, I did. If
Susan and Jinny pulled up their stockings like that, I pulled
mine up like that also. So terrible was life that I held up
shade after shade. Look at life through this, look at life
through that; let there be rose leaves, let there be vine
leaves—I covered the whole street, Oxford Street, Piccadilly Circus, with the blaze and ripple of my mind, with
vine leaves and rose leaves. There were boxes too, standing
in the passage when the school broke up. I stole secretly to
read the labels and dream of names and faces. Harrogate,
perhaps, Edinburgh, perhaps, was ruffled with golden
glory where some girl whose name I forget stood on the
pavement. But it was the name only. I left Louis; I feared
embraces. With fleeces, with vestments, I have tried to
cover the blue-black blade. I implored day to break into
night. I have longed to see the cupboard dwindle, to feel
the bed soften, to float suspended, to perceive lengthened
trees, lengthened faces, a green bank on a moor and two
figures in distress saying good-bye. I flung words in fans
like those the sower throws over the ploughed fields when
the earth is bare. I desired always to stretch the night and
fill it fuller and fuller with dreams.

'Then in some Hall I parted the boughs of music and
saw the house we have made; the square stood upon the
oblong. "The house which contains all", I said, lurching
against people's shoulders in an omnibus after Percival
died; yet I went to Greenwich. Walking on the embankment, I prayed that I might thunder for ever on the verge
of the world where there is no vegetation, but here and
there a marble pillar. I threw my bunch into the spreading
wave. I said, "Consume me, carry me to the furthest limit".

The wave has broken; the bunch is withered. I seldom think of Percival now.

'Now I climb this Spanish hill; and I will suppose that this mule-back is my bed and that I lie dying. There is only a thin sheet between me now and the infinite depths. The lumps in the mattress soften beneath me. We stumble up— we stumble on. My path has been up and up, towards some solitary tree with a pool beside it on the very top. I have sliced the waters of beauty in the evening when the hills close themselves like birds' wings folded. I have picked sometimes a red carnation, and wisps of hay. I have sunk alone on the turf and fingered some old bone and thought: When the wind stoops to brush this height, may there be nothing found but a pinch of dust.

'The mule stumbles up and on. The ridge of the hill rises like mist, but from the top I shall see Africa. Now the bed gives under me. The sheets spotted with yellow holes let me fall through. The good woman with a face like a white horse at the end of the bed makes a valedictory movement and turns to go. Who then comes with me? Flowers only, the cowbind and the moonlight-coloured May. Gathering them loosely in a sheaf I made of them a garland and gave them—Oh, to whom? We launch out now over the precipice. Beneath us lie the lights of the herring fleet. The cliffs vanish. Rippling small, rippling grey, innumerable waves spread beneath us. I touch nothing. I see nothing. We may sink and settle on the waves. The sea will drum in my ears. The white petals will be darkened with sea water. They will float for a moment and then sink. Rolling me over the waves will shoulder me under. Everything falls in a tremendous shower, dissolving me.

'Yet that tree has bristling branches; that is the hard line of a cottage roof. Those bladder shapes painted red and yellow are faces. Putting my foot to the ground I step gingerly and press my hand against the hard door of a Spanish inn.'

*The sun was sinking. The hard stone of the day was cracked
and light poured through its splinters. Red and gold shot
through the waves, in rapid running arrows, feathered with
darkness. Erratically rays of light flashed and wandered,
like signals from sunken islands, or darts shot through laurel
groves by shameless, laughing boys. But the waves, as they
neared the shore, were robbed of light, and fell in one long
concussion, like a wall falling, a wall of grey stone,
unpierced by any chink of light.*

*A breeze rose; a shiver ran through the leaves; and thus
stirred they lost their brown density and became grey or
white as the tree shifted its mass, winked and lost its domed
uniformity. The hawk poised on the topmost branch flicked
its eyelids and rose and sailed and soared far away, the wild
plover cried in the marshes, evading, circling, and crying
further off in loneliness. The smoke of trains and chimneys
was stretched and torn and became part of the fleecy canopy
that hung over the sea and the fields.*

*Now the corn was cut. Now only a brisk stubble was left
of all its flowing and waving. Slowly a great owl launched
itself from the elm tree and swung and rose, as if on a line
that dipped, to the height of the cedar. On the hills the slow
shadows now broadened, now shrank, as they passed over.
The pool on the top of the moor lay blank. No furry face
looked there, or hoof splashed, or hot muzzle seethed in the
water. A bird, perched on an ash-coloured twig, sipped a
beak full of cold water. There was no sound of cropping,*

and no sound of wheels, but only the sudden roar of the wind letting its sails fill and brushing the tops of the grasses. One bone lay rain-pocked and sun-bleached till it shone like a twig that the sea has polished. The tree, that had burnt foxy red in spring and in midsummer bent pliant leaves to the south wind, was now black as iron, and as bare.

The land was so distant that no shining roof or glittering window could be any longer seen. The tremendous weight of the shadowed earth had engulfed such frail fetters, such snail-shell encumbrances. Now there was only the liquid shadow of the cloud, the buffeting of the rain, a single darting spear of sunshine, or the sudden bruise of the rainstorm. Solitary trees marked distant hills like obelisks.

The evening sun, whose heat had gone out of it and whose burning spot of intensity had been diffused, made chairs and tables mellower and inlaid them with lozenges of brown and yellow. Lined with shadows their weight seemed more ponderous, as if colour, tilted, had run to one side. Here lay knife, fork and glass, but lengthened, swollen, and made portentous. Rimmed in a gold circle the looking-glass held the scene immobile as if everlasting in its eye.

Meanwhile the shadows lengthened on the beach; the blackness deepened. The iron black boot became a pool of deep blue. The rocks lost their hardness. The water that stood round the old boat was dark as if mussels had been steeped in it. The foam had turned livid and left here and there a white gleam of pearl on the misty sand.

'HAMPTON COURT,' said Bernard. 'Hampton Court.*
This is our meeting-place. Behold the red chimneys, the
square battlements of Hampton Court. The tone of my
voice as I say "Hampton Court" proves that I am middle-
aged. Ten years, fifteen years ago, I should have said
"Hampton Court?" with interrogation—what will it be
like? Will there be lakes, mazes? Or with anticipation,
What is going to happen to me here? Whom shall I meet?
Now, Hampton Court—Hampton Court—the words beat
a gong in the space which I have so laboriously cleared
with half a dozen telephone messages and post cards, give
off ring after ring of sound, booming, sonorous: and
pictures rise—summer afternoons, boats, old ladies holding their skirts up, one urn in winter, some daffodils in
March—these all float to the top of the waters that now lie
deep on every scene.

'There at the door by the Inn, our meeting-place, they
are already standing—Susan, Louis, Rhoda, Jinny and
Neville. They have come together already. In a moment,
when I have joined them, another arrangement will form,
another pattern. What now runs to waste, forming scenes
profusely, will be checked, stated. I am reluctant to suffer
that compulsion. Already at fifty yards distance I feel the
order of my being changed. The tug of the magnet of their
society tells upon me. I come nearer. They do not see me.
Now Rhoda sees me, but she pretends, with her horror of
the shock of meeting, that I am a stranger. Now Neville

turns. Suddenly, raising my hand, saluting Neville, I cry, "I too have pressed flowers between the pages of Shakespeare's sonnets", and am churned up. My little boat bobs unsteadily upon the chopped and tossing waves. There is no panacea (let me note) against the shock of meeting.

'It is uncomfortable too, joining ragged edges, raw edges; only gradually, as we shuffle and trample into the Inn, taking coats and hats off, does meeting become agreeable. Now we assemble in the long, bare dining-room that overlooks some park, some green space still fantastically lit by the setting sun so that there is a gold bar between the trees, and sit ourselves down.'

'Now sitting side by side,' said Neville, 'at this narrow table, now before the first emotion is worn smooth, what do we feel? Honestly now, openly and directly as befits old friends meeting with difficulty, what do we feel on meeting? Sorrow. The door will not open; he will not come. And we are laden. Being now all of us middle-aged, loads are on us. Let us put down our loads. What have you made of life, we ask, and I? You, Bernard; you, Susan; you, Jinny; and Rhoda and Louis? The lists have been posted on the doors. Before we break these rolls, and help ourselves to fish and salad, I feel in my private pocket and find my credentials—what I carry to prove my superiority. I have passed. I have papers in my private pocket that prove it. But your eyes, Susan, full of turnips and cornfields, disturb me. These papers in my private pocket—the clamour that proves that I have passed—make a faint sound like that of a man clapping in an empty field to scare away rooks. Now it has died down altogether, under Susan's stare (the clapping, the reverberation that I have made), and I hear only the wind sweeping over the ploughed land and some bird singing—perhaps some intoxicated lark. Has the waiter heard of me, or those furtive everlasting couples, now loitering, now holding back and looking at the trees which are not yet dark enough to shelter their prostrate bodies? No; the sound of clapping has failed.

'What then remains, when I cannot pull out my papers and make you believe by reading aloud my credentials that I have passed? What remains is what Susan brings to light under the acid of her green eyes, her crystal, pear-shaped eyes. There is always somebody, when we come together, and the edges of meeting are still sharp, who refuses to be submerged; whose identity therefore one wishes to make crouch beneath one's own. For me now, it is Susan. I talk to impress Susan. Listen to me, Susan.

'When someone comes in at breakfast, even the embroidered fruit on my curtain swells so that parrots can peck it; one can break it off between one's thumb and finger. The thin, skimmed milk of early morning turns opal, blue, rose. At that hour your husband—the man who slapped his gaiters, pointing with his whip at the barren cow—grumbles. You say nothing. You see nothing. Custom blinds your eyes. At that hour your relationship is mute, null, dun-coloured. Mine at that hour is warm and various. There are no repetitions for me. Each day is dangerous. Smooth on the surface, we are all bone beneath like snakes coiling. Suppose we read *The Times*; suppose we argue. It is an experience. Suppose it is winter. The snow falling loads down the roof and seals us together in a red cave. The pipes have burst. We stand a yellow tin bath in the middle of the room. We rush helter-skelter for basins. Look there—it has burst again over the bookcase. We shout with laughter at the sight of ruin. Let solidity be destroyed. Let us have no possessions. Or is it summer?

We may wander to a lake and watch Chinese geese waddling flat-footed to the water's edge or see a bone-like city church with young green trembling before it. (I choose at random; I choose the obvious.) Each sight is an arabesque scrawled suddenly to illustrate some hazard and marvel of intimacy. The snow, the burst pipe, the tin bath, the Chinese goose—these are signs swung high aloft upon which, looking back, I read the character of each love; how each was different.

'You meanwhile—for I want to diminish your hostility, your green eyes fixed on mine, and your shabby dress, your rough hands, and all the other emblems of your maternal splendour—have stuck like a limpet to the same rock. Yet it is true, I do not want to hurt you; only to refresh and furbish up my own belief in myself that failed at your entry. Change is no longer possible. We are committed. Before, when we met in a restaurant in London with Percival, all simmered and shook; we could have been anything. We have chosen now, or sometimes it seems the choice was made for us—a pair of tongs pinched us between the shoulders. I chose. I took the print of life not outwardly, but inwardly upon the raw, the white, the unprotected fibre. I am clouded and bruised with the print of minds and faces and things so subtle that they have smell, colour, texture, substance, but no name. I am merely "Neville" to you, who see the narrow limits of my life and the line it cannot pass. But to myself I am immeasurable; a net whose fibres pass imperceptibly beneath the world. My net is almost indistinguishable from that which it surrounds. It lifts whales—huge leviathans and white jellies, what is amorphous and wandering; I detect, I perceive. Beneath my eyes opens—a book; I see to the bottom; the heart—I see to the depths. I know what loves are trembling into fire; how jealousy shoots its green flashes hither and thither; how intricately love crosses love; love makes knots; love brutally tears them apart. I have been knotted; I have been torn apart.

'But there was another glory once, when we watched for the door to open, and Percival came; when we flung ourselves unattached on the edge of a hard bench in a public room.'

'There was the beech wood,' said Susan, 'Elvedon, and the gilt hands of the clock sparkling among the trees. The pigeons broke the leaves. The changing travelling lights wandered over me. They escaped me. Yet look, Neville, whom I discredit in order to be myself, at my hand on the table. Look at the gradations of healthy colour here on the knuckles, here on the palm. My body has been used daily, rightly, like a tool by a good workman, all over. The blade is clean, sharp, worn in the centre. (We battle together like beasts fighting in a field, like stags making their horns clash.) Seen through your pale and yielding flesh, even apples and bunches of fruit must have a filmed look as if they stood under glass. Lying deep in a chair with one person, one person only, but one person who changes, you see one inch of flesh only; its nerves, fibres, the sullen or quick flow of blood on it; but nothing entire. You do not see a house in a garden; a horse in a field; a town laid out, as you bend like an old woman straining her eyes over her darning. But I have seen life in blocks, substantial, huge; its battlements and towers, factories and gasometers; a dwelling-place made from time immemorial after an hereditary pattern. These things remain square, prominent, undissolved in my mind. I am not sinuous or suave; I sit among you abrading your softness with my hardness, quenching the silver-grey flickering moth-wing quiver of words with the green spurt of my clear eyes.

'Now we have clashed our antlers. This is the necessary prelude; the salute of old friends.'

'The gold has faded between the trees,' said Rhoda, 'and a slice of green lies behind them, elongated like the blade of a knife seen in dreams, or some tapering island on which nobody sets foot. Now the cars begin to wink and flicker, coming down the avenue. Lovers can draw into the darkness now; the boles of the trees are swollen, are obscene with lovers.'

'It was different once,' said Bernard. 'Once we could break the current as we chose. How many telephone calls, how many post cards, are now needed to cut this hole through which we come together, united, at Hampton Court? How swift life runs from January to December! We are all swept on by the torrent of things grown so familiar that they cast no shade; we make no comparisons; think scarcely ever of I or of you; and in this unconsciousness attain the utmost freedom from friction and part the weeds that grow over the mouths of sunken channels. We have to leap like fish, high in the air, in order to catch the train from Waterloo. And however high we leap we fall back again into the stream. I shall never now take ship for the South Sea Islands. A journey to Rome is the limit of my travelling. I have sons and daughters. I am wedged into my place in the puzzle.

'But it is only my body—this elderly man here whom you call Bernard—that is fixed irrevocably—so I desire to believe. I think more disinterestedly than I could when I was young and must dig furiously like a child rummaging in a bran-pie to discover my self. "Look, what is this? And this? Is this going to be a fine present? Is that all?" and so on. Now I know what the parcels hold; and do not care much. I throw my mind out in the air as a man throws seeds in great fan-flights, falling through the purple sunset, falling on the pressed and shining ploughland which is bare.

'A phrase.* An imperfect phrase. And what are phrases? They have left me very little to lay on the table, beside Susan's hand; to take from my pocket, with Neville's credentials. I am not an authority on law, or medicine, or finance. I am wrapped round with phrases, like damp straw; I glow, phosphorescent. And each of you feels when I speak, "I am lit up. I am glowing." The little boys used to feel "That's a good one, that's a good one", as the phrases bubbled up from my lips under the elm trees in the playing-fields. They too bubbled up; they also escaped with my phrases. But I pine in solitude. Solitude is my undoing.

'I pass from house to house like the friars in the Middle Ages who cozened the wives and girls with beads and ballads. I am a traveller, a pedlar, paying for my lodging with a ballad; I am an indiscriminate, an easily pleased guest; often putting up in the best room in a four-poster; then lying in a barn on a haystack. I don't mind the fleas and find no fault with silk either. I am very tolerant. I am not a moralist. I have too great a sense of the shortness of life and its temptations to rule red lines. Yet I am not so indiscriminate as you think, judging me—as you judge me—from my fluency. I have a little dagger of contempt and severity hidden up my sleeve. But I am apt to be deflected. I make stories. I twist up toys out of anything. A girl sits at a cottage door; she is waiting; for whom? Seduced, or not seduced? The Headmaster sees the hole in the carpet. He sighs. His wife, drawing her fingers through the waves of her still abundant hair, reflects—et cetera. Waves of hands, hesitations at street corners, someone dropping a cigarette into the gutter—all are stories. But which is the true story? That I do not know. Hence I keep my phrases hung like clothes in a cupboard, waiting for someone to wear them. Thus waiting, thus speculating, making this note and then another, I do not cling to life. I shall be brushed like a bee from a sunflower. My philosophy, always accumulating, welling up moment by moment, runs like quicksilver a dozen ways at once. But Louis, wild-eyed but severe, in his attic, in his office, has formed unalterable conclusions upon the true nature of what is to be known.'

'It breaks,' said Louis, 'the thread I try to spin; your laughter breaks it, your indifference, also your beauty. Jinny broke the thread when she kissed me in the garden years ago. The boasting boys mocked me at school for my Australian accent and broke it. "This is the meaning," I say; and then start with a pang—vanity. "Listen", I say, "to the nightingale, who sings among the trampling feet; the conquests and migrations. Believe——" and then am twitched asunder. Over broken tiles and splinters of glass I pick my way. Different lights fall, making the ordinary leopard-spotted and strange. This moment of reconciliation, when we meet together united, this evening moment, with its wine and shaking leaves, and youth coming up from the river in white flannels, carrying cushions, is to me black with the shadows of dungeons and the tortures and infamies practised by man upon man. So imperfect are my senses that they never blot out with one purple the serious charge that my reason adds and adds against us, even as we sit here. What is the solution, I ask myself, and the bridge? How can I reduce these dazzling, these dancing apparitions to one line capable of linking all in one? So I ponder; and you meanwhile observe maliciously my pursed lips, my sallow cheeks and my invariable frown.

'But I beg you also to notice my cane and my waistcoat. I have inherited a desk of solid mahogany in a room hung with maps. Our steamers have won an enviable reputation for their cabins replete with luxury. We supply swimming-baths and gymnasiums. I wear a white waistcoat now and consult a little book before I make an engagement.

'This is the arch and ironical manner in which I hope to distract you from my shivering, my tender, and infinitely young and unprotected soul. For I am always the youngest; the most naïvely surprised; the one who runs in advance in apprehension and sympathy with discomfort or ridicule— should there be a smut on a nose, or a button undone. I suffer for all humiliations. Yet I am also ruthless, marmoreal. I do not see how you can say that it is fortunate to have lived. Your little excitements, your childish transports, when a kettle boils, when the soft air lifts Jinny's spotted scarf and it floats web-like, are to me like silk streamers thrown in the eyes of the charging bull. I condemn you. Yet my heart yearns towards you. I would go with you through the fires of death. Yet am happiest alone. I luxuriate in gold and purple vestments. Yet I prefer a view over chimney-pots; cats scraping their mangy sides upon blistered chimney-stacks; broken windows; and the hoarse clangour of bells from the steeple of some brick chapel.'

'I see what is before me,' said Jinny. 'This scarf, these wine-coloured spots. This glass. This mustard pot. This flower. I like what one touches, what one tastes. I like rain when it has turned to snow and become palpable. And being rash, and much more courageous than you are, I do not temper my beauty with meanness lest it should scorch me. I gulp it down entire. It is made of flesh; it is made of stuff. My imagination is the body's. Its visions are not fine-spun and white with purity like Louis's. I do not like your lean cats and your blistered chimney-pots. The scrannel beauties* of your roof-tops repel me. Men and women, in uniforms, wigs and gowns, bowler hats and tennis shirts beautifully open at the neck, the infinite variety of women's dresses (I note all clothes always) delight me. I eddy with them, in and out, in and out, into rooms, into halls, here, there, everywhere, wherever they go. This man lifts the hoof of a horse. This man shoves in and out the drawers of his private collection. I am never alone. I am attended by a regiment of my fellows. My mother must have followed the drum, my father the sea. I am like a little dog that trots down the road after the regimental band, but stops to snuff a tree-trunk, to sniff some brown stain, and suddenly careers across the street after some mongrel cur and then holds one paw up while it sniffs an entrancing whiff of meat from the butcher's shop. My traffics have led me into strange places. Men, how many, have broken from the wall and come to me. I have only to hold my hand up. Straight as a dart they have come to the place of assignation—perhaps a chair on a balcony, perhaps a shop at a street corner. The torments, the divisions of your lives have been solved for me night after night, sometimes only by the touch of a finger under the table-cloth as we sat dining—so fluid has my body become, forming even at the touch of a finger into one full drop, which fills itself, which quivers, which flashes, which falls in ecstasy.

'I have sat before a looking-glass as you sit writing, adding up figures at desks. So, before the looking-glass in the temple of my bedroom, I have judged my nose and my chin; my lips that open too wide and show too much gum. I have looked. I have noted. I have chosen what yellow or white, what shine or dullness, what loop or straightness suits. I am volatile for one, rigid for another, angular as an icicle in silver, or voluptuous as a candle flame in gold. I have run violently like a whip flung out to the extreme end of my tether. His shirt front, there in the corner, has been white; then purple; smoke and flame have wrapped us about; after a furious conflagration—yet we scarcely raised our voices, sitting on the hearth-rug, as we murmured all the secrets of our hearts as into shells so that nobody might hear in the sleeping-house, but I heard the cook stir once, and once we thought the ticking of the clock was a footfall—we have sunk to ashes, leaving no relics, no unburnt bones, no wisps of hair to be kept in lockets such as your intimacies leave behind them. Now I turn grey; now I turn gaunt; but I look at my face at midday sitting in front of the looking-glass in broad daylight, and note precisely my nose, my chin, my lips that open too wide and show too much gum. But I am not afraid.'

'There were lamp-posts,' said Rhoda, 'and trees that had not yet shed their leaves on the way from the station. The leaves might have hidden me still. But I did not hide behind them. I walked straight up to you instead of circling round to avoid the shock of sensation as I used. But it is only that I have taught my body to do a certain trick. Inwardly I am not taught; I fear, I hate, I love, I envy and despise you, but I never join you happily. Coming up from the station, refusing to accept the shadow of the trees and the pillar-boxes, I perceived, from your coats and umbrellas, even at a distance, how you stand embedded in a substance made of repeated moments run together; are committed, have an attitude, with children, authority, fame, love, society; where I have nothing. I have no face.

'Here in this dining-room you see the antlers and the tumblers; the salt-cellars; the yellow stains on the table-cloth. "Waiter!" says Bernard. "Bread!" says Susan. And the waiter comes; he brings bread. But I see the side of a cup like a mountain and only parts of antlers, and the brightness on the side of that jug like a crack in darkness with wonder and terror. Your voices sound like trees creaking in a forest. So with your faces and their promi-nences and hollows. How beautiful, standing at a distance immobile at midnight against the railings of some square! Behind you is a white crescent of foam, and fishermen on the verge of the world are drawing in nets and casting them. A wind ruffles the topmost leaves of primeval trees. (Yet here we sit at Hampton Court.) Parrots shrieking break the intense stillness of the jungle. (Here the trams start.) The swallow dips her wings in midnight pools. (Here we talk.) That is the circumference that I try to grasp as we sit together. Thus I must undergo the penance of Hampton Court at seven thirty precisely.

'But since these rolls of bread and wine bottles are needed by me, and your faces with their hollows and prominences are beautiful, and the table-cloth and its yellow stain, far from being allowed to spread in wider and wider circles of understanding that may at last (so I dream, falling off the edge of the earth at night when my bed floats suspended) embrace the entire world, I must go through the antics of the individual. I must start when you pluck at me with your children, your poems, your chilblains or whatever it is that you do and suffer. But I am not deluded. After all these callings hither and thither, these pluckings and searchings, I shall fall alone through this thin sheet into gulfs of fire. And you will not help me. More cruel than the old torturers, you will let me fall, and will tear me to pieces when I am fallen. Yet there are moments when the walls of the mind grow thin; when nothing is unabsorbed, and I could fancy that we might blow so vast a bubble that the sun might set and rise in it and we might take the blue of midday and the black of midnight and be cast off and escape from here and now.'

'Drop upon drop,' said Bernard, 'silence falls. It forms on the roof of the mind and falls into pools beneath. For ever alone, alone, alone—hear silence fall and sweep its rings to the farthest edges. Gorged and replete, solid with middle-aged content, I, whom loneliness destroys, let silence fall, drop by drop.

'But now silence falling pits my face, wastes my nose like a snowman stood out in a yard in the rain. As silence falls I am dissolved utterly and become featureless and scarcely to be distinguished from another. It does not matter. What matters? We have dined well. The fish, the veal cutlets, the wine have blunted the sharp tooth of egotism. Anxiety is at rest. The vainest of us, Louis perhaps, does not care what people think. Neville's tortures are at rest. Let others prosper—that is what he thinks. Susan hears the breathing of all her children safe asleep. Sleep, sleep, she murmurs. Rhoda has rocked her ships to shore. Whether they have foundered, whether they have anchored, she cares no longer. We are ready to consider any suggestion that the world may offer quite impartially. I reflect now that the earth is only a pebble flicked off accidentally from the face of the sun and that there is no life anywhere in the abysses of space.'

'In this silence,' said Susan, 'it seems as if no leaf would ever fall, or bird fly.'

'As if the miracle had happened,' said Jinny, 'and life were stayed here and now.'

'And,' said Rhoda, 'we had no more to live.'

'But listen,' said Louis, 'to the world moving through abysses of infinite space. It roars; the lighted strip of history is past and our Kings and Queens; we are gone; our civilization; the Nile; and all life. Our separate drops are dissolved; we are extinct, lost in the abysses of time, in the darkness.'

'Silence falls; silence falls,' said Bernard. 'But now listen; tick, tick; hoot, hoot; the world has hailed us back to it. I heard for one moment the howling winds of darkness as we passed beyond life. Then tick, tick (the clock); then hoot, hoot (the cars). We are landed; we are on shore; we are sitting, six of us, at a table. It is the memory of my nose that recalls me. I rise; "Fight," I cry, "fight!" remembering the shape of my own nose, and strike with this spoon upon this table pugnaciously.'

'Oppose ourselves to this illimitable chaos,' said Neville, 'this formless imbecility. Making love to a nursemaid behind a tree, that soldier is more admirable than all the stars. Yet sometimes one trembling star comes in the clear sky and makes me think the world beautiful and we maggots deforming even the trees with our lust.'

('Yet, Louis,' said Rhoda, 'how short a time silence lasts. Already they are beginning to smooth their napkins by the side of their plates. "Who comes?" says Jinny; and Neville sighs, remembering that Percival comes no more. Jinny has taken out her looking-glass. Surveying her face like an artist, she draws a powder-puff down her nose, and after one moment of deliberation has given precisely that red to the lips that the lips need. Susan, who feels scorn and fear at the sight of these preparations, fastens the top button of her coat, and unfastens it. What is she making ready for? For something, but something different.'

'They are saying to themselves,' said Louis, ' "It is time. I am still vigorous", they are saying, "My face shall be cut against the black of infinite space". They do not finish their sentences. "It is time", they keep saying. "The gardens will be shut." And going with them, Rhoda, swept into their current, we shall perhaps drop a little behind.'

'Like conspirators* who have something to whisper,' said Rhoda.)

'It is true, and I know for a fact,' said Bernard, 'as we walk down this avenue, that a King, riding, fell over a molehill here.* But how strange it seems to set against the whirling abysses of infinite space a little figure with a golden teapot on his head. Soon one recovers belief in figures: but not at once in what they put on their heads. Our English past—one inch of light. Then people put teapots on their heads and say, "I am a King!" No, I try to recover, as we walk, the sense of time, but with that streaming darkness in my eyes I have lost my grip. This Palace seems light as a cloud set for a moment on the sky. It is a trick of the mind—to put Kings on their thrones, one following another, with crowns on their heads. And we ourselves, walking six abreast, what do we oppose, with this random flicker of light in us that we call brain and feeling, how can we do battle against this flood; what has permanence? Our lives too stream away, down the unlighted avenues, past the strip of time, unidentified. Once Neville threw a poem at my head. Feeling a sudden conviction of immortality, I said, "I too know what Shakespeare knew". But that has gone.'

'Unreasonably, ridiculously,' said Neville, 'as we walk, time comes back. A dog does it, prancing. The machine works. Age makes hoary that gateway. Three hundred years now seem more than a moment vanished against that dog. King William mounts his horse wearing a wig, and the court ladies sweep the turf with their embroidered panniers. I am beginning to be convinced, as we walk, that the fate of Europe is of immense importance, and, ridiculous as it still seems, that all depends upon the battle of Blenheim. Yes; I declare, as we pass through this gateway, it is the present moment; I am become a subject of King George.'*

'While we advance down this avenue,' said Louis, 'I leaning slightly upon Jinny, Bernard arm-in-arm with Neville, and Susan with her hand in mine, it is difficult not to weep, calling ourselves little children, praying that God may keep us safe while we sleep. It is sweet to sing together, clasping hands, afraid of the dark, while Miss Curry plays the harmonium.'

'The iron gates* have rolled back,' said Jinny. 'Time's fangs have ceased their devouring. We have triumphed over the abysses of space, with rouge, with powder, with flimsy pocket-handkerchiefs.'

'I grasp, I hold fast,' said Susan. 'I hold firmly to this hand, anyone's, with love, with hatred; it does not matter which.'

'The still mood, the disembodied mood is on us,' said Rhoda, 'and we enjoy this momentary alleviation (it is not often that one has no anxiety) when the walls of the mind become transparent. Wren's palace, like the quartet* played to the dry and stranded people in the stalls, makes an oblong. A square is stood upon the oblong and we say, "This is our dwelling-place. The structure is now visible. Very little is left outside."'

'The flower,' said Bernard, 'the red carnation that stood

in the vase on the table of the restaurant when we dined together with Percival, is become a six-sided flower; made of six lives.'*

'A mysterious illumination,' said Louis, 'visible against those yew trees.'

'Built up with much pain, many strokes,' said Jinny.

'Marriage, death, travel, friendship,' said Bernard; 'town and country; children and all that; a many-sided substance cut out of this dark; a many-faceted flower. Let us stop for a moment; let us behold what we have made. Let it blaze against the yew trees.* One life. There. It is over. Gone out.'

'Now they vanish,' said Louis. 'Susan with Bernard. Neville with Jinny. You and I, Rhoda, stop for a moment by this stone urn. What song shall we hear now that these couples have sought the groves, and Jinny, pointing with her gloved hand, pretends to notice the water-lilies, and Susan, who has always loved Bernard, says to him, "My ruined life, my wasted life". And Neville, taking Jinny's little hand, with the cherry-coloured finger-nails, by the lake, by the moonlit water, cries, "Love, love", and she answers, imitating the bird, "Love, love?" What song do we hear?'

'They vanish, towards the lake,' said Rhoda. 'They slink away over the grass furtively, yet with assurance as if they asked of our pity their ancient privilege—not to be disturbed. The tide in the soul, tipped, flows that way; they cannot help deserting us. The dark has closed over their bodies. What song do we hear—the owl's, the nightingale's, the wren's? The steamer hoots; the light on the electric rails flashes; the trees gravely bow and bend. The flare hangs over London. Here is an old woman, quietly returning, and a man, a late fisherman, comes down the terrace with his rod. Not a sound, not a movement must escape us.'

'A bird flies homeward,' said Louis. 'Evening opens her eyes and gives one quick glance among the bushes before she sleeps. How shall we put it together, the confused and composite message that they send back to us, and not they only, but many dead, boys and girls, grown men and women, who have wandered here, under one king or another?'

'A weight has dropped into the night,' said Rhoda, 'dragging it down. Every tree is big with a shadow that is not the shadow of the tree behind it. We hear a drumming on the roofs of a fasting city when the Turks are hungry and uncertain tempered. We hear them crying with sharp, stag-like barks, "Open, open". Listen to the trams squealing and to the flashes from the electric rails. We hear the beech trees and the birch trees raise their branches as if the bride had let her silken nightdress fall and come to the doorway saying, "Open, open".'

'All seems alive,' said Louis. 'I cannot hear death anywhere tonight. Stupidity, on that man's face, age, on that woman's, would be strong enough, one would think, to resist the incantation, and bring in death. But where is death tonight? All the crudity, odds and ends, this and that, have been crushed like glass splinters into the blue, the red-fringed tide, which, drawing into the shore, fertile with innumerable fish, breaks at our feet.'

'If we could mount together, if we could perceive from a sufficient height,' said Rhoda, 'if we could remain untouched without any support—but you, disturbed by faint clapping sounds of praise and laughter, and I, resenting compromise and right and wrong on human lips, trust only in solitude and the violence of death and thus are divided.'

'For ever,' said Louis, 'divided. We have sacrificed the embrace among the ferns, and love, love, love by the lake, standing, like conspirators who have drawn apart to share some secret, by the urn. But now look, as we stand here, a ripple breaks on the horizon. The net is raised higher and higher. It comes to the top of the water. The water is broken by silver, by quivering little fish. Now leaping, now lashing, they are laid on shore. Life tumbles its catch upon the grass. There are figures coming towards us. Are they men or are they women? They still wear the ambiguous draperies of the flowing tide in which they have been immersed.'

'Now,' said Rhoda, 'as they pass that tree, they regain their natural size. They are only men, only women. Wonder and awe change as they put off the draperies of the flowing tide. Pity returns, as they emerge into the moonlight, like the relics of an army, our representatives, going every night (here or in Greece) to battle, and coming back every night with their wounds, their ravaged faces. Now light falls on them again. They have faces. They become Susan and Bernard, Jinny and Neville, people we know. Now what a shrinkage takes place! Now what a shrivelling, what an humiliation! The old shivers run through me, hatred and terror, as I feel myself grappled to one spot by these hooks they cast on us; these greetings, recognitions, pluckings of the finger and searchings of the eyes. Yet they have only to speak, and their first words, with the remembered tone and the perpetual deviation from what one expects, and their hands moving and making a thousand past days rise again in the darkness, shake my purpose.'

'Something flickers and dances,' said Louis. 'Illusion returns as they approach down the avenue. Rippling and questioning begin. What do I think of you—what do you think of me? Who are you? Who am I?—that quivers again its uneasy air over us, and the pulse quickens and the eye brightens and all the insanity of personal existence without which life would fall flat and die, begins again. They are on us. The southern sun flickers over this urn; we push off in to the tide of the violent and cruel sea. Lord help us to act our parts as we greet them returning—Susan and Bernard, Neville and Jinny.'

'We have destroyed something by our presence,' said Bernard, 'a world perhaps.'

'Yet we scarcely breathe,' said Neville, 'spent as we are. We are in that passive and exhausted frame of mind when we only wish to rejoin the body of our mother from whom we have been severed. All else is distasteful, forced and fatiguing. Jinny's yellow scarf is moth-coloured in this light; Susan's eyes are quenched. We are scarcely to be distinguished from the river. One cigarette end is the only point of emphasis among us. And sadness tinges our content, that we should have left you, torn the fabric; yielded to the desire to press out, alone, some bitterer, some blacker juice, which was sweet too. But now we are worn out.'

'After our fire,' said Jinny, 'there is nothing left to put in lockets.'

'Still I gape,' said Susan. 'like a young bird, unsatisfied, for something that has escaped me.'

'Let us stay for a moment,' said Bernard, 'before we go. Let us pace the terrace by the river almost alone. It is nearly bed-time. People have gone home. Now how comforting it is to watch the lights coming out in the bedrooms of small shopkeepers on the other side of the river. There is one—there is another. What do you think their takings have been today? Only just enough to pay for the rent, for light and food and the children's clothing. But just enough. What a sense of the tolerableness of life the lights in the bedrooms of small shopkeepers give us! Saturday comes, and there is just enough to pay perhaps for seats at the Pictures. Perhaps before they put out the light they go into the little garden and look at the giant rabbit couched in its wooden hut. That is the rabbit they will have for Sunday dinner. Then they put out the light. Then they sleep. And for thousands of people sleep is nothing but warmth and silence and one moment's sport with some fantastic dream. "I have posted my letter," the greengrocer thinks, "to the Sunday newspaper. Suppose I win five hundred pounds in the football competition? And we shall kill the rabbit. Life is pleasant. Life is good. I have posted the letter. We shall kill the rabbit." And he sleeps.

'That goes on. Listen. There is a sound like the knocking of railway trucks in a siding. That is the happy concatenation of one event following another in our lives. Knock, knock, knock. Must, must, must. Must go, must sleep, must wake, must get up—sober, merciful word which we pretend to revile, which we press tight to our hearts, without which we should be undone. How we worship that sound like the knocking together of trucks in a siding!

'Now far off down the river I hear the chorus; the song of the boasting boys, who are coming back in large charabancs from a day's outing on the decks of crowded steamers. Still they are singing as they used to sing, across the court, on winters' nights, or with the windows open in summer, getting drunk, breaking the furniture, wearing little striped caps, all turning their heads the same way as the brake rounded the corner; and I wished to be with them.

'What with the chorus, and the spinning water and the just perceptible murmur of the breeze we are slipping away. Little bits of ourselves are crumbling. There! Something very important fell then. I cannot keep myself together. I shall sleep. But we must go; must catch our train; must walk back to the station—must, must, must. We are only bodies jogging along side by side. I exist only in the soles of my feet and in the tired muscles of my thighs. We have been walking for hours it seems. But where? I cannot remember. I am like a log slipping smoothly over some waterfall. I am not a judge. I am not called upon to give my opinion. Houses and trees are all the same in this grey light. Is that a post? Is that a woman walking? Here is the station, and if the train were to cut me in two, I should come together on the further side, being one, being indivisible. But what is odd is that I still clasp the return half of my ticket to Waterloo firmly between the fingers of my right hand, even now, even sleeping.'

*Now the sun had sunk. Sky and sea were indistinguishable.
The waves breaking spread their white fans far out over
the shore, sent white shadows into the recesses of sonorous
caves and then rolled back sighing over the shingle.*

*The tree shook its branches and a scattering of leaves fell
to the ground. There they settled with perfect composure on
the precise spot where they would await dissolution. Black
and grey were shot into the garden from the broken vessel
that had once held red light. Dark shadows blackened the
tunnels between the stalks. The thrush was silent and the
worm sucked itself back into its narrow hole. Now and
again a whitened and hollow straw was blown from an old
nest and fell into the dark grasses among the rotten apples.
The light had faded from the tool-house wall and the
adder's skin hung from the nail empty. All the colours in
the room had overflown their banks. The precise brush
stroke was swollen and lop-sided; cupboards and chairs
melted their brown masses into one huge obscurity. The
height from floor to ceiling was hung with vast curtains of
shaking darkness. The looking-glass was pale as the mouth
of a cave shadowed by hanging creepers.*

*The substance had gone from the solidity of the hills.
Travelling lights drove a plumy wedge among unseen and
sunken roads, but no lights opened among the folded wings
of the hills, and there was no sound save the cry of a bird
seeking some lonelier tree. At the cliff's edge there was an
equal murmur of air that had been brushed through forests,*

*of water that had been cooled in a thousand glassy hollows
of mid-ocean.*

*As if there were waves of darkness in the air, darkness
moved on, covering houses, hills, trees, as waves of water
wash round the sides of some sunken ship. Darkness washed
down streets, eddying round single figures, engulfing them;
blotting out couples clasped under the showery darkness of
elm trees in full summer foliage. Darkness rolled its waves
along grassy rides and over the wrinkled skin of the turf,
enveloping the solitary thorn tree and the empty snail shells
at its foot. Mounting higher, darkness blew along the bare
upland slopes, and met the fretted and abraded pinnacles of
the mountain where the snow lodges for ever on the hard
rock even when the valleys are full of running streams and
yellow vine leaves, and girls, sitting on verandahs, look up
at the snow, shading their faces with their fans. Them, too,
darkness covered.*

'Now to sum up,' said Bernard. 'Now to explain to you the meaning of my life. Since we do not know each other (though I met you once, I think, on board a ship going to Africa), we can talk freely.* The illusion is upon me that something adheres for a moment, has roundness, weight, depth, is completed. This, for the moment, seems to be my life. If it were possible, I would hand it to you entire. I would break it off as one breaks off a bunch of grapes. I would say, "Take it. This is my life."

'But unfortunately, what I see (this globe, full of figures) you do not see. You see me, sitting at a table opposite you, a rather heavy, elderly man, grey at the temples. You see me take my napkin and unfold it. You see me pour myself out a glass of wine. And you see behind me the door opening, and people passing. But in order to make you understand, to give you my life, I must tell you a story— and there are so many, and so many—stories of childhood, stories of school, love, marriage, death, and so on; and none of them are true. Yet like children we tell each other stories, and to decorate them we make up these ridiculous, flamboyant, beautiful phrases. How tired I am of stories, how tired I am of phrases that come down beautifully with all their feet on the ground! Also, how I distrust neat designs of life that are drawn upon half-sheets of note-paper. I begin to long for some little language such as lovers use, broken words, inarticulate words, like the shuffling of feet on the pavement. I begin to seek some

design more in accordance with those moments of humiliation and triumph that come now and then undeniably.
Lying in a ditch on a stormy day, when it has been raining,
then enormous clouds come marching over the sky, tattered clouds, wisps of cloud. What delights me then is the
confusion, the height, the indifference and the fury. Great
clouds always changing, and movement; something sul-
phurous and sinister, bowled up, helter-skelter; towering,
trailing, broken off, lost, and I forgotten, minute, in a
ditch. Of story, of design, I do not see a trace then.

'But meanwhile, while we eat, let us turn over these
scenes as children turn over the pages of a picture-book
and the nurse says, pointing: "That's a cow. That's a boat."
Let us turn over the pages, and I will add, for your
amusement, a comment in the margin.

'In the beginning, there was the nursery, with windows
opening on to a garden, and beyond that the sea. I saw
something brighten—no doubt the brass handle of a cupboard. Then Mrs Constable raised the sponge above her
head, squeezed it, and out shot, right, left, all down the
spine, arrows of sensation. And so, as long as we draw
breath, for the rest of time, if we knock against a chair, a
table, or a woman, we are pierced with arrows of sensation—if we walk in a garden, if we drink this wine.
Sometimes indeed, when I pass a cottage with a light in the
window where a child has been born, I could implore them
not to squeeze the sponge over that new body. Then, there
was the garden and the canopy of the currant leaves which
seemed to enclose everything; flowers, burning like sparks
upon the depths of green; a rat wreathing with maggots
under a rhubarb leaf; the fly going buzz, buzz, buzz upon
the nursery ceiling, and plates upon plates of innocent
bread and butter. All these things happen in one second

and last for ever. Faces loom. Dashing round the corner. "Hullo", one says, "there's Jinny. That's Neville. That's Louis in grey flannel with a snake belt. That's Rhoda." She had a basin in which she sailed petals of white flowers. It was Susan who cried, that day when I was in the tool-house with Neville; and I felt my indifference melt. Neville did not melt. "Therefore," I said, "I am myself, not Neville", a wonderful discovery. Susan cried and I followed her. Her wet pocket-handkerchief, and the sight of her little back heaving up and down like a pump-handle, sobbing for what was denied her, screwed my nerves up. "That is not to be borne", I said, as I sat beside her on the roots that were hard as skeletons. I then first became aware of the presence of those enemies who change, but are always there; the forces we fight against. To let oneself be carried on passively is unthinkable. "That's your course, world," one says, "mine is this." So, "Let's explore", I cried, and jumped up, and ran downhill with Susan and saw the stable-boy clattering about the yard in great boots. Down below, through the depths of the leaves, the gardeners swept the lawns with great brooms. The lady sat writing. Transfixed, stopped dead, I thought, "I cannot interfere with a single stroke of those brooms. They sweep and they sweep. Nor with the fixity of that woman writing." It is strange that one cannot stop gardeners sweeping nor dislodge a woman. There they have remained all my life. It is as if one had woken in Stonehenge surrounded by a circle of great stones, these enemies, these presences. Then a wood-pigeon flew out of the trees. And being in love for the first time, I made a phrase—a poem about a wood-pigeon—a single phrase, for a hole had been knocked in my mind, one of those sudden transparencies through which one sees everything. Then more bread and butter and more flies droning round the nursery ceiling on which quivered islands of light, ruffled, opalescent, while the pointed fingers of the lustre dripped blue pools on the corner of the mantelpiece. Day after day as we sat at tea we observed these sights.

'But we were all different. The wax—the virginal wax that coats the spine melted in different patches for each of us. The growl of the boot-boy making love to the tweeny among the gooseberry bushes; the clothes blown out hard on the line; the dead man in the gutter; the apple tree, stark in the moonlight; the rat swarming with maggots; the lustre dripping blue—our white wax was streaked and stained by each of these differently. Louis was disgusted by the nature of human flesh; Rhoda by our cruelty; Susan could not share; Neville wanted order; Jinny love; and so on. We suffered terribly as we became separate bodies.

'Yet I was preserved from these excesses and have survived many of my friends, am a little stout, grey, rubbed on the thorax as it were, because it is the panorama of life, seen not from the roof, but from the third-storey window, that delights me, not what one woman says to one man, even if that man is myself. How could I be bullied at school therefore? How could they make things hot for me? There was the Doctor lurching into chapel, as if he trod a battleship in a gale of wind, shouting out his commands through a megaphone, since people in authority always become melodramatic—I did not hate him like Neville, or revere him like Louis. I took notes as we sat together in chapel. There were pillars, shadows, memorial brasses, boys scuffling and swopping stamps behind Prayer Books; the sound of a rusty pump; the Doctor booming, about immortality and quitting ourselves like men; and Percival scratching his thigh. I made notes for stories; drew portraits in the margin of my pocket-book and thus became still more separate. Here are one or two of the figures I saw.

'Percival sat staring straight ahead of him that day in chapel. He also had a way of flicking his hand to the back of his neck. His movements were always remarkable. We all flicked our hands to the backs of our heads—unsuccessfully. He had the kind of beauty which defends itself from any caress. As he was not in the least precocious, he read whatever was written up for our edification without any comment, and thought with that magnificent equanimity (Latin words come naturally) that was to preserve him from so many meannesses and humiliations, that Lucy's flaxen pigtails and pink cheeks were the height of female beauty. Thus preserved, his taste later was of extreme fineness. But there should be music, some wild carol. Through the window should come a hunting-song from some rapid unapprehended life—a sound that shouts among the hills and dies away. What is startling, what is unexpected, what we cannot account for, what turns symmetry to nonsense—that comes suddenly to my mind, thinking of him. The little apparatus of observation is unhinged. Pillars go down; the Doctor floats off; some sudden exaltation possesses me. He was thrown, riding in a race, and when I came along Shaftesbury Avenue tonight, those insignificant and scarcely formulated faces that bubble up out of the doors of the Tube, and many obscure Indians, and people dying of famine and disease, and women who have been cheated, and whipped dogs and crying children—all these seemed to me bereft. He would have done justice. He would have protected. About the age of forty he would have shocked the authorities. No lullaby has ever occurred to me capable of singing him to rest.

'But let me dip again and bring up in my spoon another of these minute objects which we call optimistically, "characters of our friends"—Louis. He sat staring at the preacher. His being seemed conglobulated in his brow, his lips were pressed; his eyes were fixed, but suddenly they flashed with laughter. Also he suffered from chilblains, the penalty of an imperfect circulation. Unhappy, unfriended, in exile he would sometimes, in moments of confidence, describe how the surf swept over the beaches of his home. The remorseless eye of youth fixed itself upon his swollen joints. Yes, but we were also quick to perceive how cutting, how apt, how severe he was, how naturally, when we lay under the elm trees pretending to watch cricket, we waited his approval, seldom given. His ascendancy was resented, as Percival's was adored. Prim, suspicious, lifting his feet like a crane, there was yet a legend that he had smashed a door with his naked fist. But his peak was too bare, too stony for that kind of mist to cling to it. He was without those simple attachments by which one is connected with another. He remained aloof; enigmatic; a scholar capable of that inspired accuracy which has something formidable about it. My phrases (how to describe the moon) did not meet with his approval. On the other hand, he envied me to the point of desperation for being at my ease with servants. Not that the sense of his own deserts failed him. That was commensurate with his respect for discipline. Hence his success, finally. His life, though, was not happy. But look—his eye turns white as he lies in the palm of my hand. Suddenly the sense of what people are leaves one. I return him to the pool where he will acquire lustre.

'Neville next—lying on his back staring up at the summer sky. He floated among us like a piece of thistle-down, indolently haunting the sunny corner of the playing-field, not listening, yet not remote. It was through him that I have nosed round without ever precisely touching the Latin classics and have also derived some of those persistent habits of thought which make us irredeemably lop-sided— for instance about crucifixes, that they are the mark of the devil. Our half-loves and half-hates and ambiguities on these points were to him indefensible treacheries. The swaying and sonorous Doctor, whom I made to sit swinging his braces over a gas-fire, was to him nothing but an instrument of the inquisition. So he turned with a passion that made up for his indolence upon Catullus, Horace, Lucretius, lying lazily dormant, yes, but regardant, noticing, with rapture, cricketers, while with a mind like the tongue of an ant-eater, rapid, dexterous, glutinous, he searched out every curl and twist of those Roman sentences, and sought out one person, always one person to sit beside.

'And the long skirts of the masters' wives would come swishing by, mountainous, menacing; and our hands would fly to our caps. And immense dullness would descend unbroken, monotonous. Nothing, nothing, nothing broke with its fin that leaden waste of waters. Nothing would happen to lift that weight of intolerable boredom. The terms went on. We grew; we changed; for, of course, we are animals. We are not always aware by any means; we breathe, eat, sleep automatically. We exist not only separately but in undifferentiated blobs of matter. With one scoop a whole brakeful of boys is swept up and goes cricketing, footballing. An army marches across Europe. We assemble in parks and halls and sedulously oppose any renegade (Neville, Louis, Rhoda) who sets up a separate existence. And I am so made that, while I hear one or two distinct melodies, such as Louis sings, or

Neville, I am also drawn irresistibly to the sound of the chorus chanting its old, chanting its almost wordless, almost senseless song that comes across courts at night; which we hear now booming round us as cars and omnibuses take people to theatres. (Listen; the cars rush past this restaurant; now and then, down the river, a siren hoots, as a steamer makes for the sea.) If a bagman offers me snuff in a train I accept. I like the copious, shapeless, warm, not so very clever, but extremely easy and rather coarse aspect of things; the talk of men in clubs and public-houses, of miners half naked in drawers—the forthright, perfectly unassuming, and without end in view except dinner, love, money and getting along tolerably; that which is without great hopes, ideals or anything of that kind; what is unassuming except to make a tolerably good job of it. I like all that. So I joined them, when Neville sulked or Louis, as I quite agree sublimely, turned on his heel.

'Thus, not equally by any means or with order, but in great streaks my waxen waistcoat melted, here one drop, there another. Now through this transparency became visible those wondrous pastures, at first so moon-white, radiant, where no foot has been; meadows of the rose, the crocus, of the rock and the snake too; of the spotted and swart; the embarrassing, the binding and tripping up. One leaps out of bed, throws up the window; with what a whirr the birds rise! You know that sudden rush of wings, that exclamation, carol, and confusion; the riot and babble of voices; and all the drops are sparkling, trembling, as if the garden were a splintered mosaic, vanishing, twinkling; not yet formed into one whole; and a bird sings close to the window. I heard those songs. I followed those phantoms. I saw Joans, Dorothys, Miriams, I forget their names, passing down avenues, stopping on the crest of bridges to look down into the river. And from among them rise one or two distinct figures, birds who sang with the rapt egotism of youth by the window; broke their snails on stones, dipped their beaks in sticky, viscous matter; hard, avid, remorseless; Jinny, Susan, Rhoda. They had been educated on the east coast or on the south coast. They had grown long pigtails and acquired the look of startled foals, which is the mark of adolescence.

'Jinny was the first to come sidling up to the gate to eat sugar. She nipped it off the palms of one's hands very cleverly, but her ears were laid back as if she might bite. Rhoda was wild—Rhoda one never could catch. She was both frightened and clumsy. It was Susan who first became wholly woman, purely feminine. It was she who dropped on my face those scalding tears which are terrible, beautiful; both, neither. She was born to be the adored of poets, since poets require safety; someone who sits sewing, who says, "I hate, I love", who is neither comfortable nor prosperous, but has some quality in accordance with the high but unemphatic beauty of pure style which those who create poetry so particularly admire. Her father trailed from room to room and down flagged corridors in his flapping dressing-gown and worn slippers. On still nights a wall of water fell with a roar a mile off. The ancient dog could scarcely heave himself up on to his chair. And some witless servant could be heard laughing at the top of the house as she whirred the wheel of the sewing-machine round and round.

'That I observed even in the midst of my anguish when, twisting her pocket-handkerchief, Susan cried, "I love; I hate". "A worthless servant", I observed, "laughs upstairs in the attic",* and that little piece of dramatization shows how incompletely we are merged in our own experiences.

On the outskirts of every agony sits some observant fellow who points;* who whispers as he whispered to me that summer morning in the house where the corn comes up to the window, "The willow grows on the turf by the river. The gardeners sweep with great brooms and the lady sits writing." Thus he directed me to that which is beyond and outside our own predicament; to that which is symbolic, and thus perhaps permanent, if there is any permanence in our sleeping, eating, breathing, so animal, so spiritual and tumultuous lives.

'The willow tree grew by the river. I sat on the smooth turf with Neville, with Larpent, with Baker, Romsey, Hughes, Percival and Jinny. Through its fine plumes specked with little pricked ears of green in spring, of orange in autumn, I saw boats; buildings; I saw hurrying, decrepit women. I buried match after match in the turf decidedly to mark this or that stage in the process of understanding (it might be philosophy; science; it might be myself) while the fringe of my intelligence floating unattached caught those distant sensations which after a time the mind draws in and works upon; the chime of bells; general murmurs; vanishing figures; one girl on a bicycle who, as she rode, seemed to lift the corner of a curtain concealing the populous undifferentiated chaos of life which surged behind the outlines of my friends and the willow tree.

'The tree alone resisted our eternal flux. For I changed and changed; was Hamlet, was Shelley,* was the hero, whose name I now forget, of a novel by Dostoevsky; was for a whole term, incredibly, Napoleon; but was Byron chiefly. For many weeks at a time it was my part to stride into rooms and fling gloves and coat on the back of chairs, scowling slightly. I was always going to the bookcase for another sip of the divine specific. Therefore, I let fly my tremendous battery of phrases upon somebody quite inappropriate—a girl now married, now buried; every book, every window-seat was littered with the sheets of my unfinished letters to the woman who made me Byron. For it is difficult to finish a letter in somebody else's style. I arrived all in a lather at her house; exchanged tokens but did not marry her, being no doubt unripe for that intensity.

'Here again there should be music. Not that wild hunting-song, Percival's music; but a painful, guttural, visceral, also soaring, lark-like, pealing song* to replace these flagging, foolish transcripts—how much too deliberate! how much too reasonable!—which attempt to describe the flying moment of first love. A purple slide is slipped over the day. Look at a room before she comes and after. Look at the innocents outside pursuing their way. They neither see nor hear; yet on they go. Moving oneself in this radiant yet gummy atmosphere, how conscious one is of every movement—something adheres, something sticks to one's hands, taking up a newspaper even. Then there is the being eviscerated—drawn out, spun like a spider's web and twisted in agony round a thorn. Then a thunder-clap of complete indifference; the light blown out; then the return of measureless irresponsible joy; certain fields seem to glow green for ever, and innocent landscapes appear as if in the light of the first dawn—one patch of green, for example, up at Hampstead; and all faces are lit up, all conspire in a hush of tender joy; and then the mystic sense of completion and then that rasping, dog-fish skin-like roughness—those black arrows of shivering sensation, when she misses the post, when she does not come. Out rush a bristle of horned suspicions, horror, horror, horror—but what is the use of painfully elaborating these consecutive sentences when what one needs is nothing consecutive but a bark, a groan? And years later to see a middle-aged woman in a restaurant taking off her cloak.

'But to return. Let us again pretend that life is a solid substance, shaped like a globe, which we turn about in our fingers. Let us pretend that we can make out a plain and logical story, so that when one matter is despatched—love for instance—we go on, in an orderly manner, to the next. I was saying there was a willow tree. Its shower of falling branches, its creased and crooked bark had the effect of what remains outside our illusions yet cannot stay them, is changed by them for the moment, yet shows through stable, still, and with a sternness that our lives lack. Hence the comment it makes; the standard it supplies, and the reason why, as we flow and change, it seems to measure. Neville, for example, sat with me on the turf. But can anything be as clear as all that, I would say, following his gaze, through the branches, to a punt on the river, and a young man eating bananas from a paper bag? The scene was cut out with such intensity and so permeated with the quality of his vision that for a moment I could see it too; the punt, the bananas, the young man, through the branches of the willow tree. Then it faded.

'Rhoda came wandering vaguely. She would take advantage of any scholar in a blowing gown, or donkey rolling the turf with slippered feet to hide behind. What fear wavered and hid itself and blew to a flame in the depths of her grey, her startled, her dreaming eyes? Cruel and vindictive as we are, we are not bad to that extent. We have our fundamental goodness surely or to talk as I talk freely to someone I hardly know would be impossible—we should cease. The willow as she saw it grew on the verge of a grey desert where no bird sang. The leaves shrivelled as she looked at them, tossed in agony as she passed them. The trams and omnibuses roared hoarse in the street, ran over rocks and sped foaming away. Perhaps one pillar, sunlit, stood in her desert by a pool where wild beasts come down stealthily to drink.

'Then Jinny came. She flashed her fire over the tree. She was like a crinkled poppy, febrile, thirsty with the desire to drink dry dust. Darting, angular, not in the least impulsive, she came prepared. So little flames zigzag over the cracks in the dry earth. She made the willows dance, but not with illusion; for she saw nothing that was not there. It was a tree; there was the river; it was afternoon; here we were; I in my serge suit; she in green. There was no past, no future; merely the moment in its ring of light, and our bodies; and the inevitable climax, the ecstasy.

'Louis, when he let himself down on the grass, cautiously spreading (I do not exaggerate) a mackintosh square, made one acknowledge his presence. It was formidable. I had the intelligence to salute his integrity; his research with bony fingers wrapped in rags because of chilblains for some diamond of indissoluble veracity. I buried boxes of burnt matches in holes in the turf at his feet. His grim and caustic tongue reproved my indolence. He fascinated me with his sordid imagination.* His heroes wore bowler-hats and talked about selling pianos for tenners. Through his landscape the tram squealed; the factory poured its acrid fumes. He haunted mean streets and towns where women lay drunk, naked, on counterpanes on Christmas day. His words falling from a shot-tower hit the water and up it spurted. He found one word, one only for the moon. Then he got up and went; we all got up; we all went. But I, pausing, looked at the tree, and as I looked in autumn at the fiery and yellow branches, some sediment formed; I formed; a drop fell; I fell—that is, from some completed experience I had emerged.

'I rose and walked away—I, I, I; not Byron, Shelley, Dostoevsky, but I, Bernard. I even repeated my own name once or twice. I went, swinging my stick, into a shop, and bought—not that I love music—a picture of Beethoven in a silver frame. Not that I love music, but because the whole of life, its masters, its adventurers, then appeared in long ranks of magnificent human beings behind me; and I was the inheritor; I, the continuer; I, the person miraculously appointed to carry it on. So, swinging my stick, with my eyes filmed, not with pride, but with humility rather, I walked down the street. The first whirr of wings had gone up, the carol, the exclamation; and now one enters; one goes into the house, the dry, uncompromising, inhabited house, the place with all its traditions, its objects, its accumulations of rubbish, and treasures displayed upon tables. I visited the family tailor, who remembered my uncle. People turned up in great quantities, not cut out, like the first faces (Neville, Louis, Jinny, Susan, Rhoda), but confused, featureless, or changed their features so fast that they seemed to have none. And blushing yet scornful, in the oddest condition of raw rapture and scepticism, I took the blow; the mixed sensations; the complex and disturbing and utterly unprepared for impacts of life all over, in all places, at the same time. How upsetting! How humiliating never to be sure what to say next, and those painful silences, glaring as dry deserts, with every pebble apparent; and then to say what one ought not to have said, and then to be conscious of a ramrod of incorruptible sincerity which one would willingly exchange for a shower of smooth pence, but could not, there at that party, where Jinny sat quite at her ease, rayed out on a gilt chair.

'Then says some lady with an impressive gesture, "Come with me". She leads one into a private alcove and admits one to the honour of her intimacy. Surnames change to Christian names; Christian names to nicknames. What is to be done about India, Ireland or Morocco?* Old gentlemen answer the question standing decorated under chandeliers. One finds oneself surprisingly supplied with information. Outside the undifferentiated forces roar; inside we are very private, very explicit, have a sense indeed, that it is here, in this little room, that we make whatever day of the week it may be. Friday or Saturday. A shell forms upon the soft soul, nacreous, shiny, upon which sensations tap their beaks in vain. On me it formed earlier than on most. Soon I could carve my pear when other people had done dessert. I could bring my sentence to a close in a hush of complete silence. It is at that season too that perfection has a lure. One can learn Spanish, one thinks, by tying a string to the right toe and waking early. One fills up the little compartments of one's engagement book with dinner at eight; luncheon at one-thirty. One has shirts, socks, ties laid out on one's bed.

'But it is a mistake, this extreme precision, this orderly and military progress; a convenience, a lie. There is always deep below it, even when we arrive punctually at the appointed time with our white waistcoats and polite formalities, a rushing stream of broken dreams, nursery rhymes, street cries, half-finished sentences and sights— elm trees, willow trees, gardeners sweeping, women writing—that rise and sink even as we hand a lady down to dinner. While one straightens the fork so precisely on the table-cloth, a thousand faces mop and mow. There is nothing one can fish up in a spoon; nothing one can call an event. Yet it is alive too and deep, this stream. Immersed in it I would stop between one mouthful and the next, and look intently at a vase, perhaps with one red flower, while a reason struck me, a sudden revelation. Or I would say, walking along the Strand, "That's the phrase I want", as some beautiful, fabulous phantom bird, fish or cloud with fiery edges swam up to enclose once and for all some notion haunting me, after which on I trotted taking stock with renewed delight of ties and things in shop-windows.

'The crystal, the globe of life as one calls it, far from being hard and cold to the touch, has walls of thinnest air. If I press them all will burst. Whatever sentence I extract whole and entire from this cauldron is only a string of six little fish that let themselves be caught while a million others leap and sizzle, making the cauldron bubble like boiling silver, and slip through my fingers. Faces recur, faces and faces—they press their beauty to the walls of my bubble—Neville, Susan, Louis, Jinny, Rhoda and a thousand others. How impossible to order them rightly; to detach one separately, or to give the effect of the whole—again like music. What a symphony with its concord and its discord, and its tunes on top and its complicated bass beneath, then grew up! Each played his own tune, fiddle, flute, trumpet, drum or whatever the instrument might be. With Neville, "Let's discuss Hamlet". With Louis, science. With Jinny, love. Then suddenly, in a moment of exasperation, off to Cumberland with a quiet man for a whole week in an inn, with the rain running down the window-panes and nothing but mutton and mutton and again mutton for dinner. Yet that week remains a solid stone in the welter of unrecorded sensation. It was then we played dominoes; then we quarrelled about tough mutton. Then we walked on the fell. And a little girl, peeping round the door, gave me that letter, written on blue paper, in which I learnt that the girl who had made me Byron was to marry a squire. A man in gaiters, a man with a whip, a man who made speeches about fat oxen at dinner—I exclaimed derisively and looked at the racing clouds, and felt my own failure; my desire to be free; to escape; to be bound; to make an end; to continue; to be Louis; to be myself; and walked out in my mackintosh alone, and felt grumpy under the eternal hills and not in the least sublime; and came home and blamed the meat and packed and so back again to the welter; to the torture.

'Nevertheless, life is pleasant, life is tolerable. Tuesday follows Monday; then comes Wednesday. The mind grows rings; the identity becomes robust; pain is absorbed in growth. Opening and shutting, shutting and opening, with increasing hum and sturdiness, the haste and fever of youth are drawn into service until the whole being seems to expand in and out like the mainspring of a clock. How fast the stream flows from January to December! We are swept on by the torrent of things grown so familiar that they cast no shadow. We float, we float. . . .

'However, since one must leap (to tell you this story), I leap, here, at this point, and alight now upon some perfectly commonplace object—say the poker and tongs, as I saw them sometime later, after that lady who had made me Byron had married, under the light of one whom I will call the third Miss Jones. She is the girl who wears a certain dress expecting one at dinner, who picks a certain rose, who makes one feel "Steady, steady, this is a matter of some importance", as one shaves. Then one asks, "How does she behave to children?" One observes that she is a little clumsy with her umbrella; but minded when the mole was caught in the trap; and finally, would not make the loaf at breakfast (I was thinking of the interminable breakfasts of married life as I shaved) altogether prosaic—it would not surprise one sitting opposite this girl to see a dragon-fly perched on the loaf at breakfast. Also she inspired me with a desire to rise in the world; also she made me look with curiosity at the hitherto repulsive faces of new-born babies. And the little fierce beat—tick-tack, tick-tack—of the pulse of one's mind took on a more majestic rhythm. I roamed down Oxford Street. We are the continuers, we are the inheritors, I said, thinking of my sons and daughters; and if the feeling is so grandiose as to be absurd and one conceals it by jumping on to a bus or buying the evening paper, it is still a curious element in the ardour with which one laces up one's boots, with which one now addresses old friends committed to different careers. Louis, the attic-dweller; Rhoda, the nymph of the fountain always wet; both contradicted what was then so positive to me; both gave the other side of what seemed to me so evident (that we marry, that we domesticate); for which I loved them, pitied them, and also deeply envied them their different lot.

'Once I had a biographer, dead long since, but if he still followed my footsteps with his old flattering intensity he would here say, "About this time Bernard married and bought a house. . . . His friends observed in him a growing tendency to domesticity. . . . The birth of children made it highly desirable that he should augment his income." That is the biographic style, and it does to tack together torn bits of stuff, stuff with raw edges. After all, one cannot find fault with the biographic style if one begins letters "Dear Sir", ends them "yours faithfully"; one cannot despise these phrases laid like Roman roads across the tumult of our lives, since they compel us to walk in step like civilized people with the slow and measured tread of

policemen though one may be humming any nonsense
under one's breath at the same time—"Hark, hark, the
dogs do bark",* "Come away, come away, death",* "Let
me not to the marriage of true minds",* and so on. "He
attained some success in his profession. . . . He inherited a
small sum of money from an uncle"—that is how the
biographer continues, and if one wears trousers and hitches
them up with braces, one has to say that, though it is
tempting now and then to go blackberrying; tempting to
play ducks and drakes with all these phrases. But one has
to say that.

'I became, I mean, a certain kind of man, scoring my
path across life as one treads a path across the fields. My
boots became worn a little on the left side. When I came
in, certain rearrangements took place. "Here's Bernard!"
How differently different people say that! There are many
rooms—many Bernards. There was the charming, but
weak; the strong, but supercilious; the brilliant, but
remorseless; the very good fellow, but, I make no doubt,
the awful bore; the sympathetic, but cold; the shabby,
but—go into the next room—the foppish, worldly, and
too well dressed. What I was to myself was different; was
none of these. I am inclined to pin myself down most
firmly there before the loaf at breakfast with my wife, who
being now entirely my wife and not at all the girl who
wore when she hoped to meet me a certain rose, gave me
that feeling of existing in the midst of unconsciousness
such as the tree-frog must have couched on the right shade
of green leaf. "Pass" . . . I would say. "Milk" . . . she might
answer, or "Mary's coming" . . .—simple words for those
who have inherited the spoils of all the ages but not as said
then, day after day, in the full tide of life, when one feels
complete, entire, at breakfast. Muscles, nerves, intestines,

blood-vessels, all that makes the coil and spring of our being, the unconscious hum of the engine, as well as the dart and flicker of the tongue, functioned superbly. Opening, shutting; shutting, opening; eating, drinking; sometimes speaking—the whole mechanism seemed to expand, to contract, like the mainspring of a clock. Toast and butter, coffee and bacon, *The Times* and letters—suddenly the telephone rang with urgency and I rose deliberately and went to the telephone. I took up the black mouth. I marked the ease with which my mind adjusted itself to assimilate the message—it might be (one has these fancies) to assume command of the British Empire; I observed my composure; I remarked with what magnificent vitality the atoms of my attention dispersed, swarmed round the interruption, assimilated the message, adapted themselves to a new state of affairs and had created, by the time I put back the receiver, a richer, stronger, a more complicated world in which I was called upon to act my part and had no doubt whatever that I could do it. Clapping my hat on my head, I strode into a world inhabited by vast numbers of men who had also clapped their hats on their heads, and as we jostled and encountered in trains and tubes we exchanged the knowing wink of competitors and comrades braced with a thousand snares and dodges to achieve the same end—to earn our livings.

'Life is pleasant. Life is good. The mere process of life is satisfactory. Take the ordinary man in good health. He likes eating and sleeping. He likes the snuff of fresh air and walking at a brisk pace down the Strand. Or in the country there's a cock crowing on a gate; there's a foal galloping round a field. Something always has to be done next. Tuesday follows Monday; Wednesday Tuesday. Each spreads the same ripple of well-being, repeats the same curve of rhythm; covers fresh sand with a chill or ebbs a little slackly without. So the being grows rings; identity becomes robust. What was fiery and furtive like a fling of grain cast into the air and blown hither and thither by wild gusts of life from every quarter is now methodical and orderly and flung with a purpose—so it seems.

'Lord, how pleasant! Lord, how good! How tolerable is the life of little shopkeepers, I would say, as the train drew through the suburbs and one saw lights in bedroom windows. Active, energetic as a swarm of ants, I said, as I stood at the window and watched workers, bag in hand, stream into town. What hardness, what energy and violence of limb, I thought, seeing men in white drawers scouring after a football on a patch of snow in January. Now being grumpy about some small matter—it might be the meat—it seemed luxurious to disturb with a little ripple the enormous stability, whose quiver, for our child was about to be born, increased its joy, of our married life. I snapped at dinner. I spoke unreasonably as if, being a millionaire, I could throw away five shillings; or, being a perfect steeple-jack, stumbled over a footstool on purpose. Going up to bed we settled our quarrel on the stairs, and standing by the window looking at a sky clear like the inside of a blue stone, "Heaven be praised," I said, "we need not whip this prose into poetry. The little language is enough." For the space of the prospect and its clarity seemed to offer no impediment whatsoever, but to allow our lives to spread out and out beyond all bristling of roofs and chimneys to the flawless verge.

'Into this crashed death—Percival's. "Which is happiness?" I said (our child had been born), "which pain?" referring to the two sides of my body, as I came downstairs, making a purely physical statement. Also I made note of the state of the house; the curtain blowing; the cook singing; the wardrobe showing through the half-opened door. I said, "Give him (myself) another moment's respite" as I went downstairs. "Now in this drawing-room he is going to suffer. There is no escape." But for pain words are lacking. There should be cries, cracks, fissures, whiteness passing over chintz covers, interference with the sense of time, of space; the sense also of extreme fixity in passing objects; and sounds very remote and then very close; flesh being gashed and blood spurting, a joint suddenly twisted—beneath all of which appears something very important, yet remote, to be just held in solitude. So I went out. I saw the first morning he would never see—the sparrows were like toys dangled from a string by a child. To see things without attachment, from the outside, and to realize their beauty in itself—how strange! And then the sense that a burden has been removed; pretence and make-believe and unreality are gone, and lightness has come with a kind of transparency, making oneself invisible and things seen through as one walks—how strange. "And now what other discovery will there be?" I said, and in order to hold it tight ignored newspaper placards and went and looked at pictures. Madonnas and pillars, arches and orange trees, still as on the first day of creation, but acquainted with grief, there they hung, and I gazed at them. "Here," I said, "we are together without interruption." This freedom, this immunity, seemed then a conquest, and stirred in me such exaltation that I sometimes go there, even now, to bring back exaltation and Percival. But it did not last. What torments one is the horrible activity of the mind's eye— how he fell, how he looked, where they carried him; men in loin-cloths, pulling ropes; the bandages and the mud.

Then comes the terrible pounce of memory, not to be foretold, not to be warded off—that I did not go with him to Hampton Court. That claw scratched; that fang tore; I did not go. In spite of his impatiently protesting that it did not matter; why interrupt, why spoil our moment of uninterrupted community?—Still, I repeated sullenly, I did not go, and so, driven out of the sanctuary by these officious devils, went to Jinny because she had a room; a room with little tables, with little ornaments scattered on little tables. There I confessed, with tears—I had not gone to Hampton Court. And she, remembering other things, to me trifles but torturing to her, showed me how life withers when there are things we cannot share. Soon, too, a maid came in with a note, and as she turned to answer it and I felt my own curiosity to know what she was writing and to whom, I saw the first leaf fall on his grave. I saw us push beyond this moment, and leave it behind us for ever. And then sitting side by side on the sofa we remembered inevitably what had been said by others; "the lily of the day is fairer far in May";* we compared Percival to a lily—Percival whom I wanted to lose his hair, to shock the authorities, to grow old with me; he was already covered with lilies.

'So the sincerity of the moment passed; so it became symbolical; and that I could not stand. Let us commit any blasphemy of laughter and criticism rather than exude this lily-sweet glue; and cover him with phrases, I cried. Therefore I broke off, and Jinny, who was without future, or speculation, but respected the moment with complete integrity, gave her body a flick with the whip, powdered her face (for which I loved her), and waved to me as she stood on the doorstep, pressing her hand to her hair so that the wind might not disorder it, a gesture for which I honoured her, as if it confirmed our determination—not to let lilies grow.

'I observed with disillusioned clarity the despicable non-entity of the street; its porches; its window curtains; the drab clothes, the cupidity and complacency of shopping women; and old men taking the air in comforters; the caution of people crossing; the universal determination to go on living, when really, fools and gulls that you are, I said, any slate may fly from a roof, any car may swerve, for there is neither rhyme nor reason when a drunk man staggers about with a club in his hand—that is all. I was like one admitted behind the scenes: like one shown how the effects are produced. I returned, however, to my own snug home and was warned by the parlourmaid to creep upstairs in my stockings. The child was asleep. I went to my room.

'Was there no sword, nothing with which to batter down these walls, this protection, this begetting of children and living behind curtains, and becoming daily more involved and committed, with books and pictures? Better burn one's life out like Louis, desiring perfection; or like Rhoda leave us, flying past us to the desert; or choose one out of millions and one only like Neville; better be like Susan and love and hate the heat of the sun* or the frost-bitten grass; or be like Jinny, honest, an animal. All had their rapture; their common feeling with death; something that stood them in stead. Thus I visited each of my friends in turn, trying, with fumbling fingers, to prise open their locked caskets. I went from one to the other holding my sorrow—no, not my sorrow but the incomprehensible nature of this our life—for their inspection. Some people go to priests; others to poetry; I to my friends, I to my own heart, I to seek among phrases and fragments something unbroken—

I to whom there is not beauty enough in moon or tree; to whom the touch of one person with another is all, yet who cannot grasp even that, who am so imperfect, so weak, so unspeakably lonely. There I sat.

'Should this be the end of the story? a kind of sigh? a last ripple of the wave? A trickle of water to some gutter where, burbling, it dies away? Let me touch the table—so—and thus recover my sense of the moment. A sideboard covered with cruets; a basket full of rolls; a plate of bananas—these are comfortable sights. But if there are no stories, what end can there be, or what beginning? Life is not susceptible perhaps to the treatment we give it when we try to tell it. Sitting up late at night it seems strange not to have more control. Pigeon-holes are not then very useful. It is strange how force ebbs away and away into some dry creek. Sitting alone, it seems we are spent; our waters can only just surround feebly that spike of sea-holly; we cannot reach that further pebble so as to wet it. It is over, we are ended. But wait—I sat all night waiting—an impulse again runs through us; we rise, we toss back a mane of white spray; we pound on the shore; we are not to be confined. That is, I shaved and washed; did not wake my wife, and had breakfast; put on my hat, and went out to earn my living. After Monday, Tuesday comes.

'Yet some doubt remained, some note of interrogation. I was surprised, opening a door, to find people thus occupied; I hesitated, taking a cup of tea, whether one said milk or sugar. And the light of the stars falling, as it falls now, on my hand after travelling for millions upon millions of years—I could get a cold shock from that for a moment—not more, my imagination is too feeble. But some doubt remained. A shadow flitted through my mind like moths' wings among chairs and tables in a room in the evening.

When, for example, I went to Lincolnshire that summer to see Susan and she advanced towards me across the garden with the lazy movement of a half-filled sail, with the swaying movement of a woman with child, I thought, "It goes on; but why?" We sat in the garden; the farm carts came up dripping with hay; there was the usual country gabble of rooks and doves; fruit was netted and covered over; the gardener dug. Bees boomed down the purple tunnels of flowers; bees embedded themselves on the golden shields of sunflowers. Little twigs were blown across the grass. How rhythmical, and half conscious and like something wrapped in mist it was; but to me hateful, like a net folding one's limbs in its meshes, cramping. She who had refused Percival lent herself to this, to this covering over.

'Sitting down on a bank to wait for my train, I thought then how we surrender, how we submit to the stupidity of nature. Woods covered in thick green leafage lay in front of me. And by some flick of a scent or a sound on a nerve, the old image—the gardeners sweeping, the lady writing—returned. I saw the figures beneath the beech trees at Elvedon. The gardeners swept; the lady at the table sat writing. But I now made the contribution of maturity to childhood's intuitions—satiety and doom; the sense of what is unescapable in our lot; death; the knowledge of limitations; how life is more obdurate than one had thought it. Then, when I was a child, the presence of an enemy had asserted itself; the need for opposition had stung me. I had jumped up and cried, "Let's explore". The horror of the situation was ended.

'Now what situation was there to end? Dullness and doom. And what to explore? The leaves and the wood concealed nothing. If a bird rose I should no longer make a poem—I should repeat what I had seen before. Thus if I had a stick with which to point to indentations in the curve of being, this is the lowest; here it coils useless on the mud where no tide comes—here, where I sit with my back to a hedge, and my hat over my eyes, while the sheep advance remorselessly in that wooden way of theirs, step by step on stiff, pointed legs. But if you hold a blunt blade to a grindstone long enough, something spurts—a jagged edge of fire; so held to lack of reason, aimlessness, the usual, all massed together, out spurted in one flame hatred, contempt. I took my mind, my being, the old dejected, almost inanimate object, and lashed it about among these odds and ends, sticks and straws, detestable little bits of wreckage, flotsam and jetsam, floating on the oily surface. I jumped up. I said, "Fight! Fight!" I repeated. It is the effort and the struggle, it is the perpetual warfare, it is the shattering and piecing together—this is the daily battle, defeat or victory, the absorbing pursuit. The trees, scattered, put on order; the thick green of the leaves thinned itself to a dancing light. I netted them under with a sudden phrase. I retrieved them from formlessness with words.

'The train came in. Lengthening down the platform, the train came to a stop. I caught my train. And so back to London in the evening. How satisfactory, the atmosphere of common sense and tobacco; old women clambering into the third-class carriage with their baskets; the sucking at pipes; the good-nights and see you tomorrows of friends parting at wayside stations, and then the lights of London—not the flaring ecstasy of youth, not that tattered violet banner, but still the lights of London all the same; hard, electric lights, high up in offices; street lamps laced along dry pavements; flares roaring above street markets. I like all this when I have despatched the enemy for a moment.

'Also I like to find the pageant of existence roaring, in a theatre for instance. The clay-coloured, earthy nondescript animal of the field here erects himself and with infinite ingenuity and effort puts up a fight against the green woods and green fields and sheep advancing with measured tread, munching. And, of course, windows in the long grey streets were lit up; strips of carpet cut the pavement; there were swept and garnished rooms, fire, food, wine, talk. Men with withered hands, women with pearl pagodas hanging from their ears, came in and went out. I saw old men's faces carved into wrinkles and sneers by the work of the world; beauty cherished so that it seemed newly sprung even in age; and youth so apt for pleasure that pleasure, one thought, must exist; it seemed that grass-lands must roll for it; and the sea be chopped up into little waves; and the woods rustle with bright-coloured birds for youth, for youth expectant. There one met Jinny and Hal, Tom and Betty; there we had our jokes and shared our secrets; and never parted in the doorway without arranging to meet again in some other room as the occasion, as the time of the year, suggested. Life is pleasant; life is good. After Monday comes Tuesday, and Wednesday follows.

'Yes, but after a time with a difference. It may be that something in the look of the room one night, in the arrangement of the chairs, suggests it. It seems comfortable to sink down on a sofa in a corner, to look, to listen. Then it happens that two figures standing with their backs to the window appear against the branches of a spreading willow. With a shock of emotion one feels, "There are figures without features robed in beauty". In the pause that follows while the ripples spread, the girl to whom one should be talking says to herself, "He is old". But she is wrong. It is not age; it is that a drop has fallen; another drop. Time has given the arrangement another shake. Out we creep from the arch of the currant leaves, out into a wider world. The true order of things—this is our perpetual illusion—is now apparent. Thus in a moment, in a drawing-room, our life adjusts itself to the majestic march of day across the sky.

'It was for this reason that instead of pulling on my patent-leather shoes and finding a tolerable tie, I sought Neville. I sought my oldest friend, who had known me when I was Byron; when I was Meredith's young man, and also that hero in a book by Dostoevsky whose name I have forgotten. I found him alone, reading. A perfectly neat table; a curtain pulled methodically straight; a paper-knife dividing a French volume—nobody, I thought, ever changes the attitude in which we saw them first, or the clothes. Here he has sat in this chair, in these clothes, ever since we first met. Here was freedom; here was intimacy; the firelight broke off some round apple on the curtain. There we talked; sat talking; sauntered down that avenue, the avenue which runs under the trees, under the thick-leaved murmuring trees, the trees that are hung with fruit, which we have trodden so often together, so that now the turf is bare round some of those trees, round certain plays and poems, certain favourites of ours—the turf is trodden bare by our incessant unmethodical pacing. If I have to wait, I read; if I wake in the night, I feel along the shelf for a book. Swelling, perpetually augmented, there is a vast accumulation of unrecorded matter in my head. Now and then I break off a lump, Shakespeare it may be, it may be some old woman called Peck; and say to myself, smoking a cigarette in bed, "That's Shakespeare. That's Peck"—with a certainty of recognition and a shock of knowledge which is endlessly delightful, though not to be imparted.

So we shared our Pecks, our Shakespeares; compared each other's versions; allowed each other's insight to set our own Peck or Shakespeare in a better light; and then sank into one of those silences which are now and again broken by a few words, as if a fin rose in the wastes of silence; and then the fin, the thought, sinks back into the depths, spreading round it a little ripple of satisfaction, content.

'Yes, but suddenly one hears a clock tick. We who had been immersed in this world became aware of another. It is painful. It was Neville who changed our time. He, who had been thinking with the unlimited time of the mind, which stretches in a flash from Shakespeare to ourselves, poked the fire and began to live by that other clock which marks the approach of a particular person. The wide and dignified sweep of his mind contracted. He became on the alert. I could feel him listening to sounds in the street. I noted how he touched a cushion. From the myriads of mankind and all time past he had chosen one person, one moment in particular. A sound was heard in the hall. What he was saying wavered in the air like an uneasy flame. I watched him disentangle one footstep from other footsteps; wait for some particular mark of identification and glance with the swiftness of a snake at the handle of the door. (Hence the astonishing acuteness of his perceptions; he has been trained always by one person.) So concentrated a passion shot out others like foreign matter from a still, sparkling fluid. I became aware of my own vague and cloudy nature full of sediment, full of doubt, full of phrases and notes to be made in pocket-books. The folds of the curtain became still, statuesque; the paperweight on the table hardened; the threads on the curtain sparkled; everything became definite, external, a scene in which I had no part. I rose, therefore; I left him.

'Heavens! how they caught me as I left the room, the fangs of that old pain! the desire for someone not there. For whom? I did not know at first; then remembered Percival. I had not thought of him for months. Now to laugh with him, to laugh with him at Neville—that was what I wanted, to walk off arm-in-arm together laughing. But he was not there. The place was empty.

'It is strange how the dead leap out on us at street corners, or in dreams.

'This fitful gust blowing so sharp and cold upon me sent me that night across London to visit other friends, Rhoda and Louis, desiring company, certainty, contact. I wondered, as I mounted the stairs, what was their relationship? What did they say alone? I figured her awkward with the tea-kettle. She gazed over the slate roofs—the nymph of the fountain always wet, obsessed with visions, dreaming. She parted the curtain to look at the night. "Away!" she said. "The moor is dark beneath the moon."* I rang; I waited. Louis perhaps poured out milk in a saucer for the cat; Louis, whose bony hands shut like the sides of a dock closing themselves with a slow anguish of effort upon an enormous tumult of waters, who knew what has been said by the Egyptian, the Indian, by men with high cheekbones and solitaries in hair shirts. I knocked: I waited; there was no answer. I tramped down the stone stairs again. Our friends—how distant, how mute, how seldom visited and little known. And I, too, am dim to my friends and unknown; a phantom, sometimes seen, often not. Life is a dream surely. Our flame, the will-o'-the-wisp that dances in a few eyes, is soon to be blown out and all will fade. I recalled my friends. I thought of Susan. She had bought fields. Cucumbers and tomatoes ripened in her hothouses. The vine that had been killed by last year's frost was putting out a leaf or two. She walked heavily with her sons across her meadows. She went about the land attended by men in gaiters, pointing with her stick at a roof, at hedges, at walls fallen into disrepair. The pigeons followed her, waddling, for the grain that she let fall from her capable, earthy fingers. "But I no longer rise at dawn", she said. Then Jinny—entertaining, no doubt, some new young man. They reached the crisis of the usual conversation. The room would be darkened; chairs arranged. For she still sought the moment. Without illusions, hard and clear as crystal, she rode at the day with her breast bared. She let its spikes pierce her. When the lock whitened on her forehead she twisted it fearlessly among the rest. So when they come to bury her nothing will be out of order. Bits of ribbons will be found curled up. But still the door opens. Who is coming in? she asks, and rises to meet him, prepared, as on those first spring nights when the tree under the big London houses where respectable citizens were going soberly to bed scarcely sheltered her love; and the squeak of trams mixed with her cry of delight and the rippling of leaves had to shade her languor, her delicious lassitude as she sank down cooled by all the sweetness of nature satisfied. Our friends, how seldom visited, how little known—it is true; and yet, when I meet an unknown person, and try to break off, here at this table, what I call "my life", it is not one life that I look back upon; I am not one person; I am many people; I do not altogether know who I am—Jinny, Susan, Neville, Rhoda, or Louis; or how to distinguish my life from theirs.

'So I thought that night in early autumn when we came together and dined once more at Hampton Court. Our discomfort was at first considerable, for each by that time was committed to a statement, and the other person coming along the road to the meeting-place dressed like this or that, with a stick or without, seemed to contradict it. I saw Jinny look at Susan's earthy fingers and then hide her own; I, considering Neville, so neat and exact, felt the nebulosity of my own life blurred with all these phrases. He then boasted, because he was ashamed of one room and one person and his own success. Louis and Rhoda, the conspirators, the spies at table, who take notes, felt, "After all, Bernard can make the waiter fetch us rolls—a contact denied us". We saw for a moment laid out among us the body of the complete human being whom we have failed to be, but at the same time, cannot forget. All that we might have been we saw; all that we had missed, and we grudged for a moment the other's claim, as children when the cake is cut, the one cake, the only cake, watch their slice diminishing.

'However, we had our bottle of wine, and under that seduction lost our enmity, and stopped comparing. And, half-way through dinner, we felt enlarge itself round us the huge blackness of what is outside us, of what we are not. The wind, the rush of wheels became the roar of time, and we rushed—where? And who were we? We were extinguished for a moment, went out like sparks in burnt paper and the blackness roared. Past time, past history we went. For me this lasts but one second. It is ended by my own pugnacity. I strike the table with a spoon. If I could measure things with compasses I would, but since my only measure is a phrase, I make phrases—I forget what, on this occasion. We became six people at a table in Hampton Court. We rose and walked together down the avenue. In the thin, the unreal twilight, fitfully like the echo of voices laughing down some alley, geniality returned to me and flesh. Against the gateway, against some cedar tree I saw blaze bright, Neville, Jinny, Rhoda, Louis, Susan, and myself, our life, our identity. Still King William seemed an unreal monarch and his crown mere tinsel. But we—against the brick, against the branches, we six, out of how many million millions, for one moment out of what measureless abundance of past time and time to come, burnt there triumphant. The moment was all; the moment was enough. And then Neville, Jinny, Susan and I, as a wave breaks, burst asunder, surrendered—to the next leaf, to the precise bird, to a child with a hoop, to a prancing dog, to the warmth that is hoarded in woods after a hot day, to the lights twisted like white ribbon on rippled waters. We drew apart; we were consumed in the darkness of the trees, leaving Rhoda and Louis to stand on the terrace by the urn.

'When we returned from that immersion—how sweet, how deep!—and came to the surface and saw the conspirators still standing there it was with some compunction. We had lost what they had kept. We interrupted. But we were tired, and whether it had been good or bad, accomplished or left undone, the dusky veil was falling upon our endeavours; the lights were sinking as we paused for a moment upon the terrace that overlooks the river. The steamers were landing their trippers on the bank; there was a distant cheering, the sound of singing, as if people waved their hats and joined in some last song. The sound of the chorus came across the water and I felt leap up that old impulse, which has moved me all my life, to be thrown up and down on the roar of other people's voices, singing the same song; to be tossed up and down on the roar of almost senseless merriment, sentiment, triumph, desire. But not now. No! I could not collect myself; I could not distinguish myself; I could not help letting fall the things that had made me a minute ago eager, amused, jealous, vigilant, and hosts of other things, into the water. I could not recover myself from that endless throwing away, dissipation, flooding forth without our willing it and rushing soundlessly away out there under the arches of the bridge, round some clump of trees or an island, out where seabirds sit on stakes, over the roughened water to become waves in the sea—I could not recover myself from that dissipation. So we parted.

'Was this, then, this streaming away mixed with Susan, Jinny, Neville, Rhoda, Louis, a sort of death? A new assembly of elements? Some hint of what was to come? The note was scribbled, the book shut, for I am an intermittent student. I do not say my lessons by any means at the stated hour. Later, walking down Fleet Street at the rush hour, I recalled that moment; I continued it. "Must I for ever," I said, "beat my spoon on the table-cloth? Shall I not, too, consent?" The omnibuses were clogged; one came up behind another and stopped with a click, like a link added to a stone chain. People passed.

'Multitudinous, carrying attaché-cases, dodging with incredible celerity in and out, they went past like a river in spate. They went past roaring like a train in a tunnel. Seizing my chance I crossed; dived down a dark passage and entered the shop where they cut my hair. I leant my head back and was swathed in a sheet. Looking-glasses confronted me in which I could see my pinioned body and people passing; stopping, looking, and going on indifferent. The hairdresser began to move his scissors to and fro. I felt myself powerless to stop the oscillations of the cold steel. So we are cut and laid in swaths, I said; so we lie side by side on the damp meadows, withered branches and flowering. We have no more to expose ourselves on the

bare hedges to the wind and snow; no more to carry
ourselves erect when the gale sweeps, to bear our burden
upheld; or stay, unmurmuring, on those pallid noondays
when the bird creeps close to the bough and the damp
whitens the leaf. We are cut, we are fallen. We are become
part of that unfeeling universe that sleeps when we are at
our quickest and burns red when we lie asleep. We have
renounced our station and lie now flat, withered and how
soon forgotten! Upon which I saw an expression in the tail
of the eye of the hairdresser as if something interested him
in the street.

'What interested the hairdresser? What did the hairdresser see in the street? It is thus that I am recalled. (For
I am no mystic; something always plucks at me—curiosity, envy, admiration, interest in hairdressers and the
like bring me to the surface.) While he brushed the fluff
from my coat I took pains to assure myself of his identity,
and then, swinging my stick, I went into the Strand, and
evoked to serve as opposite to myself the figure of Rhoda,
always so furtive, always with fear in her eyes, always
seeking some pillar in the desert, to find which she had
gone; she had killed herself.* "Wait", I said, putting my
arm in imagination (thus we consort with our friends)
through her arm. "Wait until these omnibuses have gone
by. Do not cross so dangerously. These men are your
brothers." In persuading her I was also persuading my
own soul. For this is not one life; nor do I always know if
I am man or woman, Bernard or Neville, Louis, Susan,
Jinny, or Rhoda—so strange is the contact of one with
another.

'Swinging my stick, with my hair newly cut and the
nape of my neck tingling, I went past all those trays of
penny toys imported from Germany that men hold out in

the street by St Paul's—St Paul's,* the brooding hen with
spread wings from whose shelter run omnibuses and
streams of men and women at the rush hour. I thought
how Louis would mount those steps in his neat suit with
his cane in his hand and his angular, rather detached gait.
With his Australian accent ("My father, a banker at Brisbane") he would come, I thought, with greater respect to
these old ceremonies than I do, who have heard the same
lullabies for a thousand years. I am always impressed, as I
enter, by the rubbed noses; the polished brasses; the
flapping and the chanting, while one boy's voice wails
round the dome like some lost and wandering dove. The
recumbency and the peace of the dead impress me—
warriors at rest under their old banners. Then I scoff at
the floridity and absurdity of some scrolloping* tomb;
and the trumpets and the victories and the coats of arms
and the certainty, so sonorously repeated, of resurrection,
of eternal life. My wandering and inquisitive eye then
shows me an awe-stricken child; a shuffling pensioner; or
the obeisances of tired shop-girls burdened with heaven
knows what strife in their poor thin breasts come to solace
themselves in the rush hour. I stray and look and wonder,
and sometimes, rather furtively, try to rise on the shaft of
somebody else's prayer into the dome, out, beyond, wherever they go. But then like the lost and wailing dove, I
find myself failing, fluttering, descending and perching
upon some curious gargoyle, some battered nose or absurd
tombstone, with humour, with wonder, and so again
watch the sightseers with their Baedekers shuffling past,
while the boy's voice soars in the dome and the organ now
and then indulges in a moment of elephantine triumph.
How then, I asked, would Louis roof us all in? How
would he confine us, make us one, with his red ink, with

his very fine nib? The voice petered out in the dome, wailing.

'So into the street again, swinging my stick, looking at wire trays in stationers' shop-windows, at baskets of fruit grown in the colonies, murmuring Pillicock sat on Pillicock's hill,* or Hark, hark, the dogs do bark,* or The World's great age begins anew,* or Come away, come away, death*—mingling nonsense and poetry, floating in the stream. Something always has to be done next. Tuesday follows Monday: Wednesday, Tuesday. Each spreads the same ripple. The being grows rings, like a tree. Like a tree, leaves fall.

'For one day as I leant over a gate that led into a field, the rhythm stopped; the rhymes and the hummings, the nonsense and the poetry. A space was cleared in my mind. I saw through the thick leaves of habit. Leaning over the gate I regretted so much litter, so much unaccomplishment and separation, for one cannot cross London to see a friend, life being so full of engagements; nor take ship to India and see a naked man spearing fish in blue water. I said life had been imperfect, an unfinishing phrase. It had been impossible for me, taking snuff as I do from any bagman met in a train, to keep coherency—that sense of the generations, of women carrying red pitchers to the Nile, of the nightingale who sings among conquests and migrations. It had been too vast an undertaking, I said, and how can I go on lifting my foot perpetually to climb the stair? I addressed myself as one would speak to a companion with whom one is voyaging to the North Pole.

'I spoke to that self who had been with me in many tremendous adventures; the faithful man who sits over the fire when everybody has gone to bed, stirring the cinders with a poker; the man who has been so mysteriously and with sudden accretions of being built up, in a beech wood, sitting by a willow tree on a bank, leaning over a parapet at Hampton Court; the man who has collected himself in moments of emergency and banged his spoon on the table, saying, "I will not consent".

'This self now as I leant over the gate looking down over fields rolling in waves of colour beneath me made no answer. He threw up no opposition. He attempted no phrase. His fist did not form. I waited. I listened. Nothing came, nothing, I cried then with a sudden conviction of complete desertion, Now there is nothing. No fin breaks the waste of this immeasurable sea. Life has destroyed me. No echo comes when I speak, no varied words. This is more truly death than the death of friends, than the death of youth. I am the swathed figure in the hairdresser's shop taking up only so much space.

'The scene beneath me withered. It was like the eclipse* when the sun went out and left the earth, flourishing in full summer foliage, withered, brittle, false. Also I saw on a winding road in a dust dance the groups we had made, how they came together, how they ate together, how they met in this room or that. I saw my own indefatigable busyness—how I had rushed from one to the other, fetched and carried, travelled and returned, joined this group and that, here kissed, here withdrawn; always kept hard at it by some extraordinary purpose, with my nose to the ground like a dog on the scent; with an occasional toss of the head, an occasional cry of amazement, despair and then back again with my nose to the scent. What a litter— what a confusion; with here birth, here death; succulence and sweetness; effort and anguish; and myself always running hither and thither. Now it was done with. I had no more appetites to glut; no more stings in me with which to poison people; no more sharp teeth and clutching hands or desire to feel the pear and the grape and the sun beating down from the orchard wall.

'The woods had vanished; the earth was a waste of shadow. No sound broke the silence of the wintry landscape. No cock crowed; no smoke rose; no train moved. A man without a self, I said. A heavy body leaning on a gate. A dead man. With dispassionate despair, with entire disillusionment, I surveyed the dust dance; my life, my friends' lives, and those fabulous presences, men with brooms, women writing, the willow tree by the river—clouds and phantoms made of dust too, of dust that changed, as clouds lose and gain and take gold or red and lose their summits and billow this way and that, mutable, vain. I, carrying a notebook, making phrases, had recorded mere changes; a shadow, I had been sedulous to take note of shadows. How can I proceed now, I said, without a self, weightless and visionless, through a world weightless, without illusion?

'The heaviness of my despondency thrust open the gate I leant on and pushed me, an elderly man, a heavy man with grey hair, through the colourless field, the empty field. No more to hear echoes, no more to see phantoms, to conjure up no opposition, but to walk always unshadowed, making no impress upon the dead earth. If even there had been sheep munching, pushing one foot after another, or a bird, or a man driving a spade into the earth, had there been a bramble to trip me, or a ditch, damp with soaked leaves, into which to fall—but no, the melancholy path led along the level, to more wintriness and pallor and the equal and uninteresting view of the same landscape.

'How then does light return to the world after the eclipse of the sun? Miraculously. Frailly. In thin stripes. It hangs like a glass cage. It is a hoop to be fractured by a tiny jar.

There is a spark there. Next moment a flush of dun. Then a vapour as if earth were breathing in and out, once, twice, for the first time. Then under the dullness someone walks with a green light. Then off twists a white wraith. The woods throb blue and green, and gradually the fields drink in red, gold, brown. Suddenly a river snatches a blue light. The earth absorbs colour like a sponge slowly drinking water. It puts on weight; rounds itself; hangs pendent; settles and swings beneath our feet.

'So the landscape returned to me; so I saw the fields rolling in waves of colour beneath me, but now with this difference; I saw but was not seen. I walked unshadowed; I came unheralded. From me had dropped the old cloak, the old response; the hollowed hand that beats back sounds. Thin as a ghost, leaving no trace where I trod, perceiving merely, I walked alone in a new world, never trodden; brushing new flowers, unable to speak save in a child's words of one syllable; without shelter from phrases—I who have made so many; unattended, I who have always gone with my kind; solitary, I who have always had someone to share the empty grate, or the cupboard with its hanging loop of gold.

'But how describe the world seen without a self? There are no words. Blue, red—even they distract, even they hide with thickness instead of letting the light through. How describe or say anything in articulate words again?—save that it fades, save that it undergoes a gradual transformation, becomes, even in the course of one short walk, habitual—this scene also. Blindness returns as one moves and one leaf repeats another. Loveliness returns as one looks, with all its train of phantom phrases. One breathes in and out substantial breath; down in the valley the train draws across the fields lop-eared with smoke.

'But for a moment I had sat on the turf somewhere high above the flow of the sea and the sound of the woods, had seen the house, the garden, and the waves breaking. The old nurse who turns the pages of the picture-book had stopped and had said, "Look. This is the truth."

'So I was thinking as I came along Shaftesbury Avenue tonight. I was thinking of that page in the picture-book. And when I met you in the place where one goes to hang up one's coat I said to myself, "It does not matter whom I meet. All this little affair of 'being' is over. Who this is I do not know; nor care; we will dine together." So I hung up my coat, tapped you on the shoulder, and said, "Sit with me".

'Now the meal is finished; we are surrounded by peelings and breadcrumbs. I have tried to break off this bunch and hand it to you; but whether there is substance or truth in it I do not know. Nor do I know exactly where we are. What city does that stretch of sky look down upon? Is it Paris, is it London where we sit, or some southern city of pink-washed houses lying under cypresses, under high mountains, where eagles soar? I do not at this moment feel certain.

'I begin now to forget; I begin to doubt the fixity of tables, the reality of here and now, to tap my knuckles smartly upon the edges of apparently solid objects and say, "Are you hard?" I have seen so many different things, have made so many different sentences. I have lost in the process of eating and drinking and rubbing my eyes along surfaces that thin, hard shell which cases the soul, which, in youth, shuts one in—hence the fierceness, and the tap, tap, tap of the remorseless beaks of the young. And now I ask, "Who am I?" I have been talking of Bernard, Neville, Jinny, Susan, Rhoda and Louis. Am I all of them? Am I one and distinct? I do not know. We sat here together. But now Percival is dead, and Rhoda is dead; we are divided; we are not here. Yet I cannot find any obstacle separating us. There is no division between me and them. As I talked I felt, "I am you". This difference we make so much of, this identity we so feverishly cherish, was overcome. Yes, ever since old Mrs Constable lifted her sponge and pouring warm water over me covered me with flesh I have been sensitive, percipient. Here on my brow is the blow I got when Percival fell. Here on the nape of my neck is the kiss Jinny gave Louis. My eyes fill with Susan's tears. I see far away, quivering like a gold thread, the pillar Rhoda saw, and feel the rush of the wind of her flight when she leapt.

'Thus when I come to shape here at this table between my hands the story of my life and set it before you as a complete thing, I have to recall things gone far, gone deep, sunk into this life or that and become part of it; dreams, too, things surrounding me, and the inmates, those old half-articulate ghosts who keep up their hauntings by day and night; who turn over in their sleep, who utter their confused cries, who put out their phantom fingers and clutch at me as I try to escape—shadows of people one might have been; unborn selves. There is the old brute, too, the savage, the hairy man who dabbles his fingers in ropes of entrails; and gobbles and belches; whose speech is guttural, visceral—well, he is here. He squats in me. Tonight he has been feasted on quails, salad, and sweetbread. He now holds a glass of fine old brandy in his paw. He brindles, purrs and shoots warm thrills all down my spine as I sip. It is true, he washes his hands before dinner, but they are still hairy. He buttons on trousers and waistcoats, but they contain the same organs. He jibs if I keep him waiting for dinner. He mops and mows perpetually, pointing with his half-idiot gestures of greed and covetousness at what he desires. I assure you, I have great difficulty sometimes in controlling him. That man, the hairy, the ape-like, has contributed his part to my life. He has given a greener glow to green things, has held his torch with its red flames, its thick and smarting smoke, behind every leaf. He has lit up the cool garden even. He has brandished his torch in murky by-streets where girls suddenly seem to shine with a red and intoxicating translucency. Oh, he has tossed his torch high! He has led me wild dances!

'But no more. Now tonight, my body rises tier upon tier like some cool temple whose floor is strewn with carpets and murmurs rise and the altars stand smoking; but up above, here in my serene head, come only fine gusts of melody, waves of incense, while the lost dove wails, and the banners tremble above tombs, and the dark airs of midnight shake trees outside the open windows. When I look down from this transcendency, how beautiful are even the crumbled relics of bread! What shapely spirals the peelings of pears make—how thin, and mottled like some sea-bird's egg. Even the forks laid straight side by side appear lucid, logical, exact; and the horns of the rolls which we have left are glazed, yellow-plated, hard. I could worship my hand even, with its fan of bones laced by blue mysterious veins and its astonishing look of aptness, suppleness and ability to curl softly or suddenly crush—its infinite sensibility.

'Immeasurably receptive, holding everything, trembling with fullness, yet clear, contained—so my being seems, now that desire urges it no more out and away; now that curiosity no longer dyes it a thousand colours. It lies deep, tideless, immune, now that he is dead, the man I called

"Bernard", the man who kept a book in his pocket in which he made notes—phrases for the moon, notes of features; how people looked, turned, dropped their cigarette ends; under B, butterfly powder, under D, ways of naming death. But now let the door open, the glass door that is for ever turning on its hinges. Let a woman come, let a young man in evening-dress with a moustache sit down: is there anything that they can tell me? No! I know all that, too. And if she suddenly gets up and goes, "My dear", I say, "you no longer make me look after you". The shock of the falling wave which has sounded all my life, which woke me so that I saw the gold loop on the cupboard, no longer makes quiver what I hold.

'So now, taking upon me the mystery of things, I could go like a spy without leaving this place, without stirring from my chair. I can visit the remote verges of the desert lands where the savage sits by the camp-fire. Day rises; the girl lifts the watery fire-heated jewels to her brow; the sun levels his beams straight at the sleeping-house; the waves deepen their bars; they fling themselves on shore; back blows the spray; sweeping their waters they surround the boat and the sea-holly. The birds sing in chorus; deep tunnels run between the stalks of flowers; the house is whitened; the sleeper stretches; gradually all is astir. Light floods the room and drives shadow beyond shadow to where they hang in folds inscrutable. What does the central shadow hold? Something? Nothing? I do not know.

'Oh, but there is your face. I catch your eye. I, who had been thinking myself so vast, a temple, a church, a whole universe, unconfined and capable of being everywhere on the verge of things and here too, am now nothing but what you see—an elderly man, rather heavy, grey above the ears, who (I see myself in the glass) leans one elbow on the table, and holds in his left hand a glass of old brandy. That is the blow you have dealt me. I have walked bang into the pillar-box. I reel from side to side. I put my hands to my head. My hat is off—I have dropped my stick. I have made an awful ass of myself and am justly laughed at by any passer-by.

'Lord, how unutterably disgusting life is! What dirty tricks it plays us, one moment free; the next, this. Here we are among the breadcrumbs and the stained napkins again. That knife is already congealing with grease. Disorder, sordidity and corruption surround us. We have been taking into our mouths the bodies of dead birds. It is with these greasy crumbs, slobbered over napkins, and little corpses that we have to build. Always it begins again; always there is the enemy; eyes meeting ours; fingers twitching ours; the effort waiting. Call the waiter. Pay the bill. We must pull ourselves up out of our chairs. We must find our coats. We must go. Must, must, must—detestable word. Once more, I who had thought myself immune, who had said, "Now I am rid of all that", find that the wave has tumbled me over, head over heels, scattering my possessions, leaving me to collect, to assemble, to heap together, summon my forces, rise and confront the enemy.

'It is strange that we, who are capable of so much suffering, should inflict so much suffering. Strange that the face of a person whom I scarcely know save that I think we met once on the gangway of a ship bound for Africa— a mere adumbration of eyes, cheeks, nostrils—should have power to inflict this insult. You look, eat, smile, are bored, pleased, annoyed—that is all I know. Yet this shadow which has sat by me for an hour or two, this mask from which peep two eyes, has power to drive me back, to pinion me down among all those other faces, to shut me in a hot room; to send me dashing like a moth from candle to candle.

'But wait. While they add up the bill behind the screen, wait one moment. Now that I have reviled you for the blow that sent me staggering among peelings and crumblings and old scraps of meat, I will record in words of one syllable how also under your gaze with that compulsion on me I begin to perceive this, that and the other. The clock ticks; the woman sneezes; the waiter comes—there is a gradual coming together, running into one, acceleration and unification. Listen: a whistle sounds, wheels rush, the door creaks on its hinges. I regain the sense of the complexity and the reality and the struggle, for which I thank you. And with some pity, some envy and much good will, take your hand and bid you good-night.

'Heaven be praised for solitude! I am alone now. That almost unknown person has gone, to catch some train, to take some cab, to go to some place or person whom I do not know. The face looking at me has gone. The pressure is removed. Here are empty coffee-cups. Here are chairs turned but nobody sits on them. Here are empty tables and nobody any more coming to dine at them tonight.

'Let me now raise my song of glory. Heaven be praised for solitude. Let me be alone. Let me cast and throw away this veil of being, this cloud that changes with the least breath, night and day, and all night and all day. While I sat here I have been changing. I have watched the sky change. I have seen clouds cover the stars, then free the stars, then cover the stars again. Now I look at their changing no more. Now no one sees me and I change no more. Heaven be praised for solitude that has removed the pressure of the eye, the solicitation of the body, and all need of lies and phrases.

'My book, stuffed with phrases, has dropped to the floor. It lies under the table, to be swept up by the charwoman when she comes wearily at dawn looking for scraps of paper, old tram tickets, and here and there a note screwed into a ball and left with the litter to be swept up. What is the phrase for the moon? And the phrase for love? By what name are we to call death? I do not know. I need a little language such as lovers use, words of one syllable such as children speak when they come into the room and find their mother sewing and pick up some scrap of bright wool, a feather, or a shred of chintz. I need a howl; a cry. When the storm crosses the marsh and sweeps over me where I lie in the ditch unregarded I need no words. Nothing neat. Nothing that comes down with all its feet on the floor. None of those resonances and lovely echoes that break and chime from nerve to nerve in our breasts, making wild music, false phrases. I have done with phrases.

'How much better is silence; the coffee-cup, the table. How much better to sit by myself like the solitary sea-bird that opens its wings on the stake. Let me sit here for ever with bare things, this coffee-cup, this knife, this fork, things in themselves, myself being myself. Do not come and worry me with your hints that it is time to shut the shop and be gone. I would willingly give all my money that you should not disturb me but let me sit on and on, silent, alone.

'But now the head waiter, who has finished his own meal, appears and frowns; he takes his muffler from his pocket and ostentatiously makes ready to go. They must go; must put up the shutters, must fold the table-cloths, and give one brush with a wet mop under the tables.

'Curse you then. However beat and done with it all I am, I must haul myself up, and find the particular coat that belongs to me; must push my arms into the sleeves; must muffle myself up against the night air and be off. I, I, I, tired as I am, spent as I am, and almost worn out with all this rubbing of my nose along the surfaces of things, even I, an elderly man who is getting rather heavy and dislikes exertion, must take myself off and catch some last train.

'Again I see before me the usual street. The canopy of civilization is burnt out. The sky is dark as polished whale-bone. But there is a kindling in the sky whether of lamplight or of dawn. There is a stir of some sort—sparrows on plane tree somewhere chirping. There is a sense of the break of day. I will not call it dawn. What is dawn in the city to an elderly man standing in the street looking up rather dizzily at the sky? Dawn is some sort of whitening of the sky; some sort of renewal. Another day; another Friday; another twentieth of March, January, or September. Another general awakening. The stars draw back and are extinguished. The bars deepen themselves between the waves. The film of mist thickens on the fields. A redness gathers on the roses, even on the pale rose that hangs by the bedroom window. A bird chirps. Cottagers light their early candles. Yes, this is the eternal renewal, the incessant rise and fall and fall and rise again.

'And in me too the wave rises. It swells; it arches its back. I am aware once more of a new desire, something rising beneath me like the proud horse whose rider first spurs and then pulls him back. What enemy do we now perceive advancing against us, you whom I ride now, as we stand pawing this stretch of pavement? It is death. Death is the enemy. It is death against whom I ride with my spear couched and my hair flying back like a young man's, like Percival's, when he galloped in India. I strike spurs into

my horse. Against you I will fling myself, unvanquished
and unyielding, O Death!'

The waves broke on the shore.

THE END

EXPLANATORY NOTES

3 *The sun*: VW's Quaker aunt, Caroline Emelia Stephen, wrote *Light Arising: Thoughts on the Central Radiance* (Cambridge: W. Heffer, 1908). See Introduction p. xxxi.

7 *I am the stalk*: the game of hide-and-seek produces metamorphosis. VW's description recalls the language of Ovid's *Metamorphoses* when Daphne, daughter of the river god, escapes the pursuit of Apollo by changing into a tree. (Ovid, *Metamorphoses*, vol. i, ed. Frank Justus Miller (Loeb Classical Library, Boston, Mass.: Harvard University Press, 1977), 40–1.) Throughout *The Waves* VW freely switches the genders in mythological stories; cf. pp. 76–7.

10 *'I love,' said Susan, 'and I hate'*: this is Susan's recurrent refrain. See Introduction, p. xxx. 'I hate and love': *Catullus*, ed. F. W. Cornish (Loeb Classical Library, Boston, Mass.: Harvard University Press, 1962), 162–3.

13 *One sails alone*: during the last stage of writing *The Waves* VW saw a crashed plane in which three men were killed. She commented in her diary: 'But we went on, reminding me of that epitaph in the Greek anthology: when I sank, the other ships sailed on.' 'I am the tomb of a shipwrecked man; but set sail, stranger: for when we were lost, the other ships voyaged on': Theodoridas, no. 282 in book VII of *The Greek Anthology*, Loeb edn. *Diary*, iv. 7 and note. Rhoda's ship sails on.

17 *Queen Alexandra*: wife of Edward VII, king from 1901 to 1910. Cf. pp. 24–5.

18 *the implacable tree*: after her stepsister Stella's death VW records: 'I always see when I think of the month after her death the certain leafless bush; a skeleton tree in the dark of a summer night. . . . And the tree, outside in the dark garden, was to me the emblem, the symbol, of the skeleton agony to which her death had reduced him; and us; everything.' 'A Sketch of the Past', in *Moments of Being: Unpublished Autobiographical Writings of Virginia Woolf*, ed. Jeanne Shulkind (Brighton: Sussex University Press, 1976), 121; see also 'Reminiscences', 56.

[249]

Neville's association of a tree with death is repeated at the news of Percival's death, p. 124. Compare also Introduction, p. xxx concerning Matthew Arnold, 'Thyrsis'.

19 *little children*: see *Hymns Ancient and Modern*, from the section For the Young, Evening, no. 346, 'Now the day is over', headed 'When thou liest down thou shalt not be afraid; yea, thou shalt lie down and thy sleep shall be sweet'. Verse 4 becomes entangled in Rhoda's drowsing visions:

> Grant to little children
> Visions bright of Thee;
> Guard the sailors tossing
> On the deep blue sea.

20 *my Armadas*: Rhoda's 'Armadas' also allude to her later visit to Spain.

22 *the moon-faced clock regards me*: the line appears to be Bernard's own.

23 *Virgil ... Lucretius ... Catullus ...* : the children are now about 13, the age at which English public (i.e. private) boarding-schools accept pupils. VW's brothers went to Clifton School, Bristol. The syllabus of such schools was, until very recently, dominated by Latin and Greek learning. *The Waves* is saturated with the vocabulary of these writers. Vergilius Maro (Virgil), b. 70 BC, most famous for the *Aeneid* which records the sea-adventures of Aeneas on his way to found a nation in Italy. Lucretius, b. 95 BC, author of *De Rerum Natura*, a founding text in philosophical science. Catullus, b. 87 BC, love poet. Catullus was imitated and translated by three of the English poets who are named in the novel: Meredith, Byron, and Tennyson. His work, alongside that of Shelley, moves persistently just beneath the surface of *The Waves*. See Introduction, p. xxx for discussion.

28 *the Duke's birthday*: probably the birthday of Edward VII's second son, later George V, king from 1910 to 1936.

36 *brake*: an open conveyance.

37 *Pope, Dryden, even Shakespeare*: Pope and Dryden are extra-ordinarily skilled metrical innovators: the suggestion seems to be that Neville can mimic technique but not write feeling, whereas Percival cannot read but can understand.

40 *Richelieu*: Cardinal Richelieu, chief minister of Louis XIII, 1628–42; the Duke of St Simon. Consummate politician and pithy thinker, both in the service of Louis' kingly namesake.

41 *Plato's*: VW herself was reading Plato's *Republic* at 16; cf. p. 76).

44 *May, wild roses and ivy serpentine*: Rhoda is reading Shelley's 'The Question' (*The Complete Works of Percy Bysshe Shelley*, ed. Thomas Hutchinson (Oxford: University Press, 1934), 614): 'And wild roses, and ivy serpentine' is line 21. The poet gathers a nosegay of these visionary flowers. The phrase 'Oh! to whom?' from the last line of the poem becomes Rhoda's leitmotiv. For discussion see Introduction, p. xxxi).

I faint, I fail: this summons another Shelley poem, 'The Indian Serenade':

> Oh lift me from the grass!
> I die! I faint! I fail! (*Works*, 580)

45 *Horace, Tennyson ... Keats and Matthew Arnold*: canonical writers who escape their hidebound function as school prizes to become part of the novel's linguistic exploration. All memorably evoked the sea: for example, Arnold's 'Dover Beach' and 'To Marguerite—Continued': 'Yes! in the sea of life enisled', alluded to in *The Waves*, Draft 2, p. 693.

quit ourselves like men: 1 Samuel 4: 9.

50 *I came to the puddle*: compare, for example, p. 130, and 'Again those moments of being. There was the moment of the puddle in the path; when for no reason I could discover, everything suddenly became unreal; I was suspended; I could not step across the puddle; I tried to touch something ... the whole world seemed unreal.' (*Moments of Being*, 78.) In this passage VW is describing her experience in the winter of 1894.

56 *I shall become a don*: Neville self-denigratingly—and with a certain caustic comedy—foresees his life as a classical scholar. His distaste for 'one of those University women' is part of his distaste for heterosexual love. Sophocles and Euripides: two of the three most famous Greek tragic dramatists.

59 *lovelily*: perhaps with a reminiscence of Byron, 'So lovelily the morning shone' ('The Bride of Abydos', 1. iii).

62 *a self who does not come*: Compare p. 65 and Bernard's soliloquy where he describes, in age, calling for a self who does not come, pp. 236–7.

63 *Byron*: Bernard's self-identification with Byron in youth (cf. pp. 67, 70–3) may also be a thread in the novel's submarine system of elegiac allusion. The death of Byron, like that of Thoby, is associated with Greece.

67 *Gray's Elegy*: Thomas Gray, *Elegy in a Country Churchyard* (1750).

70 *Byron's . . . Meredith's young man*: repeated p. 227; perhaps like Levin in *Anna Karenina*, Byron's Childe Harold, Meredith's Richard Feverel or Harry Richmond.

75 *Worcester sauce*: a pungent sauce used, often indiscriminately, to pep up bland food in workaday restaurants. On p. 105 Louis recalls this repeated scene: 'I . . . prop my poet—is it Lucretius?—against a cruet .'

77 *tea-urn . . . eternity*: in a lexical twist that will become pronounced in *Between the Acts* 'tea-urns' here become 'eternity'.

91 *How fair . . . London lies*: there are glancing allusions throughout this paragraph to Wordsworth, 'Upon Westminster Bridge'.

96 *who goes to India*: the first mention that Percival is going to India.

   Rhoda the Nymph of the fountain always wet: Arethusa, one of Diana's attendants, bathed in the Alpheus. Pursued by the enamoured god of the river she was changed into a fountain by Diana. The characterizing phrase occurs several times: Louis and Rhoda become lovers but, p. 170, 'I left Louis; I feared embraces'. Compare Bernard's soliloquy, p. 216.

104 *a seven-sided flower*: the seven-sided flower is complete only on this occasion; in the next section Percival has died. Seven is a magic number. The seven here also calls up Wordsworth's poem of continuance past death, 'We are seven'.

111 *The Oriental problem is solved*: the ensuing images of Percival in India lightly mock imperialism, calling on Leonard Woolf's novel about Ceylon, *The Village in the Jungle* (London: Edward Arnold, 1913) and, perhaps, E. M. Forster's *A Passage to India*. Percival's is another passage to India, and a pointless death.

115 *The procession passes*: VW owned and read an abridged copy of James Frazer, *The Golden Bough* (London: Macmillan, 1922). She knew the work well and was a friend of the anthropologist Jane Harrison. See, for example, Harrison's *Prolegomena to the Study of Greek Religion* (Cambridge: Cambridge University Press, 1903) for her description of Olympian and Chthonic ritual, and the placation of ghosts.

124 *He died where he fell*: compare note to p. 18. The fall of Percival is likened to the death of Hector in *The Iliad*, dragged behind a horse.

128 *these pictures make no reference*: London, above and below ground, becomes important in this section in providing a topography for private emotion and a sense of communal life continuing. The Tube is the underground railway system. Bernard visits the National Gallery in Trafalgar Square at the heart of London and enters first the Italian room. Percival is dead; Bernard's son, his first child, is born. Images of crucifixion, annunciation, nativity relate to Bernard's present experience.

129 *Titian*: Venetian painter, *c.* 1487–1576, famous above all for his innovative use of primary colours, especially blues and reds. The picture referred to is probably *Bacchus and Ariadne* in the National Gallery, whose patterns of movement are similar to his earlier religious paintings.

130 *Hampton Court*: the first mention of Hampton Court. A later section describes the communal visit there without Percival. See note to p. 175. Bernard had failed to go with Percival to Hampton Court when he asked him to: see p. 221.

131 *Oxford Street*: the great department stores in Oxford Street were at this period among the most elegant in London.

violets: 'There grew pied wind-flowers and violets', Shelley, 'The Question'. Compare note to p. 44 and Introduction. Rhoda's repeated question 'Oh! to whom?' is answered. She can offer flowers to Percival, but only after his death. Compare p. 132: 'This is my tribute to Percival; withered violets, blackened violets.'

132–3 *Where shall I go then?*: Rhoda goes to the Wigmore Hall just

behind Oxford Street. Bernard finds comfort in pictures, Rhoda
in music.

134 *And what is a cry?*: the singer's primal cry 'Ah!' goes beyond
words—the repeated yearning of the book's language. The
musicians make creative order, 'a perfect dwelling place': 'We
have made oblongs and stood them upon squares. This is our
triumph; this is our consolation.' Compare Lily Briscoe's picture
with its line and triangle at the end of *To the Lighthouse*.

I will go to Greenwich: Rhoda's bus and tram journey out to
Greenwich from the centre of London is also a journey out
towards the sea and port from which ships then sailed to India,
and so enters the wave that sweeps across the world.

139 *Pitt, Burke and Sir Robert Peel*: Louis is now a powerful figure
in the commercial world of the city, with aspirations to enter
parliament 'where Chatham stood, and Pitt, Burke and Sir
Robert Peel'. All the figures mentioned were much involved with
the development of the Indian empire, for example, Chatham
was associated with its founding, Pitt with its expansion and
commercial exploitation through the East India Company.

140 *Percival died in Egypt*: on Saturday, 7 Feb. 1931 VW reached
the end of *The Waves* and wrote in her diary: 'I have been sitting
these 15 minutes in a state of glory, & calm, & some tears,
thinking of Thoby & if I could write Julian Thoby Stephen
1881–1906 on the first page. I suppose not.' VW describes their
relationship in 'A Sketch of the Past' (*Moments of Being*,
115–20).

146–7 *Jug, jug, jug*: many Elizabethan lyrics thus denote the nightingale's song and repeat the detail of her leaning her breast
against a thorn, producing a phallic pun on 'prick-song'. Compare Norman Ault (ed.), *Elizabethan Lyrics* (New York: Capri-
corn, 1960), e.g., Brathwaite, 'Jug! jug! fair fall the nightingale',
502–3. T. S. Eliot in *The Waste Land* emphasized Philomel's
rape by Tereus:

> The change of Philomel, by the barbarous king
> So rudely forced; yet there the nightingale
> Filled all the desert with inviolable voice

And still she cried, and still the world pursues,
'Jug Jug' to dirty ears.

(*The Complete Poems and Plays of T. S. Eliot*
(London: Faber, 1969), p. 64)

Here in Jinny's thoughts of sexual penetration and climax VW divests the myth of martyrdom and emphasizes the animal energy of the deer. VW also refers to the nightingale's thorn: 'One has pierced me. One is driven deep within me.'

147 *a lion in Trafalgar Square*: Neville and his male lover walk through London, past Nelson's column with its stone lions in Trafalgar Square; they separate at the Tube and are reunited, despite Neville's fears, in the afternoon.

149 *Alcibiades, Ajax, Hector and Percival*: Neville's new lover is not Percival, but he is like all such brave active heroes as Alcibiades, the Athenian general and disciple of Socrates, Ajax, second only in valour to Achilles, and Hector, most valiant of the Trojans. He is also unique: 'You are you.'

152 *a great moth*: VW's first intention was to call the book 'The Moths' and to organize the intermezzi around that idea. Comparatively few references to moths remain in the final version.

154 *a ticket for Rome*: Bernard is in Rome. Compare Shelley's elegy for John Keats, 'Adonais', xlix, 'Go thou to Rome' (*Works*, 442).

157 *A fin turns*: cf. *Diary*, 30 Sept. 1926: '. . . frightening and exciting . . . One sees a fin passing far out. . . . I used to feel this as a child—couldn't step across a puddle once . . . See Introduction, p. xii.

160 *Piccadilly . . . Haymarket*: still the signboards in the central hall at Piccadilly Underground.

163 *Cleopatra*: Enobarbus's description of Cleopatra in Shakespeare's play lies behind the first line also of Eliot's 'A Game of Chess' in *The Waste Land*: 'The Chair she sat in, like a burnished throne' (*Works*, 64). The 'figures of the damned' and 'wait the divine moment' suggest Dante, *The Divine Comedy*, whose *Inferno* VW was reading nightly in late 1930 as she wrote *The Waves*.

165 *To read this poem . . . when the door opens accept absolutely*: the sentiments and methods of the poem that Neville reads recall the

'withdrawn' poet T. S. Eliot. Compare the last part of 'What the Thunder Said' in *The Waste Land*, particularly 'The awful daring of a moment's surrender' and

> I have heard the key
> Turn in the door once and turn once only
> We think of the key, each in his prison. (lines. 411–13)

166 *O western wind*: the medieval lyric 'O westron wind', 'O western wind', is the first poem in *The Week-End Book* 'Great Poems', *The Week-End Book* (London: Nonesuch Press, 2nd ed., 1928), 3. This 'little book' was a publishing phenomenon in the 1920s, the 1924 first edition being reprinted seventeen times. VW's modernized version follows the *Week-End Book* punctuation.

169–71 *I climb this mountain*: Rhoda is now in Spain. She has left Louis. This passage is rare in being in the past tense and bids farewell to her memories. She imagines her own suicidal fall yet enters the inn.

175 *Hampton Court*: the night visit to Hampton Court has erotic as well as humdrum memories and fantasies attached to it: 'Look here Vita—throw over your man, & we'll go to Hampton Court & dine on the river together & walk in the garden in the moonlight & come home late & have a bottle of wine, & I'll get tipsy, & I'll tell you all the things I have in my head, millions, myriads—They won't stir by day, only by dark on the river. Think of that.' (*Letters*, iii. 393 [1927?]) Hampton Court is a wonderful architectural *mélange* as well as a summary history of English power-politics, built by Cardinal Wolsey, given by him under duress to Henry VIII in 1525 who demolished parts and added to it. Later Christopher Wren began new building under William III, but this plan was never completed. Hampton Court can be approached by river from the centre of London.

181 *A phrase*: compare '& still I say to myself instinctively "Whats the phrase for that?" & try to make more & more vivid the roughness of the air current & the tremor of the rooks wing' (*Diary*, iii. 191; Sunday, 12 Aug. 1928).

184 *scrannel beauties*: 'scrannel' is substituted for 'disembodied' in the first draft of *The Waves*. See Virginia Woolf, *The Waves: The*

Two Holograph Drafts, transcribed and edited by J. W. Graham (London: Hogarth Press, 1976), 293. An extremely rare word, it is another elegiac allusion. It occurs in Milton's elegy for his drowned friend, 'Lycidas': 'Grate on their scrannel pipes of wretched straw' (1. 124).

189 *Like conspirators*: VW may well have had in mind that the life of Charles I was threatened by conspirators at Hampton Court: *Hampton Court Conspiracy, with the Downfall of the Agitators and Levellers ... Together with the horrid resolution of Geo. Greenland to murder his Majesty at Hampton Court* (London, 1647).

a King, riding, fell over a molehill here: in *The Waves*, Draft 2, Percival's death is caused when 'His horse stumbled over a molehill'. See Graham, *The Waves: The Two Holograph Drafts*, 560–617.

190 *King George*: William and Mary added Dutch influence to the formal gardens of Hampton Court at the end of the seventeenth century: wildernesses, parterres, and fountains. The grandiose scale of Hampton Court and its gardens momentarily turns Neville, self-consciously and with irony, into a patriot, a subject of King George V. The same scene makes Louis think of the unnamed ordinary people (p. 192).

The iron gates: the gates of Dante's Inferno.

the quartet: Rhoda compares the creative and ordering symmetries of Christopher Wren's architecture to the quartet she heard earlier.

191 *a six-sided flower; made of six lives*: the seven-sided flower has become six-sided after Percival's death; it is no longer a sept-foil or Tormentilla, nor a magic number.

yew trees: of the Great Fountain Garden and the water-lilies of the Long Water at Hampton Court.

199 *we can talk freely*: an unknown companion from an unrecorded voyage of Bernard's; the reader. VW first imagined the conclusion as an immense conversation. It resolves as an inclusive soliloquy.

207 *laughs upstairs in the attic*: something of Bertha Rochester in *Jane Eyre* and the wicked fairy in *The Sleeping Beauty*.

208 *some observant fellow who points*: the problem of the observer, the outside: compare Introduction, p. xvii.

Shelley: the first mention of Shelley by name, though quotations from his poetry have been seamed through the work.

209 *pealing song*: a song such as Rhoda heard on p. 133. The group of friends becomes a symphony, p. 214.

211 *He fascinated me with his sordid imagination*: for this passage, compare Eliot's early poems, particularly 'Prufrock', 'Rhapsody on a Windy Night', 'Sweeney Erect'. Leonard Woolf describes the pleasure of constantly rereading single lines as he handset the early poems for publication by the Hogarth Press. He and VW handset *The Waste Land* themselves. A response to Joyce's *Ulysses*, which VW initially found distasteful, may also be present.

213 *India, Ireland or Morocco*: major international problems surface only as small talk.

217 *Hark, hark, the dogs do bark*: 'The beggars are coming to town': a nursery rhyme often interpreted as having a political sub-text.

Come away, come away, death: Shakespeare, *Twelfth Night*, II. iv. 52, sung by Feste. See also note to p. 236.

Let me not to the marriage of true minds: the opening line of Shakespeare's Sonnet 116.

221 *the lily of the day is fairer far in May*:

> It is not growing like a tree
> In bulke, doth make man better bee;
> Or standing long an Oake, three hundred yeare,
> To fall a logge, at last, dry, bald, and seare:
> A Lillie of a Day,
> Is fairer farre, in May,
> Although it fall, and die that night;
> It was the Plant, and flowre of light.
> In small proportions, we just beauties see:
> And in short measures, life may perfect bee.

Ben Jonson, 'To the immortal memorie, and friendship of that noble paire, Sir Lucius Cary, and Sir H. Morison', l. 69. *The*

Complete Poetry of Ben Jonson, ed. William B. Hunter, Stuart Editions (New York: New York University Press, 1963), 226.

222 *love and hate the heat of the sun*: a fugitive allying of the phrase from Catullus that typifies Susan (compare note to p. 10) with the dirge from Shakespeare's *Cymbeline*, 'Fear no more the heat of the sun'.

229 *Away! . . . The moor is dark beneath the moon*: another Shelley poem, of loss, ageing, and melancholy: see *passim*. Note particularly stanza 3:

> Away, away! to thy sad and silent home;
>   Pour bitter tears on its desolated hearth;
> Watch the dim shades as like ghosts they go and come,
>   And complicate strange webs of melancholy mirth.
>
> (*Works*, 521)

See discussion in Introduction, p. xxxii.

234 *she had killed herself*: we never know when. The event seems outside narrative sequence.

235 *St Paul's*: Christopher Wren's great domed cathedral is in the commercial heart of London. Bernard observes the funeral brasses and monuments, the boy chorister singing, the tourists with their Baedeker guidebooks. In 1930, while VW was writing *The Waves*, St Paul's had just been extensively restored: 'I almost went into St Paul's & saw Dr Donne, now uncovered again' (*Diary*, 23 Oct. 1930). The poet Donne was Dean of St Paul's for ten years and his monument is there.

scrolloping: a humorous word of VW's invention which occurs also in the *Diary* and in *Orlando*. See *Oxford English Dictionary*, 2nd edn. *OED* suggests that it combines 'scroll' and 'lollop'.

236 *Pillicock sat on Pillicock's hill*: the Fool in *King Lear*, III. iv. 79, the scene of the mock trial of Lear's cruel daughters. The Fool's doggerel is often, as here, full of sexual innuendo.

Hark, hark, the dogs do bark: see note to p. 217.

The World's great age begins anew: Shelley, 'Hellas', ll. 1060 ff.

> Heaven smiles, and faiths and empires gleam,
> Like wrecks of a dissolving dream.

236 *Come away, come away, death*: the clown Feste in *Twelfth Night*, II. iv. 52. The mingled 'nonsense and poetry' here all has to do with the overturning of established order and the fleetingness of life and death. Rhythm takes precedence of sense in linking the passages together. See also p. 217 where Bernard adds to the list Shakespeare's sonnet 'Let me not to the marriage of true minds'.

237 *like the eclipse*: compare the long account of the Woolf's expedition to Yorkshire to see the complete solar eclipse, the first for two hundred years: *Diary*, Thursday, 30 June 1927. The next eclipse will occur, as VW remarks, in 1999.

PELICAN BOOKS

A193

THE SIZE OF THE UNIVERSE

BY F. J. HARGREAVES, F.R.A.S.